TERRA INCOGNITA

TERRA INCOGNITA

A Novel of the Roman Empire

RUTH DOWNIE

BLOOMSBURY

Published by Bloomsbury USA, New York
Distributed to the trade by Macmillan

All papers used by Bloomsbury USA are natural, recyclable products made from wood grown in well-managed forests. The manufacturing processes conform to the environmental regulations of the country of origin.

Library of Congress Cataloging-in-Publication Data

Downie, Ruth, 1955–
Terra incognita : a novel of the Roman Empire / by Ruth Downie.—1st U.S. ed.
p.   cm.
ISBN-13: 978-1-59691-232-8
ISBN-10: 1-59691-232-4
I. Rome—History—Hadrian, 117–138—Fiction.   2. Murder—
Investigation—Fiction.   I. Title.

PR6104.O94T47   2008
823'.92—dc22
2007044474

First U.S. Edition 2008
Published in the United Kingdom with the title *Ruso and the Demented Doctor* by Penguin Books Ltd. in 2008

1 3 5 7 9 10 8 6 4 2

Typeset by Westchester Book Group
Printed in the United States of America by Quebecor World Fairfield

To Bill and Lyn Hancock

TERRA INCOGNITA

A NOVEL

IN WHICH our hero will be . . .

puzzled by
> Felix—a silenced trumpeter

troubled by
> Tilla—his housekeeper
> a wagon driver
> a carpenter
> Lydia—the carpenter's girlfriend
> Thessalus—retiring medic to the Tenth Batavians
> bedbugs

hindered by
> Gambax—assistant medic to the Tenth Batavians
> Ness—a domestic servant

challenged by
> a baker's wife
> Decianus—prefect of the Tenth Batavians
> Metellus—Decianus's aide, assigned to "special duties"

Postumus—a centurion from the Twentieth Legion
Rianorix—a basket maker

distracted by
Dari—a waitress

assisted by
Albanus—a clerk
Ingenuus—a hospital bandager
Valens—a colleague

welcomed by
Catavignus—a local brewer
Susanna, who serves the best food in town
Veldicca—a single parent
a shopkeeper
several civilians with ailments

disdained by
Audax—a centurion with the Tenth Batavians
Trenus—a man from the north
the ladies of the bathhouse
several other civilians with ailments

endangered by
a mysterious rider
Festinus—a barber
a large number of locals

embarrassed by
Claudius Innocens—a trader

surprised by
Aemilia—Catavignus's daughter

missed by
Lucius—his brother
Cassia—Lucius's wife

their four (or five) children
Arria—his stepmother

not missed at all by
his two half sisters
Claudia—his former wife

ruled by
the emperor Hadrian

ignored by
the governor of Britannia

thanked by
nobody

Nec tecum possum vivere, nec sine te.

I can't live with you—nor without you.

—Martial

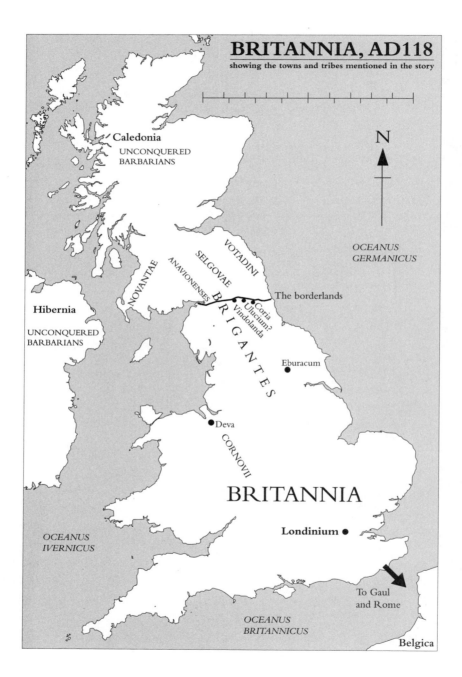

BRITANNIA, AD118

showing the towns and tribes mentioned in the story

Caledonia
UNCONQUERED
BARBARIANS

N

OCEANUS
GERMANICUS

VOTADINI

SELGOVAE

ANAVIONENSES

NOVANTAE

B R I G A N T E S

The borderlands

Coria
Ulucium?
Vindolanda

Hibernia

UNCONQUERED
BARBARIANS

Eburacum

Deva

CORNOVII

BRITANNIA

OCEANUS
IVERNICUS

Londinium

To Gaul
and Rome

OCEANUS
BRITANNICUS

Belgica

*H*E HAD NOT *expected to be afraid. He had been fasting for three days, and still the gods had not answered. The certainty had not come. But he had made a vow and he must keep it. Now, while he still had the strength.*

He glanced around the empty house. He was sorry about that barrel of beer only half drunk. About the stock of baskets that were several weeks' work, and that he might never now sell at market.

He had nothing else to regret. Perhaps, if the gods were kind, he would be drinking that beer at breakfast tomorrow with his honor restored. Or perhaps he would have joined his friends in the next world.

He would give the soldier a chance, of course. Make one final request for him to do as the law demanded. After that, both their fates would lie in the hands of the gods.

He closed the door of his house and tied it shut, perhaps for the last time. He walked across and checked that the water trough was full. The pony would be all right for three, perhaps four days. Somebody would probably steal her before then anyway.

He pulled the gate shut out of habit, although there was nothing to escape and little for any wandering animals to eat in there. Then he set off to walk to Coria, find that foreign bastard, and teach him the meaning of respect.

1

MANY MILES SOUTH of Coria, Ruso gathered both reins in his left hand, reached down into the saddlebag, and took out the pie he had saved from last night. The secret of happiness, he reflected as he munched on the pie, was to enjoy simple pleasures. A good meal. A warm, dry goatskin tent shared with men who neither snored, passed excessive amounts of wind, nor imagined that he might want to stay awake listening to jokes. Or symptoms. Last night he had slept the sleep of a happy man.

Ruso had now been in Britannia for eight months, most of them winter. He had learned why the province's only contribution to fashion was a thick cloak designed to keep out the rain. Rain was not a bad thing, of course, as his brother had reminded him on more than one occasion. But his brother was a farmer, and he was talking about proper rain: the sort that cascaded from the heavens to water the earth and fill the aqueducts and wash the drains. British rain was rarely that simple. For days on end, instead of falling, it simply hung around in the air like a wife waiting for you to notice she was sulking.

Still, with commendable optimism, the locals were planning to celebrate the arrival of summer in a few days' time. And as if the gods had finally relented, the polished armor plates of the column stretching along the road before him glittered beneath a cheering spring sun.

Ruso wondered how the soldiers stationed up on the border would greet the arrival of men from the Twentieth Legion: men who were better trained, better equipped, and better paid. No doubt the officers would make fine speeches about their united mission to keep the Britons in order, leaving the quarrels to the lower ranks, and Ruso to patch up the losers.

In the meantime, though, he was not busy. Any man incapable of several days' march had been left behind in Deva. The shining armor in front of him was protecting 170 healthy men at the peak of their physical prowess. Even the most resentful of local taxpayers would keep their weapons and their opinions hidden at the sight of a force this size, and it was hard to see how a soldier could acquire any injury worse than blisters by observing a steady pace along a straight road. Ruso suppressed a smile. For a few precious days of holiday, he was enjoying the anonymity of being a traveler instead of a military—

"Doctor!"

His first instinct was to snatch a last mouthful of pie.

"Doctor Gaius Petreius Ruso, sir?"

Since his other hand was holding the reins, Ruso raised the crumbling pastry in acknowledgment before nudging the horse to the edge of the road where there was room to halt without obstructing the rest of the column. Moments later he found himself looking down at three people.

Between two legionaries stood a figure that gave the unusual and interesting impression of being two halves of different people stuck together along an unsteady vertical line. Most of the left half, apart from the hand and forearm, was clean. The right half, to the obvious distaste of the soldier restraining that side, was coated with thick mud. There was a bloodied scrape across the clean cheek and a loop of hair stuck out above the one braid that remained blond, making the owner's head appear lopsided. Despite these indignities, the young woman had drawn herself up to her full height and stood with head erect. The glint in the eyes whose color Ruso had never found a satisfactory word to describe—but when he did, it would be something to do with the sea— suggested someone would soon be sorry for this.

All three watched as Ruso finished his mouthful and reluctantly rewrapped and consigned the rest of his snack to the saddlebag. Finally he said, "Tilla."

"It is me, my lord," the young woman agreed.

Ruso glanced from one soldier to the other, noting that the junior of the two had been given the muddy side. "Explain."

"She says she's with you, sir," said the clean man.

"Why is she like this?"

As the man said, "Fighting, sir," she twisted to one side and spat on the ground. The soldier jerked her by the arm. "Behave!"

"You can let go of her," said Ruso, bending to unstrap his waterskin. "Rinse the mud out of your mouth, Tilla. And watch where you spit. I have told you about this before."

As Tilla wiped her face and took a long swig from the waterskin, a second and considerably cleaner female appeared, breathless from running up the hill.

"There she is!" shrieked the woman. "Thief! Where's our money?" Her attempt to grab the blond braid was foiled by the legionaries.

Ruso looked at his slave. "Are you a thief, Tilla?"

"She is the thief, my lord," his housekeeper replied. "Ask her what she charges for bread."

"Nobody else is complaining!" cried the other woman. "Look! Can you see anybody complaining?" She turned back to wave an arm toward the motley trail of mule handlers and bag carriers, merchants' carts and civilians shuffling up the hill in the wake of the soldiers. "I'm an honest trader, sir!" continued the woman, now addressing Ruso. "My man stays up half the night baking, we take the trouble to come out here to offer a service to travelers, and then *she* comes along and decides to help herself. And when we ask for our money all we get is these two ugly great bruisers telling us to clear off!"

If the ugly great bruisers were insulted, they managed not to show it.

"You seem to have thrown her in the ditch," pointed out Ruso, faintly recalling a fat man behind a food stall—the first for miles—at the junction they had just passed. "I think that's enough punishment, don't you?"

The woman hesitated, as if she were pondering further and more imaginative suggestions. Finally she said, "We want our money, sir. It's only fair."

Ruso turned to Tilla. "Where's the bread now?"

Tilla shrugged. "I think, in the ditch."

"That's not our fault, is it, sir?" put in the woman.

Ruso was not going to enter into a debate about whose fault it was. "How much was it worth?"

There was a pause while the woman appeared to be assessing his outfit and his horse. Finally she said, "Half a denarius will cover it, sir."

"She is a liar!" put in Tilla, as if this were not obvious even to Ruso.

He reached for his purse. "Let me tell you what is going to happen here," he said to the woman. "I will give you one sesterce, which is—"

"Is too much!" said Tilla.

"Which is more than the bread was worth," continued Ruso, ignoring her. "My housekeeper will apologize to you—"

"I am not sorry!"

"She will apologize to you," he repeated, "and you will go back to your stall and continue charging exorbitant sums of money to travelers who were foolish enough not to buy before they set out."

Ruso dismissed the grinning soldiers with a tip that was not enough to buy their silence but might limit the scurrilous nature of their exaggerations when they told the story around tonight's campfires. The women seemed less satisfied, but that was hardly surprising. Ruso had long ago learned that the pleasing of women was a tricky business.

By now the bulk of the legionaries had gone on far ahead, followed by a plodding train of army pack ponies laden with tents and millstones and all the other equipment too heavy to be carried on poles on the soldiers' backs. Behind them was the unofficial straggle of camp followers.

Ruso turned to Tilla. "Walk alongside me," he ordered, adding quickly, "Clean side in." She sidestepped around the tail of the horse and came forward to walk at its shoulder. Ruso leaned down and said in a voice which would not be overheard, "None of the other civilians is causing trouble, Tilla. What is the matter with you?"

"I am hungry, my lord."

"I gave you money for food."

"Yes, my lord."

"Was it not enough?"

"It was enough, yes."

She ventured no further information. Ruso straightened up. He was not in the mood for the I-will-only-answer-the-question-you-ask-me game. He was in the mood for a peaceful morning and some more of last night's chicken in pastry, which he now retrieved and began to eat. He glanced sideways. Tilla was watching. He did not offer her any.

They continued in silence along the straight road up and down yet another wooded hill. British hills, it seemed, were as melancholic as British rain. Instead of poking bold fingers of rock up into the clouds, they lay lumpy and morose under damp green blankets, occasionally stirring themselves to roll vaguely skyward and then giving up and sliding into the next valley.

Somewhere among those hills lay the northern edge of the empire, and even further north, beyond the supposedly friendly tribes living along the border, rose wild cold mountains full of barbarians who had never been conquered and now never would be. Unless, of course, the new emperor had a sudden fit of ambition and gave the order to march north and have another crack at them. But so far Hadrian had shown no signs of spoiling for a fight. In fact he had already withdrawn his forces from several provinces he considered untenable. Britannia remained unfinished business: an island only half-conquered, and Ruso had not found it easy to explain to his puzzled housemate back in Deva why he had volunteered to go and peer over the edge into the other half.

"The North? Holy Jupiter, man, you don't want to go up there!" Valens's handsome face had appeared to register genuine concern at his colleague's plans. "It's at—it's *beyond* the edge of the civilized world. Why d'you think we send foreigners up there to run it?"

Ruso had poured himself more wine and observed, "When you think about it, we're all foreigners here. Except the Britons, of course."

"You know what I mean. Troops who are used to those sorts of conditions. The sort of chap who tramps bare chested through bogs and picks his teeth with a knife. They bring them in from Germania, or Gaul, or somewhere."

"I'm from Gaul," Ruso reminded him.

"Yes, but you're from the warm end. You're practically one of us." This was evidently intended as a compliment. "I know you haven't exactly shone here in Deva, after all that business with the barmaids—"

"This has got nothing to do with barmaids," Ruso assured him. "You know I spent half of yesterday afternoon waiting for a bunch of men who didn't turn up?"

"I believe you did mention it once or twice."

"And it's not the first time, either. So I tracked down their centurion today. Apparently he and his cronies have been telling the men they can go for first aid training if they want to."

"If they *want to*?"

"Of course they don't want to. They want to spend their spare time sleeping and fishing and visiting their girlfriends."

"I hope he apologized."

"No. He said he couldn't see the point of teaching ordinary soldiers first aid. He said it's like teaching sailors to swim—just prolongs the agony."

Valens shook his head sadly. "You really shouldn't let a few ignorant centurions banish you to the—" He was interrupted by a crash from the kitchen and a stream of British that had the unmistakeable intonation of a curse. He glanced at the door. "I suppose you're intending to take the lovely Tilla as well?"

"Of course."

"That *is* bad news. I shall miss her unique style of household management." Valens peered down at his dinner bowl and prodded at something with the end of his spoon. "I wonder what this was when it was alive?" He held it up toward the window to examine it, then flicked it off the spoon and onto the floor. One of the dogs trotted forward to examine it. "So," continued Valens. "Where exactly is this unholy outer region?"

"It's a fort called Ulucium. Apparently you go up to Coria and turn left at the border."

"You're going to some flea-bitten outpost beyond the last supply depot?"

"I'm told the area's very beautiful."

"Really? By whom?"

Ruso shrugged. "Just generally . . . by people who've been there." He took refuge in another sip of wine.

Valens shook his head. "Oh, Ruso. When I told you women like to be listened to, I didn't mean you should take any notice of what they say. Of course Tilla says it's very beautiful. She probably wants to go home to visit all her little girlfriends so they can paint their faces blue and dance around the cooking pot, singing ancestor songs. You didn't promise you'd take her home?"

"It's only for a few months. There's a couple of centuries going up to help revamp the fort, fix their plumbing, and encourage the taxpayers."

"You did! You promised her, didn't you?"

Ruso scratched the back of his ear. "I think I may have," he confessed. "It seemed like a good idea at the time."

Ruso took another mouthful of cold pie and wondered whether he should have listened to Valens rather than Tilla. From what he could gather, the principal activities of Tilla's tribe were farming and fighting, fueled by rambling tales about glorious ancestors and a belief that things you couldn't see were just as real as things you could. None of this had mattered much down in the relatively civilized confines of Deva, but as they traveled farther north, Tilla's behavior had definitely begun to deteriorate.

Ruso glanced downward. Tilla's muddy tunic was flapping heavily around her ankles. Thick brown liquid squelched out of her boots with every step.

He sighed, and balanced the remains of the pie on the front of the saddle. He reached out and touched her cheek just above the scrape. "I'll clean that up when we stop. Are you hurt anywhere else?"

"It was a soft landing, my lord. I do not see him coming, or I would fight back."

Ruso was not as sorry about this as his housekeeper seemed to be. "Why didn't you buy food before we set out this morning?"

"There was a woman in labor in the night. I forgot."

"One of the soldiers' women?"

"Yes."

"What on earth was she doing traveling in that condition?"

Tilla shrugged. "When a man marches away, who knows if he will come back? He might find a new woman. The army might send him across the sea. Then what will she do?"

Ruso, who had no idea what she might do, said, "So what happened to her?"

His slave jerked a thumb backward over her shoulder. "She is giving her daughter a bumpy welcome on a cart."

"She's a very lucky woman," observed Ruso.

"The goddess has been kind to her."

Ruso retrieved the crumbling remains of the snack and passed them across. "It's a bit dry. Sorry."

She wiped her mouth and hands on a clean patch of tunic before accepting it. "Thank you, my lord."

"There's to be no more stealing from now on, Tilla. Is that quite clear?" He gestured toward the mud. "You see where it leads."

A smile revealed white teeth in the unusually brown face. "I know where it leads." She patted the outside of her thigh. From beneath her clothing he heard the chink of money. Ruso was not impressed. "I had to pay that woman more than you saved to get you out of trouble," he said.

Tilla eyed him for a moment as if she were considering a reply, then crammed the remains of the food into her mouth, dropped into a crouch at the roadside, and began to scrabble about under her clothing. Ruso glanced around to see one or two people watching, and decided the most dignified reaction was to ride on and pretend he had not noticed.

Moments later he heard her running up behind him. He turned. "Was that really necessary?"

She nodded, and drew breath before announcing, "I have been waiting a long time to tell you something, my lord."

A sudden and deeply worrying thought crossed Ruso's mind. A thought he had been trying to ignore for some months.

He had been careful. Extremely careful. Far more careful than his slave, who on first being introduced to modern methods of contraception had fallen into a fit of disrespectful and uncontrollable laughter. He had insisted, of course, citing three years of successfully child-free marriage—something Tilla evidently thought was nothing to boast about. He had finally persuaded her to complete her part by squatting on the floor, taking a cold drink, and sneezing, but over the months Tilla had proved just as reluctant as Claudia to face the chill of a winter bedroom. Her sneezing too had shown a disappointing lack of commitment. He had given up trying to argue with her. Now he supposed he was going to have to face the consequences.

The horse, sensing his tension through the reins, tossed its head.

"Do you really think," Ruso said, "that this is the best time to tell me?"

"No, but you must know one day, and you will be happy."

"I see."

"Close your eyes, my lord."

"What for?"

"It is nothing bad."

"But why—"

"Is nobody looking."

Ruso glanced around to verify this before obeying. As the view faded away he was conscious of his body shifting with the pace of the horse. Something touched his thigh with a chink, and rested there.

"Is for you, my lord."

He opened his eyes. Hooked over one of the front saddle horns was the leather purse he had given her for the housekeeping money. He felt the muscles in his shoulders relax. Whatever this was, it was not what he had feared.

As he lifted the purse he glanced at his slave. Tilla was watching him, and looked very pleased with herself.

He loosened the drawstring, slid two fingers into the pouch, and pulled out a large warm coin. "What's this?"

"A sesterce."

"I can see that." He really must have a word with Tilla about this literal interpretation of questions. It was bordering on insolence, but so far he had failed to find a way to phrase the reprimand that did not suggest he could have worded his questions better. "Why," he tried again, framing the sentence with care, "are you stealing when you have this much cash?"

Her smile broadened. "I know my lord has no money."

"That's my business, not yours. You aren't going to help by pinching bread and getting into fights."

She pointed at the purse. "All for you."

Ruso tugged at the drawstring and peered inside.

'Gods above!' he exclaimed, weighing the purse in his hand again. He lowered it quickly as an army slave leading a string of pack ponies looked across to see what was happening. When the man had lost interest he investigated the contents of the purse again and leaned down to murmur, "This is a lot of money. Where did you get it?"

Tilla's shrug turned into an expansive gesture that suggested the coins had mysteriously fallen upon her in a rain shower.

"This can't possibly belong to you!"

"I save up."

Ruso sat up and frowned. He had little spare cash. He had certainly not offered any of it to his slave. He assumed she was sometimes paid for helping to deliver babies, and it was quite normal for slaves to try and build up enough funds to buy their freedom. But why would she hand him her personal savings? Besides, this was too much for a handful of babies, no matter how grateful their parents. He glanced at her. "Tilla, how have you . . ." The answer crept up on him as he spoke, stifling the final words of the question.

Tilla had become his housekeeper not long after his arrival in Britannia. Since she knew more about shopping than he did—in fact, almost everyone knew more about shopping than he did—he had never bothered to inquire too deeply into the relationship between cash and catering. He had begun by insisting that she render a weekly account. But after the first week she seemed to have forgotten about it and he had been too busy to insist. In any case, what was the point of having a slave to look after the house if he still had to do all the thinking himself?

A voice rose unbidden from the depths of his memory. *For goodness' sake, Gaius,* it said. *If it weren't for me the staff would walk all over us!*

He was glad Claudia was not here to see him now.

"Tilla," he murmured, "Tell me you don't make a habit of stealing."

She looked surprised. "Oh no, my lord."

"Good. So what is this?"

"I am your servant," she continued. "I will not let you be cheated."

"What?"

"I make things fair."

"Are you telling me," said Ruso, glancing around again to make sure he could not be overheard, "that if you don't approve of the price you help yourself?"

"Is not right that people grow fat on cheating when my lord is a good man and has no—"

"That's hardly the point, Tilla!" Ruso sat back in the saddle, frowned at the whiskery ears of his horse, and wondered how to explain something so fundamental it had never occurred to him to question it. "Ever since I began my work as a doctor," he observed, "I have done my best to build up a good reputation."

"Yes, my lord."

"I want men to say, 'There is Gaius Petreius Ruso, the medicus who can be trusted.'"

"Yes, my lord."

"'He doesn't pretend to know everything, but he does his best for his patients.'"

"Yes, my lord."

"This has been my ambition."

"Yes, my lord."

"If it ever becomes my ambition to have them say, 'There is Gaius Petreius Ruso, the man who sends his servant out to steal for him,' I will let you know."

"I understand this," came the reply. "I am doing it before you tell me."

*F*ELIX WAS GOING *to have to do something about the native. The man had been pestering him for days. Now he had stepped right up to the table in front of everyone in Susanna's and started jabbering again about honor. About the law. About compensation. Felix had explained, politely, that he couldn't be breaking his promise, because he'd never made one.*

That was when the native had begun to shout about cows. Felix began to lose patience with him. He didn't have one cow to hand over, let alone five, even if he'd wanted to. "Sorry, pal. It's not that I don't want to help, but it's not really my problem, is it?"

Any normal native would have shut up and slunk off home to his smoky house and his skinny children, glad that he hadn't been taken outside for a beating. This one started yelling about gods and shame and vengeance.

Felix held his hands up. "Look, pal, I've said it nicely. I'm sorry if you think I've been plowing your field, but she never said a word about you to me. You can have her. I'll back off."

Instead of calming down, the native had tried to climb over the table and grab him. The other lads had thrown the man out into the street. What had he been thinking of? One basket maker taking on four Batavian infantrymen? Especially four Batavian infantrymen who found themselves in a bar where the beer had run out. When he came back for more, already with one eye swelling up and blood dribbling from a split lip, they were all so surprised that they burst out laughing.

They were pretty soft with him, considering. They left him in a fit state to run away, still shouting to the street that everyone would see what happened around here to men who didn't honor their debts.

More beer arrived. They were still laughing and searching for imaginary cows under the table when they heard the trumpet announcing the approach of curfew. The others got to their feet. Felix glanced across to where Dari the waitress was showing more than a glimpse of cleavage as she stretched forward to clear tables. "I'll be in later," he said. "I've got some business."

When they had gone, Felix slid his arm around Dari's waist. "You're not going to let me down, are you?" he said.

2

FROM THE WAY the medicus was hunched over the writing tablet,
Tilla guessed he was either making the wax speak to his brother
across the sea, or doing his accounts. She restrained an urge to stride
across the bedroom, wrench the stylus out of his hand, and poke him in
the eye with it.

As far as she had been able to work out, the medicus's family lived in a
fine house whose roof baked beneath the everlasting sunshine of southern Gaul, while its foundations stood in a deep and perilous pool of debt.
When she had found this out she had felt sorry for him. She knew that
he sent most of his money home to his brother, and she knew that it was
never enough. In the same way, she knew, she could never fully repay
what she owed him for saving her life. More than once, while he
frowned over the latest letter from the brother, she had slipped away and
brought out the purse from its hiding place, secretly adding up how
much she had saved for him and imagining his pleasure when she pre-
sented it.

But now he had taken the money that she had spent months building
up for him and squandered half of it on the best room that the surprised
innkeeper could offer. Worse, the smug expression on his face as he had
patted the fine large bed suggested he expected her to be grateful. It was

one of those moments when, no matter how loyal she knew she should feel toward this man, she found him utterly exasperating.

She had squinted at the covers and said, "There will be bugs."

He had assured her that this room was usually kept aside for important travelers.

"Rich men's bugs," she had said, surveying the painted walls.

"Sleep on the floor, then," he had replied. "The bugs and I will have a quiet night." But she had seen him opening a bag from his medical case and sprinkling something under the bedding. As if that would make any difference.

The water in which she was standing was like gritty brown soup. She balanced on one foot while she rinsed the other with fresh water from the jug. Brown smudges mingled with older, unknowable stains on the linen of the innkeeper's towel.

She did not want to curl up with the medicus in that borrowed bed, bugs or no bugs. She would rather have been outside in the yard, bedding down under the canopy of the hired cart in the company of the woman who had just had the baby. It was not wise for any woman to be left with only a boy driver for protection in a place like this. Especially not a woman with a new baby. But the medicus's patience had been wearing thin today, and by the end of the journey she had felt too tired and dirty to point out to him that Lydia's needs were just as important as his own.

Instead she had waited obediently for him outside the army transit camp, feeling the mud stiffen on her skin, ignoring the curious passersby and the loudmouths who thought their comments were funny. By the time he had finished doing whatever it was soldiers did and they had walked down to the inn, the lamps were being lit.

The inn's bathhouse had turned out to be a small and not very clean set of rooms occupied by sweaty latecomers scraping off the dirt of their day's journey. She had only paused long enough to collect water and towels. So now here they both were, trapped in a costly privacy neither of them seemed to be enjoying.

The medicus was still sitting on the rented bed, scratching out his letters by the light of the lamp. He would certainly not be telling his brother how much money he had just handed over to the landlord of the Golden Fleece.

Tilla reached for her clean undertunic and dragged it over her head. He had not thanked her for saving him from cheats and liars. He had not even thanked her for the money. No matter what he used it for now, the gift was spoiled.

She unwrapped the towel from around her hair. A silent blaze of white appeared around the window shutters. In less than a heartbeat it pulsed again and was gone.

The Medicus glanced up. "Was that lightning?"

"Yes." There. Now she could not be accused of refusing to speak to him.

He went back to his writing. He began adding up on his fingers and muttering. Accounts, then. That was one of the odd things about Romans. Everything was valued in useless metal discs.

She had never stolen any real wealth. Nothing anyone could actually use—tools or cows or a winter seed store or clothes to keep the cold out. All she had done was to even up the barter occasionally so that the medicus got a fair deal. And yes, she had included the money she had been given for helping three new lives safely into this world. He had taken it without a thought, and wasted it.

There was a distant rumble of thunder. She began to rub the wet snakes of her hair with the towel. She hoped Lydia and the baby were safe. Her man had rushed across to admire his new daughter this morning before the march set off, but now he would be sharing a tent with the other soldiers. He had promised the driver extra money to make sure the cart in which his new family was sleeping was parked somewhere secure overnight. The boy, who knew the road, had agreed to bring it into the yard at the inn.

Tilla wrung drips out of the ends of her hair and felt ashamed. At the very least, she should have taken the trouble to check that the driver had followed his orders.

She glanced at the big bed and the wooden chest in which her meager possessions would have fitted twenty times over. This was not right. She and the medicus, two healthy adults, had all this to themselves. They were safe from thieves behind a barred door. Meanwhile outside, a newborn baby and its mother were huddled under the canopy of a hired cart that smelled of old vegetables.

Tilla got to her feet and tossed the damp towels into the corner. Behind the window, lightning flashed and vanished. Giving the bed a wide berth, she went across and unlatched the shutters. As she pushed them open, a crash of thunder made her flinch. She stretched one arm out between the window bars, flexing the stiff fingers of her right hand into the chilly air. The first drops of rain struck cold on her skin.

She would go and invite them in. The medicus, whose duty it was to help people, would not be able to turn them out in the storm. It would be a good use of the money. And it would serve him right.

"Close the window, will you?"

She fastened the shutters as ordered. Then, ignoring his "Where are you going dressed like that?" she snatched up her shawl and hurried out of the room.

3

B Y T H E T I M E Tilla had found the yard door and struggled with the latch, the storm was overhead. Rain was beating on the roofs and spluttering in the drains. No one else was about. Staff, guests, and slaves would be huddled in their rooms, praying for the storm to pass safely over them. From the shelter of the doorway she squinted out into the blustery dark, trying to distinguish the shapes of the vehicles lined up along the far side.

"Lydia?"

Another flash of lightning captured pale streaks of rain in mid fall and veiled everything beyond them. She had barely counted five paces when she had to clap her hands over her ears. She shook her head like a dog as the thunder drilled through her skull.

When it was over she shouted, "Lydia! Are you out here?"

There was no answer.

The spatter of raindrops on tarpaulin told her she was nearing the vehicles. She ducked around to shelter between the first hulk and the wall, and called in Latin, "Are you there? Lydia? Don't be afraid. Is the midwife. Come indoors with me."

Still no reply. She moved on, calling at the second shape and then waiting for more thunder to die away before trying the third. It seemed smaller, more like the cart her patient had hired, but in the dark it was difficult to tell. Whatever it was, no one was replying from inside. There was nobody else out here.

Tilla shivered. Her wet scalp felt as though it was shrinking in the cold. She pulled the shawl over her head and told herself the woman must be safe indoors with the baby. She had worried for nothing. Surely not even the most money grabbing of innkeepers would turn away a newly delivered mother in a storm. Only her guilt-ridden midwife was alone in the dark, getting wet. Unless, of course, the driver had not brought the cart into the yard at all. Lydia could be anywhere among the houses huddling around the army's camp.

Wrinkling her nose at the stench of flooded drains, Tilla turned to splash back across the courtyard and stubbed her toe. Her feet were so cold that the pain took a couple of paces to register. When it did, it reached her mind at the same time as the thought that there was still one thing she could do to help the mother and baby.

Raising her hands to the gods roaring in the sky, she cried in the language they had given to her people, "Great Taranis, god of the thunder, come to visit us this night! I am your servant, here to greet you!"

The rain lashed at her face. She stood with her arms stretched out, trying not to shiver. Perhaps she had said the wrong things. Prayer was a difficult business at the best of times, and even harder when the worshipper was growing numb with cold. "Listen to me, great god of thunder!" she shouted into the rain. "I have no gift today, but I will make one if you keep safe the woman Lydia and the—"

She was silenced by a white flash that left her blinking, staring, wiping the water out of her eyes, unable to take in what she had just seen. Summoning her courage, she peered into the darkness and called, "Who is there? Speak to me!"

Something brushed against her. She shrank away, lost her footing, and landed with a splash. She lay with her hands over her ears as another crash of thunder buffeted the yard.

When the thunder god's voice rolled away, she scrambled to her feet. Someone was calling out. It was not the strange creature she had seen in the lightning. It was a recognizable voice, speaking in Latin, and definitely not heavenly.

"Tilla, where the hell are you? What are you doing?"

She turned toward the medicus. "I am looking for someone who is not here!"

She heard the splash of approaching footsteps. She felt herself seized and lifted and pressed against his warmth as he carried her back toward the safety of the doorway.

He said, "Who were you talking to?"

Tilla closed her eyes, picturing the creature who had the form and face of a young man but growing from his head there had definitely been . . ."You will not believe me," she said.

They both lurched sideways as the medicus kicked the door open. "Try me."

She saw again the angles of the antlers in the harsh light. *Antlers.* The sign of Cernunnos, king of the beasts. But she had seen the hand on the wheel of the cart. . . . The wheel was the sign of Taranis, ruler of the thunder. She did not know whom her prayer had conjured in the yard. But she knew what. As the medicus stumped up the stairs, she whispered, "It is a powerful god."

CENTURION AUDAX OF the Tenth Batavians had stumbled over nasty things in back alleys before, but none quite like this. He took a step backward, unable to believe what he was looking at. Then, glancing around to see if anyone else was watching, he unfurled his cloak and bent to drape it over what remained of Felix the trumpeter.

The only sign of life in the street was the huddled figure of a woman making an early start out of town with a bundle on her back. A swelling chorus of birdsong was heralding a clear dawn. The rest of Coria was either still in bed or yawning over its breakfast.

Audax rapped on the door of the butcher's shop. "Go over to the fort," he ordered the bleary-eyed slave who finally responded to his knocking. "Tell them Audax needs Officer Metellus down here right away. And tell him I said to come alone."

He tramped back through the stink of the alley and crouched beside the body, pulling out a fold in the cloak to hide another inch of pale leg. It was pointless, but until Metellus turned up he did not know what else he could do.

It was a while before he noticed the drawing. Scratched in charcoal on the plastered wall above Felix's body was a crude sketch of a man. Audax *scowled. Whoever had done it wasn't much of an artist. He supposed those things that looked like two trees sprouting from the man's head were meant to be antlers. It was not a good picture, but that didn't matter. It didn't have to be a good picture to make a great deal of mischief.*

4

L AST NIGHT'S STORM seemed to have washed the sky clean but already a stiff breeze was blowing fresh clouds in from the west. Beneath them, a cavalry outrider had stationed himself in a dramatic pose on the top of a distant hill from whence he could see not only the column but also the approach of any potential marauders. Ruso, whose horse was ambling along as if it were asleep, wished he could join him. Instead he was expected to keep pace with infantry. The goods convoy the infantry was escorting on this last-but-one stage of their journey included a wagon carrying lead for replumbing Ulucium's leaky latrines, so the pace of the column was excruciatingly slow.

Ruso rubbed at an itch on his elbow, muttered, "Pick your feet up, will you?" to the horse, and urged it into a trot. As he passed up the hill along the column he scanned the glum faces of the Twentieth. The prospect of drying out in Coria this evening seemed to offer little cheer. It occurred to him, not for the first time, that the man who invented a tent that could fend off rising as well as falling water would have a statue erected in his honor in every army camp in the empire.

Finally spotting the soldier he wanted, Ruso allowed his mount to relax into a walk. " 'Morning, Albanus."

A slight figure in a damp tunic looked up from the ranks. "Good morning, sir."

The clerk did not look quite as weary today. Ruso suspected that Albanus had suffered on this march. No matter how keen a man might be, and how regularly he attended physical training, a life of writing letters and organizing medical records was poor preparation for carrying a full pack across the hills in all weather for days on end. Rubbing his elbow again, Ruso said, "Just as well nobody called me out last night, eh?"

"Very lucky, sir."

He wondered what Albanus would think if he knew that he had been paid with Tilla's stolen money for being willing to get up and fetch Ruso—who should have been in one of the tents—if a doctor were needed. "I don't suppose you got much sleep anyway," he ventured.

Albanus smiled. "Oh, I was fine, sir. My mother says I've always been the same. Once I'm off, nothing ever wakes—" He stopped.

Ruso hid his amusement. "I see."

"I would have got up, sir, of course—"

"I'm sure you would," said Ruso, truthfully. There was no fun in teasing Albanus. It was like poking a kitten with a stick. He slapped at his elbow. The itch shrank away for a few seconds, then crept back.

The road was still running along high ground, offering views to either side that would have been dramatic had there been anything new to look at. But even native house fires were no longer a novelty. There was another one now. A fresh plume of thick black smoke rushing skyward from a settlement in the middle distance. It was hardly surprising that people who insisted on lighting fires in the middle of thatched huts would have mishaps, but as they drew closer he could make out a squad of men clad in armor marching away down the valley, ignoring the frantic figures who were trying to beat out the flames.

It occurred to him that perhaps some of the other fires had not been accidents either. Everyone said the natives were more difficult to manage in the north.

Ruso yawned. He had not slept well. Tilla had finally consented to join him in the bed, but his efforts to warm her up had led to an unexpected cry of "Cernunnos!" at a crucial moment, and somehow despite her insistence that this was the name of the god she had seen in the yard, it had still put him off his stroke. Unabashed, she had proceeded to speculate about what this divine visitation might mean. His insistence on resuming his own more earthly visitation was greeted with tolerance rather than enthusiasm.

She had woken him again in the middle of the night, babbling in British. It was a moment before he realized she was talking in her sleep, no doubt to some god with antlers. After she fell silent he had lain awake in the dark, telling himself that it was completely irrational to be jealous of a trick of the light, and that he was only starting to wonder if she really had seen something because he was not properly awake himself.

Another itch had sprouted in the hollow between his shoulder blades. When the column stopped for water, he would have to dig out his baggage and try and find some calming ointment. In the meantime, his fingers slid up between two of the layers of iron plates, but they were now trapped at an awkward angle and he could not move them enough to have any effect. Twisting sideways, he tried plunging the hand down the back of his neck instead. The probing fingers fell just short of their destination.

Several instruments that would have done the job safely were in his medical case, but that was back on one of the carts. He tried grabbing the top and bottom of his tunic, and pulling it taut while wriggling against it like a cow trying to scratch itself on a gate. That did not work either.

Finally he thumped at his back with his fist before noticing that several of the legionaries tromping up the slope beside him were watching with interest. Among them was his clerk.

"Are you all right, sir?"

"Fine, thank you, Albanus." He wondered whether to add, "Just doing some morning stretches," but decided that would make it worse.

He urged the horse forward, musing upon the pointlessness of formal education. Instead of wasting time arguing over dilemmas unrelated to real life, bright young minds should be set useful questions. Questions such as: *A man is offered a chance to share a room with a bad-tempered woman and several biting insects, or a tent with his comrades and a large quantity of rainwater. Which should he choose?*

Moments later he was level with a centurion whose nose appeared to have been attached to his face as an afterthought. This was Postumus, the man in whose tent he had failed to appear last night. Ruso was anticipating some cutting comment on his absence, but Postumus was busy scowling at the horizon.

"Little bugger," Postumus observed.

Following the centurion's gaze, Ruso saw the lone rider still silhouetted against the gathering clouds. "There's something to be said for joining the cavalry," he said.

"He's not cavalry."

"No?" At this distance, it was impossible to make out whether the horseman was carrying weapons. "Who is he, then?"

"That's exactly what he wants us to ask."

"Ah," said Ruso, surprised to find he had fallen into some sort of trap. Then, as the outline of the horse narrowed and began to sink into the rise of the hill, "He's going."

"He'll pop up again farther along," said Postumus. "Always where we can see him and always just out of range. He's following us."

"I've seen him before," said Ruso.

"One of the patrols went after him yesterday and he outran them. Vanished into the woods and couldn't be tracked."

"What do you think he wants?"

"Well, he's not a lookout," said Postumus. "They'd use some snot-nosed little goatherd for that."

"They?"

"The natives," said Postumus. "I reckon all that one wants is to get on our nerves."

"Ah."

"Which is why, for the time being, we're ignoring him."

"Right," said Ruso, guessing that the watcher's presence had been the cause of yesterday's unexplained order to don helmets. "So we *do* know who he is."

"If you'd been where you were supposed to be last night, you'd know what I know. Nice and cozy up at the inn, were you?"

"Very," said Ruso, suddenly unable to resist wriggling under his armor. "Kind of you to ask."

Postumus was looking at him oddly. "Something the matter with you?"

"Me? No."

"Uh."

They rode on in silence for a while, then Postumus said, "You haven't heard what's going on, then?"

"What?"

"You might want to think about making an offering to Fortuna next time you get a chance," added Postumus. "Or whatever god you think might be listening up here."

"I'll bear it in mind," promised Ruso, deducing that he was being punished for sleeping under a solid roof last night.

"Not that our lads are worried," added Postumus.

"Of course not," agreed Ruso.

"But the units stationed up here are pretty jumpy."

Ruso felt his resolve slipping away. Eventually he said, "What aren't we worried about, exactly?"

"You really want to know?"

"Go on then."

"The story I heard . . ."

The story Postumus had heard began with an army transport convoy making its way to a base at the opposite end of the border. The convoy had been delayed by a breakdown and was still an hour away as darkness fell. They were making good progress when a sudden shower of burning arrows rained down on the carts, and a fire broke out in the straw packing around a consignment of oil jars. Postumus described what ensued as "a fine old fry-up" and in the chaos that followed nobody noticed that the guards on the rear vehicle had been knifed and the cargo stolen. Nobody could remember seeing any of the attackers.

"So next morning they do a security roundup and most of the natives don't know a thing, as usual. But after a bit of expert prompting they start talking about a strange figure riding past in the half-light, and they swear he had antlers and he's a messenger from the gods."

"Antlers?"

"Nobody took much notice until a couple of the guards on the transport said they saw the same thing, only they didn't speak up in case people thought they were crazy."

"It was dark when they saw this—thing?"

"But every one of them described it the same way. That's not all. There's an outpost where the whole unit fell ill, including the medic."

Ruso ignored the gibe.

"Turned out there was a dead wolf in the water channel," said Postumus. "But it couldn't have got in there by itself. Someone had replaced the cover stone and laid a set of antlers on top. Then there's a tax collector who got ambushed. He saw him too."

"Who's going to believe a tax collector?"

The centurion grunted. "I'm just telling you what I heard. Don't say I didn't warn you. But like I said, I don't reckon matey on the horse is anything to worry about."

"No," agreed Ruso. "The lack of antlers would seem to support you there."

"I reckon," continued Postumus, "that he's some scabby little Brit who thinks he's clever. We'll go across and give him a surprise later on. When we're good and ready."

Privately Ruso thought that if the scabby little Brit really were clever, he would play along with the rumors by strapping something spiky to his head. Deciding not to bother Postumus with this thought, he said, "So we've been sent up here to steady a few nerves."

"*I've* been sent," corrected Postumus, edging his horse sideways to steer around a minor landslip where the curb had begun to collapse into the ditch. "I heard *you* volunteered. Don't know what the hell for. Specially with that girl of yours."

"I heard there's more action up on the border," said Ruso, not keen to get into a discussion about Tilla.

A grin made its way around the nose. "Not enough bodies for you back at base, eh?"

Ruso sighed. He had never wanted to get tangled up in that business of the murdered barmaid. Now, no matter how often he denied it, it seemed everyone in the Twentieth legion knew him as the medicus with as much interest in dead patients as live ones. "Last month," he explained, "a man turned up on my doorstep with the corpse of his girl-friend's cat, and asked me to find out who'd poisoned it."

"And did you?"

"No."

"Heard you didn't have much luck pinning down who killed that barmaid, either."

"I don't investigate dead cats," said Ruso, who knew far more about the barmaid than Postumus suspected. "I've got better things to do."

"Well, perhaps you can track down matey with the antlers." Postumus was scanning the horizon, presumably looking out for the scabby little Brit so he could carry on ignoring him.

Ruso let the centurion ride on ahead before making another futile attempt to scratch his back. There was a suspicious tickling sensation on the lower right-hand side of his ribcage now. Almost as irritating as the itching was the fact that he had not noticed any of this until after they had set out this morning. Otherwise he would have cornered that lying innkeeper and demanded a refund.

For a moment he had been alarmed by the way Postumus's stories echoed Tilla's. Now, thinking about it logically, he realized that Tilla must have heard those same stories from other travelers. Her vision in the yard last night had not been an apparition sent to inspire her or to terrorize the army, but the result of frightening rumors working on the uneducated native imagination. The only mysterious creature at the inn had been the common but strangely invisible bedbug—and if she did not mention the bites, neither would he. She would only gloat.

*O*FFICER *METELLUS WAS* able to name Felix's murderer by the start of the third watch. It was a native. His identification had not been difficult, since he was not the brightest of men. Plenty of people had heard him pick a quarrel with the victim in a local snack bar only hours before the body was found. Several of the witnesses could remember the exact wording of the threats he had made.

Unfortunately, as Prefect Decianus of the Tenth Batavians observed over his lunch tray, naming the murderer did not solve the problem.

"We'll pick him up soon, sir," promised Metellus, who had not been invited to share the frugal offering of bread and black olives. "All our contacts know who to look for, and I've got men watching the house."

Decianus tore a chunk off the bread. "Audax wants to round up twenty natives and execute one every watch until someone tells us where he is."

Metellus frowned. "I don't think the governor would approve, sir. His orders are—"

"I don't need you to tell me what the governor's orders are, Metellus. Obviously we aren't going to do that. Not without approval. I'll send a message down and see what he says."

"I've already done that."

Decianus glanced at him. "I don't suppose we'll get much of an answer till he *gets here to see for himself. And I want to have this cleared up by that time any-way."* He dropped the bread back onto the tray. *"Where's the body now?"*

"In the mortuary. Audax is guarding the door. Nobody else has been allowed anywhere near it."

Decianus pondered that for a moment. *"What are the men saying?"*

Metellus said, *"We're putting it out that it was just a quarrel in a bar, sir."*

"And do they believe it?"

"Probably not."

"I want it made absolutely clear that we're dealing with a simple backstreet brawl. There's nothing mysterious about the way the native cursed our man, and there is no connection between this business and anything else they may have heard."

"I'll do my best sir," agreed Metellus. *"But judging by the number of civilians lining up to make devotions to the gods, it's not going to be easy."*

Decianus sighed. *"Tell me this isn't happening, Metellus."*

"It'll be better when we arrest the native, sir."

"It'll be better when you find our missing item."

Metellus said, *"It's nowhere in his house. I've got two men covering the road between here and there, and another three covering the streets, spreading out from where the body was found."* He raised a hand to silence the objection the prefect was about to make. *"It's all right, I haven't told them anything. Their orders are to search for evidence of anything the native might have stolen from the victim, then bring it back and say nothing."*

Decianus picked up an olive, examined it for a moment, then flung it back into the bowl. It bounced off the rim, missed the desk, and skittered across the floor-boards. *"We should have seen this coming."*

"My people can't be everywhere, sir. The native wasn't on our list as anybody important."

As Decianus was saying, *"Well he's found a way of making himself important now,"* there was a knock on his office door. Apparently the fort doctor urgently wished to speak with him.

Decianus frowned. *"I suppose he's come to complain about having a centurion keeping him out of his mortuary."*

The young soldier in the doorway hesitated, evidently not sure whether the pre-fect was always right or whether his staff were expected to warn him when he wasn't. Finally he said, *"Not exactly, sir."*

Decianus brushed breadcrumbs from his tunic. He had not been impressed by Doctor Thessalus's recent performance. The man was due to be replaced in a few days when the governor arrived, and Decianus was not sorry. *"Very well,"* he said, sliding the tray aside. *"Send him in."*

The state in which Thessalus appeared before him did nothing to improve his opinion. "Stand easy," he ordered.

Thessalus, who had not been standing as straight as he might, relaxed even further. The glare of the guard who had marched him in suggested that he would very much like to seize this excuse for an officer and straighten him up again.

Thessalus seemed to be having difficulty staying awake. He squeezed his eyes shut and then opened them again. Decianus followed his gaze and saw that a fly had settled on the tray and was now busy cleaning its back legs. Decianus dismissed the guard and waved away the fly. Metellus, who had retreated to sit in the corner, said nothing.

"So, doctor," said Decianus, "Tell me what's so urgent."

"Yes, sir," agreed the doctor. "Right away, sir." The silence that followed was broken by a hiccup. "Oops," he said, a faint grin creasing his thin face. "Sorry, sir."

Decianus reflected that it was very early in the day to be drunk. He nodded to Metellus, who approached the doctor and leaned close to repeat the order into his ear.

Thessalus's smile faltered. He blinked several times. His mouth opened, closed again, and then, in an accent that betrayed a better education than everyone else in the room, offered the words, "I've come to confess to a murder, sir."

Decianus leaned his elbows on the desk, placed his fingertips together, and eyed the unsteady Thessalus over the top of them. "You might want to reconsider what you've just said, doctor."

The young man rubbed his unshaven jaw and appeared to be pondering this question. Then he said, "No, sir. I have to tell the truth. I was the man who killed Felix."

Decianus sighed. "We already know who killed Felix, Thessalus. It wasn't you."

The dark eyes widened. "Holy gods! That wasn't Felix?" The fingers that rose toward his mouth were trembling. "This is even worse than I thought. Is there another man missing, sir?"

A swift glance at Metellus assured Decianus that there was not. "What," he said, "exactly, do you think you did to Felix?"

Thessalus swallowed. His eyes attempted to focus on the edge of the desk. Finally he said, "I think I may have, ah—I may have . . ." The words had failed but the meaning of the collision between the outer edge of the hand and the back of the neck was unmistakable.

Decianus glanced at Metellus again, then returned his attention to the doctor. "Tell me what you did with the body."

Thessalus appeared to be pondering the meaning of this question. Finally he said, "The local people believe the soul resides in the head, sir."

"I see. So where is the soul of Felix residing now?"

"They take the enemy's head home with them. They keep it on display as a trophy. Sometimes they make a cup out of the skull and drink from it."

"That was years ago," put in Metellus. "Even the northerners don't get up to that sort of thing now."

Instead of replying, Thessalus swayed alarmingly and grabbed hold of the desk for support.

"Stand up straight, man! Why on earth would you want to murder Felix?"

Thessalus's eyes closed. His knees buckled. His body slumped to the floor.

"He's relieved of duty," said Decianus, leaning over the desk. "He's to be confined to quarters until further notice. And he's not to talk to anyone."

When the semiconscious doctor had been dragged out, Decianus turned to Metellus. "Search his rooms."

"It can't have been him, sir. He's not the type."

"Then how does he know?"

There was a soft tap at the door. A servant scurried in and removed the tray. When he had gone Metellus said, "Audax must have talked."

"That doesn't seem likely."

"Well, it wasn't me, and it wasn't you either."

Decianus looked him in the eye. "It might have been better to tell the truth in the first place."

"You're doing the right thing, sir," Metellus assured him. "We'll keep Thessalus quiet, arrest the native, and it'll all blow over."

"It had better blow over before the governor gets here."

"Do you want some ideas for the funeral speech?"

Decianus scowled at him. "No," he said. "I want you to concentrate on keeping this thing under control."

When he was alone, Decianus walked across to the small wooden shrine on the side wall of his office, sprinkled some more incense in the burner, and prayed that this mess was not about to get considerably worse.

5

JUST AS POSTUMUS had predicted, the lone rider reappeared—
on a low rise to their right this time—just after the column had
stopped for water. The officers continued to ignore him. When everyone
moved on, he disappeared.

Ahead of Ruso, Postumus was berating a marcher for some misdeed or
other. Ruso found it difficult to see how anyone could get into trouble
simply by putting one foot in front of another, but some remarkably cre-
ative men seemed to manage it. Indeed, a man on a long journey could
begin to think and do all manner of bizarre things. He could start to
wonder if his housekeeper truly had seen something strange in the yard
at the inn. Tilla was no fool: perhaps he should have been more sympathetic. He could wonder what he should do with the rest of the stolen
money. He could even, after he had exhausted all other possibilities,
begin to wonder if he should have listened to his ex-wife. Certainly,
since he had discovered the true extent of his family's debts, Ruso had
begun to see—too late—the sense of Claudia's plans to expand his
business.

"I'm not a businessman," he had objected. "I'm a doctor."

"But you never try to make yourself *known*, Gaius. Do you? I keep
telling you!"

"I don't want to be known. I've plenty of work already. If I make myself more known, I'll have more patients than I can cope with."

"Of course you will! That's the idea. Take on an apprentice to deal with the easy cases and—"

"But if people want me, they want *me*. Not some apprentice."

"Oh, Gaius, for goodness' sake! All you have to do is hire somebody who'll be nice to people! You said yourself that lots of patients get better by themselves and all you have to do is try not to kill them while they're doing it!"

"I said *what*?"

In the course of the argument that followed, it became clear that some unguarded and long-forgotten remark of his had been horribly mangled on its journey through the space between his wife's ears and her mouth. Finally, unable to shake her belief that she was repeating his exact words, he said,

"I hope that's not what you go around telling people?"

"Of course not! I care about your career, even if you don't!"

Ruso scowled at the ears of his horse. He needed a promotion. Distracted by Tilla and entangled in that business about the barmaid, he had failed to impress the right people in Deva. He could not allow that to happen a second time. In the future he must avoid dabbling in matters that were none of his business. And he must make it clear to everyone at this temporary posting that Tilla was not the troublesome sort of native who met gods in stable yards or spread rumors about men with antlers, but a respectable housekeeper who was under proper control.

It was starting to spatter with rain again. Ruso leaned back in the saddle as the horse began to pick its way down a long slow drop that had been cut into the side of the hill. To his right, a bank loomed above the road. To the left, a grassy slope fell away into a thickly wooded valley.

The column must have been descending for at least half a mile when he drew the horse to a standstill. For some reason the pace had slowed to a crawl, and there seemed to be a line of stationary vehicles ahead. He heard Postumus bellow the order to halt.

It was not a wide stretch of road, and the cavalryman coming up the hill had to weave his mount through the queue of men and carts.

"What's the holdup?" asked Ruso.

"The river's burst its banks," explained the cavalryman. "Taken part of the bridge with it. They've got a team patching it up, but—" He broke off, distracted by shouting farther down the hill.

Stationary and bored, soldiers who had had nothing interesting to look at for some miles were craning to their left and yelling abuse. A rider was galloping at full tilt along the margin of the woods not 150 paces below the road. Ruso blinked. He rubbed his eyes. The rider definitely had the head of a stag. And the stag had antlers.

The cavalryman wheeled his horse around and plunged headlong down the hillside to join his comrades in pursuit. Ruso was wondering whether to follow them when over the shouting he heard someone farther back in the line roar, "Clear the road! Out of the way!"

What happened next was over in seconds and seemed to take hours. Ruso urged his own horse aside to the sound of screams and the bellowing of frightened animals. People were trampling over one another in the rush to escape the path of a heavy wagon careening down the road out of control. The axles were shrieking, the oxen galloping and skidding in a vain attempt to outrun the vehicle to which they were still yoked.

Ruso grabbed a fistful of mane as the terrified horse reared beneath him. One of the front oxen fell. The others were dragged down around it. The wagon collided with the thrashing tangle of black bodies. It slewed off the road, crashed onto its side, and rolled down the hill. For a moment there was a terrible silence. Then came the sound of men screaming.

Finally bringing the trembling horse to a standstill, Ruso surveyed the chaos. Further back, two carts had tipped off the road. One had a pair of mules still struggling and kicking in their harness. A boy had slid down from the bank above them where he must have leaped for safety, and was wiping the mud from his hands. A woman was comforting her sobbing children. People were calling the names of friends and of gods, gathering their scattered possessions or sitting dazed at the roadside while drivers set off toward the woods in pursuit of fleeing animals.

Legionaries were running to form a guard as two men with bloodied swords stepped away from the carcasses of the oxen. Down by the stricken wagon, Postumus was barking orders and a squad was struggling to heave the cargo of lead out of the wreckage.

He could not see Tilla.

He dismounted and put his hand on the shoulder of a pale boy who was standing motionless with his fingers in his mouth. "Are you hurt?"

The boy shook his head, still staring at the scene.

"Hold her steady for me," ordered Ruso, pressing the reins into the boy's hand. The child looked relieved to have something to do.

As he strode up to retrieve his medical case from one of the stricken carts, Ruso glanced down at the woods. The Stag Man, or Cernunnos, or whoever he was, had vanished.

6

THE GRAY-FACED CARPENTER laid out on the grass gave a moan of pain. Ruso had not revealed the severity of his injuries to the man, nor to his hysterical girlfriend, who turned out to be Lydia, Tilla's patient from yesterday. The tiny bundle of cloth she was clutching had the sort of persistent rasping cry that set one's teeth on edge. Finally the man himself had summoned the strength to tell her to go away and see to the child: He would be fine. Ruso, knowing the state of the leg hidden beneath the blanket and suspecting further internal injuries, could not imagine that he really believed it.

"We'll get you down to the sick bay at the fort," he promised, relieved to see that the man he had dispatched with a message to the fort by the river was already weaving his way back up through the jammed traffic on the road.

The news was not good. The sick bay had flooded during the storm. The patients had been evacuated. The building was full of orderlies padding about in mud with mops and buckets.

Ruso checked the state of the leg again. The bleeding was more or less under control, but the man would not survive the journey across the hills to Coria without surgery.

He helped the stretcher bearers maneuver the carpenter across the slippery remains of the damp bridge, then strode ahead up the road, examining the line of vehicles waiting to cross in the opposite direction. Picking out an empty carriage that had the luxury of suspension, he commandeered it with the optimistic promise to the driver that the army would pay the owner well for his trouble. The vehicle was maneuvered out of the line and parked farther up the hill away from the traffic. One of the stretcher bearers lit a fire at the roadside.

Ruso began to lay out the instruments: needle and thread, hooks, scalpel, cautery. . . . Finally alerted to the enormity of what was happening by the appearance of the bone saw, the driver had to have his objections quieted by the promise of more cash and an imminent flogging if he refused to cooperate. The carpenter was in turn quieted with mandrake and held steady by two less-than-confident stretcher bearers as Ruso cleaned up the mess that had been a leg and prepared for the drastic surgery that might save its owner.

Later, as the carriage rumbled up out of the river valley in the direction of Coria, it held four men in addition to the disgruntled driver. Ruso was tending the carpenter, whose truncated thigh was now neatly sewn over with a flap of skin hidden by a temporary dressing. Behind them, a bandager plucked from the ranks of the Twentieth was looking after the unfortunate slave who had been in charge of the wagon when it ran out of control.

"Not long now," Ruso promised the carpenter as a particularly nasty pothole caused the man to groan. "We'll have you properly patched up in the hospital."

The slave's injuries were less serious. He had leaped clear just as his vehicle tipped over, and escaped with cuts and bruises only to find himself chained and beaten up by the soldiers who found him weeping beside his fallen animals. Postumus had asked Ruso to get him away from the scene before somebody killed him.

The slave had tears welling in his swollen eyes, but to Ruso's surprise they were neither of pity for himself nor sorrow for the trouble he had caused. "Poor old Speedy and Star," he was mumbling through broken teeth. "Poor little Holly. Never a bit of trouble. Even old Acorn. Poor old boys. They didn't deserve to go like that. I wouldn't have let them go like that, sirs."

"Wiggle your toes," grunted the bandager. "Right. Now flex that knee."

Ruso gave the carpenter another sip of honeyed water. The slave bent his knee as far as his chains would allow, shrinking away from the injured man as if he were afraid he would leap up and attack him. "It weren't my fault, sirs," he insisted. "Honest it weren't. I tried the brake at the top, I swear I did. I always try the brake. I don't know what went wrong. It was holding all right yesterday and the hills was just as bad."

"Keep still," grunted the bandager, splashing more cheap wine onto the bloodstained cloth and wedging the flagon in the corner of the cart behind him. "And shut up. You're bothering me."

Ruso glanced down at the carpenter to check that there was no more bleeding, and scratched at his own ribs. The man was very weak. He might survive, and he might not. Nine walking wounded were being patched up by the medical staff back at the flooded fort. The hillside was littered with shattered cargoes, damaged vehicles, and the carcasses of one mule and four oxen. Nobody—for the moment—was going to be very interested in hearing the slave's excuses.

"It weren't the animals, sirs," the man was continuing, glancing from the bandager to Ruso and back. "They're steady old boys. I trained them myself. I looked after them like—ow!"

"I said, shut up."

But the slave was clearly desperate to get his point across before someone decided to punish him again. "They've never run off like that before, officers. Never!" He reached out and grabbed Ruso's arm, evidently deciding he was the more sympathetic of the two. "It was the Stag Man, sir! I saw him."

"Everybody saw him," pointed out Ruso, pushing aside the memory of Tilla crying out, *"Cernunnos!"* "He was nowhere near the wagon."

"Somebody's put a curse on me. The Stag Man said a spell and made the team bolt and the brake give way." Tears began to spill down the slave's cheeks. "Oh, holy Jupiter! My master's going to kill me!"

Ruso eyed the battered and tearstained face. The slave had chosen to take a vehicle creaking under the weight of lead down a long and difficult hill while the road was still crowded with travelers. He should have known better.

"Sir!"

A horse was following them up the hill at a shambling half trot. The rider was kitted out like an ordinary member of the infantry, and instead of steering he seemed to be using both hands to cling to the horns of the saddle.

"Sir!"

"Albanus? What are you doing on my horse?"

"I'm having a very uncomfortable time, sir!" cried Albanus, bouncing to one side and adding "Whoa!" as the animal showed no signs of slowing down.

"Sit back," suggested Ruso. "Use your reins."

"I've tried that, sir. It just ignores me."

The horse finally slowed to a walk, although it was doubtful whether Albanus had influenced its decision. It seemed that, with uncharacteristic deviousness, he had managed to avoid the riding lessons that were supposed to be the lot of every well-trained soldier.

"Sir, I thought I'd better come and tell you Centurion Postumus wants to talk to Tilla."

Ruso frowned. "To Tilla? What about?"

"I don't know, sir, but he doesn't look very happy. That's why I thought I ought to tell you."

"I can't deal with it now," said Ruso, not bothering to add that Postumus never looked very happy.

"So what shall I say to the centurion, sir?"

"You'll have to find her," said Ruso, wondering what Tilla had done that would interest Postumus during the current crisis. "She was helping the civilians the last time I saw her. She might be with a mother and a baby. And when you find her, tell her I said she's to do exactly what she's told for once, will you?"

"I'll tell her that, sir."

"I'll keep the horse," said Ruso. "Hitch her to the carriage and walk back."

When a relieved Albanus had dismounted awkwardly and headed back toward the scene of the accident, Ruso turned to the miserable slave. "Where was your wagon parked overnight?"

"In the yard at the inn, officer, sir. All secure. I always look after my master's property, sir."

Ruso sighed. He didn't know how Postumus had found out, but he could guess why the grimfaced centurion wanted to talk to Tilla.

7

THE RAIN HAD stopped now, thank the gods, and all around people were busy clearing up the mess made by the accident. Baggage was being reloaded onto righted vehicles. A mule had been fetched from the army post down the hill and was being persuaded into the harness vacated by the one lying at the roadside. A family rounded up from the nearest farm were struggling to shift the carcass of an ox while a couple of legionaries leaned on their shields and watched. Other soldiers were standing guard on the top of the bank and facing outward down the valley, as if they were expecting followers of the mystery rider to burst out of the woods and attack.

The civilian victims of the accident, closer to the wagon's slow start, had mostly gotten away with bumps and scrapes. Tilla had been trying to clean gravel out of a small girl's knee when the medicus's weedy clerk had arrived with the summons from the centurion. She might have ignored it, but the weedy one had also brought very firm instructions from the medicus that she should do as she was told. She could see how much Albanus enjoyed passing that on. So now, again, she was standing in damp clothes at the roadside under the guard of soldiers.

The nose poking out beneath the metal rim of the centurion's helmet made her want to laugh, but the black stones of his eyes suggested that this conversation was not going to be amusing.

He said, "You were seen at the inn last night. Not the sort of place slaves usually sleep."

"I fell in some mud, sir. My master takes me to the baths to clean myself."

"But you didn't go to the baths, did you?"

How did he know this? More worryingly, why did he care? "The baths are full of men," she explained. "And not clean. I take water and wash privately."

Farther down the road, they had managed to move the first animal. There was no sign of the medicus, who had rushed up to her, hugged her, and then looked embarrassed and hurried away to deal with the injured. "If you will just tell me what you need to know, sir . . ."

"What were you doing in the yard?"

"I went to look for a friend. But she is not there."

"And then?"

"Then I went back inside, sir."

"You're lying."

"I am not!"

The stick moved so fast she barely saw it coming. Just felt the blow and the pain flowing into her shoulder as the shock died away. She tried to steady herself. "I pray to the gods of the storm, sir. That is all. Then I go back inside with my master."

The eyes assessed her while the mind seemed to be thinking over the next question. "How long were you alone out there? I'll be asking your master as well."

She was confused. She wished they would let go of her arms so she could rub the pain out of her shoulder. "I was not alone in the yard, sir."

The eyes betrayed a flicker of interest.

"I think I am alone but then I see . . ." She stopped. How was she going to explain to this foreigner that she had brought the god upon them with her prayers?

"What?"

"A man."

"If you're lying, you'll be sorry."

"I am not lying, sir. I was praying. He was there. I saw him."

"Describe him."

She frowned. "I do not know him." It was true, she did not know him, but every time she pictured the faintly quizzical dark brows and shadowed eyes, she had the feeling she had seen them somewhere before. She dared not say so. The centurion would only hit her again for failing to remember where. Perhaps it was in a dream. The gods visited people in dreams. Everyone knew it.

"Tall, short, fat, thin, young, old? What were his clothes like?"

She closed her eyes and murmured a prayer to Cernunnos for courage.

"Speak up, girl. What did he look like?"

She opened her eyes. "He is the man-god we saw on the horse, sir. He is the god with the antlers."

This time she had braced herself for the stick, but the pain of the second blow on top of the first still made her gasp.

"I don't want to hear that rubbish. Was there a man or wasn't there?"

"It was the god Cernunnos, sir, I swear. I felt him brush past me."

"Tell me what he looked like."

"He had antlers!" What more could anyone need to know?

The centurion gave an exaggerated sigh. "Try telling me what he was doing."

"He is standing with his hand on the wheel of a wagon. One moment he is there, the next he is vanish in the dark."

The centurion glanced at his men. "All right. Let her go."

The grip on her arms was released.

"Stay where I can find you," he ordered. "I'll be talking to your master later. And if you've lied to me, I'll have you flogged."

8

THE HOSPITAL, SIR?"

Ruso had unfastened his armor, slung his riding breeches over one shoulder, and was clad in a creased and sweaty tunic whose edges were splattered with mud and bloodstains. The Batavian soldier from whom he had just asked directions looked at him with mingled concern and confusion, then glanced up and down the busy street of the fort in the apparent hope that he might spot a building he had failed to notice before. Since the stronghold at Coria had turned out to be extremely small—an energetic sentry atop the timber turret of the east gate could have held a shouted conversation over the clang of the smithy with one on the west—this did not seem likely.

"I think the nearest hospital's at Vindolanda, sir," the man suggested. "Shall I go and ask somebody for you?"

"Vindolanda?"

"Out on the west road, sir. You could be there by dinnertime on a fast horse."

"But you must have a hospital!" insisted Ruso. "The gate guard told me it was next to headquarters. I've got an injured man arriving any minute."

The man frowned. "Not more trouble, sir?"

"Traffic accident," explained Ruso.

The man pointed to a long low wood-framed building across the road. "They must have meant the infirmary. You won't find a medic there now, though, sir. Not at this time of day."

"I *am* the medic," explained Ruso. The man did not look entirely convinced.

The closed door of the infirmary had painted carvings of gods nailed up on either side. The uglier of the two must be some sort of protector that the Tenth Batavians had brought with them from wherever Batavia was. The other, with a snake curled around his stick, was Aesculapius, the god of healing. At least the carpenter would find a familiar helper here. The artistic effect was spoiled by an untidy message chalked on the door: "Days to Governor's Visit" was followed by a cloudy blur slashed over with a white "IV."

Ruso stepped forward, rapped on the wood, and lifted the latch. The door did not budge. Squinting at the latch to see if it were jammed in some way, he knocked again. Surely the Batavian had not meant that in the absence of the doctor, nobody at all would be running the infirmary?

Somewhere beyond the building the tramp of boots grew louder. An order was bellowed and the tramp changed rhythm. Evidently "Days to Governor's Visit IV" was inspiring some serious marching practice.

He knocked again.

From inside came a shout of, "We're closed. Come back in an hour."

Ruso slammed the flat of his hand three times against the door. From somewhere within came a roar of "Answer the bloody door, Gambax!"

There was the scrape of something being removed from the latch. A slack-jawed creature with lank brown hair appeared and stopped chewing for long enough to say, "What do you want?" in the same fluent but guttural Latin as the other men Ruso had met on the way through the fort.

"Gaius Petreius Ruso, medicus with the Twentieth. There's an urgent casualty coming in. Didn't you get the message?"

The soldier pulled open the door and managed something that might have been a salute. "Gambax, sir. Deputy medic. What message?"

Ruso stepped into the dingy corridor. At the far end he could make out a square soldierly shape planted outside one of the doors. The shape showed no interest in him as he followed Gambax into a cramped and ill-lit room that seemed to be both an office and a pharmacy.

"I was just having some lunch," explained Gambax.

"At this hour?"

"Busy morning, sir." The man scooped up the remains of a raisin pastry and brushed crumbs off the desk. "We've had a murder. The body was brought in this morning."

"Sorry to hear that," said Ruso, noting that it did not seem to have affected his appetite. "Where's the doctor?"

"Gone sick, sir."

This was not good news. "I've done an emergency amputation on the road. Crushed femur, and I think there are broken ribs and bruising to the lungs. He'll be here any minute. Where is everybody?"

"The lads have gone off to get a bite to eat, sir."

Ruso took a deep breath and reminded himself that he was not in Deva now. He could not expect a country outpost serving six hundred men to be run in the same way as a legionary hospital serving five thousand.

"Don't you worry, sir," Gambax assured him, reaching for a cup and swilling the pastry down with something that smelled very much like beer. "The watch'll give them a shout when your lads come in over the bridge. How about a drink while you're waiting?"

"No thanks," said Ruso. He glanced across at what must be the pharmacy table. Above it, a cobweb billowed gently in the breeze from the open window. Three shelves held a jumble of pots and bottles and bags and boxes. A few had labels indicating their contents, written in a large untidy script. Most did not. The table itself held a weighing scale and an abandoned mortar bowl containing some sort of brown paste. Beneath it were a couple of wine amphorae—medicinal wine, he assumed—and a wastebasket crammed with wilted greenery. The basket was topped with a selection of broken pots projecting from a pale crusted mass of green slime. Some of the slime had dripped down the side of the basket and hardened into a small semicircular pancake on the floorboards. Ruso said, "Who's the pharmacist?"

"That would be me, sir."

Somehow this was not a surprise. "What medicines have you got for pain relief and postoperative treatment?"

"All the basics, sir. And plenty of poppy tears and mandrake."

Ruso hoped the man knew which containers they were in. He glanced down at the desk. A few stray crumbs remained. Black inkstains had spread themselves along the grain of the wood, running into the circular imprints of cups bearing drinks long ago consumed. A wooden tablet addressed in the same large hand as the medicines lay to one side.

"I keep the records as well, sir."

"I thought you might."

"Yes, sir. We're an auxiliary unit here. We don't have lots of staff like you're used to in the legions. Would you like to take a look at the treatment room, sir? Just through that door, next on the left."

Now that Ruso's eyes had adjusted to the gloom he could make out that the figure at the end of the corridor was a squat centurion with a savage haircut. The man's glare suggested that whoever was behind the door he was guarding was not receiving visitors.

Evidently Gambax was not in charge of the treatment room, where two cobweb-free glass windows allowed the surgeon enough light to see what he was doing on the operating table. This was good news, but within seconds the warmth from the brazier in the corner had reawoken the itches on Ruso's back and ribs along with the smell of horse in his clothing. He placed his medical case on the side table, slid a bronze probe down his spine, and enjoyed a few blessed moments of relief.

His concentration was interrupted by a voice from the doorway.

"Everything to your liking in here, is it, sir?"

"Very good," said Ruso, hastily removing the probe. "Is there usually a centurion in the corridor?"

"That's Audax, sir," said Gambax, adding, "It's one of his men lying murdered in the mortuary. Would you like to see the rest of the facilities?"

The rest of the facilities consisted of a steamy kitchen containing a ruddy-faced cook with a limp and two fingers missing, a couple of untidy storerooms, the smaller of which contained a vast barrel, and a latrine with the usual stench defying the usual effort to mask it. The mortuary was behind the centurion, and thus inaccessible. These were the facilities to service four smelly and stuffy wards containing seventeen beds and fifteen patients, four of whom were sitting around a table with a jug of beer. Judging by the speed at which they concealed the evidence of gambling when Ruso appeared, the four were not terribly sick.

One of the patients in the next room looked up from a board game with his neighbor and offered Ruso an unexpectedly warm welcome. "A doctor! Good to see you, sir! How's Doctor Thessalus?"

"About the same," put in Gambax from the doorway.

"What's the matter with him, sir?"

"He's ill," said Gambax.

"Doctor Thessalus saw to both of us, sir," said the man, indicating his comrade, whose shoulder was heavily bandaged. "But we haven't seen anybody since." He leaned forward and flung back the blankets to reveal a splinted leg. "Would you like to start with me, sir?"

"Not just now," said Ruso, not wanting to trespass uninvited on a colleague's territory. "I've got a casualty arriving in a moment."

"Ah!" said the man, nodding, as if that explained the state of Ruso's attire. He lowered his voice. "Wasn't that Stag Man again, was it, sir?"

"Traffic accident," said Ruso, then, realizing there was no hope of swearing 170 legionaries to silence, added, "There was a rider who'd put some sort of animal thing on his head. But he was nowhere near the accident."

The man and his friend exchanged glances. "You want to be careful around here, sir," he said. "He's just left one of our lads dead in a back alley."

"He's got powers," put in the man with the shoulder injury. "The locals are saying the gods have sent him from the Other World."

Ruso said, "Well, when I saw him, he was very firmly in this one."

Back in the office, the Batavians' deputy medic was still keeping company with his beer. "Have you called the staff in, Gambax?"

Gambax looked at him over the rim of the cup. "Don't you worry, sir. Your lads aren't over the bridge yet."

"I need men here now. I need a room scrubbed out and aired and a fresh mattress brought in."

"What—right now, sir?"

"Right now. And while they're doing it maybe you could find me some calamine, or alum in honey?"

There was a slight twitch at one side of Gambax's mouth as he said, "You didn't happen to stay at the Golden Fleece last night, sir?"

"Never again."

"Yes," said Gambax. "That's what they all say."

9

A S SOON AS the cart rumbled in beneath the wooden towers of Coria's west gatehouse, the slave who had been driving the runaway cart was marched to the fort lockup and the groaning carpenter carried into the infirmary. His breathing was definitely worse, although nothing seemed to have penetrated the lungs.

Ruso did what he could to ease the breathing, cleaned up the minor cuts and scrapes, and supervised the dressing of the amputation site. He had just finished settling his patient into a hastily cleaned room under the care of the bandager from the Twentieth when he received a summons to report immediately to the prefect of the Tenth Batavians.

The yelling and clatter of weapons practice and the arrhythmic clang of the forge barely seemed to disturb the peace of the prefect's courtyard. Ruso waited in a space between two tall amphorae that the household staff had reused as plant pots, and wished he had taken the time to borrow some clean clothes. In front of him, marooned on a stone plinth in a rectangular pond, stood a two-foot-high statue of a nymph whose skimpy attire was no more appropriately designed for life in the north than the house surrounding her. Ruso wondered what it must be like for the prefect and his family—assuming he had one—to have to scuttle from room to room via an open walkway in the depths of a British winter. He was eyeing the nymph with some sympathy when one of the doors under the walkway opened and he was summoned to enter the prefect's office.

Prefect Decianus turned out to have all the finest qualities of Roman manhood except that he wasn't—by blood—a Roman. His jaw was square, his shoulders were broad, and he had the air of solid dependability more reliably found in centurions than in the aristocratic holders of high office. When he said, "Doctor. You're traveling with the vexillation from the Twentieth Legion?" his Latin had only the faintest of Batavian accents. Evidently he was one of those provincial leaders who were permitted to command their own troops overseas in the service of Rome.

"I was sorry to hear about the accident," the prefect continued. "I'm told the men from the Twentieth will camp here tonight, then move up the road to Ulucium in the morning. Will your casualty be fit to travel by then?"

"No, sir."

"What do you think about trusting him to our medical service?"

"I hear your regular medic is ill, sir," said Ruso, hoping not to have to venture an opinion on the patchy regime at the infirmary and wondering if the silent man sitting at Decianus's elbow was something to do with it.

"And you don't want to leave your man in the care of our deputy," observed Decianus.

Ruso looked him in the eye. "I think the patient needs experienced supervision, sir."

"Good." The prefect settled back in his chair and folded his arms. "Our own medic is due to move on in a few days," he said. "His replacement is traveling up here with the governor. I'm told he's keen to see military experience. I suppose that means he wants to explore the insides of my men. In the meantime we have nobody to fill the gap. I'm putting in a request to keep you until then."

So unless Postumus objected—which was unlikely—it seemed Ruso would be here for at least the next four days. He would be able to look after the carpenter. That was good. He would have to work with Gambax. That wasn't. He said, "Thank you, sir."

"Don't thank me. I want you to do a job of work. Our man Thessalus has not been . . ." the prefect paused, searching for a word. "He has not been on top of things for some time. One of our escorts was attacked by

bandits the other day and it took three hours to organize a team to operate on the wounded. My men deserve better than that. You're with the
Legion, so you must be reasonably competent. While we have you, I
want you to sort out the shambles that calls itself a medical service."

"Thank you, sir," said Ruso, less sincerely than before and realizing
that the room was beginning to smell as though he had brought his horse
in with him.

"Are you a hunting man, Ruso?"

Perhaps the prefect had noticed it too. "Not really, sir."

"A pity. Never mind. The other thing I want you to do is connected
with the body now under guard in the mortuary. I expect you've been
told that one of our trumpeters was found murdered this morning."

Ruso, who had often felt the urge to murder an enthusiastic trumpeter
first thing in the morning, reminded himself that this was a serious matter. "I'll have the postmortem report ready by the end of the day, sir," he
promised.

"What? We don't need you to go near the body."

"No?" What did they want him for, then?

"Sorry to disappoint. I know how much you medics enjoy the chance
for a dig about, but any fool can see how he died and we already know
who did it."

Afterward, Ruso blamed the bedbugs. He would normally have kept
his mouth shut. But today he had woken up tired, he had witnessed a
shocking accident, performed harrowing surgery, seen a strange creature
he did not believe in, and worst of all, despite Gambax's ointment—
alum boiled in cabbage juice, apparently—he was still itchy. He was used
to his profession being insulted, but today he was not in the mood to put
up with it.

"I don't enjoy it, sir," he insisted. "I've got better things to do. I was
only offering because a close inspection of the body might offer you
some more evidence for the murder case."

The prefect's eyebrows rose. "Evidence?"

"What sort of weapon was used," said Ruso, improvising wildly.
"Whether the victim put up a fight and might have injured the attacker.
Whether he was killed where he was found, or whether he was moved
afterward. That sort of thing."

"I see."

A soft voice pointed out, "We already know what the weapon was, sir."

The prefect glanced at the man beside him. "But the rest might be useful, don't you think, Metellus?" He returned his attention to Ruso. "You can do all that?"

"Sometimes, sir," said Ruso, realizing he had now advanced too far to retreat. "It depends on the circumstances."

The man leaned across and whispered something in the prefect's ear. Moments later Ruso found himself admiring the nymph from the shelter of the covered walkway while the prefect and the other man were arguing on the other side of the office door. He hoped the prefect would lose. He didn't want to meet a dead trumpeter. He wanted to go and check on the amputee and then track down a good masseur followed by a hot meal. Preferably washed down with a glass of decent wine.

When he was summoned to return the prefect said, "You can examine the body and report your findings back to Metellus."

"Yes, sir."

"The circumstances are unusual," said the prefect.

As Ruso wondered what the usual circumstances of murdered trumpeters might be, Decianus confirmed most of the gossip he had already picked up at the infirmary: that the body of a Batavian soldier had been found this morning about a hundred paces outside the fort, in an alleyway between a butcher's shop and a general store. "At the moment," continued Decianus, "relations with the natives are tense, and a rumor has gone around that this death was something to do with the rebel horseman I'm told you saw this afternoon. Metellus has investigated, and it turns out to be a simple brawl outside a bar. The culprit is a native who will be arrested very soon and tried by the governor when he arrives in four days' time. In the meantime I don't want my men unsettled. Any suggestions that the murder is something to do with the local gods are to be firmly denied."

"Yes, sir."

"Despite anything you may think you find during your examination."

"Yes, sir."

"So just to avoid any confusion, Metellus will help you with your report. Now, what I really wanted you for in connection with the murder is something else. Tell me what you know about treating madness."

Ruso realized, too late, that he was scratching the back of his ear instead of replying. At length he said, "Not a great deal, sir. I've met some cases in the past. I can offer comfort, but I can't promise a cure. Frankly, I think anyone who tells you they can is lying."

"Hm." Evidently this was not what the man was hoping to hear. "Your predecessor, Thessalus, is locked in his rooms convinced he's the one who did the murder. Which he isn't, but he does seem to know more than he should about the details. The natives are a bit overexcited at the moment with this Stag Man business, and if they find out we're charging one of their people with murder when one of our officers has confessed, it won't go down well. Metellus has questioned him but can't get any sense out of him. So, we need to get him to withdraw his confession before anyone hears about it, and find out who told him how the victim was killed. See if you can settle him down, will you?"

"I'll do my best, sir," said Ruso, hoping his voice did not betray his lack of enthusiasm. He had arrived here with one patient and a few questions about visions of the gods. Now he had a sloppy health service to shape up, a politically sensitive postmortem to carry out, and a deranged colleague. The holiday was definitely over.

10

"I CARRY OUT special duties for the prefect," explained Metellus as
Decianus's guards stepped smartly aside to let them out of the official
residence.

"Special duties?" inquired Ruso.

"Whatever he wants done."

"I see," said Ruso, admiring this splendidly evasive reply and failing to
trace Metellus's origins from his neutral accent, or to detect any sign of
character or background in an even-featured, unmemorable appearance that
was only marred by a few flakes of dandruff on the shoulders of an ordinary blue tunic.

Metellus led him away from the headquarters building. As they were
passing a line of men waiting for rations outside the granaries he said,
"Haven't I heard of you somewhere, Ruso?"

"I doubt it."

"Really? I'm sure the name . . ." the man shrugged. "No matter. Where
are you from?"

"Gallia Narbonensis. You?"

"Rome," said Metellus, with the casual air of a man who has no need
to prove his superiority. "Appointed by the governor."

"The new one?"

"No, Bradua. I've been here for four years now."

Ruso wondered what the Batavians made of having a governor's man foisted upon them. And how secure Metellus's position now was, since the man who had appointed him was no longer in charge. No doubt he would be anxious to make the right impression when the new governor came to visit.

"Four years is a long time to spend this far from Rome," observed Ruso.

"It's not as remote as you think," said Metellus. "Londinium keeps a close eye on what happens up here. And Hadrian's known for taking an interest in the provinces. If a man does well here, it's noticed."

Presumably if he didn't, that would be noticed too.

Just inside the west gate they turned and crunched along the gravel of the perimeter road, passing the din of a metal workshop and a yard where men were stripping down a heavy mechanical bolt launcher for repair. Behind it, a line of wooden spear shafts were propped against the wall, ready to have their iron heads attached.

They clattered up the steps to the top of the ramparts and Metellus said, "Take a good look."

A faint waft of boiled cabbage drifted past as Ruso rested his elbows on the rough wood. Twenty feet below him, a couple of tethered horses were grazing pale spheres in the grass of the security zone. A line of carts was waiting to be allowed entry through the gates. Beyond them lay a jumble of civilian buildings leading down to the bridge. On the far side of the river, three vehicles were crawling along the thin streak of road that led along a valley dotted with grazing animals and the odd cone of native thatch.

It struck Ruso that the whole of Coria could have been picked up and set down within the stout walls of Deva's legionary fortress and there would still be room to spare.

"This place is sometimes described as a brown oasis in a desert of green," said Metellus. "A lot of the men from the forts up in the hills come down to enjoy their leave here. Coria is where the north and the east–west roads meet."

Ruso wondered what sort of posting would lead a man to think of a road junction as an exciting holiday destination, and scanned the bridge for any sign of the Twentieth's arrival. "So where's the border?" he asked.

"Just turn a little to your right."

Ruso frowned. All he could see was another road, with a dispatch rider just out of the west gates urging his horse into a canter.

"That's more or less it," said Metellus.

Looking from one side of the road to the other, Ruso failed to discern any difference. He felt a faint slump of disappointment. Was this what he had traveled all those miles to see? "Where are the barbarian hordes?"

"The tribes just across the border are officially friendly," explained Metellus. "And just to make sure, we offer the usual incentives."

"Which are?"

"We're giving some of their sons a free education down in Londinium, and we send advisers to their meetings."

"I see," said Ruso, assuming that the sons were effectively hostages and "advisers" meant "spies."

"In exchange, we ignore the odd cattle raid and their head men get invited to dinner when the governor comes to visit."

"It's not quite how I'd imagined it."

"Oh, the hordes are out there, believe me," said Metellus. "On both sides of the border. Sulking and skulking, most of them looking like perfectly innocent hill farmers. According to my informers, this Stag Man business has them all very excited. That's why this murder has come at the worst possible time, and why the prefect's being scrupulous about investigating it. We have to make it clear that the culprit's getting a fair trial. We don't want to give them an excuse to dig out the weapons they aren't supposed to have and march on the nearest fort demanding justice for Our Poor Innocent Boy chained up by the Evil Romans."

"I'm beginning to wish I hadn't gotten involved in this."

"Frankly, my view is that the fewer people involved the better," agreed Metellus. "But a report from a medical officer won't do any harm. We can be seen to be taking the inquiry seriously."

Ruso watched the dispatch rider growing smaller in the distance. A road patrol was approaching in the opposite direction. As they passed, he saw arms raised in greeting. He wondered how many soldiers were holding the string of isolated forts and watchtowers that must lie out along that border road, compared to the number of sulkers and skulkers lurking in the surrounding hills—although why anyone should bother to fight over land that seemed to contain nothing but a few peasants and sheep was a mystery.

"I had imagined the border would be more . . ." he paused, searching for a word. "Watertight."

"We don't want it watertight," said Metellus. "We want it porous. We want long strings of well-laden merchants traveling in and out of the province paying border taxes. We station men here to run the customs posts, the men spend their wages, and that gives the locals a chance to turn a profit. It all works very nicely as long as everybody behaves themselves."

"I see," said Ruso, wondering what the northerners could offer to sell or afford to buy. "So this business with travelers being ambushed—"

"It's making things very difficult," said Metellus. "There's been an interesting change in language up here lately," he said. "Travelers are no longer talking about *arriving* at their destination. They're starting to call it *getting through*."

"I'm told there are people who think the Stag Man is some sort of god," said Ruso, not adding that his housekeeper was one of them.

"The locals are a superstitious bunch," explained Metellus. "They think stags are messengers from another world. You don't have to go back too many generations before you find human sacrifice and all manner of magic and mayhem in the name of religion. That's another reason for keeping a watchful eye on their get-togethers."

Ruso decided this was not the time to request a gate pass to allow Tilla in and out of the fort.

"Not everything you'll hear about the Stag Man is true," continued Metellus. "But as you'll find when you've been up here awhile, what's true is less important than what people believe."

"Well, I believe I've got a body to examine."

Metellus turned to head toward the steps, and waited for a man to lead a mule laden with firewood past before continuing, "So, we don't want our men putting all that together with the murder and imagining there's some sort of mad Druid revival going on right outside the gates."

"Where their families live."

"Exactly. It would cause unnecessary alarm."

It would also cause a serious discipline problem. The fine balance of the border would be a distant memory, and so would Metellus's hopes of making a good impression on the new governor.

As he followed him back toward the shambles that called itself a medical service, Ruso pondered the man from Rome. Average height, average weight, age somewhere between late twenties and midthirties. Being so unremarkable made him the sort of man who could notice things without himself being noticed. The sort of man who would have had written on his recruitment documents, "no distinguishing features." An ideal man for special duties.

"The trouble with the Britons, Doctor," Metellus continued as they approached the twin gods of the infirmary, "is that you can never quite rely on them. But fortunately for us, the tribes have a long tradition of falling out with each other. In addition to which, some of them don't take much notice of their own leaders." Metellus paused. "So the last thing we need is a troublemaker who's going to unite them."

11

RUSO HAD ALREADY guessed from the shape what he was going to find when he pulled the sheet back, but it was still a shock. He dragged the sheet down to the end of the table and folded it with unaccustomed neatness while he struggled to control the urge to walk out of the incense-filled mortuary and fill his lungs with fresh air. He had been a fool to open his mouth in the prefect's office. He should never have got himself involved in something like this. He understood now what the prefect had meant about Metellus helping with his report. This was some sort of ritual killing, and he was being asked to help cover it up.

The wave of nausea passed. Regaining his composure, he turned to Metellus. "Why didn't you tell me?"

"Security," said Metellus. "You never know who's listening."

"So," said Ruso, turning back toward the naked corpse which had been so thoroughly washed that any incidental evidence would be long gone, "Where *is* his head?"

"We're hoping to find it when we get hold of the murderer," said Metellus. "Just tell us what you can from what you have here."

Ruso walked slowly around the table, examining what remained of the body from all angles, and glancing at the polished military belt and dagger that had been laid out beside him. "I'm not going to be able to do much with this," he said. "Who cleaned him up?"

"Audax."

Centurion Audax had gone to fetch the bowl of water and cloths Ruso had asked for, and which he now realized were superfluous.

Ruso flipped open a note tablet and reflected that it was just as well Albanus was still some miles back on the road with Postumus and the other men from the Twentieth. The clerk would be deeply offended to find Ruso writing his own notes.

"The victim's name is Felix," prompted Metellus, "And the cause of death is *head injuries*."

Ruso glanced up. "Without a head to examine, that's rather difficult to prove. For all we know he could have been poisoned. Died of natural causes. Choked on a radish. This could have been done afterward. How much blood was there?"

"The cause of death in the report needs to be consistent with the statements already made. With no mention of anything missing."

"What's true is less important than what people believe?"

"You were the one who asked to be involved."

"If I put down the cause of death as head injuries," pointed out Ruso, "And then the head turns up—"

"If it turns up, Doctor, particularly if it turns up in native hands, your professional reputation will be the least of our problems. Now if you have everything you need, I'll leave you with Audax. As you'll appreciate, I'm having a rather busy day."

As Ruso was wondering whether he could possibly write a postmortem report that left out "cause of death" altogether, Centurion Audax entered, bringing the water and a welcome waft of slightly clearer air from the corridor.

"You're another of these doctor fellers, then," the centurion observed, eyeing Ruso as if he were some kind of interesting insect. "Not mad, are you?"

"Not as far as I know."

"Well, you won't find anything wrong with me. Or my men."

"Good," said Ruso, placing the water on a side table.

The centurion lifted his chin slightly, narrowing his eyes as if he was not sure whether Ruso was being sarcastic. "Want to know why?"

There were several things that Ruso wanted to know. They included the whereabouts of the rest of the corpse, the circumstances of its discovery, what it had looked like before it was washed, and what the hell he was going to put on his report. The reasons for Audax's good health were not of immediate relevance, but clearly he was going to have to listen to them before he could find out anything else.

"Doctor Scribonius's Tonic," announced Audax.

"Really?" Ruso had never heard of this particular medicine, but he was not surprised. A public desperate for health and wary of doctors provided a willing market for any number of wonder cures. A few were genuine, most useless, and some positively dangerous.

"A dose of Doctor Scribonius," said Audax, "and a swim in the river every morning."

"That sounds very healthy," said Ruso, turning back to the body. "Can you tell me—"

"Take a look at this." The centurion had lifted one leg in the air as if he were about to perform a dance. "See?"

Ruso guessed that he was supposed to be admiring the ragged four-inch scar that ran from just above the knee to the outside of the thigh. "How did that happen?"

"Arrow," said Audax, as casually as another man might have said, "Splinter." "Pulled it out and stitched it myself."

"Very impressive," said Ruso, wondering if the centurion cut his hair himself too.

The leg was lowered. "That's what the doctor said."

There was a pause. Ruso suspected he was supposed to fill it by announcing that he had decided to give up wasting his time with medicine and become a plumber. "Well," he said, "it sounds as though I won't be seeing many of your men while I'm here. Now, about this—"

"If you get one and he's fit to stand, you send him straight back to me. It's no good me training them up if they can sneak across to you and have every sniffle blamed on breathing bad air and eating the wrong thing for dinner."

"I'll bear that in mind," said Ruso, recognizing a garbled parody of other men's careful and considered work on the causes of disease. "When you found this body—"

"My men's job is to eat what they're given, go where they're told, and do what I tell them when they get there. It won't do them a scrap of good to lie around the infirmary feeling sorry for themselves."

It was the second time this afternoon that Ruso had been told what his diagnosis should be. "So, as one of your men, Felix was in good health?"

he asked, finally seeing a way to corral Audax and steer him toward the subject.

Audax at last paid some attention to the body. One hand rose to finger a charm on a leather thong around his neck. "You're the doctor," he said.

"You were his centurion," retorted Ruso. "I don't want to waste my time guessing at things other people already know."

Audax finally conceded that Felix had no known health problems that might have prevented him from defending himself against an attacker, but despite a careful examination of the body Ruso could find no sign that he had done so. There were only some yellowed bruises that could have been training or sports injuries, and a fresh graze on his knee that probably happened when he fell.

"And Metellus says this is the murder weapon?" Ruso picked up the gleaming dagger lying beside the body and laid its edge against the victim to test the shape of the blade.

"I've cleaned it up," explained Audax, grasping the charm around his neck again. "We're cremating him tonight. That'll be sent to his family back home along with the rest of his kit."

"This doesn't look like the work of anyone who's studied anatomy," observed Ruso, checking the sharpness of the dagger and bending down to take a closer look at the corpse. "Why didn't he put up more of a fight? Had he been drinking?"

"He wasn't a big drinker."

Ruso scrawled, "Four cut marks on fifth cervical vertebra, division between fifth and fourth cervical," *vertebrae* into his notes. At least they would be accurate, even if his official conclusion was questionable. "Did you notice the temperature of the body?"

Audax sniffed and replied that it was about what you would expect from a man who had been lying dead in a back alley all night. And yes, he did seem to have been killed where he was found. "I should know. I got sent down by matey from Rome to clean up the alley."

"Metellus?"

"While he sat on his ass in here waiting for me to come back and wash the body."

"The body was only ever seen by the two of you? Not the infirmary staff?"

"We decided not to invite the neighbors in for a look," retorted the centurion, inadvertently trampling over Ruso's theory of how the disturbed doctor had learned the details of the murder.

"And you haven't spoken to anybody about what you found?"

Audax scowled. "Who's running this, you or Metellus?"

"I'm supposed to be helping him."

"So help him by telling us something we don't know already. Like why some bastard native would do this sort of thing to one of my men."

"Can I take a look at his clothes?"

"They're burned."

"Really? Why?"

Audax shrugged and said it had been done on Metellus's instructions. Well, they hadn't known a medic was going to come along asking questions, had they? And no, nothing much had been found on the body.

"Nothing at all?" asked Ruso, surprised.

"Just his belt and his purse with his money still in it. The money's gone back into the camp bank."

The young man's hands were surprisingly uncalloused for a soldier. One of his fingernails had been blackened some time ago. Ruso imagined him cursing when that had happened. Imagined him expecting to live long enough for the injury to heal. Imagined him hurrying into that alley between the butcher's and the general store, perhaps worried about getting back to the barracks in time for curfew. Instead, his night out had ended with him being turned into some sort of ghastly sacrificial victim.

Ruso told his imagination to get back into its place. He must think clearly. He must find something useful enough to justify his insistence on a postmortem, but not so useful that he would look like a threat.

He allowed himself a small glow of self-congratulation. After several months of sharing quarters with Valens he was beginning to get the hang of this politics business.

"Thanks," he said to Audax. "I'll write up my report now."

Alone in the mortuary with his note tablet and his thoughts, Ruso found that his eyes were still irresistibly drawn to the place where Felix the trumpeter's head should be. It was just—not right. Every time he looked away, his imagination replaced the head and each new look was a fresh shock.

He stood up and pulled the linen sheet back over the length of the table. Then he sat on a stool, balanced the note tablet on his knee, and tapped the point of the stylus against the wooden frame.

He needed to have discovered *something*. Stating, "No sign of resistance," and refusing to speculate on an unknown cause of death would only confirm what seemed to be a generally poor opinion of doctors here.

The point came to rest on the corner of the wax. The murderer had not used his own weapon, which suggested the crime—or at least, the method—was not premeditated. Somehow, the murderer had managed to take Felix's knife and use it against him without an obvious fight. Ruso dismissed the idea of an overpowering god and told himself he must be tired. A god would surely have used a more efficient manner of execution. No, Felix had fallen forward onto his knees . . .

Ruso dug the point of the stylus into the wax. On the evidence he had found, it was not impossible that someone had approached the victim from behind and overpowered him by knocking him out.

He readjusted his grip on the stylus and scraped, "Possible cause of death: head injuries," and told himself the word *possible* meant he was not compromising his standards.

12

TILLA PAUSED AT the top of the slope, taking in the sight of the broad meadows and the river snaking between the willows and dividing around the little islands. Home was just beyond the wooded ridge on the far side of the valley, not yet in sight. Perhaps that was a good thing. She would not spoil this moment by thinking about what she might find there. Instead, she would enjoy the memories of paddling in those stony shallows with her brothers and the other children while their parents exchanged goods and gossip at the market.

She had assured the medicus that this valley was beautiful, but in truth the memory of its beauty had faded with use. Now, seeing it basking in the afternoon sun, with the skylarks spilling music into the air like silver and the yellow splashes of gorse on the hillsides celebrating her return, she wanted to shriek with delight and run laughing down the road, leaving behind the sour-faced soldiers still tramping in their miserable column like a row of iron wood lice.

Instead she took in a deep breath of the precious air and told herself, "I am home!" before walking on, keeping pace with the baggage train. She had a duty to make sure Lydia was safe. Lydia would not be running around laughing today. Her man would not be running for a long time. Perhaps never. This morning he had been a healthy young Roman with a new daughter and a steady trade as a carpenter with the legion. By midday he had become a body lying in a cart with a crushed leg that the medicus had covered up so as not to frighten him. She tried not to think about what the medicus might have done to him while other men held him down. She had assured Lydia that her master was a fine doctor. This had seemed to comfort her. Evidently the girl knew very little about surgery.

She shifted her bruised arm to ease the ache that echoed the blows from the centurion's stick. She would ask the medicus for some salve to-night. Perhaps she would also ask him to explain to the centurion that she had nothing to do with the accident, and that she was not in league with Cernunnos the horned god or with Taranis the god of thunder against anybody. The figure had simply appeared to her in answer to her prayers for another woman's safety. It was not her fault if he had come back the next day and brought about a terrible accident. And if he had a face that was vaguely familiar, what of it? She must have seen him in a dream.

"Is that it?" Lydia was clutching the side of the cart with both hands and peering at the buildings on the low rise beyond the river.

"Yes." Tilla followed her gaze, seeing the familiar mud brown rectangle of the fort and the jumble of thatched houses that spread out from it like a stain. The clang of a smithy echoed across the valley, interrupted by the distant whinny of a horse.

"It's very small."

Tilla had to agree. Yet the fort had not seemed small when she lived here. It had seemed massive and ugly and overwhelming.

She could make out tiny figures moving along the streets outside the fort. She wondered if she knew any of them. How many of the girls she had grown up with had been seduced by Roman money? What had happened to the girls who should have married her brothers?

She would not think about her family. She would not think about them because when she did, the sparkling river and the birds and the splendid yellow of the gorse became a hollow joy: a reminder of all that she had lost.

The civilians who had traveled with the Twentieth were barely across the bridge when a gaggle of residents—mostly women of assorted ages, sizes, and colors—surged down the slope to greet them. Bags were grabbed, with or without the owners' permission. A blather of multi-accented Latin promised fine rooms, dry rooms, cheap rooms, rooms with no bother with the neighbors, rooms with good views of the river, snug and secure rooms, nice quiet rooms, rooms handy for the shops, rooms only a short stroll from the waterspout. . . . Nobody, Tilla noticed, even bothered to try the local tongue. These women were living their lives on the land her own people had farmed for generations, yet now it was she who was the stranger.

The mule's bridle was seized by a shawled woman with badly bleached hair who assured them in Latin that she had a very comfortable loft room, and they should hurry now before someone else took it. "Close to the baths, over a very respectable eating house," she assured them, tugging the animal past an official-looking inn and up the slope toward the houses while the driver protested in vain.

She did not release her grip until she had led them past the wooden ramparts of the fort, taken another turn down a side street and reached the grand doors of a gleaming white bathhouse. She waved an arm toward a snack bar opposite with an awning sagging over a couple of outside tables. "A week's rent in advance," she said, "and the back of the loft is yours."

"I have no money," whispered Lydia.

"Don't worry," Tilla assured her. "I know who has."

13

RUSO RETURNED FROM delivering his weasel-worded report to headquarters to find the infirmary office crowded with men and smelling of beer and stale sweat. He gave them a cursory glance and went across the corridor to visit the amputee.

The man was horribly pale. Ruso checked his pulse, which was as fast and faint as he expected. The man's hands and remaining foot were cold. Ruso renewed the compresses on the rib cage and sat watching the labored breathing for a few minutes. "There isn't much more we can do at the moment," he said to the bandager. "Get the cook to feed you. I've got to go to a funeral this evening, but I'll take over after that. Fetch me right away if there's any change."

After a swift visit to the bedridden patients in the four scruffy wards (four! Seventeen beds should present no challenge to a man who was used to supervising dozens . . .), Ruso went to inspect the state of the treatment room.

As he stepped into the room he realized he was not alone. A large man crawled out from under the heavy operating table, scrambled to his feet and performed a salute that would have looked more impressive had he remembered to let go of the brush first.

"Stand easy," said Ruso, recognizing the big Batavian who had helped with the carpenter that afternoon: a man who seemed to be perpetually stooping to duck under a lintel that wasn't there.

The man's arm returned to his side and the brush clattered onto the floorboards.

"Remind me of your name."

"Ingenuus, sir."

Ruso nodded. "Do the bandagers usually sweep the floors here, Ingenuus?"

The man looked flustered. "Sorry, sir. Only I thought in case the room was needed—"

"And nobody else here is getting on with it?"

Ingenuus glanced toward the door and muttered, "Well, somebody's got to do it, sir."

The table had been scrubbed, the instruments and bowls washed and dried, the shelves restacked with linen bandages and dressings, the restraints neatly coiled and put to one side.

"Very good," said Ruso. "You can leave it there. Are you on duty this evening?"

"No, sir."

"If you weren't here, what would you be doing?"

Ingenuus thought about that for a moment. "We're getting ready for the governor's visit, sir. So I'd be doing a little polishing."

"Right. Come down to the office for a moment, then you can go and polish."

Ruso shouldered his way into the office past a couple of men who were lolling against the doorposts. "Gentlemen," he announced, glancing around to make sure all the members of staff slumped against the furniture were gathering themselves into upright positions. Several cups were quietly put down or concealed behind backs, but the smell of beer lingered in the air. "Thank you for your help this afternoon."

The murmurs of appreciation were decidedly wary. Ingenuus, unable to get his bulk past the men in the doorway, was listening in the corridor.

"I think we did as well as could be expected," continued Ruso, aware that he was supposed to be making a motivating speech and that he had no idea how to make one. "The patient's made a good start. Now, as you all know, Doctor Thessalus is out sick. In the meantime the prefect has asked me to take over temporary responsibility for the medical service."

He let that sink in for a moment before adding, "I'm looking forward to working with you." He suspected this sounded like the lie it was, and certainly it did not seem to inspire his audience. There were more murmurs of something that might or might not have been assent. It occurred to him that some of these men were the ones he had seen gambling in the ward that afternoon.

Finally Gambax made a show of clearing his throat and said, "You don't have to worry, sir. You just leave everything to us."

The murmurs were much more enthusiastic this time.

"Thank you, Gambax. Although if I were to leave *everything* to you, it wouldn't be worth me being here, would it?"

Silence.

"So, can we establish who's on duty at the moment?"

Three hands rose.

"Right," said Ruso. "And which of you are patients?"

One hand rose. Realizing too late that he was alone, its owner cast around for support. Finally four hands were in the air.

"You can go back to your room. The rest of you are dismissed. Thanks again for your help this afternoon and I'll see you when you're next on the roster."

When Ingenuus and the hangers-about had shuffled away, he was left with Gambax, one orderly, and a bandager. He delegated the bandager to apply fresh dressings, the orderly to finish sweeping the treatment room and begin tidying the wards, and Gambax to remain to talk about "how we're going to get ready for the governor's visit."

Gambax did not look thrilled.

"Over a beer," suggested Ruso.

Gambax looked marginally less disgruntled. He retrieved his cup from its hiding place behind a box of medical records.

"And I'd like one too," Ruso pointed out.

His new deputy produced a flagon and another cup from behind the box. "There you are, sir," he said, pouring the beer himself and handing it over. "You know, for a minute there I thought we weren't going to get along."

The beer, although possibly safer to drink than the local water, was as awful as Ruso had feared. The conversation was not much better. It seemed Gambax was loyal to Doctor Thessalus, whose regime seemed to have consisted of letting the men do whatever they wanted, and he resented having a legionary doctor imposed upon him. He had more sense than to try the "leave it all to us" line again, but instead managed to give all the appearance of cooperation while finding Ruso's questions strangely difficult to answer. When Ruso had heard, "I wouldn't know, sir. Doctor Thessalus deals with all that," for the fifth time, he gave up and asked about Doctor Thessalus instead. It seemed that the doctor had been looking tired lately and had just taken some leave, but it hadn't seemed to help.

Ruso said, "What's the matter with him?"

"Hard to say, sir."

"Try."

"I think he's just out of balance from overworking, sir."

This was not a problem that was likely to trouble Gambax. "Any idea what treatment he was trying?"

Gambax shook his head. "Sorry, sir. There aren't any records."

Ruso, who usually dealt with his own minor ailments and never quite got around to writing up his own records either, was in no position to criticize. "Did you know he went to see the prefect today?"

Gambax looked blank.

"When did you last see him?"

"A couple of hours ago, sir. I took him some lunch. I thought he'd like to see a familiar face."

"And how was he?"

"About the same, sir."

Ruso gritted his teeth.

"But you go and see him if you want," said Gambax, in a tone that suggested it would be a waste of time.

"I'll take him something to cheer him up. What does he like?"

Gambax scratched his chin. "He's quite fond of music, sir. Can you sing?"

"Not in a way that would make anyone feel better." Nor did he have the time to round up anyone who could, although it might be a useful therapeutic approach later. Music was supposed to soothe sufferings of the mind, and it certainly sounded as though Thessalus was suffering. "Anything else? Favorite food? Wine?"

Gambax looked vacant.

"Never mind," muttered Ruso. "I'll work it out for myself."

"Right-oh, sir. Anything else I can help you with? More beer?"

"No thanks," he said, glancing into his cup. "One's enough."

"Very wise, sir," agreed Gambax, standing to collect the cup and feign-ing surprise at the amount that remained inside. "Sorry, sir. Take your time. I don't suppose you gentlemen in the legions get much practice at drinking beer, do you?"

"It's not our first priority," said Ruso, suspecting from the look in the as-sistant's eye that this was some sort of challenge. Legionaries versus Bata-vians. As he tipped back his head to drain the cup he was vaguely aware of a knock and a door opening. When the room was the right way up again, he found his clerk gazing at him with barely concealed disapproval.

"Albanus."

"Reporting for duty, sir." Albanus cast a professional glance around the room and was clearly unimpressed.

Ruso turned to Gambax. "This is my clerk. He's very good. Albanus, you'll be able to give Gambax here a hand with the records."

The two men eyed each other. Gambax looked as though he did not want any help and Albanus looked as though he had no intention of of-fering it.

"Perhaps," said Ruso, breaking the silence, "You and I might have a word outside, Albanus?"

When they were standing outside by the twin—or possibly rival—gods, the clerk said, "Sorry, sir. But are you absolutely sure he wants me to help out?"

"Of course not," said Ruso, "But I do. And there isn't going to be much else here to keep you busy."

Albanus glanced around him. Ruso followed his gaze. The ramparts at the end of the street were stout enough but somehow the unevenness of the limewashed daub that filled the wooden frames of the fort buildings, and the fact that the infirmary building was not the only one still topped with lumpy thatch instead of tiles, gave the fort an air of quaintness and vulnerability. As if the place had been put up by enthusiastic amateurs.

"Tell me, Albanus. Where exactly is Batavia?"

"It's in the north of Gaul, sir."

"These people are Gauls?" Ruso, who had spoken enough Gaulish to communicate with the farm servants at home only last summer, found that hard to believe.

"Not really, sir. They migrated to Gaul from Germania."

That explained the accent.

"They're supposed to be very tough men, sir. Used for the emperor's bodyguards and good on difficult terrain—swimming across rivers fully armed and so on. I think it might have been Batavians who led the final assault when our people finished off the Druids."

"Hm," said Ruso, imagining Audax plunging into a river in pursuit of raving Druids and wondering whether Gambax would have been off sick that day.

"It's rather remote up here, isn't it, sir?" observed Albanus.

"I did warn you."

"Never mind, sir. I've brought some good long books to read."

"You've been lugging books around as well as all your kit?"

"Just a couple, sir."

Ruso shook his head. The last thing the average legionary would do was think of concealing lengthy and expensive scrolls among the already considerable weight of equipment he was required to carry. No wonder Albanus had been looking weary.

"Don't read when you're on duty," he warned. "Or somebody will find you something else to do. You don't want to be scraping bandages and emptying bedpans."

Albanus looked alarmed.

"Now tell me what's happened to Tilla."

Unfortunately all Albanus knew was that Centurion Postumus had interviewed Tilla earlier that afternoon about something he seemed to think was serious, but Albanus did not know what it was. No, she was not under arrest and no, Albanus did not know where she had gone. As if in an attempt to redeem himself, the clerk added, "But I've located all your luggage, sir. They'll be bringing it along any moment."

At last: a cheering thought. The fort might be small, the natives vicious, the infirmary badly run, and the restoration of his new colleague's mind unlikely, but a lone legionary officer here at the request of the prefect would be assigned decent quarters. While Tilla was practicing her unconventional approach to cookery, that officer would be able to retreat to his room, relax in his favorite chair, and think deep thoughts with no danger of Valens wandering in and distracting him with wine and gossip.

"They might as well take it straight to my quarters," said Ruso. "You don't happen to know where they are, do you?"

"There was a letter waiting for you, as well, sir," continued Albanus, a little too brightly. "Here."

Whoever it was had gone to the trouble of writing out several sheets that were now tied and sealed together in an offering of ominous width.

Ruso took it and tucked it into his belt. "Albanus, what are you trying not to tell me?"

Albanus looked apologetic. "I asked about the medic's quarters, sir, but some other doctor's in them and they said you wouldn't want to share."

"He's ill."

"You'll be very close to your work, sir."

"Everywhere here is close to my work. Everywhere's close to everything. What's the problem?"

Albanus cleared his throat. "They said you'll have to bed down in the infirmary, sir."

"*What?*"

"Sorry, sir."

"But there aren't any empty rooms! I'm not sharing with the patients. And I'm not bloody sleeping in the treatment room. I'd rather camp outside in a tent."

"They said one of the storerooms could be cleared out, sir."

"Has anybody from headquarters actually been into the infirmary recently?"

"I don't know, sir."

Ruso shook his head. "No, of course you don't. Rhetorical question. Well. The infirmary it is, then."

When Ruso returned to the office, Gambax had lit a fire in the hearth and was standing by the pharmacy table weighing out a pile of torn leaves.

"Tell me," said Ruso, "when Felix's body was brought in, who was on duty?"

"Me, sir."

"So you and the other staff helped to lay it out?"

"Audax did it, sir, all by himself," said Gambax, confirming what the centurion had said. "Wouldn't even let us in there to pay our respects. We offered to help, but he thinks medics are a waste of time. If you're not happy, you need to talk to him."

"I will," said Ruso. Fortuitously, it seemed the infirmary staff had thought they were being kept away from the body because of Audax's prejudices rather than any more sinister reason. "Tonight I want you to organize a roster."

Gambax's eyes registered alarm.

"By the time the lamps are lit tomorrow, I want every patient to have had a wash. All over. I want the wards properly aired, every floor and wall scrubbed, every mattress replaced with one that's got a clean cover and fresh straw, and clean bedding on every bed."

Gambax's jaw dropped even farther than normal.

"You don't have to do it all yourself," explained Ruso. "Just organize the staff. And if those four malingerers are still here in the morning, they can clean out the latrine."

"Me and the staff will see what we can do, sir."

"Good," said Ruso. "If anybody needs me, I'm going across to visit Doctor Thessalus, then I'm heading for a quick cleanup at the baths. Then I'll come back here to see my amputee before I go to Felix's funeral."

"Right you are, sir," agreed Gambax. "You take your time. Don't worry about us. We'll keep an eye on everything while you're gone. I'll see if I can find a pen in a minute and make a start on that roster you want."

"If there's any change with the amputee, call me right away. And did you know about the billeting arrangement?"

The deputy poured a measure of cold water on top of the leaves. "Billeting arrangement, sir?"

"I'll be sleeping here. So while I'm out, you'll need to get the smaller storeroom cleared out and a clean bed put in there too."

Gambax reached down to balance the pot on the iron grid by the hearth. "I'll get a room ready for you, sir."

"The smaller one," insisted Ruso. "And leave the barrel where it is."

Gambax's "Yes, sir," was not heartfelt, and Ruso knew why. The smaller storeroom was the one housing the infirmary's beer supply.

14

"GOOD AFTERNOON!" THE young man's cheerful smile belied both the gravity of his situation and the pallor of his thin face. Ruso guessed that the smell filling the gloomy little entrance room was rising from the hair oil glistening on his dark curls.

"Very good of you to call," the man continued. "I'm Thessalus. I expect you know that. The guard tells me you're called Ruso. Odd sort of name. Did you bring the fish?"

"I'm a doctor," explained Ruso, who had been mistaken for many things before but never a cook. "Gambax will be bringing your dinner later."

"Yes, I know. So did you bring the fish?"

Ruso glanced at the guard, hoping for some guidance, but the man did not seem to feel his duties extended beyond announcing the visitor and standing at attention by the door. "I didn't know I had to bring a fish," said Ruso, wondering why Gambax had failed to warn him. "Was it any particular sort of fish?"

"Well, of course it was a particular sort of fish!" exclaimed Thessalus, ushering him through a doorway to where the very little light edging around a cloth nailed over the window revealed the domestic confusion of a single man not expecting visitors. "You can't get much use out of a salmon, can you? Or a trout? They would just lie there and flop about a bit."

"I'll see about a fish next time," Ruso promised, making a mental note to ask Gambax what on earth the man was talking about. "How are you feeling today?"

"In need of a fish. A fish around the head. A fish on a dish around the head until it's dead." Thessalus giggled, then clamped a hand over his mouth before indicating a chair and saying with exaggerated politeness, "Do sit down, Doctor."

Ruso cleared away a scatter of scroll cases, upon some of which he could just make out the names of medical writers. Turning, he found Thessalus perched on the edge of a folding stool.

"Now," said Thessalus, rocking the stool toward him with his hands clasped together but remaining out of reach. "How are you feeling today? Is it any better?"

Ruso sniffed the air in the untidy room, picking up a waft of wine mingled with the hair oil. It was clear he was not going to get much help—or even sense—from Thessalus. "I am well. Are you feeling ill?"

Thessalus giggled again. "No, I'm lovely. Are you? You look tired. It's tiring being a medic, isn't it? All those problems. All that misery. They all want a miracle, don't they?"

"True."

"I've run out of miracles. I told them. I looked in the miracle jar and, oh dear, someone's left the stopper off and all the miracles have flown out."

"I heard you went to see the prefect today."

"Did I really?" This seemed to be a great surprise. "Is he ill?"

"I heard you went to talk about a man called Felix."

"Felix? Oh dear, you want to stay away from him. There's nothing you can do for him now."

"Where is he?"

Thessalus frowned. "Where's who?"

"Felix."

Thessalus looked around the room. "He isn't here, is he?"

Knowing Metellus had searched the rooms, Ruso could say with confidence that he was not. "I'm told you might know where he is."

Thessalus shook his head. "Doctors don't know all the answers, you know. What color is time? Where do the thoughts of the dead go? How is it diseases spread but miracles don't? Have you ever thought of that?"

"No, I can't say I have."

Thessalus tapped his chest. "Greek, you see. The race of thinkers. Romans do; Greeks think. And write rather good books."

"My grandfather was Greek," said Ruso.

"Ah, you understand! Welcome, philosopher! Well, a quarter of a philosopher. Torn between thought and action, I suppose."

Ruso cleared his throat. He needed to take charge of this conversation. "How long have you been stationed at Coria, Thessalus?"

"Ah, the Roman practicality. Back to the facts. Take the patient's history. To tell you the truth, I arrived here some time ago and I've been at a junction ever since. Of course, if we don't hold firm at the join we might as well all go home." Thessalus paused. "Do you ever find you wake up in the wrong bed, Doctor? Or is that just me?"

"The wrong bed?"

"You wake up and the bed's wrong, the walls have moved, you can smell things that shouldn't be there, the sounds are different, and you think, *Where am I? Who's put me here?*"

Worryingly, Ruso could recall exactly that sensation. "I think it's when you've been dreaming about a place where you used to live—"

"Ah, you *think* that. But how do you know? How does any of us know? Who's to say that while our bodies are resting, our souls don't go wandering somewhere else? Back into the past? What about the future? Do you ever have the feeling that you've seen something before, even when you know you can't have? What if our souls travel into the future before our bodies do, Doctor? Have you thought of that?"

Ruso suspected that Thessalus's soul often went on trips unaccompanied by his body. He said, "Do you find this happening a lot?"

"Oh dear me, no." Thessalus clasped his hands together. The dark eyes narrowed and his head tilted slightly on one side in a way that implied concern. "Do you?"

Ruso wondered whether he adopted the same pose himself, and whether his patients found it as unnerving as he now did. "Not often, no."

"It's so nice to be able to chat with a fellow medic, you know. Such a joy to talk to someone who understands. Between you and me—" Here the young Greek leaned forward to the point where the stool was about to overturn and seized Ruso's left knee, digging his fingernails into the flesh—"I think I've been alone here far too long. My triangles are getting blunt."

"Ah—very possibly," said Ruso, prizing the fingers off his knee and wondering if the prefect and Metellus might be wrong about the man being incapable of violence. "It can be a lonely job."

"Oh!" Thessalus, motionless, was staring at his hand as if he were seeing it for the first time. He withdrew it, sat back on the stool, and glanced into his palm as if to check that nothing else unexpected was lurking inside. "Dear me. Sorry about that. And I was going to try my new approach."

"New approach?"

"Talking. You must never touch the patient. You just talk to him until he feels better."

"Look, is there anything I can do to help?" said Ruso, not optimistic. "The prefect said something was worrying you.'

"To help? Well, that's very decent of you. But no, not really. I'm absolutely fine. If you really want to help somebody, you might find a few men in the infirmary. I think I left some behind in there."

Ruso got to his feet. He could no longer remember any of the questions he had wanted to ask Thessalus. "I'll see to the men," he promised. This patient did not seem to be in need of any immediate help. In fact, despite being as mad as a bee in a bottle, he was the most cheerful person Ruso had met since arriving there.

"Do come back and see me again, Doctor."

"I will," he promised, not adding, *And I'll be better prepared.*

"Excellent!" Thessalus smiled. "Next time, make sure you remember the fish!"

15

R USO INTERCEPTED HIS luggage on its way into the infirmary and extracted a clean tunic and his bathing kit. Then he went
out through the fort gates, past more tethered horses, and into the civilian street. On his left a gang of grubby children eyed him from a doorway. Opposite was a shop front bearing crude pictures of a saucepan, a
shoe, and what might have been a cabbage beneath the flaking legend,
We Sell Everything. A cockerel was poised to strut inside the shop when
a man emerged from the doorway, aimed a kick at the bird, and sized up
Ruso before deeming him worthy of a gap-toothed smile. Ruso nodded
an acknowledgment. The shopkeeper was too dark to be a native. He
wondered how far the man had traveled to end up selling everything on
the edge of the empire, and why he had bothered.

In front of the next shop, a crippled boy was flapping a branch over a
carcass to keep the flies off it while an angular woman and a man in a
blood-smeared leather apron were haggling in a Latin that was clearly
the first language of neither.

It had just struck him that the narrow passageway between the two
shops must be the scene of the murder, when a squad of soldiers appeared, marching a scruffy pair of civilians toward the fort. Butcher and
customer glanced around briefly and then went back to haggling. One

of the children shouted something and the others giggled. Evidently the sight of locals under arrest was nothing unusual. As soon as they had passed, Ruso followed his curiosity into the alley.

He had imagined the murder scene as a backstreet, but the gap between the buildings was only about three feet wide. A few weeds straggled down either side of a worn strip of mud, and the place was gloomy even in daylight. Why the victim would have chosen to walk down here late on a night when he had already been threatened with violence was a mystery.

Ruso sniffed. The usual alleyway stench of urine and dog droppings was blanketed by heavy layers of incense and rose oil. Evidently the priests had been around to purify the place. Even so, he suspected it would be a long time before many people ventured down this unlucky shortcut again.

About ten paces in, he paused. Behind him, a couple of small windows overlooked the passageway. Ahead, the sides of the buildings were blank. Another five or six paces and he guessed the freshly scrubbed walls and the battered state of the weeds at their feet were the only remaining indicators of the murder site. If there had been any evidence, either Audax or last night's storm had done another fine job of destroying it. Ruso bent and picked up a broad flat stone about as big as his fist. If the cause of death really were head injuries, it was a plausible murder weapon, unhelpfully washed clean by the centurion or by the rain. The bang-on-the-head theory would, he supposed, explain why the victim had not been heard to shout for help. No doubt Tilla would say he had been struck dumb by a native god.

Ruso dropped the stone, lengthened his stride, and emerged into the street at the far end of the alley. He passed a crowded bar, ignored a brothel, nodded to a gaudy and surprisingly busy shrine honoring a god he didn't recognize, and walked on in pursuit of a cheering aroma that told him someone was cooking sausages.

The bathhouse, a big building gleaming with fresh lime wash, was the most—in fact, the only—impressive structure outside the fort. At the back, it must have a pleasant view across the meadows towards the river. A barber's shop was tucked into the frontage, and on the corner opposite was a snack shop. He had found the source of the cooking smell. He had also found something else.

Seated at one of the tables beneath a sagging canvas awning were two women. The one clutching a baby-shaped bundle was Tilla. The dark-skinned girl now scrambling to her feet was the carpenter's girlfriend.

"Sir! Is there news?"

He nodded, approaching the table so they could not be overheard. "He's as well as can be expected," he said, and explained about the amputation. "The next few days will be dangerous. There are other injuries inside that we can't see."

"But he is alive!"

"I told you," said Tilla, who had not bothered to stand, despite the presence of her master. "That one is a good medicus."

"May I see him?"

"Tomorrow," promised Ruso. "I'll arrange a gate pass."

"I will pray for him to Apollo." The girl reached down and took the baby from Tilla's arms. "Please tell him his daughter is well."

The girl retreated indoors. When she had gone, Ruso found himself faced with an interesting social dilemma. He was standing. Tilla was still sitting at the table. If he sat down to eat next to her in public, it would be tantamount to declaring her his social equal. If he didn't, he would look ridiculous: the master dancing attention on the slave. He considered asking her to stand, but there was a strong chance she would not cooperate, and being defied in public would be even more awkward. In the end he compromised by perching himself on the end of the rough table, and vowed to have words with her later. "I hear Postumus wanted to see you," he said.

"That man is not as funny as his nose."

"What did he want?"

Instead of replying, she pushed up her sleeve and revealed a heavy purple and red bruise.

Ruso ran a finger over the surface of the arm whose shattered lower bones he had pieced back together, and from which he had cut off the copper slave band. He frowned. "Postumus did this to you?"

"He thinks slaves tell more truth when you beat them."

"I'll talk to him. He was probably angry about the accident."

"I did not make the accident, the gods did."

"I'll put some salve on that bruise later," he promised, aware that it would be futile to argue about the gods. "What did he want to know?"

"He says somebody has seen me in the yard with the cart. He asks what I am doing. So I tell him about the god who appears when I pray, and he hits me for lying."

"I'll talk to him," Ruso repeated, knowing an apology would be out of the question. "I came to tell you we'll be here for a few days. I want to keep an eye on Lydia's man, and while I'm here they've asked me to run the infirmary."

Her expression brightened. "Because you are a good medicus."

"Because the one they have is crazy," he explained, "And his deputy is spectacularly idle."

The woman approaching with the tray was plump, dark, and, judging by her cheerful expression, had forgiven her hairdresser for the very bad bleaching job that the shawl failed to hide.

"Wine," he said. "Something decent if you have it. And what's quick to eat?"

"Lamb pies, sir? Beef sausages? Raisin pastry? We have some very good stuffed hens' eggs."

He chose the eggs.

Instead of going to fetch them, the woman said to Tilla, "Did you ask him?"

Ruso hoped whatever ailment the woman was about to describe to him was not going to delay the eggs.

"My lord," said Tilla, "I have said you will pay Susanna the money for Lydia's rent."

"Ah." She did not want advice. She wanted cash.

"Her man cannot give anything," continued Tilla. "She only has a room because I promised Susanna an officer from the legion would pay."

Their eyes met. He knew she had not approved of the way he had spent her savings at the inn. They both knew how much was left. He reached for his purse. "Of course," he said, as if she had offered him a choice.

When the woman had gone, he said, "So. You are back home."

"Home is across the hill," Tilla said, pointing north. "And I think much is changed." It was a reminder, had he needed one, about the loss of her family.

"Do you still have friends here?"

She shrugged. "Perhaps. I have an uncle and a cousin, if they are still alive."

He said, "I am sorry about your family, Tilla." The words seemed stiff and inadequate. He wanted to hold her hand, but they were in a public snack bar and the woman was arriving with the food. "You can stay with me in the infirmary," he said. "It's a bit of an odd arrangement, but nobody approves of me anyway, so I don't suppose it'll matter." He took a sip of the wine, swilled it around his mouth, stared into the cup, lifted it again, and sniffed. In this remote valley, miles from civilization, he had just been served the best wine he had tasted since he left Gaul.

"This is Aminaean," he said, impressed. "It's very good for you. Just the thing for colds. I haven't had this since . . ." he paused. Finally he said, "I can't remember." This was not true, but it was better than, *Since the night my wife threw a jug at my head and told me I was impossible to live with.*

Tilla was chewing her lower lip. "Do you think my family will see me going into the soldiers' fort?"

Ruso took another sip of the surprising wine and decided Tilla would not be interested in knowing that it was good for bowel trouble too. "I don't know," he said. "Why, do you think they wouldn't approve?"

"My uncle has been inside the fort many times," she said. "My uncle is a friend of the army."

This was good news. He had wondered what Tilla's remaining friends and family would make of their relationship. Evidently it was not going to be as awkward as he had feared.

"Your family ought to be pleased," he said. "You'll be safer in the fort."

"I am safe here," she assured him. "Trenus would not dare to come here."

Ruso busied himself spooning filling out of the egg while he tried to remember who Trenus was. One of the many difficult things about women was that they tended to pick the most unsuitable times to tell you something they considered to be important, and then became irrationally upset when you failed to remember it. On the other hand, they sometimes dropped oblique hints about something they were eager to tell you, expecting you to show an interest. When you failed to take the hint, instead of simply saying what it was they wanted you to know, they were upset because you had not asked.

Consequently he was rather pleased with the ambiguity of "Tell me more about Trenus."

"Trenus," said Tilla, evidently glad to be asked, "is a man without honor. He has the body of a bear, the brain of a frog, and he makes love like a dying donkey with the hiccups."

Ruso inhaled a lump of egg by mistake and began to cough.

Tilla placed the wine cup in his hand and carried on talking about Trenus while he gasped for air. He was not listening.

"It's not that simple now, Tilla," he said, recovering his composure and taking another drink of soothing wine. "You've become a friend of the army yourself. There are people who won't like that."

Tilla stood up. Those eyes looked into his own. "You are a good medicus," she said, "And a good man. But you are mistaken about this. I am not a friend of the army. Now if you have no work for me, I am going to talk with Lydia."

16

RUSO COMPLIMENTED THE woman on the wine when he went to pay for his food. She shook her head sadly. "It's the last we'll get, sir. We lost our supplier today. A terrible, terrible thing."

"Felix?" he guessed.

She nodded. "Did you know him?"

"Not really."

"He'll be missed," she said. "Always a friendly face. Whatever they say about him, we never had any trouble with him. It's a sad way to lose a young man, like that."

"It is," agreed Ruso, wondering how much information had escaped from the fort. "What did happen to him, exactly?"

The woman hesitated.

"I just don't want to say the wrong thing to his friends," he explained.

"He was hit over the head," she said. "His centurion found him in an alleyway over by the fort first thing this morning."

"So have they caught the man who did it?"

She looked at him oddly. "*I* don't think so," she said, and bent down to pick up something from behind the counter. Ruso took the hint.

Across the road, a middle-aged native with a cascade of iron gray hair was sitting outside the barber's in the late afternoon sun, having his mustache trimmed by a barber's slave. In the gloom of the shop behind him, a man and a woman were staring silently at the floor. The way their chairs were turned toward each other reminded Ruso of those awful social occasions—usually instigated by Claudia—where he and some stranger had run out of conversation but could not find an excuse to move apart.

As Ruso headed for the bathhouse doors, a voice called, "Good afternoon, sir!"

The man, more alert than he seemed, had sprung to his feet.

"How are you today?"

"Dirty," said Ruso.

"Well, you've come to the right place, sir!" The barber was beside him now, making ushering motions with his arms as if he were hoping to round Ruso up and pen him into the shop like a sheep for shearing. "What can we do to help? Haircut? Shave?"

Ruso rubbed his chin. What he felt beneath his fingers was no longer stubble. Unfortunately, from what he had seen of the chins of the Tenth Batavians this afternoon, Hadrian's famous beard had so far failed to inspire any imitators here. Since he was now in charge of the infirmary until the new man turned up in four days' time, he supposed he should make an effort to resemble the Batavians' image of an officer.

"Take a seat, sir." The barber had trotted ahead and was indicating a stool next to the native. "Guaranteed the best in town, or your money back!"

"Just a shave," he said, subsiding onto the stool and adding, "Take it steady, will you?" lest this should be one of those enthusiastic razor-wielders who valued speed above accuracy.

"Don't you worry, sir!" chirped the barber, draping a stained cloth across Ruso's chest and pulling his own stool closer. "You just close your eyes, relax, and it'll be over in no time."

This sounded alarmingly like the sort of thing surgeons said to patients: not because there was nothing to worry about, but because worrying would make no difference.

Ruso checked that the letter Albanus had given him was still safely in his belt, and closed his eyes.

"So," said the barber, slapping cold water onto the doomed beard, "have you come a long way, sir?"

"Deva," said Ruso, making no effort to stimulate the conversation since in a moment he would only be able to answer in grunts.

"Deva! Well!"

Ruso heard the water bowl being put down.

"You'll be with the Twentieth, then, sir?"

Presumably the razor had been picked up. Just to be on the safe side, Ruso's reply was confined to, "Uh."

A voice close to his left ear said, "Just keep still now, sir," and he felt the scraping begin at the lower left-hand side of his jaw. "It's an honor to shave an officer from the legions, sir. Especially the Twentieth. It's a grand legion, the Twentieth, isn't it?"

"Uh."

"A lot of people will be very pleased to have you here, sir. What with all the bother we've been having lately.'

Ruso, unable to explain that most of his comrades were leaving in the morning, said, "Uh."

"We have to expect a few robbers and thieves around, I suppose, sir, don't we? Low types too lazy to earn an honest living. And if people don't keep an eye on their things in the bathhouse, they've only got themselves to blame, haven't they? But it comes to something when the roads aren't safe to travel in daylight, and now an innocent man's been horribly murdered right in the middle of—"

"Festinus!"

The rich bass voice could only have come from the native. Ruso opened his eyes, but his head was being held over to one side and all he could see was glinting light alternating with the shadow of a hand as the blade scratched at his left cheek.

"Festinus," continued the voice, "don't alarm our guest."

In truth Ruso was less alarmed by talk of horrible murders than by the discovery that he was being shaved by a man whose nickname was Hasty.

"I'm not trying to alarm him," said Festinus, pausing briefly to wipe his blade. "I'm just making conversation. And it's only fair to warn visitors if there's something funny going on. You'd rather be warned than murdered, wouldn't you, sir?"

Ruso grunted an assent. He wished he could find a way of asking the stranger not to distract the man who was sliding a razor up under his left ear.

"Nobody knows what they did to him, but it must have been nasty. They won't let no one see the—"

"Festinus!"

"'Course, I don't expect you'll have no bother at all, sir," the barber continued. "I always said Felix would get into trouble one day. He was a bit too clever, sir; that was his problem."

"No danger of you being in trouble, then, is there?" put in the woman's voice. "Don't you listen to him, sir. Poor Felix was a nice friendly young man. Not like some of them we get around here."

The barber snorted. "A bit too free with his friendship, if you ask me."

"Nobody did ask you," pointed out the woman. "And you shouldn't be talking like that before he's even buried."

The barber, ignoring her, urged Ruso to "Straighten up a little, please, sir," just as a gray mustache appeared in his line of vision and its owner said, "Pleased to meet you, officer. Catavignus. I represent the local people in the guild of caterers.'

Ruso had the vague sensation that he had seen him somewhere before, but could not think where.

The barber paused again to wipe the razor. Ruso seized the moment to introduce himself to Catavignus, who was evidently a native who had added a Latin ending to his name.

Catavignus bowed. "Welcome to Coria, Doctor. Sorry to hear about the accident. I hope you're not hurt?" The accent was similar to Tilla's, but his Latin demonstrated a grasp of grammar that Tilla seemed to have decided was not worth the effort.

Ruso offered a double-barreled "Uh-uh," and a wave of the hand to indicate that he had survived the accident unscathed.

"Good. Don't let this blabbermouth bother you."

The slave repositioned the stool in front of Ruso, who hoped the sudden waft of beer was coming from Catavignus and not the barber.

"If you'll allow me to explain," continued Catavignus, seating himself and indicating his remarkably fine head of hair to the slave, who reached for a pot of lotion. "This is a decent, law-abiding place. A safe place to run a business and raise a family. We welcome the army. Losing one of our soldiers like this is a great shock to everybody. We don't expect that sort of thing around here."

Evidently Catavignus's opinion of the natives' loyalty was much higher than that of Metellus, although Ruso supposed a lot of the residents of this decent law-abiding place wouldn't be Britons anyway. They would be relatives of the soldiers, or veterans, or the traders Metellus was so eager to welcome in exchange for their taxes.

"The caterers are keen to help the investigation in any way we can," continued Catavignus. "Felix was well known to all of us."

"We've been over to pray to Apollo Maponus," said the barber's wife. "You can't be too careful."

"I heard it was a native what done it," put in the barber. "Chin up, please, sir."

Catavignus cleared his throat. "If it is, then he's a disgrace."

Ruso clenched his teeth as the blade scraped another channel up the underside of his chin.

"Fell out with him over at Susanna's," continued the barber.

"At Susanna's?" Catavignus seemed surprised.

"I told you you should have gone and seen what that shouting was about," put in the barber's wife.

"I must go and speak to Susanna," put in Catavignus, getting to his feet. "She will need the support of the guild after something like this."

"I told you, didn't I?" continued the woman. "I said, 'There's something going on over there.'"

"If I got up every time you heard something in the street I might as well sleep on the doorstep," said the barber. "Besides, if I'd got involved that native might have gone for me too. He was wild, sir, that's what I heard. Raving. Shouting about sheep. Or was it cows?" The man paused. "Perhaps it was goats."

"Never mind what he was raving about," retorted the woman. "The point is, if somebody had stepped in, Felix might still be alive."

"Oh, so it's my fault now, is it?"

Catavignus paused in front of Ruso, who was willing the barber to keep a steady hand while arguing with his wife. "Doctor. The caterers are giving a private dinner across at Susanna's snack bar on the eve of the governor's visit. Celebrating the start of the British summer in a modern style. We'd be honored if you'd join us."

"Uh," said Ruso, who had once responded to his wife's suggestion that they attend a dinner party by pointing out that he would rather leap naked into a tankful of starving lampreys.

"We'll look forward to it. Tell me. Are you treating civilians during your visit?"

"Uh." Ruso did not want the complications, but he did want the money.

"I ask because my daughter Aemilia is not well. If she's no better tomorrow, can I refer her to you?"

Ruso decided he could risk saying, "Do."

"Thank you. I'm sure you know what these young women are like."

"Mm," said Ruso, not sure whether knowing what young women were like was a sign of medical competence or something less desirable.

"A pleasure to meet you," continued Catavignus. "Call on me anytime you're passing the brewery. Aemilia and I will be happy to welcome you."

"There he goes. Look," muttered the woman after he had left. "Straight over to Susanna's. Any excuse. Well, she'll be thrilled."

"More slime than a bucket of slugs, that one," said the barber. "Never turn your back on the natives, sir, that's my advice. Even if they are in some fancy guild of caterers. They're all the same. Women as well. Smile at your face and stab you in the back. I said to that centurion what was in here earlier, what we want around here is a few more patrols on the streets. You only ever see them marching past on the way to somewhere else. I said to him, I'll offer free services to any man what—oops! Sorry, sir. Just put that on it for a moment, will you?'

Ruso held the cloth against the right-hand side of his jaw, removed it, assessed that the damage was not life threatening, and replaced it quickly before the blood dripped onto his clean tunic.

"Ready again, sir? Nearly done. Lean that way a minute for me, please. . . ."

"So you're the new doctor, sir?" inquired the woman.

"Aah."

"Will it be you or Doctor Thessalus tomorrow at the clinic?"

"Uh?"

"*Doctor Ruso,*" mused the barber. "Haven't I heard of you some-where?"

Before Ruso could respond the woman continued, "Doctor Thessalus does a clinic here every market day, sir. It's always very popular."

"It's free," added the barber, explaining its popularity.

"Ah," said Ruso.

17

Ruso's jaw had more or less stopped bleeding by the time he paused on the threshold of the bathhouse, eyeing the occupants of the main hall.

The grunts echoing around the walls came from a young man lifting weights in the middle of the floor, evidently keen to give his small audience every chance to admire his oiled biceps. The audience must have been a disappointment to him: It consisted of a couple of white-haired men hunched over a game of dice in the corner, a fat man ogling his young manicurist, and a lone attendant sweeping the floor.

The door swung back with unexpected ease. It hit the wall with a crash that reverberated around the room. Everyone stopped what they were doing and looked at Ruso, then lost interest as he stepped into the less-than-appealing atmosphere of sweat and damp and overperfumed oils.

Forewarned by the pessimistic barber, he paid the attendant to guard his clothes and helped himself to a towel.

He gasped as he entered the hot room, instantly regretting the gasp as burning air scorched the back of his throat. The attendant's assurance that it was "still good and hot in there" had been an understatement. Ruso clopped safely across the searing floor on wooden sandals and laid

his towel out on a bench beneath a window before sitting down to face
the alarming prospect of what he now saw, on perusing the address on the
reverse, was a long letter from his stepmother.

The letter ran expensively over several thin leaves of wood bundled together. He frowned. He had never before received a letter from Arria,
and this neat handwriting was certainly not her own. He cracked open
the seal, unwound the cord, and began to read.

Dearest Gaius,

*I send greetings and hope you are in good health. How I wish you were here
with us, although we are glad that you can enjoy the green hills of Britannia,
away from the cares of everyday life that burden us here. We always look forward to your letters, but it is hard to bear both the loss of your dear father and
your absence.*

*I am delighted to tell you that the shrine to Diana that your dear father
commissioned and he and I designed together*

(*So that,* thought Ruso, *explained the catastrophic expense.*)

*is now complete, and we have received many compliments on your father's
good taste and generosity.*

*Since your father's death your poor brother has been doing his best, but it is
difficult for your sisters and I without anyone in authority here to care for us.
I am sorry to say that although dear Publius left many investments, Lucius's
management of them is uncertain. The simplest pleasures are often unreasonably denied to us.*

Since Arria's idea of a simple pleasure was a new suite of baths or a
summer dining extension, that was hardly surprising. And as Publius Petreius had died secretly bankrupt, Lucius's denial of them was not at all
unreasonable.

*These small pleasures could of course in no way make up for the loss of a happy
marriage such as Publius and I shared for a few all-too-brief years and that I
know he also enjoyed in earlier times with your dear and respected mother.*

What did Arria know about his mother? Nothing. Ruso gritted his
teeth and read on, realizing that the steamy atmosphere was not good for

the letter and hoping the ink would melt into an illegible blur before he
reached the request for money that no doubt lurked near the end.

*Your father understood the joys of a happy union—such as I trust you will
yourself enjoy again one day soon, dearest Gaius—and I know he wished the
same for all of his children. I am especially anxious for your beloved sisters.
Although they are, as you know, both beautiful and charming, how will they
find the right sort of husbands if no suitable dowry is offered? As I have explained to your brother, one has to sow in order to reap. This is something I
felt that he, as a farmer, would understand, but it seems not. Of course there
is no reason why he should listen to me, but I am sure that if you, dearest
Gaius, as head of the family, were to explain it to him, he would immediately
understand what is required.*

*Naturally I have not yet mentioned this matter to your sisters, as I am hop-
ing to avoid disappointing them. See, am signing this letter myself and send
you the very kindest of greetings.*

Your loving stepmother, Arria
Beneath the uneven signature,
squeezed in tiny letters, was:
Lucius and Cassia baby boy very small

Ruso slapped the letter shut, dropped it on the floor, and eyed it with
all the affection he would offer a large and poisonous spider. He and Lucius had always been careful to keep their correspondence discreet, with
references to their dire financial state carefully coded. No matter how
firmly a letter was sealed there was no way of making sure it would not
"fall open" in transit and be read by someone who would pass the contents on to one of their many creditors. Now Arria had not only written
a letter that suggested Lucius was mismanaging the family finances, but it
seemed she had been into town and dictated it to a public scribe.

Maybe they had been wrong not to tell Arria the exact situation in
which her husband had left the family coffers. Maybe they should have
told her the truth and frightened her into silence with the warning that
public bankruptcy would sweep away their home, their dignity, and possibly even their freedom.

He would have to write an urgent letter to Lucius congratulating him
on the birth of a son and delegating the challenging task of getting their
stepmother under control.

The rattle of the door latch warned him someone was about to come in. He picked up the letter, slid it under his thigh, and closed his eyes.

The clatter of sandals tracked the passage of a bather picking his way across the floor. To Ruso's dismay the footsteps passed the empty seating and came closer. Moments later his bench rocked as a heavy body lowered itself down next to him. A long breath was followed by a familiar voice. "Ruso."

"Postumus." Ruso acknowledged him, not bothering to open his eyes. "I was going to come and find you later."

"Flashy room with your floozy again tonight, I suppose?" inquired Postumus in a tone that suggested this would be deeply tedious.

"Sharing a store cupboard with a beer barrel."

"Lucky you. I'm still sharing a tent with the bloody wildlife. And I hear you're staying on to look after my carpenter. Tell me what you've done for him."

"Amputation, I'm afraid. No choice."

"What are his chances?"

"Mixed. He's a strong man. Most people wouldn't survive being run over by a wagonload of lead. We'll be able to tell over the next few days."

"I suppose I'll have to get a message to his woman."

"I've done that," said Ruso. "I hear you've been talking to Tilla?"

"I asked her some questions."

"I can still read them on her arm."

"She needed some encouragement."

"Next time Tilla needs some encouragement," said Ruso. "Leave her to me."

Postumus grunted. "Next time I need a doctor's advice on security, I'll let you know."

Ruso opened his eyes. There was a pale form on the bench in the corner. The man, who must have entered without making a sound, nodded a greeting and closed his eyes as if he was not listening. It was a moment before Ruso realized it was Metellus the aide. He wondered how long he had been there.

Postumus glanced at the door before sliding closer to Ruso so that their shoulders stuck together in the heat.

"That wagon business," he growled in what seemed to be the nearest he could manage to a whisper, "wasn't an accident."

Ruso looked at Metellus, conscious that the sound was echoing off the hard surfaces of the room and the aide was taking in every word.

"It's all right," said Postumus. "He knows. Some bastard had sawed halfway through the brake."

"So the driver was right?"

"Hmph." Postumus did not sound inclined to be charitable. "Should've kept his eyes open. Sonny with the antlers had an accomplice. There was a lump of lead slingshot in one of the oxen. That would have got them trotting along all right. Then, once a heavy load got going down that hill, there was no way of stopping it."

"The accomplice must have been hiding somewhere up on the bank," mused Ruso. "And all our escorts . . ."

"Were busy chasing the Stag Man," said Postumus, finishing the sentence for him. "Bloody cavalry. All of 'em want to be heroes. S'pose we'll have to let the driver go, then."

"So was Tilla's evidence useful?"

Postumus sniffed. "My sources say she was hanging around the vehicles in the yard during the storm."

"What are your sources?"

Postumus looked askance at him. "You're not the only one who's sick of sleeping in a tent. I sent a couple of lads up there to escort the wagon in and they seemed to think that meant they could stay the night."

"Ah."

"Now they wish they hadn't. And they didn't even guard the bloody wagon. Just stuck their heads out in the rain from time to time to make sure it wasn't floating away."

"Why didn't they do something when they saw her?" demanded Ruso, wondering when Metellus was going to have the decency to either join the conversation or leave.

Postumus shrugged. "Said they were thinking about it when somebody came and took her away. They did a lot more thinking when I'd finished with them."

"That was me," said Ruso. "She went to look for your carpenter's girlfriend and her baby. I followed her out into the yard."

The centurion's "Hm," did not sound entirely convinced. "See anybody else out there?"

"I heard her calling out. But it was pitch dark and pelting with rain. I couldn't see a thing."

"What was she saying?"

"I don't know. It was in British."

"So who was she talking to?"

"She told me she was praying to her gods."

Postumus snorted. "Bit unusual in the middle of a thunderstorm, isn't it?"

"Not for Tilla."

To Ruso's relief, the centurion shifted his weight and their shoulders peeled apart. A long breath whistled out down the misshapen nose. "My lads tell me," said Postumus, "that she could have unbolted the gate and let somebody in."

"Your lads are trying to cover their own backs," said Ruso. "Those gates weren't impossibly high. Somebody could have climbed over them and not been noticed in the storm."

"True," agreed Postumus. "But all I know is, that wagon was all right yesterday. It's parked in the yard at the inn all night, the only person seen near it is your woman, and today it flattened some of my best men."

"Why would Tilla help someone interfere with a wagon?"

"She's a native," said Postumus, as if that explained everything.

"She's my housekeeper."

"So you think you can trust her?"

"Of course!" In the silence that followed Ruso wondered if he had said it a little too quickly. "She's very loyal," he insisted, uneasily recalling *I am not a friend of the army.*

"We hope so," put in Metellus from the corner. "Because she's told Postumus she was out there with the god Cernunnos."

"Oh, for goodness' sake!" Ruso's exasperation was as much with Tilla as with her questioners. If she could not manage to control her imagination, why could she not at least learn to control her tongue? "She's very religious," he said. "Superstitious. You know what the natives are like. She heard the stories. She saw him outrun the cavalry this afternoon. She probably got confused with something she saw in the lightning."

"You just said she was reliable," pointed out Postumus.

"She is."

"I heard she was caught stealing."

"That was a misunderstanding. She was just trying to save me some money."

"Save you money? A woman? That's a first."

"I told you she was unusual," said Ruso.

"Our friend Metellus here," said Postumus, "wants to get his hands on whoever this Cernunnos is and ask him a few questions. I want to get my hands on him and kill him. Trouble is, nobody's got much to go on."

"This is all very interesting, Ruso," said Metellus. "I'm surprised you didn't mention any of it earlier."

"I didn't know," Ruso said, feeling sweat trickle down his spine and wishing he had at least said something about Tilla being local.

"She didn't tell you she saw the antlered man in the yard? That's interesting."

"She told me she saw something," said Ruso. "I didn't take much notice, frankly."

"We all know what the natives are like," said Metellus. "But now if she's telling the truth, we have a witness who's seen this man—which undoubtedly he is—close up. So we're rounding up a few suspects and we'll get her to take a look at them in the morning."

"I see," said Ruso, making a mental note to urge Tilla to cooperate.

"I thought as her owner you ought to be kept informed. But you won't mention it to her, of course."

"Er—no."

"We don't want anyone having advance warning. If we can get ahold of him, the man in the yard should be able to tell us a lot of things we'd like to know. Who knows? Maybe your housekeeper will solve our problems at a stroke."

Ruso said nothing, entranced by the prospect of Tilla solving problems rather than causing them. Then he retrieved Arria's letter and got to his feet. He wanted to go and check on the carpenter.

"Off to investigate your latest body?" said Postumus.

"I was asked to do a postmortem," Ruso assured him, marveling at the speed with which gossip could travel. "I'm not involved in the investigation."

Postumus snorted. "That's what you told everybody last time."

Ruso's glare was wasted, since the centurion had his eyes closed.

"Last time?" inquired Metellus, a little too casually.

"There was an unexplained death at Deva," Ruso said. "There was a misunderstanding about the inquiries."

"Like his housekeeper being a thief," put in Postumus. "That was a misunderstanding too." He leaned back against the painted wall. Instantly he jerked forward. "Hercules, that's hot!"

"The Second Spear ran the investigation," Ruso pointed out, retrieving his towel. "Not me. Now if you've finished, I've patients to see."

"Hey!" said Postumus when Ruso was halfway out the door. "Where did you get that shave?"

Ruso jerked a thumb toward the exit. "Out there," he said. "He's very good. Tell him you're in a hurry and you'll be done in no time."

18

RUSO RETURNED TO the infirmary to find that little had improved in the few hours since he had performed the amputation at the roadside. The carpenter had woken but was weak and incoherent, which did not bode well. He wondered whether he should send for the girlfriend tonight. When Tilla turned up—what was taking her so long?—he would ask her to fetch her.

The malingerers had taken to their beds. Albanus was diligently walling himself into a corner behind stacks of half-sorted record tablets and Gambax was sitting beside the chaotic pharmacy table apparently doing nothing at all.

Ruso beckoned Albanus out from behind the wall. "That can wait," he said, summoning him out into the corridor. "Go and sort your quarters out and finish the records tomorrow. Otherwise you're going to end up being given a scrubbing brush."

Albanus grinned and left. Gambax was still sitting by the pharmacy table as if he was waiting to be told to move.

"Well?"

"I'm stuck, sir."

Ruso went across and picked up a writing tablet that read,

Patients must wash
Air
Floors and walls
Mattresses

"Is this as far as you've got?"

"I couldn't remember the other thing, sir. So I was waiting to ask you. I didn't want to get it wrong."

"Bedding," said Ruso, understanding why centurions were equipped with solid and knobby vine sticks and wondering whether he could borrow one to goad Gambax into action. "Next time, get on with what you can remember."

Gambax's "Yes, sir!" made it sound as though Ruso had just made a brilliant suggestion that had never occurred to him before.

"I've been to see Doctor Thessalus," continued Ruso. "He was very confused. Has he been like this before?"

"Confused, sir?"

"Confused," confirmed Ruso, aware that Gambax's habit of repeating the question rather than answering it, combined with the secrecy of Thessalus's confession to murder, was going to make it extremely difficult to find out anything useful.

"I wouldn't say he was confused, sir. Not really."

"Was he all right when he was on duty last night?"

Gambax shook his head. "I don't know, sir. We take turns doing night duty."

"So when was the last time you saw him, apart from taking his food across?"

"He was all right when we came back from Susanna's."

"And that was last night?"

"Yes, sir. It was my birthday. Doctor Thessalus took a few of us out to celebrate. He's very good to his staff, sir."

"And when you came back here, was he all right then?"

"I don't know. I went to my quarters and Doctor Thessalus went out on an emergency call."

"Out? Outside the fort?"

"I don't know where," said Gambax, anticipating the next question. "You'd have to ask him that."

Ruso managed to establish that an emergency summons from a patient

living out in the civilian housing would have to be delivered as a message
at one of the fort gates. Beyond that, Gambax's mind seemed to be as
blank as his face. He decided to try a different approach.

"Gambax, do you know anything about Doctor Thessalus and fish?"

The deputy considered this for a moment, then offered, "He's partial
to a bit of fish, sir."

"He didn't seem to want to eat it," said Ruso. "He seemed to want to
do something—ah!" He paused, rerunning the conversation in his memory. *A fish around the head. A fish on a dish around the head until it's . . .*
"Have you heard of the torpedo fish?"

"I don't think so, sir."

"It gives a shock to the nerves. I've heard of it being prescribed for
headaches. And it's quite successful with gout, apparently."

"A fish that gives a shock to the nerves, sir?"

"Yes," insisted Ruso, aware that he was sounding almost as delusional
as his patient.

"Some sort of poison, sir?"

"No, just a sort of—shock. A jolt. Like lightning. Only not as big, obviously."

"No," agreed Gambax. "I suppose not. And it's definitely a fish?"

"Yes," said Ruso.

"You won't find it around here, sir."

"Does he suffer from headaches?"

"Not particularly, sir."

"Gout?"

"Not as far as I know."

Ruso scratched one ear. "He must have read about it in a book."

"I don't think so, sir," said Gambax. "We don't have that sort of book
here."

Ruso was beginning to wonder why Thessalus's strange fantasies about
murder had not fixed themselves upon Gambax. "I hear there's a public
clinic over at the baths tomorrow," he said. "Will you be deputizing for
Thessalus?"

"Me, sir?" A faint smirk appeared, as if Ruso had just suggested something ridiculous. "'Fraid I can't help you there, sir. Army medical training. I don't know anything about women and children. But don't you
worry. I'll find you a good bandager to help out."

The main thing Ruso knew about the ailments of women and children was that he wasn't very confident with them either. "I'll think

about it," he conceded. "And you'll have time to supervise the cleanup back here. Is my room cleared?"

To his surprise the reply was, "All done, sir."

"Good. If my housekeeper turns up, show her to it. You haven't seen her, have you? Blond girl. Local."

Gambax's brief flash of helpfulness had faded. The smirk reappeared. "Sorry, sir," he said. "Can't help you there."

Finally, he was alone. A shaft of late afternoon sunlight revealed a sparkle of dust motes dancing in the space above a narrow bed. It also illuminated the fat barrel that blocked access to the rest of the room. Bed and barrel fit perfectly into the space provided, but with the barrel in its present position, the only way to reach the chair at the far end of the room was to clamber across the mattress, and the only way Ruso could sit on the chair and still have room for his feet was to remove the trunk resting on the seat and place it on top of the bed. On the other hand, if he shifted the barrel to the far end of the room everyone would have to climb over his furniture to reach the beer. This had not been one of his better ideas. Unfortunately, it was too late to back down now.

He surveyed the small space into which his belongings were crammed and wondered how he was going to fit Tilla into it as well. He would have to explain to her that one of the first steps in restoring the infirmary to working order was to establish control of the beer supply, and what better way to do so than to have it under his own personal supervision? Besides, she would probably want to spend most of the few days they were here with her remaining family.

He would insist on more comfortable arrangements down the road at Ulucium. Maybe Postumus would save him a decent place. On reflection, maybe not. Definitely not, if he'd followed Ruso's recommendation to visit Festinus the barber.

Ruso made the necessary furniture removals to get to his chair. The room looked no better from this end than the other. There was not even room to rock the chair onto its back legs, which was a pity, because he needed to do some serious thinking.

There were several things he did not want to think about. One was the question of exactly who, or what, Tilla had seen in the yard of the inn. Another was what the sulkers and skulkers might at this moment be doing with the head of Felix the trumpeter. Ruso shuddered. He was not going to like the north of Britannia very much.

What he *did* need to think about was Doctor Thessalus. Apparently
Thessalus knew the dreadful details of the murder even though they
seemed to be a secret from everyone else—but the prefect and Metellus
were adamant that he was not guilty. The chances of getting any sense
out of Thessalus himself were minimal. He needed to track down the
guard who had taken that urgent call for a doctor and find out from him
where Thessalus had gone that night after he returned from the bar. In
the meantime, if he was to stand any chance of sorting out the infirmary
before the governor's new medic arrived, he needed to find a way of
spurring Gambax into action.

That barrel would be better six inches nearer the door. Ruso got to his
feet and gave it an experimental shove. It did not move. He turned and
braced his back against it with his feet on the floor beneath the chair,
and heaved. The barrel gave way suddenly, tipping away from him and
almost overturning to block the door as he tried not to fall backward. As
he recovered himself it landed back into place with a thud. He was
wondering whether to call for reinforcements when there was a knock
on the door. The bandager from the Twentieth was worried about the
carpenter.

19

THE LOG WALLS surrounding the fort were more silvered with age now. The steep grassy ramparts that rose up beneath them were spattered with spring flowers. Little had changed since the last time Tilla had seen this place. But everything was different.

When she left, the soldiers' fort had been impressive. Now that she had lived in Deva, it looked almost puny. She wondered if the men who were busy clearing out the rampart ditch knew that their fort was nothing to be proud of. Probably not. What would they say if somebody told them?

She walked on. Ahead of her, beneath two wooden towers, was a dark rectangle surrounding a splash of late afternoon sunlight. The gates were open. In a moment she would be able to see inside.

Her parents and grandparents had watched from the top of the ridge as soldiers stacked turf into ramparts and hammered in posts around a patch of land that their people had walked over freely for generations. Once the walls were up none of them had ever set foot on that land again apart from her uncle, who usually had more wisdom than to boast of it when her father was around. Like most sensible people, the rest of them had done their best to avoid Rome's intrusions into what—according to the very old—had once been a peaceful valley. Although you could never trust old people not to exaggerate. Any peace must have always been fragile with the Votadini tribe as neighbors. Perhaps this was why some people had imagined that the arrival of the Romans might be a good thing.

The truth, of course, was quite different. The truth was that when foreigners desecrated your land, cut down your trees, fouled your water supply, and made impressive speeches about bringing peace in return for taxes, nothing good could possibly come of it. She could imagine what her family would be saying now if they were watching her walking toward the gates, knowing there was a soldier waiting for her inside.

"It was all I could do, Mam," she whispered. "He is a good man. He helps people."

She was almost at the gatehouse now. It was nowhere near as grand as the smallest of the gatehouses at Deva. The irrepressible grass had crept up around the feet of the supporting timbers, reminding any soldiers who took the trouble to read the signs that the spirit of the land could not be destroyed. Beyond it, through the open gates, she could see two men slapping clean white lime wash onto the end of a building as a squad marched past them and—

"Halt!"

The crossed spears in her path had appeared so quickly from the shadows that the soldiers holding them must have been watching her approach.

"Password?" demanded the shorter of the two.

"I do not know it. My master is only just arrived."

"Password," he repeated, perhaps thinking she had not heard the order, although she was close enough to see the yellow teeth and the black hairs sprouting from his nostrils.

She backed away to a more comfortable distance. "I do not know the password," she explained again. "My master is a doctor with the Twentieth Legion. He comes today with an injured man."

"Gate pass?"

"I am just arrived too."

"No entry without a pass."

"I cannot get a pass without going in."

"Not our problem."

"But I am his housekeeper!"

The two men exchanged glances. They seemed to find this amusing. The symmetry of the crossed spears wavered as they relaxed.

"Come to cook his dinner, have you?" inquired the taller one.

She lifted the bag that contained damp clothes needing to be hung out to dry, and now two apples and the pastries she had brought from Susanna's snack bar for supper. "Yes."

"Tuck him into bed?" suggested hairy nose.

Tilla pointed past them to the white buildings. "I will live in there."

"Then you'll have to get a job with the prefect's family."

"Or marry him," suggested the taller one.

"We don't know what you've been getting up to with the legion," said hairy nose, "But 'round here, women and children live out there." He shifted his spear to indicate the road outside. "Run off and find yourself a bed, and the doctor will come and give you the treatment later."

Tilla had met enough ignorant guards to know that showing annoyance would make matters worse. The only things that would impress them were fear of their superiors, and cash. "My master," she said, trying the cheaper option, "is Senior Medical Officer Gaius Petreius Ruso. My name is Tilla. I ask you to send a message—"

"We're the Tenth Batavians," the taller one interrupted. "We don't run messages for the legions."

"Why don't you put your request in writing, Tilla?" suggested his companion: a remark they both seemed to think was extremely witty.

Tilla, who could no more write than fly—and they knew it—placed her hands behind her back, gripped them tightly, and counted to five. Then she reached into her purse and brought out the last coin she possessed. As hairy nose hid it somewhere on his person, she said, "Tell my master—"

"Sorry, love," he said. "We're not allowed to run messages for girl-friends."

"But I have paid you!"

"Have you?" He held his hands wide and looked down his chest as if he was searching for it. "Are you sure?"

"Take the message, or give me my money back."

"I didn't see any money." He jerked a thumb toward his friend. "He didn't see any either."

"I will report you to my master and you will be in trouble!"

"Tell you what," he suggested. "I'll try doing a trick. Give me a kiss and I'll see if I can make it reappear."

Tilla looked them both up and down. "You are not worth it," she said, turned on her heel, and strode away down the gravel road.

As she was passing the men who were clearing the ditch, the taller guard called after her, "Hey, whatsyourname!"

"Tilla," prompted hairy nose.

"Tilla! Do you want to leave a message or not?"

"Go on, Tilla!" urged some interferer from the depths of the ditch.

"You can give me a message any day, Tilla!" added one of his comrades.

Tilla was tired. She was hungry. She was at the end of a long journey. The thought that her family was in the next world was no consolation for the fact that they were not here to greet her in this one. Now she had been humiliated by the men her master thought of as comrades. She stopped. She turned to face the men in the ditch. In her own dialect, speaking fast so they would not understand, she said, "I have a message for you."

There was a chorus of cheers.

"You are very stupid and ugly men," she informed them, smiling sweetly, "and the gods of this land will curse you for the disrespect you show when you hack holes in it."

This time the cheers were more uncertain. Someone said, "What did she say?"

"She says she loves me!" roared one of the men, scrambling up the side of the ditch toward her. "Come here, Tilla—"

"Back to work!" bellowed a voice from farther along the ditch. "And you, girl, clear off before I feed you to them."

20

RUSO SLUMPED DOWN the roughly plastered wall until he was sitting on the floorboards with his legs stretched out in front of him. His eyes were level with the body of the carpenter, whose pulse had faded some time ago but whom he had tried desperately and hopelessly to revive. He stared at the body, which could have been asleep. He knew from experience that amputations were best performed on the spot: Crushed legs did not travel well. But he now realized the internal injuries would have killed the man eventually wherever the surgery was carried out. His fate had been sealed from the moment the wagon hit him. His doctor's insistence on interfering had merely prolonged his suffering and given false hope to his comrades and his family.

There were sound reasons why Ruso had made the decisions he had made, but he knew only too well that logic would not lift the burden of failure. Nor would the memories of past successes: the amputees who survived to swing out through the hospital doors on their crutches; the fevers cured; the eyesight saved; Tilla, whose shattered right arm had seemed almost beyond hope. There was no relief to be found in reason. The only comfort he could offer himself was a reminder that *this feeling will pass.*

He got to his feet. Postumus would be here in a moment. He neatened the bedding and drew the sheet up over the carpenter's face. Then he went to the door and summoned Albanus to take a report.

He was just finishing dictation when Postumus arrived. The centurion was freshly shaved. He had a heavy red scrape down one side of his face. In other circumstances, Ruso would have enjoyed that.

Once the centurion had paid his respects to the corpse, he and Ruso withdrew to the corner of the room. The men of the Twentieth had been scheduled to march out at dawn, but now they would stay for a funeral.

"There's a child," said Ruso.

"I know. Didn't even have time to name it, poor sod."

"Yes he did," insisted Ruso, hoping Postumus would not demand the details. "I was there. They did it early."

"What were you doing there?"

"Tilla was the midwife."

"What did he name it?"

"I can't remember."

The black eyes met his own. "He must have had a premonition."

"So it seems," agreed Ruso, suspecting Postumus knew full well that the carpenter hadn't officially named his daughter—why would he, when he would have expected to be alive eight days later to do it at the proper time?

Postumus frowned. "Even if he did, the girlfriend's not entitled to anything. We're not a bloody benevolent fund."

"But if he's named the child, and there isn't any other family . . ."

Postumus glanced across at the bed. "I'll see what I can do."

Standing on the threshold between the images of the healing gods, the centurion paused and turned. "I've just lost one of my best men," he said. "When we catch that bastard who cut the brake, I'll nail him up myself. And if you ever recommend another barber like that one, I'll do the same to you."

21

THE SOUNDS OF the fort had faded in the distance now. Tilla paused by the beech tree that had been split by lightning. She hid the pin of her shawl down inside the cleft trunk, in gratitude to Taranis, god of thunder, for keeping Lydia safe. Perhaps for sending a messenger in the shape of Cernunnos too, although she could not think why he had come or what he had wanted to tell her. But the next day he had appeared on a horse in front of everyone, and no one could explain why the cavalry had been unable to catch him. The spears had fallen short. The slingshots had missed. And although he had not touched it, that wagon had crashed just after he appeared. It was a mystery.

She sat on a stone and ate one of the pastries she had bought for supper and one of last season's apples grown soft and wrinkled with age. It occurred to her that perhaps she should have left a message for the medicus with Lydia. It was too late now. She smoothed out the holes where the pin had pierced the shawl, knotted it in place, and carried on.

Just above the dell where the sacred spring rose, she laid the remaining pastry she had bought for the medicus at the foot of the oak as a gift to the goddess. Then she stood and raised her hands to the tree, which, Mam always said, was not the goddess but showed her strength. She gave thanks for a safe journey home. She prayed for courage to face what she would find here. She prayed for her lost family in the next world, and for protection for herself and for the medicus. She prayed that Lydia's man would live, but that he would be of no further use as a soldier to the emperor, who should never have sent him to desecrate this land in the first place. Then she waited in silence, in case the goddess wished to speak.

A soft breeze rustled the new leaves of the oak. A movement to one side caught her attention and she saw a robin perched on the rock that marked the spring. It eyed her for a moment, then flew off.

It was not a clear message. But it was a sign that she had been heard. Tilla picked up her bag and set off along the stony path that led to her uncle's house and to the place she had once called home.

She was walking behind a long shadow of herself. A chill in the breeze lifting the shawl reminded her that the night would be cold and that nothing in her bag would keep her warm. She quickened her pace.

She could see the house now. On her left was the flat land where the stream rested before taking its journey down the hill. Cows were grazing with their young around tufts of marsh grass. The far end of the field had been fenced off, and a couple of sheep were settling down for the night in the shelter of the hurdles. Beyond them, the field was empty. As she approached, she could see that someone seemed to have been digging up the ground. A pile of stone had been collected and dumped on the far side of the enclosure. Propped against the stone were a hand cart, two spades, and a pick. Drawing closer, she could make out orange rust on the blade of the pick. *Careless,* she thought. Da would never have allowed that. Tools were precious. They should be oiled and put away.

She dropped her bag into the long grass and leaned over the wall. Slashed through the rough turf in front of her were two long straight ditches that met at a right angle. Heavy foundation stones had been laid in them. The ditches followed lines marked out by twine stretched between wooden pegs. More twine and pegs formed the other sides of a large rectangle, with its long side facing south toward the path and out over the green valley. Tilla frowned. She knew what this was, but she had never seen anything like it here before. She could not imagine what Da would have said about it. Mam would have warned whoever it was about the anger of the gods. Her brothers would have scoffed. What a stupid place to put a grand Roman house.

She shouldered her bag again, calling out a greeting as she approached her uncle's home. A skinny hound appeared from an outbuilding, rushed

across the yard, and flung itself at the gate, barking furiously. She drew
back. She and this dog did not know each other.

"Hush!" she urged it. "I have not come to hurt you!" But the animal
could hear nothing over its own din.

From inside the round house, someone yelled at the dog to shut up. It
took no notice. Moments later a lank-haired woman in a dingy tunic
emerged, folded her arms, and shouted, "What do you want?"

Evidently the gods had not favored her uncle. This was not the stan-
dard of welcome—or of woman—anyone would have found here in the
old days.

The woman snatched up a stick, shrieked, "Will you *shut up,* dog?" and
strode down toward the gate. The animal saw her approach, gave a last
defiant bark, and slunk away.

"He is a good guard dog," remarked Tilla, not adding that he would be
better if he were properly fed and trained by someone who knew what
they were doing.

"He is a nuisance," retorted the woman, placing a protective hand over
the top of the gatepost. "What do you want?"

Tilla, dispensing with the usual greetings since the woman clearly
knew nothing about politeness, said, "I have come to visit my uncle."

"We haven't got any uncles here."

"Who is your master?" demanded Tilla, realizing with relief that this
was a servant and not a wife.

The woman's eyes narrowed. "We work for Catavignus the brewer."

"Catavignus is my father's brother. My family used to live up on the
hill."

The woman backed away. "That family are all dead. Killed."

Tilla frowned. "How do you know this?"

"Everyone knows it."

"Everyone is wrong," she said. "My name is Darlughdacha, niece of
Catavignus." She could not help the smile from showing. "And I am
come home at last!"

Instead of smiling back the woman looked around as if she was hoping
someone would appear to tell her what to do. "I wouldn't know," she
said. "We've only been here two years."

"Where is my uncle?"

"He lives in town."

"You mean outside the fort?"

"Near the bathhouse."

Tilla stared at her in disbelief. "I have just come from there!" It seemed her uncle was in a house yards away from the one where she had left Lydia. She had walked all the way up here for nothing.

The woman eyed her for a moment. "I expect you're wanting to come in, then?"

"I am tired."

The woman shifted her hand on the gate. "I suppose, if you really are the master's kin . . ."

"My uncle will thank you," promised Tilla, hoping it was true.

The woman untwisted the frayed loop of twine that held the gate to the post. "The master doesn't allow strangers on the land," she explained, dragging the gate just wide enough to let Tilla squeeze through. "We don't want trouble 'round here."

Tilla had seen plenty of trouble here in the past, none of which would have been stopped by an inhospitable woman with a half-starved dog.

"We don't want to get tangled up with the rebels," said the woman, tying the gate and setting off up the yard toward the house. "The gods have sent us enough problems already. We sacrificed a lamb but it didn't make any difference. My husband says we're cursed."

"What rebels?"

"There isn't much to offer you. Only a drop of beer, or milk."

"I will have milk," said Tilla. "What rebels?"

The woman seemed surprised that she needed to ask the question. "I hear they *call* themselves warriors. Followers of some Messenger of Cernunnos."

"I have seen him!"

The woman frowned. "I do not want to."

Tilla followed her past a scrubby vegetable patch. The thatch above her uncle's porch was collapsing and there were unfilled cracks in the walls. Evidently the curse these people were suffering from was laziness.

"Nobody knows the name of this messenger," said the woman. "He wants to throw the army off our lands. His warriors turn up asking for hospitality and no sooner is it given than the soldiers come and arrest everyone for harboring criminals. Sometimes they burn the house and take all the livestock."

"The warriors?"

"The soldiers. To teach a lesson. That's why the master says we mustn't let anyone in. If there's any trouble here we will be turned out."

"I have not come to cause trouble."

"Wait there," said the woman, pushing open the door and kicking something out of the way as she entered the house.

Tilla seated herself on a heavy log set under the eaves. Her feet were aching. Her shoulder was stiff from the weight of the bag. She leaned back against the cracked wall and closed her eyes. Last night's grand room at the inn seemed a thousand miles away, and not so bad after all.

"This is all we have."

Tilla opened her eyes to see a very small cup of milk being offered. She wondered if the household was genuinely short of milk. With three cows in the paddock, it did not seem likely. But perhaps Catavignus had most of his produce delivered into town.

"Nobody told us you were coming."

"No," agreed Tilla. "I am sure they did not."

"My husband will have to talk to the master. This is only a poor house for servants now."

"Who is building the house with corners?"

The woman frowned. "That house has nothing to do with us. We don't know anything about it. The builders do as they please. We just look after the master's land."

"The house is for Catavignus?"

"He never said we were supposed to watch them. One day they were here putting in foundations, and the next they were gone. It's not our fault."

"I did not say it was." Wearily, Tilla eyed the path that led back toward the fort. If she hurried, she could make it down to her uncle's new house before the lamps were lit. She finished the milk and reached for her bag of damp clothes. "I thank you for the drink," she said, getting to her feet. "There will be no need to talk to Catavignus. I shall see him myself."

"We could make you up a bed," said the woman, suddenly seeing a new reason to be anxious. "You must not tell the master we turned you away. Of course it would be a poor bed compared to what you are used to—"

"I am used to many things," Tilla informed her. "And now I shall need to get used to having come back from the dead. But you have orders not to invite people in, and I will not ask you to disobey."

"But—"

"There is no need to worry," said Tilla. "I shall say nothing about you to my uncle."

"But mistress—"

"I am not your mistress," pointed out Tilla. "I am not anybody's mistress anymore. But if I were, I would tell you that the thatch needs mending, those tools should be put away even if they are not yours, and someone needs to hoe the vegetable patch."

"But what will the master say if he knows we let you wander off by yourself at sunset?"

"I don't know," said Tilla, swinging her bag onto her shoulder and heading for the gate. "Perhaps I shall be eaten by wolves on the way back, and then nobody but you will ever know, will they?"

22

THE SKY WAS orange above the silhouette of the western hills by
the time Ruso left Lydia in the infirmary with Postumus. The shutters of We Sell Everything had been pulled across. The barber's shop was
locked and there was no sound from the bathhouse. The awning outside
the snack shop rose with a brief gust of wind, then collapsed again. It
seemed everyone had gone to pay their last respects to Felix.

Ruso arrived at the small cemetery on the road out of town and
slipped in at the back of the crowd gathered around the bier, glad of the
approaching dusk. Distracted and late, he had not thought of changing
into better clothes. Audax, easily distinguished by the centurion's plume
across his helmet, was standing at attention among the ranks of Batavians
whose full formal turn-out displayed a polished range of antique but
fearsome-looking weaponry. Over the heads of the crowd he saw the
prefect move forward and step up onto some sort of platform.

As Decianus announced that every man was born mortal, Ruso was
distracted by the gaggle of young women in front of him. Several were
clinging to one another and sniffling. All seemed to have spent much
time inconsolably wrecking their fancy hairstyles, and had he been
closer, their torn mourning clothes might have revealed some interesting sights.

Decianus moved on to extol the virtues and the necessity of good military trumpeters, while Ruso craned to look around at the rest of the civilians. He wondered if Tilla had come to watch the funeral before delivering his supper. He would have asked her to visit Lydia, but in the fading light he recognized only Susanna from the snack bar and the barber's wife.

Decianus was commending Felix as a true Batavian, a man of four years' loyal service to Rome and to the Tenth and a man who would be much missed, when he was interrupted by a stray wail from one of the young women. There was an audible intake of breath from the crowd. Decianus ignored the intrusion and went on to explain that Felix was now freed from the pains and difficulties of life, and that we must all prepare ourselves—

Another wail rose into the air, followed by sobbing and furious hisses of "Sh!" Decianus was still talking, but quite possibly no one was listening as a plump and bedraggled female howled, "Oh, Felix!" The ensuing commotion suggested that either she had collapsed, or one of her wiser friends had wrestled her to the ground. Ruso sighed. Since everyone knew he was the doctor, he supposed he had better step forward.

Catavignus got there first. Evidently this was Aemilia, the daughter who was not well. Grabbing the apparently unconscious girl under the arms, he dragged her away from the mourners onto the grass beyond the gravestones. The angular woman Ruso had seen haggling with the butcher separated herself from the crowd and limped across to kneel beside her. Catavignus waved Ruso away. "We'll just get her home, Doctor. This has been a very difficult day."

As Ruso walked away from them he heard the slap of a hand on human flesh, and a wail of pain. Catavignus was administering his own treatment.

Ruso rejoined the funeral just as the speech came to an end. There was another blast of the trumpets. Decianus stepped up to the bier, raised a staff of office, and sprinkled something on the corpse, reciting a chant in what Ruso now recognized as Batavian. A fat man who had been blocking Ruso's view shifted and for the first time he could make out the full shape of the body. Either the head had been found, or a convincing dummy placed under the shroud. A command was yelled, the troops saluted, the horns blared, and flames began to lick up around what remained of Felix the trumpeter.

Decianus stepped back and stood at attention. A couple of men moved the platform safely away from the flames. The fire cast a flickering light on the impassive features of Audax, who was watching the disappearance of the body that he had been guarding since early morning. Perhaps he was hoping that the fire had been well set, so that the flames would obscure what lay beneath when the shroud burned away. It took Ruso a while to spot Metellus. In the end it was not his face that betrayed his identity beneath the anonymous shell of the helmet, but his stance. All other eyes looking out from under the polished brims were trained on the pyre as Felix's comrades oversaw his departure to the realms of the dead. Only the prefect's aide was more interested in watching the crowd.

23

R USO WAS ON the way back to the infirmary for his first evening in charge, when he heard a familiar voice bawling orders. Exactly what the orders were was a mystery, since half of the syllables
seemed to have been swept away in the tidal wave of sound, but the infantrymen tromping down the street understood the need to wheel
right, march forward a few paces, and then halt.

"Dismissed!"

That was clear enough.

Ruso was threading his way through the crowd of men heading for
their barrack rooms when the same voice called, "Hey, Doc! I want a
word!"

Audax's office displayed a predictable lack of interest in home comforts.
The furniture looked old, hard, and lonely. Around it, a selection of no-
tices hung from nails that had cracked the plaster. The only extrava-
gances, all the more striking because of the plain surroundings, were the
crested helmet and scarlet cloak that Audax was now unloading onto the
wooden frame in the corner.

Ruso assumed he had been called in to hear the latest news about the
search for the missing remains of Felix the trumpeter, but he was wrong.

"I'm telling you this," announced Audax, kicking the door shut and not bothering with a greeting, "Since you don't seem to be as much of an idiot as some of the others. You want to keep an eye on that lazy smear of grease that works over in the infirmary."

"Gambax?" suggested Ruso, reflecting that Audax was not a man one would choose to lead a stealth mission.

"That's him. The other one never got him under control. Don't suppose you'll do much in a few days, but I thought you ought to be warned."

"Thank you."

"He's another one who thinks he can do what he likes."

"Another one?" queried Ruso.

Audax snorted. "The other one was my problem. Still is. Problem alive, problem dead. Typical. Should have done what he was bloody told for once and come in before curfew. None of this would have happened."

"Felix."

Audax shrugged. "Ah well. Shouldn't speak ill of the dead. Specially not under the circumstances."

Ruso glanced around to confirm that the door was firmly shut and murmured, "That head on the corpse . . ."

"Fake."

"I assumed from his funeral that he was pretty popular."

"Half of 'em probably owed him money and wanted to make sure he wasn't going to collect."

This did not seem to explain the distress of the disheveled girls. "Felix was a moneylender?"

"He was a trader. Buying and selling. Everybody's mate."

"Can you think of any reason why Doctor Thessalus would have a grudge against him?"

"No more than anybody else. Thessalus wouldn't harm a fly. No wonder being in the army's driven him crackers."

"You don't happen to know where Thessalus was called out to on the night of the murder?"

Audax did not.

"What did you mean by 'no more than anybody else'?"

Audax glanced around the shadowy corners of the room. "You believe in spirits?"

"You're not speaking ill of him," Ruso assured him, curious. "You're telling the truth." It was a distinction fine enough for a prefect's aide.

"Hmph." Audax pondered that for a moment, and fingered the charm around his neck. Finally he said, "When I got here six months ago, Felix was paying other men to toot his horn for him so he could wander off doing his fancy business deals. You wanted it, Felix could get it. At a price, and no questions asked. Now, my lads don't get paid as much as you boys in the legions and I don't mind them making a bit extra, but they've got to do it in their own time. And the minute I put a stop to Felix skipping off duty, he took to going sick with invisible ailments."

"Bad back?" suggested Ruso, familiar with the list of conveniently unprovable disorders. "Headaches?"

"That sort of thing. Sets a bad example to the others."

"And he was seen at the infirmary by Thessalus?"

"Gambax."

Ruso was beginning to see why the medical service commanded scant respect among the Tenth. "You really excused him from duty on Gambax's say-so?"

"Twice," said Audax. "Then I cured him myself. Sent him on a twenty-mile run. And d'you know, he was never ill again. Felix was a lazy bugger, Doc. But he was my lazy bugger, and he didn't deserve to go like that."

24

IN THE RAPIDLY fading light the sensible thing to do would be to hurry straight back to—no, the sensible thing would have been to accept the woman's grudging offer of a bed for her first night back at home. The second most sensible thing would be to hurry back to her uncle's house by the fort. Tilla did neither of these sensible things. Instead, she set off up the path to a place she had not seen for three winters and where there would be nothing to welcome her except memories. The woman had made it clear that even if any others had survived, they were not there.

She glanced back at the paddock with the strange ditches cut into a rectangle. With the Votadini for neighbors, this was probably a stupid place to build any sort of a house. She shook her head. Her uncle had always had some very odd ideas. Like giving his daughter a Roman name and insisting that she learn to speak fluent Latin. Her own father had always said it was pointless: The Romans had finally abandoned their attempts to control the northern tribes a few years ago and any fool could see that it was only a matter of time before they gave up here too.

Time, had they known it, was the one thing her family would not be given.

The Votadini had come in the dark. Bandits, thieves—perhaps they too called themselves warriors. Warriors who were too cowardly to show their faces in daylight. She had imagined their approach countless times since that night. Threading their way up through the woods, crouching behind the field wall and listening to Trenus whispering last words of encouragement. Clambering across the ditch and creeping silently over the bank. Excited, perhaps, by their own daring. Slinking across the yard in the dark to surround the house where the family lay dreaming by the warmth of the dying fire.

The dog alone had sensed the danger. He had raised the alarm, but there were too many of them, and this time they had not just come to steal a few cows.

The walls were in poor repair, as she had expected. Yet one paddock was still properly fenced, and a shaggy pony, nothing like the fine horses Trenus had stolen from her family, lifted its head to watch her as she passed.

Someone was living here.

Whoever had built the small round house had set it on the same patch of level ground as the old one. She scanned the earth at its feet for the scars of the burning. Instead the gods had sent new growth. She saw only spring grass, with a couple of chickens pecking for food. The land, it seemed, had a shorter memory than those who tilled it.

She called a soft greeting but there was no reply. Not even a dog. She unlooped the twine and pushed the gate open.

Her ancestors had fought alongside Venutius in the failed struggle for freedom, and her father kept an ancient sword oiled and hidden in the thatch, ready for the day when a new leader would rise up and call them to victory. But the thatch had been ablaze before they realized it. The sword could not be reached.

In the light of the flames she had seen her mother struck down in the doorway. She knew then that the raiders would show no mercy. She had expected to die herself. Instead the knife had been torn from her hand and she had been dragged away into the darkness, still screaming threats she could not carry out.

For the first days and weeks among the Votadini she had waited. Ready to run. She had closed her eyes and her mind whenever she lay crushed beneath the grunting mass of Trenus, and told herself it would not be for much longer. When she was alone, she watched the woods for any sign of the warriors from the south who would come to help her escape. Or even of the army, come to enforce the law they claimed to uphold. But the weeks had turned into months and autumn hardened into winter, and still there was neither a raid nor even any word of anyone offering a deal to buy her back. The melting of the winter snows and the opening of the roads had brought no news. Gradually, deliberately, she had buried all hope of seeing her family again. If they were alive, they would have come for her. She had comforted herself with thoughts of them waiting for her in the next world. But perhaps she was wrong. Perhaps someone was still waiting here.

A lone blackbird was warbling his evening song. The dark bushes behind the house shivered in the breeze. Tilla told herself not to hope too much. Hope would mean disappointment. She looked around her. The sun was gone behind the black skeletons of the trees on the horizon.

That family are all dead.

Dead. As if a family could be summed up and done away with in one word.

She pulled the knotted shawl tighter around her shoulders. Surprised to realize she was trembling, she put her bag down on the stone outside the door—the stone where the water bucket used to rest—and called, "Who is here?"

There was movement from behind the house. Someone was limping toward her carrying a horse harness. A man. A man she had known from childhood . . .

But the hair was too fair. The frame was too broad. The walk—

The walk had stopped. He was standing there with his mouth open. There was dried blood on his upper lip. Bruising around one eye. He reached one hand out toward the wall as if trying to steady himself.

She said, "Are they all dead, Rianorix the basket maker?"

"All dead, daughter of Lugh," he whispered. "Have you come to haunt me?"

"No," she said, pushing the door open. "I have come home!"

25

SHE HAD DONE her best to treat what the soldiers had done to him at the bar last night, but he had no herbs in store and it had been too late to search for any growing around the house. She had cleaned up the cuts and put cold compresses on the vicious bruises, struggling to see what she was doing in the uneven light of the fire and the smelly rush taper that was almost burned out. "I could do better with some herbs," she assured him. "I will go and see what there is outside tomorrow. Mam used to grow lots of things. They might have seeded themselves."

He eased himself into a more comfortable position on the bracken bed, closed his eyes, and murmured, "Your touch is healing, daughter of Lugh."

"Your flattery is still as clumsy, I see."

"I am out of practice."

She said, "You should have gone to your sister. She would have medicines."

"I have no sister."

She sighed. "You are still not speaking to Veldicca?"

"She is still not speaking to me."

She shrugged his spare overshirt back up over her shoulder. Her own clothes were at last put out to dry, draped across a chair by the fire. Running the cool damp rag down the small of his back, she said, "I am surprised you have no wife to do these things."

He gave a tentative smile: a careful move to avoid reopening the split lip. "If you had been here, things would have been very different." The faint lisp reminded her that he was still learning to form his words without the shattered tooth.

"I suppose Aemilia would not have you?"

She felt his body stiffen.

"How did you know?"

"I am not a fool, Rian. I used to see how you looked at her when you thought I was not watching." It was the way all men looked at Aemilia. Tilla had frequently thought that if men were obliged to choose their partners with their eyes closed, they would make far more sensible decisions. She said, "I did not expect you to mourn me forever. But I could have told you Aemilia was not interested in marrying a basket maker."

"If you had been here, I would never have tried."

"So tell me. Has she married an officer?"

"Not yet." He gave a snort of disapproval. "No doubt Catavignus is eyeing the legionaries who marched in this afternoon."

"And nobody else suited you?"

"I am a busy man with a business to run. Have you not noticed the stock of baskets over by the door? I shall go to sell at the market in Coria tomorrow."

"With your warhorse between the shafts of the cart."

"One day I will have a warhorse," he promised.

"You have been saying that for a long time."

He sighed. "When I think of the horses we rode when your Da was alive . . ."

"Trenus kept Cloud for a while," she said. "I tried to steal her and ride home."

"What happened?"

"I got lost. His men caught us."

"Bastard," muttered Rianorix. "You can never trust the Votadini. What Trenus did to your family was an outrage. Did he apologize when he released you?"

"Trenus did not release me," she said. "It is a long story. I will save it for tomorrow."

His hand sought hers. "It is not easy to remain strong when your enemies prosper," he said. "Your family was kind to me. I came here and rebuilt the house in their honor. And now you are home, we can begin again."

After a moment she wrested her hand free. "You are very thin," she said. "Was the harvest bad?"

"I am fasting."

"You have made a vow?"

"I am sworn to protect someone."

"Who?"

"Never mind," he said. "That was why the fight happened at the bar. There is a soldier who shamed this person and will not pay compensation."

"Then the soldier must be punished," she agreed, feeling the warm muscles of his shoulders begin to relax beneath her fingertips. "Have you spoken to his officer?"

His body jerked. "His *officer?*"

"Sometimes if a man needs to be disciplined—"

He chuckled. "Daughter of Lugh, you have been away a long time. Have you forgotten how things are here?" He touched his split lip. "This is the only answer you get from the army when you ask for justice."

She said nothing. Her experience with the gate guards suggested he was right. On the other hand, Rianorix's efforts to negotiate were probably as well-meant but clumsy as his flattery.

He said, "What does my eye look like?"

"People will be afraid of you," she said. "Small children will run away crying."

The half smile returned. "Is it very bad?"

"The swelling will go down by tomorrow. The bruise will get worse." She traced a faint line around the base of his eye socket with her forefinger. "It is all around here, black and purple. And part of the white is red."

"This is nothing."

"It does not look like nothing."

"It is nothing to what they have done to others." He indicated the graze along her cheek. "We make a matching pair."

"I upset a baker," she explained. "He was trying to cheat my—" She stopped herself. "He was asking more than I wanted to pay."

"Did you win?"

"No."

The bloodshot eye gave her a glance that was probably more alarming than he intended. "Three winters gone by, daughter of Lugh, and neither of us is much the wiser."

"And what else has happened while I have been away?"

"The usual things," he said. "The harvests have been poor, but they still take the taxes. What little people have is being saved for the feast at the Gathering, but nearly everyone is running out now. Except the soldiers in the fort. The emperor's men will be the last to starve."

She dared not confess that she too would be one of the last to starve. She sat him up and wrapped strips torn from an old linen undershirt around his wounds. Then she lay beside him on the bracken bed and gazed into the dying firelight, thinking of how very differently things had turned out from the way they had expected, and of how sad it would be to hear the old songs and stories at the summer Gathering without the family they had both loved. The family that had been sent so violently to the next world.

"Their bodies were treated with honor," he said suddenly, thinking the same thing. "At least we could do that."

"But you had no body for me. Why did you believe I was dead?"

"Catavignus said you must have been inside when the house burned down. There would be nothing but ash."

"Surely someone tried to find out?"

"I asked him what he was doing. He said he sent messages north to ask if you were a prisoner, and heard nothing." He paused. "Ash has never been treated with such reverence."

"But I was waiting!"

"If you had sent a message to say you were alive, we would have come."

"If I could have sent a message I would have come myself!" She rolled over. "And what about Trenus?" The memory of her captor made her shudder. "I saw no sign of punishment for Trenus, and he was the leader."

"I said we should gather up men and act. Catavignus said we should leave Trenus to the army because he is a Votadini and we mustn't start a war between the tribes."

She sat up. "They were the ones who started it!"

"I know," he said, his hand seeking hers again. "I know. But Catavignus was next of kin, so his wishes were respected." After a moment he added, "Lie down, you are letting the cold air in."

She threw herself back down onto the bed. "Did you fast against Trenus?"

"Of course. We made a curse against him, and I fasted until your cousin persuaded me to stop. She said five lives were enough to lose."

Aemilia. She might have guessed. "So while you were cursing and starving, what did the army do about Trenus raiding and murdering on the land they are supposed to protect?"

"What do you think?"

"I know what I think. I am asking you."

"You know how it is. They're only interested if one of them is involved. Or if we don't pay the taxes. They sent some men up to look at what was left of the house."

"And did nothing, I suppose."

"And did nothing," he agreed. "But things are beginning to change now. You will see when you come to the Gathering. The gods are waking. People are remembering where they hid their courage. The army is learning to fear us again."

She wondered whether to tell him about the god in the yard, but he would ask questions and she was not sure she understood it herself yet. Instead she said, "You must be careful. Frightened men are dangerous."

"It is the Romans and their friends who should be careful. A leader has come at last who hunts with the power of the gods. The army cannot catch him, and they never know where he will strike next."

"He struck today," said Tilla. "One legionary is very badly hurt and others are injured."

"Really? How badly hurt?"

"He has lost a leg. He may not live."

"A man from the legions!" Rianorix chuckled. "Well, that's one that won't be bothering us for a while."

"He had just become a father," she said.

Rianorix observed that it was a pity he had not been injured before he had time to spawn. "The soldiers are afraid. They are looking for friends. I hear they are fetching Trenus down to dine with the new governor when he comes to visit."

"What?"

"Daughter of Lugh, this blanket will only cover us both if you lie still."

She pushed a fold of blanket down into the gap between them. "Tell me it's not true."

"Trenus is a head man of a friendly tribe."

"He is a thief and a murderer!"

"He's useful to them. His people lie between the army and the tribes they never managed to conquer."

"I know that," she said, unable to keep the bitterness out of her voice. "I had to live there."

A log tumbled in the fire, sending up a fountain of sparks.

He said, "I thought about you often, daughter of Lugh. I prayed to meet you in the next world so that I could ask your pardon for being too late to save you."

"Did you come to help?"

"As soon as I heard the alarm. When I got here the house was a furnace, and you were gone."

She supposed he had done his best. Under the circumstances. Believing that she was dead and that it was not his place to overrule her kin and seek vengeance. "Well," she said. "I am home now."

He circled his fingertips lightly on the back of her hand. "And even more beautiful than I remembered."

"Yes," she said. "I am also very tired, and if you move, the bandages will shift and all my work will be wasted."

His hand slid across her thigh. "Do you remember when we did it just by lying still and—"

"No," she lied. "Go to sleep."

26

WHATEVER HIS INEPTITUDE at managing staff, it seemed Thessalus was a competent medic. By the time Ruso had finished an evening tour of the wards, admired his predecessor's handiwork on the splinted leg, and diagnosed the malingerers as in need of various gruesome therapies that he promised to administer first thing in the morning, the long hours of the spring day were at last coming to an end. He needed to visit Thessalus, but he was more immediately concerned with what had happened to Tilla. Quite possibly she had gone to visit her family, or been called to deliver a baby, but surely she would have left a message—or at least the supper she was supposed to be bringing—at the gate?

The fort had the customary four entrances, and in the customary fashion the information Ruso wanted was at the last one he tried. He had two questions, but as soon as he introduced himself the gate guard did not stop to find out what they were. Instead, the man groped inside the folds of his tunic and handed Ruso a coin. "I didn't mean no offense, sir. It was all just a bit of a joke. Only she took umbrage and walked off before I could explain."

"Ah," said Ruso, imagining the scene.

"And I asked if she wanted to leave a message, but she didn't. And I couldn't let her in without a gate pass. So if you could let her have the money back, sir, and tell her it was all just a bit of fun?"

Ruso glanced down at the profile of the late emperor Trajan and back up at the less impressive head of a sentry with an odd shadow under his nostrils that turned out to be a vigorous sprouting of black hairs.

"Next time," he said, "just take a message when you're asked. And if you don't want this to go any farther, try to be a little more helpful about something else. I need to know about an emergency call for the doctor that came in last night."

The guard, who had not been on duty at the time, went to fetch the watch captain. He returned with the captain and a youth who looked barely old enough to be sent around the corner to buy a pound of figs, let alone serve overseas with the army.

"Oh yes, sir!" the youth exclaimed in answer to Ruso's question. "I saw the doctor and Gambax come in before curfew. I remember because Gambax was drunk."

The watch captain glared at him.

"And then Doctor Thessalus went out on his horse and I remember thinking I was glad I wasn't ill, sir, because—"

"The officer doesn't want to know what you were thinking!" interrupted the watch captain. "This is the army, not a bloody philosophy club." He glanced at Ruso. "Sorry, sir. He's new."

Ruso said, "I'm trying to find out who took the message calling for a doctor." Realizing this sounded like a threat, he added, "The patient wanted to say thank you." He hoped this did not sound as lame to his listeners as it did to him.

"Would that be the call for Doctor Thessalus or the call for Gambax, sir?"

"There was only one call, surely?"

"I don't know, sir. We didn't get either of them. You'd have to ask at the other gates. But Gambax went out just after Doctor Thessalus."

Ruso frowned. "Out?"

The youth's head bobbed. "His case must have been nearer, though, 'cause he was on foot. And he was back before long, but I didn't see Doctor Thessalus again."

When the youth had gone Ruso observed, "He looks very young," and realized with horror that it was the sort of remark he and Lucius used to deride from their father.

"They'll be sending them straight out of the cradle soon," observed the watch captain, who could not have been much over twenty-five himself.

"While I'm here," said Ruso, "how do I go about getting a gate pass for my housekeeper?"

The man shook his head. "You'd have a hard time sir. The only civilians allowed in with no escort are the prefect's family. Security policy. Because of the way the natives are."

"But she's only a woman!"

The watch captain shook his head again. "So was Helen of Troy, sir. Look what she started."

27

To Ruso's relief, Thessalus seemed to have forgotten about the fish. He gestured Ruso to the stool while he himself sat on the chair, crushing the scroll cases. He frowned at them, made an ineffective attempt to pull one of them out from beneath him, and gave up.

Ruso tried, "How are you this evening?"

Thessalus gave a slow smile. "You don't need to keep coming to see me, Doctor," he said. "Don't worry. All will be well. I have seen to it."

In the light of the one lamp it took Ruso a moment to realize that Thessalus was smiling not at him but at a spot a few inches beyond his left ear. Ruso turned. The wall was bare. He wished he could see whatever was giving Thessalus the confidence that all would be well, because from his own point of view things were not good at all. During his first visit this afternoon, his patient's mind had been scuttling about like a startled lizard. Now it was moving more like a . . . like a slow thing. Ruso had had a long and trying day.

"I have seen to it," Thessalus repeated, sounding much as Ruso imagined an oracle might sound. "This is my answer. Ambitions, hopes . . . it all comes to the same thing in the end."

"I've met some of your patients. The men speak very highly of you."

"They will not speak highly of me when they know."

Outside the main door, the guard coughed and shuffled his feet.

Ruso said gently, "You have been troubled, brother."

"This is true."

"Your mind has not served you well of late."

"My hands have served me worse. I did no harm with my mind."

"You think you have done someone harm?"

Thessalus looked puzzled. "You think it is all in my mind, that it is a dream?"

"We all dream things we do not do."

"And sometimes we do things we would not dream of." Thessalus put his head in his hands. His shoulders began to shake.

"Gently, brother." Ruso leaned forward and grasped the man's thin arms. Thessalus drew back as if in pain.

"Don't touch me!"

"I was only—"

"I told you, you must never touch the patient!"

Ruso sat back. He wished he had left this visit until tomorrow. The man had been calm. Now he was in distress.

"All gone now," Thessalus mumbled. "All over. I am a murderer. I know. I saw it. I felt it." He began to rock backward and forward. "I can feel it now."

"Open your eyes, Thessalus. Look at me."

Without lifting his head Thessalus began to moan softly, "No, no . . ."

"Look at me, Thessalus. Open your eyes and look up. I am real. Put aside the visions. Just for a moment."

Slowly, the man's head lifted.

"What if I can prove to you that you were somewhere else on the night Felix died? What if we find people who saw you?"

"You wish to prove me insane. I am condemned either way."

"I wish to prove you ill, brother. And soon to be restored to health."

"But never again trusted."

"In time, when you are well—"

"You are wasting your time," Thessalus continued.

"Metellus will find out the truth," insisted Ruso. "The man who killed Felix will be punished."

"They will find an innocent native to execute in my place."

"Not innocent. Nobody believes you did it, Thessalus."

The glistening dark eyes looked again into his own. "Then you must convince them."

"First," said Ruso carefully, "You must convince me. What reason would you have to attack Felix?"

"I don't know. I don't know. He was there. His friends beat the native. They ask for justice and cows and we beat them."

"What did you do with the body?"

Thessalus sighed. "I'm very tired."

"We'll talk about this tomorrow. I expect they'll bring your supper in a minute. Do you want something later to help you sleep?'

"I want something to stop me dreaming. Do you have that in your case? Freedom from one's own dreams?'

Ruso wished he could place a comforting hand on that of his colleague. "Tomorrow we will begin to sort this out," he promised. "Tomorrow we will begin to work on a cure."

"His head," whispered Thessalus.

"Sleep tonight, brother," said Ruso. "We will find a way through."

"What did I do with his head?" said Thessalus.

28

RUSO WANDERED BACK through the dark streets of the fort to the infirmary, still pondering what to do with Thessalus.

He had met patients with problems of the mind before, but even in the spring—known to be a dangerous time for people prone to madness—he had never come across one displaying both mania and melancholy on the same day. It was as if his two visits had been to two different men. And although no one believed Thessalus to be capable of murder, he was so utterly convinced he had done it that Ruso was beginning to wonder himself.

Normally he would have shared his concerns about a difficult patient with a colleague, but the nearest one was half a day's ride away. Besides, the confession and Thessalus's position as a fellow medic made it too delicate a matter to broach with an untried stranger.

He would have liked to write to Valens about the case, but the only way to get a reply before the governor's arrival would be to use the official dispatch service. A humble medic was as likely to have access to that service as he was to have Mercury fly in through the window and offer to deliver the message in person. No: Whatever he did, he would have to do it on his own.

Back in his room, he scrambled down to the end of the bed and opened the trunk. Picking out one of the scrolls, he held it dangerously close to the lamp and began to scan it for diseases of the mind.

When he found it, the passage proved of doubtful use. The author contended, not unreasonably, that the treatment to be offered must depend upon the diagnosis. Given the symptoms he had exhibited so far, Thessalus was simultaneously in need of a day's starvation, and a moderate diet. He needed to have blood let, and not to have blood let. He needed to be given a serious fright, and to be kept calm. He needed cold water poured over his head, and to have his head gently moistened with rose oil and thyme. He also, apparently, needed a good vomit.

Ruso slid the scroll into its container and threw it back into the trunk. His body was tired but his mind was still churning over the events of the day. Without Tilla, bed held little appeal. He decided to go for a late walk to clear his head.

Ruso had intended to ask the guard whether there was still any sign of movement behind Thessalus's door, but as he approached he heard a crash, followed by a shout of "How long are you going to keep this up, you mad bastard?"

The voice was familiar. If Thessalus replied, Ruso did not hear it.

"This isn't a game!" yelled the voice. "I'm not bringing you any more until you stop messing about!" There was a thump on the inside of the door and a shout of "I'm done here, let me out!" presumably aimed at the guard. Seconds later Gambax emerged and strode off down the dark street, oblivious to Ruso approaching from the opposite direction.

"What's happened?" demanded Ruso, taking in the sight of a pale Thessalus cowering under his blankets. On top of the bed was an overturned tray. Liquid had streamed across the floor from a shattered cup and a loaf of bread had come to rest against the doorpost.

Ruso crouched by the bed. "Are you all right?"

Thessalus's hand was shaking as he reached to turn the tray upright. "I'm sorry. Tell him I'm sorry."

"You don't have to be sorry," said Ruso grimly. "Don't worry, it won't happen again. I'll get someone else to bring your meals."

"No!"

He was surprised at the strength of the man's response. "You'll still get your food," he explained. "Just from somebody—"

"I want Gambax to come." Thessalus glanced wildly around the room.

"The others . . ." His voice sunk even lower as his thin fingers gripped Ruso's arm. "They're trying to poison me."

"I promise I'll make sure they don't poison you. We'll have your food tasted before it arrives."

"No—oh!" Thessalus withdrew his hand. "Mustn't touch. Mustn't— sorry."

"I'll bring it myself and taste it in front of you. How about that?"

Thessalus shook his head. "No. Please. You don't understand. He doesn't mean to shout. I want Gambax."

"Perhaps we could eat out tomorrow," suggested Ruso. "Is there anywhere you'd like to go, or shall I choose?"

"They have a guard at the door."

"I'll talk to them," said Ruso, encouraged by the logic of this objection and confident that he would be able to get permission to take his patient out of this miserable confinement. "Perhaps we could go to the baths."

"Gambax. I need to see Gambax. He understands."

"I always find that a massage—"

"No."

Ruso nodded. "We'll stay here, then."

"Rocking," said Thessalus suddenly.

"How about taking me out for a ride tomorrow? You could show me around."

"Rocking," persisted Thessalus. "Rocking is good."

Ruso, possibly recalling the same passage as his patient about the treatment of the insane, glanced up at the rafters. "We could suspend some sort of swing from up there," he said. "So you think rocking in a swing might make you feel better?"

"No," said Thessalus. "But it will keep you happy."

Ruso was beginning to suspect that Thessalus knew much more than he did himself about problems of the mind. "I'll see what I can arrange."

"My head," said Thessalus, staring at the rafters, "is full of words."

"What sort of words?"

"All the words," explained Thessalus. "Jumping around like frogs." He lifted one hand and made a slow circling motion in the air. " 'Round and 'round like frogs, bumping against the edges." He turned to look at Ruso. "Hellebore for madness," he said. "Thyme vinegar for clearing the head. Don't drink it, Doctor. Only sniff. Vinegar shrivels the mouth." He pulled a face. "Is it time to get up yet?"

"It's evening."

"Mustn't get up in the dark. Bad things happen in the dark."

"What sort of bad things?"

"Dreams. Bad dreams."

"Can you tell me what you see in the dreams?"

Thessalus reached up a thin arm and grasped the back of the couch, hauling himself into a sitting position. Slowly, he eased his feet down toward the floor without throwing off his blanket, so that he was swathed in gray wool with one skeletal set of toes poking out at floor level. He ran both hands roughly through his hair, springing out the dark curls from where they had lain flattened over his ears, then rested his elbows on his knees and leaned closer to Ruso. Their eyes met. "I can see what you see," he whispered.

"What's that?"

"Blood." Thessalus's eyes were still locked on Ruso's as if he were trying to gaze past their surface and into the soul.

Ruso swallowed. "Blood?"

"All that blood. All that pain. Don't tell me you don't hear them screaming in your dreams."

He could not deny it. He had thought the nightmares would fade with experience, but while his rational mind tucked his own fears away in a corner during his waking hours, there were times when the ghastly things he had done to living human beings returned to haunt his sleep. The worst times were when he dreamed he had made a catastrophic mistake. Even when he woke and reassured himself that it was not true, the guilt remained over him like a shroud, as it had this afternoon when the carpenter died. "Sometimes, I have trouble sleeping," he concurred. "But the things we do—"

"Are *always done* for the *best*," said Thessalus, tilting his head from side to side and reciting the words in the singsong voice of a platitude. "No they're not. Have you ever been told to revive a man so he could feel pain, doctor? 'We need information, doctor. Our men are in danger if you don't wake him up for questioning, doctor. . . .' "

Ruso shook his head. "I haven't." But what would he have done, had he been asked? That must have been what Audax had meant when he said, "No wonder being in the army's driven him crackers."

"I said no," said Thessalus. "They threw a bucket of water over him."

"Tomorrow," said Ruso, getting to his feet, "we will begin to work on a cure."

He retrieved the bread and placed it on the tray. He cleared up as many of the broken shards of the cup as he could find in the lamplight, and sniffed at the contents. Gambax had been delivering a late supper of bread and wine.

He sniffed again. He ran his forefinger along an inside surface of the cup. He put the finger in his mouth, and smiled. Suddenly, Thessalus's diagnosis had become clearer—and he might just have found the lever with which to shift Gambax.

29

R USO UNBUCKLED HIS belt and placed it on top of the beer barrel. Then he sat down on his solitary bed and wondered if Tilla were missing him. He supposed the confusion about access was his own fault: He should have checked the regulations here before giving her instructions. Well, it was too late now. A man couldn't think of everything. Especially a man who had begun the day with no cares beyond a few bug bites and ended it with a surgical failure, a grim secret, a lazy underling to discipline, and a clinic full of women and children to face tomorrow. Not to mention a mother-in-law who sent dangerously indiscreet letters and an absent housekeeper who seemed to be the army's only link with some sort of violent Druid revival.

He unlaced his boots and set them together under the bed so that he could find them easily in the dark. Gambax was officially on duty, but he had left orders that he was to be called himself if there were a problem. Audax's warning had only served to confirm Ruso's unease about Gambax. It seemed he had been extending his slovenly influence over the infirmary for some time, usurping the ineffective Thessalus, and, by the sound of it, taking bribes from men who wanted to avoid duty. Tomorrow, he would confront him about the drug he had tasted in Thessalus's wine. The trouble was, Gambax was the only person who knew what was in those unlabeled jars and packets in the pharmacy, and until today he had been the sole guardian of the records system. The man had dug himself in like a tick. He was unpleasant to have around, but wrenching him out too suddenly would leave a worse mess. Ruso would have liked to send him out to do the public clinic, but the local women and children probably hadn't done anything to deserve him.

They probably hadn't done anything to deserve Ruso either. What he had meant by promising to think about it was that he would announce his decision not to run the clinic when he had wrestled his conscience into accepting a good excuse. But now his conscience was telling him he was a coward. A public clinic run by an army medic (as opposed to passing quacks) probably provided a useful service. He would have the help of an experienced man, and he would get out of this miserably cramped infirmary for the afternoon.

Thinking of misery reminded him that he was supposed to be doing something about replying to Arria. The challenge of sorting out Arria made him feel weary. So weary that he was going to have to close his eyes for a moment and consider it from a horizontal position.

As soon as he lay down, Ruso discovered a new problem: The bed was not only narrow, but too short. He lay with his heels suspended in the cool air beyond the end of the mattress, wondering if this was Gambax's revenge for having the staff's access to the beer barrel curtailed.

He rolled over. Now his toes were dangling in the air instead of his heels. Perhaps it was just as well Tilla was not here. This bed would never allow two people to sleep at the same time, even if they liked each other a great deal. Especially if one of them had extremely cold feet.

At the memory of his last encounter with Tilla's feet, the bite on his elbow began to itch. He slapped at it, sat up, and groped for the pen and inkpot he had borrowed from Albanus.

Dearest Mother,

It grated to write this, but it would annoy Arria even more, as she was only seven years older than he was. With a son his age, how old would that make her?

I was surprised to have the pleasure of my first ever letter from you, which was forwarded to me at a temporary posting. I cannot send greetings to my sisters as I am writing in confidence, but you know my feelings for them.

Arria could make of that whatever she wanted. Ruso found his half sisters almost as exasperating—and twice as incomprehensible—as their mother.

I understand your anxiety but not your decision to confide in me via a market-place scribe. I hope nobody has been given the false impression that no dowry is offered with my sisters. How I wish I could say this to you in your presence

—and din some sense into your silly head—

Do NOT worry, mother. I admit I have been eager to protect my sisters

—and their unfortunate future spouses—

from rushing into marriage at the first opportunity. However, be assured that I am making useful investments here on the girls' behalf and suitable dowries will be settled on them when the time comes.

He then scrawled an urgent letter to Lucius congratulating him and his wife on the birth of their new son and warning him to try and put a stop to Arria's public complaining. *As I have explained to her,* he said, *I am making useful investments here on the girls' behalf.*

He stared at the letter and realized he had sunk to a new low: Now he was lying to his brother. The place to make investments—if he had had any spare money—was Deva. It definitely wasn't here on the crumbling edge of the empire, no matter how law-abiding and loyal the mustachioed Catavignus and his guild of caterers might consider themselves to be.

He reached for the third writing tablet he had persuaded Albanus to part with. He would cheer himself up by writing to Valens.

Ruso to his old friend and colleague Valens at Deva, greetings.

He paused. What next? The business of the murder was too sensitive to be entrusted to a letter, although it was just the sort of salacious gossip Valens would enjoy. He certainly could not convey his suspicion that the local unrest was more widespread than anyone was allowed to know, and that the governor had sent orders not to provoke the locals because if this Cernunnos business got out of hand there were not enough troops here to hold the roads. Once the roads were cut, the small border forts could be picked off one by one. No wonder the men from the Twentieth had been sent here. If Ruso's suspicions were right, the governor would be sending a lot more troops up the north road very soon to impose order. There was a strong chance that far from being sent back to Deva, he would have his stay here extended indefinitely.

He surveyed the blank sheet and wished he had written the greeting in larger letters. Finally he settled on,

Bogs very pleasant at this time of year, and chest getting a fine tan. Tilla looking lovely in blue.

There was still plenty of blank space. It would be a waste not to use it. Maybe he would feel more inspired tomorrow.

He placed the letter on top of the barrel, blew out the lamp, lay down, and wondered where Tilla was sleeping tonight. He hoped wherever it was, it was better than this. An experimental shuffle up the bed confirmed that with his head pressing against the wall, his feet were almost on the mattress. He had just closed his eyes when a sudden idea made him fling back the covers and crawl down to the end of the bed on all fours. He groped about in the darkness, lifting the trunk off the chair and maneuvering it around so that the longest side was pressed against the end of the mattress. Then he rearranged the blankets. Finally he settled back down and stretched his feet experimentally past the end of the bed.

Ruso smiled to himself. At least one problem was solved.

30

TILLA WAS RETRIEVING her share of the narrow blanket when the door caved in.

For an absurd moment she thought it was the medicus come to wreak revenge on them. Then she knew Trenus had come back to kill her, yelling, "Don't move!"—in *Latin*?

Something fell over with a crash. Torches advanced, light glancing off the straight lines of weapons and curves of helmets. The point of a sword was cold against her throat. Next to her, Rian tried to get up and was pushed down again.

"Rianorix the basket maker?" demanded a quiet voice from beyond the torchlight.

His agreement was hoarse.

"Get up. And tell us where it is."

"He has done nothing wrong!" cried Tilla, grabbing his arm and trying to hold him down beside her.

Soldiers had seized the other arm. Rianorix, naked apart from the gleaming white stripes of bandage, was on his feet. She heard the rattle of chains.

"Don't hurt him!"

The soldier with his sword at her throat hooked the toe of his boot under the blanket. "Move over, love."

Rianorix's shout of "Leave her alone!" was followed by a sickening crack as someone swung a weapon against the side of his head. The basket maker reeled. The quiet voice said, "Where is it?"

Tilla said, "Where is what?"

A couple of the soldiers were pulling down baskets from the creaking stock pile and flinging them aside. Others were clambering through them to prod the thatch with spears. Someone tipped over the beer barrel and the contents hissed and spat and stank across the hearth in the middle of the floor.

The soldier was grinning down at Tilla. The blade was withdrawn from her throat. She scrambled upright, pulling the blanket around herself and wishing she were wearing proper clothes instead of one of Rian's old shirts. The soldier, still keeping the sword pointed toward her, kicked apart the pile of bracken that had made the bed. "Where is it, eh?"

"What?"

"What you took."

"We have done nothing wrong!" She was about to say, "I will tell my master how you have behaved!" when she realized that if she told them who her master was, they would tell him where they had found her. Instead she said, "Please do not hurt him, sir."

"That's better," said the soldier, patting her bottom with the flat of his sword. "Now, save yourself a lot of bother and tell the nice officer where it is."

Another man in a better uniform stepped forward. The torchlight made the blond in his hair gleam. When he spoke she knew he was the quiet one in charge. "I remember you," he said. "You used to live here."

She did not care whether he thought he knew her or not. "Why are you arresting us?"

"Not you," he said. "We only want the basket maker. And what he has stolen."

"But he is a good man! He pays his taxes, he keeps the law—" At least, she supposed he did. More or less. It could not be illegal to fast against someone, surely?

"He is accused of the murder of a member of the emperor's auxiliary forces."

As Tilla was protesting that they were wrong, she heard Rian's voice from the doorway. "Felix? Felix is dead?"

"You should know," said the quiet one.

"Yes!" The chains rattled as Rianorix tried to fling his hands in the air, was pulled up short, and stumbled sideways. It did not stop him from laughing. "He's dead, daughter of Lugh! Dead! The gods have answered!"

"Get out!" retorted one of the soldiers, giving him a kick in the direction of the door.

Tilla ducked around the soldier who was supposed to be guarding her and ran across to cling to Rianorix, pretending to kiss him good-bye. A couple of the soldiers cheered.

"It worked!" whispered Rianorix as more hands reached in through the entrance of the house and dragged his pale form away into the dark while others held her back.

"The gods killed that soldier!" she shouted after them. "They will kill all of you if you hurt their favored one!"

"Oh, those lads won't hurt him, miss," her guard assured her. "We've got experts back at base who do that." He seized her bruised arm and pushed her backward, his foul breath in her face. "Back to bed, eh?"

"Leave her," ordered the quiet one.

"Won't be a minute, sir."

"I said, leave her."

The man flung Tilla down on the bracken bed and growled, "Tart."

The officer was already out of the house by the time the soldier kicked a brand out of the fire and into the jumble of baskets by the door.

She would have run after them, but by the time she had put out the flames and rescued what remained of Rian's stock, she was exhausted and the soldiers were long gone.

She had used the blanket to beat out the fire. Now she retrieved her damp clothes from the chair, wriggled into them, and huddled by the hearth, afraid to sleep lest the scorched thatch begin to smoulder again.

There was a long cold night ahead. The only very small consolation was that under the guise of that desperate kiss, she had managed to slip the last apple into Rianorix's hand and whisper, "No need to fast now. You are right. The gods have woken."

31

THE ASHES OF Felix's pyre were still smoldering on one side of the road as the flames rose from the brushwood stacked beneath the body of the carpenter on the other. The man's eyes had been opened so that he could see the heavens as his comrades watched the smoke rising into the pale morning sky. Ruso stood at attention with the men of the Twentieth, uncomfortable in the knowledge that many of them would be blaming him for the death. The civilians who had traveled up from Deva with them were huddled together, silent and grim faced. One or two of the women were weeping. Lydia stood impassive, a dark shawl covering her head, one hand patting the back of the child mewling over her shoulder. Next to her Ruso recognized Susanna from the snack bar, stolidly attending her second funeral in two days. To his surprise, Tilla was not with them.

As soon as the ceremony was over, Postumus's men shouldered their packs and marched westward, leaving a squad of eight legionaries to stand guard over the pyre. Most of the civilians loaded up their belongings and set off after them. Susanna patted Lydia on the shoulder and hurried away to open up. Lydia seated herself on the ground in front of the collapsed pyre. As Ruso crouched beside her, he could see the glint of the flames in her dark eyes.

"We will catch the person who did this, Lydia."

"Ask him to give me my man back," she said, not looking at him.

As he returned to the fort, he passed a makeshift potter's stall at the roadside. A linen merchant was setting out his wares and two old women were squabbling as they hung up a display of leather bags and belts. Someone had laid four scraggy cabbages on a cloth beside a crate containing a hen. He stepped aside to allow a girl to pass with a clumsy handcart loaded with bread. Today was market day, and everyone else's life would go on.

Ruso dropped in to see Thessalus on the way back from the funeral, and discovered him hunched over his breakfast. Gambax seemed to have taken a more conventional approach to delivery this time, and the crockery was intact. Ruso stole a sip of the wine. Thessalus, drizzling oil onto a hunk of bread with an unsteady hand, did not seem to notice him. The wine tasted the same as last night: army vinegar laced with something that shouldn't be there.

Ruso hoped Gambax knew what he was doing with the dosage. He said, "I'm on the way to the infirmary. Any advice?"

"Lock the door," said Thessalus, drizzling the oil in a circle. "Keep them out. You can't do anything for them."

"Thanks," said Ruso. "I'll bear that in mind. I came to tell you: There's good news. Metellus has arrested a native for the murder of Felix. Whatever you dreamed up, Thessalus, you have nothing to feel guilty about. Just concentrate on getting well. I'll be back to see you as soon as I can."

To his surprise, when Thessalus looked up from the bread his eyes were glistening with tears. "I told you this would happen," he said. "They will find someone else to blame. Now I have killed two men."

This was not the reaction Ruso had expected to his good news. Wishing he had kept quiet until later, he knelt beside Thessalus and handed him a cloth. "Courage, brother."

"Don't touch me! Don't come near me!"

Ruso backed away. "Sorry. Would you like anything to read? Something else to eat?"

"I want to sleep with no dreams."

"We will make you well," Ruso promised, although he was not entirely sure how.

32

THE TWIN GODS guarding the infirmary door (which now read: "Days to Governor's Visit III") had been busy overnight. Miracles had been performed. The four malingerers had all enjoyed sudden cures and been discharged back to their units, and Gambax had actually managed to complete a rota before heading off to some administrative meeting or other at headquarters.

The newly vacated ward was descended upon by orderlies bearing scrubbing brushes and buckets and bedding in a manner that suggested intention if not efficiency. Ruso put his head around the door frame and declared their efforts to be splendid.

Only slightly less miraculously, the splinted leg still had no inflammation. The man with the shoulder wound was still pessimistic, and the morning sick parade offered the usual coughs and stomach complaints, bad backs, sore eyes, and dodgy knees. All seemed genuine. Ruso chose not to ask if any of their owners was under the command of Audax.

He sent a junior officer with a wrecked knee hobbling out, moved his chair into the treatment room, and was reading *The Varieties and Uses of the Poppy* when Albanus came to tell him that Gambax had returned. Ruso put his scroll aside and braced himself for a difficult interview.

"You wanted to see me, sir." Gambax's expression as he appeared in the doorway of the treatment room suggested the summons was very inconvenient.

"Shut the door, Gambax."

The man glanced back into the corridor as if hoping to find an excuse to go somewhere else, then dropped the latch.

"Will this take long, sir? I've got a list of—"

"That depends on how long you take to tell me the truth."

Alarm showed in Gambax's eyes, but only for a moment.

"When I asked you what was wrong with Doctor Thessalus, you told me you thought he was just in need of a rest."

"Yes, sir."

"Is there anything you'd like to add to that?"

"No, sir."

"No ailments that you're aware of?"

"No, sir."

"How long have you been giving him poppy tears?"

A blink was the only betrayal of emotion. "About three months, sir, off and on."

"But you don't think there's anything wrong with him?"

"I was obeying orders. He asked me for them."

"And you didn't think to wonder whether this was a good idea?"

There was pause before, "I respect the doctor's judgment, sir."

"I see. What would you think of an orderly who shouted at a patient and threw a meal tray at him?"

Gambax's throat moved as he swallowed. "I didn't throw it at him, sir. I threw it on the floor."

"Why?"

"I was trying to help him, sir."

"What?"

"I was trying to shock him back into sanity."

"By telling him to stop messing about and threatening not to bring his happy juice anymore?"

"It probably wasn't a good idea, sir."

"Cutting down his supply would have been a good idea months ago. You're supposed to be both pharmacist and record keeper here. You've kept doling out powerful medicine to a man you know isn't sick—or wasn't when you started—and not even bothered to keep a note of it."

When the man did not reply, he prompted, "Haven't you?"

"He said it helped him sleep, sir."

"At breakfast?"

Ruso sighed. *The Varieties and Uses* had warned against using poppy tears in the eyes, and everyone knew that too much would be fatal. But the author was only one of several authorities who recommended poppy as a miracle cure for all kinds of ailments. Many remedies included it in small doses. He often prescribed it himself to relieve pain, and it would certainly help the patient sleep. However, for a healthy man to be taking regular and heavy doses of poppy over a period of three months was surely abnormal, and Gambax must have known that. The deputy had deliberately lied to him.

In other circumstances, Ruso would have relieved him of duty. But as the sole pharmacist, Gambax was a necessary evil. And the last thing Ruso wanted was to suggest to a man in charge of dangerous medicines that he had nothing to lose.

"While the staff are sorting out the wards," said Ruso, "I want that mess around the pharmacy table tidied up. I want everything properly and clearly labeled. I want a complete, up-to-date record of everything you've got there, and I want you to make a list of what gets dispensed every day. I'll be inspecting the area and checking the records on a regular basis. In the meantime you're not to go near Thessalus without me present. If I hear that you've so much as looked at barrack block two, I'll have you charged with insubordination. Is that clear?'

"Yes, sir."

"Good. Now go and get on with it."

When he had gone Ruso stared at the cloak hanging on the back of the closed door. *I respect the doctor's judgment,* indeed! Of course he did. As long as Thessalus was happily doped up and dependent on Gambax for his supply, the staff had been left to manage the infirmary in whatever way suited them best. And what had suited most of them was to sit in the office with the door barred, drinking beer.

I was trying to help him, sir. Gods above.

Still, he had Gambax on the run at last. He was making progress with the prefect's order to sort out the medical service. Even if he was beginning to sound worryingly enthusiastic about the sort of administrative procedures he could never usually be bothered to follow himself.

Gambax had failed to shut the door. He could see movement in the corridor outside.

"Albanus, you're lurking."

The clerk grinned, stepped into the treatment room, and closed the door. "Could I possibly come in here for a moment, sir? It's safer than out there."

Ruso indicated a seat. "Tell me, Albanus," he said, tipping back his chair so that the front legs left the ground, "have you ever heard of the torpedo fish?"

"It gives some sort of shock, sir."

"Excellent," said Ruso, wishing Gambax were there to hear himself proved wrong. "You haven't by any chance got a remedy for a man whose triangles are falling apart, have you?"

"I think the only remedy for that is death, sir."

"No doubt," said Ruso, mildly surprised. Albanus was not in the habit of making jokes.

Seconds later it became apparent that no joke was intended. "It's a bit of an obscure piece, sir. Plato. My father was a teacher. He made me translate it once. I can't remember much about it, but I think when your triangles finally crumble they release your soul to fly to . . . somewhere."

"What triangles?"

"I never really understood it. But I think Plato thought everything was based on mathematics and people are made out of little triangles and the sharp edges help you digest your food."

"Gods above," said Ruso, scratching one ear. "No wonder people are rude about the Greeks."

"I probably haven't explained it terribly well, sir."

"No, I'm sure that's right. It explains something Doctor Thessalus said to me yesterday."

There was a thump from the corridor, then a curse and the sound of something cumbersome being dragged along the floor. Ruso guessed the orderlies had finally realized they needed to change the mattresses before they put on the fresh bedding.

"I've finished sorting the records, sir," said Albanus. "There's lots of gaps but at least you can find what there is now."

"Excellent," said Ruso. "I'll come and have a look." He caught Albanus's eye. "Maybe it's better not to disturb Gambax at the moment. But I'd like you to start checking the rest of the infirmary paperwork. Find out how they've been placing the orders, paying the bills, and so on."

Albanus was chewing his lower lip. "I don't think Gambax will like me interfering in that very much, sir. He's a bit agitated already."

"That's why you'll have to do it discreetly when he's not there. In the meantime, I want you to nip around to the gatehouses and see if you can find a guard who can remember where Doctor Thessalus was called to on the night of the murder, and what time he arrived back. I tried last night but I didn't get very far. While you're there, see if they've had any messages from Tilla. If they haven't, I think you'd better go out and try to track her down."

"Right-oh, sir. What do I say if they ask why I want to know about the doctor?"

"Say 'medical reasons,'" said Ruso. "That usually works." He tipped his chair forward again. "Now I suppose I'd better go and encourage the scrubbers."

33

THE THORN HEDGE finally came into sight on the far side of the river meadow. Tilla looked above her shoulder again to make sure that there was no one following her before she forced herself to slow down and recapture her breath. Beyond the thorn hedge, smoke was seeping lazily skyward from a dumpy cone of thatch. As she drew closer she could make out the tops of the beehives.

Nobody noticed her approach. Veldicca was on her knees, ripping early weeds out of one of the herb beds. There was a green shawl tied across her back, sheltering the shape of a sleeping baby. In the doorway of the house a small girl was grinding flour while two hens loitered, waiting to lunge at the spilled grains of wheat.

"Veldicca!" called Tilla as she pushed open the gate.

The young woman took one look, scrambled to her feet, and backed away in alarm.

"It is me," Tilla assured her.

"Daughter of Lugh?"

"Alive. May I come in?"

Veldicca peered at her for a moment, then hurried forward, slapping the worst of the mud off her hands before embracing her. "They told us you were dead!"

"And you have a baby!"

They drew back for a moment, each appraising the other. Veldicca was thinner, and a dull red scar ran across her left cheekbone. But whatever troubles had assailed her in the last three years, they had not repressed her smile.

"Come and sit and talk." Veldicca turned to the girl. "Leave the corn and fetch us some mead—and some of the dried apple?" She looked to Tilla for approval.

"That would be very good," agreed Tilla, realizing she had not eaten since last night.

"A friend's child," explained Veldicca, indicating the girl before she dipped her hands into the washing bowl by the door. "She is here to help and learn about the herbs. Where have you been? We mourned for you—it is a joy to see you!"

"I have been in many places. But last night I went to visit your brother."

The smile faded. "I have no—"

"Never mind about that. He has been arrested. The soldiers have taken him."

Veldicca shook her hands dry and wiped them on her skirt. Then she said, "I am sorry, but I am not surprised. From what I hear, it is better not to be Rianorix's sister at present."

They seated themselves side by side on the shaped log under the eaves. Tilla said, "The gods have woken, Veldicca. But doing their will has brought your brother serious trouble."

Veldicca adjusted the shawl so that the child lay in her lap for her visitor to admire. "A girl," she said, stroking the child's dark hair. "Four months. Much has happened while you have been gone."

"You must be proud," said Tilla, reaching to snatch away the abandoned bag of grain just as the first hen stabbed at it. "About your brother—"

"I should be proud," agreed Veldicca. "But mostly I am just busy and tired. You know I am widowed?"

"I am sorry. Your brother said nothing."

"That is no surprise. Even in death, Rianorix does not approve of my choice of husband."

"They say your brother killed a soldier," said Tilla. "But all he did was curse him. He does not know how the curse was fulfilled. It must be a sign."

"Well, if the curse did harm, then he has brought this on himself. You know what a fool he is."

"Veldicca—"

"It has never given me pleasure to be estranged. But he has always been stubborn."

"And you are . . . ?"

"As I said. Busy and tired. To speak openly, daughter of Lugh, we do not need my brother's trouble at our hearth. He is not wise in the company he keeps, and if you want to stay away from trouble, do not go with him to the Gathering that he thinks I do not know about. Have you heard about this creature who is hunting down soldiers?"

Tilla took the cup the girl was offering, and took a deep swallow of the rich sweet mead. "My own brothers would have been just as yours is. Act first, think later. Or not at all."

"I grieved for your family."

"I thank you."

A robin flitted down into the patch that Veldicca had been weeding and began to stab for worms.

"You never know how long the gods will allow you in this world," said Tilla. "At least try to send a message to him."

Veldicca bent and kissed the sleeping baby on the forehead. "I will think about it," she said.

It was a concession. Tilla acknowledged it with silence, stretching her legs out in the grass and watching a white butterfly dancing above the vegetable patch. Moments later the child noticed it too and ran over to chase it away.

Veldicca said, "So, tell me. We heard you were killed. Then we heard a rumor you were alive. Surely you have not been all this time with the northerners?"

"Two years in Trenus's household that are best forgotten," Tilla said. "Then I went south and lived much better in the lands of the Cornovii." That was true, if misleading. The Roman fort at Deva was on stolen Cornovii land. "They are a good people." That was more honest: She had made friends in the surrounding villages.

Veldicca laid a hand on hers. "It is good to have you home."

"There were times when I thought I would never see home again."

"Trenus should have been punished."

"Instead I hear he is invited to dine with the governor."

Veldicca said, "You remember Dari, the girl both your brothers lay with in one night?"

"Big breasts and small brain."

"She is working over in the town now. Selling drinks and pastries to soldiers and their families."

"At Susanna's?"

"You have met Susanna?"

"My friend is lodging there."

They exchanged news of other mutual friends and acquaintances: of births and deaths, weddings and betrayals and divorces. All the news Rianorix had not thought interesting enough to tell her. Finally Veldicca asked if she was married.

Tilla shook her head. "My life is complicated."

"Mine also," said Veldicca. "Now you are here, will you stay?"

Tilla paused to dip the apple in the mead and lick it. "That depends. I have not seen my cousin yet. Or my uncle. I hear they are living over by the fort."

"You will be surprised. Your uncle Catavignus is a rich man now. He is leader of the guild of caterers."

"The what?"

"They worship Apollo-Maponus, the god who pleases everybody. He has one Roman name and one of ours."

"I did not know my uncle was religious."

"Nor did anyone else," said Veldicca. "But I hear the caterers hold some very fine dinners and are loyal to the emperor. And of course they all help one another. They buy whatever beer Cativignus has left after he has supplied the soldiers. I hear he is having a grand house in the Roman style built up on the hill."

"I have seen the house on the hill. It is just a hole in the ground."

"Really? I had thought from what your cousin Aemilia said—"

"You know Aemilia." Tilla dipped the apple again. "I am surprised to hear she is not yet married."

"Hah! Did my brother not tell you what all this is about?"

"He said he is sworn to protect—surely not Aemilia?"

"Of course it's Aemilia! I told you, he is a fool. Now see where it has got him."

Tilla listened in silence as her friend explained how Aemilia had been convinced that a soldier had promised to marry her. "And this false soldier is the one who died?"

Veldicca nodded. "Felix, the man my brother cursed. So whoever killed him, Rianorix will be in trouble for it and Aemilia will be the cause."

Tilla shook her head. It was plain that Aemilia had not changed.

"I hear Catavignus still has hopes of marrying her to a centurion," said Veldicca.

"After this, about as likely as your family's hopes of marrying you to that blacksmith."

Veldicca sniffed. "I should have listened."

"Your soldier was not a good husband?"

"It turned out he had more patience with his bees than with his woman." Veldicca ran one mud-ingrained fingertip along the scar on her cheek. "This is what happened when I left his boots to dry by the fire and the leather went hard. I could show you others."

"I am sorry."

"But last winter he died of a fever. So now I do what I want."

Tilla glanced toward the beehives. "Now you are the beekeeper."

"I am the bee-loser. Whatever he was, that man knew how to charm the bees. After he died one swarm went and left no king, and another died of cold in the winter when I forgot to feed them. This is the last of the mead. I am glad to celebrate your homecoming with it."

Tilla glanced down at the sleeping child. "I have seen your brother's house, Veldicca. It is difficult for one man to manage alone. The house is very untidy and he lives on bought food and beer and lets other men's ideas grow around him with no one to show him any sense."

"My brother made his choice. I made mine."

"And are you content?"

"Which of us is ever content?"

Tilla watched the hens pecking at the grass. "I have a friend in the army," she said. "I will ask his help to release your brother."

"I will pray for your success. Then you can go and sort out his house and his ideas. See if he thanks you."

The baby stirred, opened a pair of deep brown eyes, and crinkled her small face as if she did not like what she had just seen. Veldicca unpinned her tunic and put the child to her breast just as it began to cry.

"So," said Tilla, looking around, "how will you live without the wages of your angry soldier? Two hens, a little honey, and a few herbs for sale are not going to keep you through the winter. You have no cow. You do not even have a goat."

"I have a little saved. Perhaps I shall buy a cockerel and become the champion hen breeder of Coria."

"But—"

"And if I grow tired of hens," Veldicca continued, "I will find myself a blacksmith. Or maybe a centurion."

34

THESSALUS WAS ASLEEP. Over at the infirmary, there was no one in the office. The cobweb above the pharmacy table was gone, the wastebasket was empty, and the green pancake had been scraped off the floorboards. A lone bottle with no label rested on the desk. Ruso picked it up, removed the stopper, and sniffed at the brown powder inside.

An orderly with strands of straw caught in his hair—presumably Gambax had assigned him to stuffing mattresses—wandered in and told him the deputy had gone to fetch some stationery supplies.

No doubt finding a clean stock of labeling materials would occupy him until lunchtime. It was a pity Albanus was not here to start investigating the rest of the paperwork. Ruso put the bottle back where he had found it. Gambax seemed to know what he was doing, even if he was doing it painfully slowly. Ruso had once had the misfortune to work with an apprentice pharmacist who had decided to tear off all the labels at once, throw them into the fire, and start again.

As he left the office the trumpet sounded the next watch. There was still no sign of Albanus. Ruso would have suspected most men of deliberately spinning out his missions to find out about Thessalus's night call and track down Tilla, but not Albanus. The clerk's deeply rooted sense of duty would compel him to get on with the job and report back, even if it did mean facing the rest of the day in the office with Gambax. No: It was far more likely that Tilla was proving elusive.

Just as he reached this conclusion, the clerk reappeared. He was not happy.

"Every door in the town, sir," said Albanus, slumping back against the table in the treatment room. "Every single door. And I explained that I'd been sent by an officer. In case they thought I was hunting down a runaway girlfriend."

"Very wise."

"I had to stop telling people you were a doctor," he said. "Some of them wanted to tell me what was wrong with them." He winced. "One even wanted me to *look* at it."

"I know," agreed Ruso. "That's why I don't tell them either."

"A couple of them said they wouldn't talk to me because a doctor had murdered that trumpeter they found in the alley."

"Really?" said Ruso. Evidently Thessalus's confession was no longer a secret. He wondered whether anybody had told Metellus.

"Then some ignorant clod in the vehicle repair shop said if I was snooping around his woman I would end up in the alley too. And some people wouldn't talk to me at all. I suppose they were hoping for a bribe."

"Probably," said Ruso, wondering how the news about Thessalus had leaked out.

"But I didn't have any money, sir," the clerk pointed out, clearly feeling his officer did not appreciate the difficulty of the fool's errand on which he had wasted most of the morning. "And I had no idea she might be using a native name."

"Albanus," said Ruso, who had forgotten to warn his clerk beforehand that Tilla's current name had only been adopted after he met her, "I'm sorry."

"That's all right, sir."

"Never mind. I think neither of us knows quite how things work around here."

"I think it helps if you're Batavian, sir."

This was not encouraging. "Apparently I have to go down to the bathhouse and face a clinic full of the Batavians' friends and relations. I can't think of a good excuse not to go."

Albanus seemed to be on the verge of coming up with one when Gambax put his head around the door frame of the treatment room to announce that he had put together a box of the sort of medicines and dressings Doctor Thessalus usually took with him. The regular assistant was on leave but he had assigned a bandager to clinic duty. Clearly, to back out now would be a sign of weakness. No Batavian was going to be allowed to accuse him of that.

Albanus, offered a choice of activities, decided that despite his complaints he would rather resume the search for Tilla than face the ailing families of the Batavians. "While you're out," suggested Ruso, handing him some small change, "just listen out for any gossip about the murder, will you?"

Albanus's eyes widened. "Are you doing another investigation, sir?"

"No," said Ruso. "I'm just trying to help Doctor Thessalus. Officer Metellus is . . . it's ah . . . it's just that there seem to be some rumors going around that may be . . ."

He stopped. If he told Albanus the rumors were false, the clerk would quite reasonably want to know what the truth was. And since almost everything about this wretched business was supposed to be a secret, Ruso would not be able to tell him. Finally he said, "What have you heard?"

Albanus was apologetic. He had not heard anything new, apart from the suggestion that a doctor had been the murderer, which was obviously ridiculous. "And I spoke to lots of gate guards but I still can't find anyone who remembers what time Doctor Thessalus came back in that night, sir. Or where he went. Several of them told me where I could go, though. I'm not doing very well, am I?"

"Never mind," said Ruso. "Have you mentioned any of this to anybody?"

Albanus observed glumly that he didn't know anybody to mention anything to.

"Good. Don't discuss the murder. Just let me know anything you happen to pick up."

35

THE DESIGNATED BANDAGER for this morning's clinic was the oversized Ingenuus, from whom Ruso rapidly discovered that the rumor about Thessalus's confession had reached the infirmary. Ruso's attempt to trace the source produced a list of names. To his relief none were infirmary staff. Maybe Thessalus had repeated his confession to his guard. Whatever the source, Metellus would have to deal with it. As they tramped out of the east gate in the direction of the bathhouse, the big man was eager to insist that nobody believed a word of it.

"Somebody should have arrested that local when he started playing up in the bar, sir. We're too soft with 'em, that's the trouble. You can't treat a barbarian like a civilized man. They can't understand it. You have to think of them like dogs. They need to know who's boss."

"So why do you think Doctor Thessalus might have confessed?" asked Ruso, "If he has."

"Ah, but has he, sir?" said Ingenuus, lowering his voice to a conspiratorial whisper. "That's what they want us to think."

Ruso returned the nod of the owner of We Sell Everything. "What who want you to think?" he said, wondering what the distant shouting was about. It seemed to be coming from the direction of the river.

"The officers, sir," said Ingenuus, shifting the weight of his box of medicines to get a better grip.

"I really don't think that's very likely."

"They put that story out before they found that native to arrest, just to stop us thinking it might be the Stag Man. But if it wasn't the Stag Man, why wouldn't they let us see the body?"

Fortunately he did not wait for an answer before continuing. "Doctor Thessalus is off sick and he's leaving anyway, so it won't matter what they accuse him of, will it?"

Evidently the military rumor mill had been turning at quite a rate this morning. "He's certainly ill," said Ruso, moving onto safer ground. "Have you noticed him behaving oddly lately?"

"He's been looking a bit tired, sir. And he's a bit forgetful. Sometimes he forgets he's on duty and we have to fetch him. But that's no reason to blame him for murdering Felix."

The commotion was growing louder. "I'm looking into the arrangements for night calls," said Ruso, who wasn't, but supposed that as part of his overhaul of the infirmary he should be. "You don't happen to know where Doctor Thessalus was called out to on the night of the murder, do you?"

Ingenuus looked uncomfortable. "I don't know where he went, sir. He was supposed to be on duty. But when I went to remind him, his door was locked and he didn't answer."

"So who was working at the infirmary that night? Gambax?"

"It was a quiet night, sir. Me and one of the orderlies managed on our own."

"I see." Ingenuus had understandably chosen not to call on Gambax if he didn't have to. "That was until Doctor Thessalus got back?"

Ingenuus coughed. "That was until Gambax came on duty in the morning, sir. I expect Doctor Thessalus went straight to bed."

"I see."

"We'd have called him if we needed him," insisted Ingenuus. "He's a good man. And a good doctor. He wouldn't hurt anybody. Speaking frankly, sir, not everybody in the Tenth thinks you can cure the sick with cold baths and—" He broke off. "What's that?"

This time they had both heard the blare of an alarm horn.

"Come on, sir!" urged Ingenuus, breaking into a run. "Someone's in trouble!"

Ruso sprinted after him, grasping the hilt of his knife. There was more shouting. He could hear the medicines rattling in the box as Ingenuus lumbered along ahead of him. The alarm sounded again. They turned onto another street. Other men were running in the same direction. One of them yelled something at him and he shouted, "What?" as they joined them, but nobody answered. Ingenuus was towering over the rest of the mob, still clutching the box, and dodging around an old man waving a stick. What brought Ruso to a lone halt moments later was the sudden realization that the old man had not been shouting encouragement to the pursuers, but the words, "They're in here! Come back!"

The mob disappeared around the corner with a trail of small boys and dogs in its wake.

"In there, officer!" cried the old man, jabbing his stick toward another of the narrow alleyways.

Inside the depths of the alley a knot of men was lurching about, cursing and grunting in some kind of struggle.

Ruso drew his knife. Around him, the street was deserted apart from the old man and a woman clutching a toddler in each hand.

"You get 'em, sir!" urged the man. "I'll call for help!"

Ruso glanced at the medical case in his left hand. "Look after that for me," he said, dropping it at the feet of the old man. Then he took a deep breath, yelled, "You four men, follow me. Audax, take the others around to the far end and cut them off!" and charged.

Faces turned toward him in alarm. The curses were louder as the knot rapidly disentangled itself and three or four plaid-trousered natives fled, escaping from the far end of the alley. Left behind, writhing on the ground, was a figure in Batavian uniform.

The man was wild-eyed, clutching at his chest, shaking his head and gasping for air as if he were drowning. Ruso looked for blood and failed to find any.

"Have you swallowed something?" asked Ruso, kneeling beside him and running through the possibilities. Choking. Poison. Stab wounds to the lungs. Heart failure. All sorts of things that could kill a man while a doctor was still trying to work out what he was dealing with.

The man shook his head in denial and pushed him away.

"I'm a doctor. Where are you hurt?"

The man jabbed a finger toward his abdomen.

"Stomach punch?" said Ruso, hopefully.

The man nodded.

"You're winded," said Ruso, relieved. "Curl up into a crouch. Don't worry, it'll settle down in a minute."

While the soldier was recovering his breath the shouting by the river reached a crescendo and then seemed to die down. Ruso glanced out of both ends of the alley into peaceful streets. There was no sign of the man's attackers, nor of any other assault upon the town. Ruso went back to the victim just to make sure there wasn't an injury he had missed.

The soldier was now beginning to take in some air but his face still suggested that he was not in a fit state to listen to the old man's account of how he had seen three of them natives grab him off the street and bundle him into an alley and how he'd have come after them himself if the officer hadn't turned up.

Neither man, fortunately, had yet noticed what Ruso had seen scratched in stark black charcoal on the grubby lime wash of the wall above the victim: a line sketch of a two-legged figure with antlers sprouting from his head.

Ruso, who had been silently critical of Audax for destroying evidence, leaned hard against the wall and slid his shoulders first from side to side, then up and down, rubbing off the loose surface of the charcoal. The old man looked up and asked if he was all right.

"Just an itch," explained Ruso, leaning back against the wall. "You did well, father."

"If I'd have been ten years younger, I'd have had 'em!" the man assured him, waving his stick in the direction of the natives' flight. "Barbarians. Savages. Oughtn't to allow 'em in the streets."

A thunder of hooves announced the approach of a cavalry patrol. Moments later a blur of color passed the end of the alley, heading toward the river.

Unable to spend the rest of the afternoon blocking the view of the wall, Ruso distracted the old man with a request for help in getting the soldier up, and together they shuffled back toward the street. The old man seemed delighted to hear that the authorities might want to ask him some questions. The soldier complained that he didn't want a fuss.

"You want to make all the fuss you can, boy," insisted the old man. "You might have ended up cracked over the head like that Felix." He turned to Ruso. "You tell them to come and ask questions any time. It'll make a change from listening to the wife."

"Nosy old bugger," muttered the soldier after he had gone. "What's it got to do with him?"

"Did you know who those men were?"

"Didn't see their faces."

Something about the manner of the reply suggested that he was lying. "But you knew what they wanted."

"I never said that!"

"I'm going to have to report it anyway," Ruso told him, "so you'd better think what you're going to say."

The man winced and clutched at his abdomen. Ruso told him to come over to the infirmary later for a checkup.

"It was only a bloody hen," the man muttered. "Everybody does it. How was I supposed to know it belonged to somebody?"

"Hens usually do belong to somebody," pointed out Ruso. "When did you last see a flock of wild hens?"

The man scowled. "Whose side are you on?" he said.

Ruso made his way back through the alley and finished rubbing off the worst of the charcoal figure before going in search of his assistant.

The stampede seemed to have come to a halt at the end of a muddy lane leading to the river meadows. He could see the top of Ingenuus's head above an excited mob who were all too busy shouting questions to listen to the answers. Other men were walking back up from the willows along the riverbank. In the far corner of the field, a couple of grooms were trying to round up some horses who were cavorting around in circles and far too excited to let anyone approach.

The dogs had wandered off. The small boys, having seen all there was to see, had fallen to wrestling with one another. Nobody appeared to be hurt.

As Ruso heard the next watch being sounded from inside the fort walls, it occurred to him that Metellus had been waiting to see Tilla for his identity parade since breakfast, and it was now midmorning. Well, he would have to wait. He stepped forward and extricated Ingenuus from the melee, relieved to see he was still clutching the medicine box.

"Broad daylight!" the bandager grumbled as they made their way back up the slope toward the bathhouse. "Broad daylight! They're getting more uppity by the day, sir. That's two good stallions gone, and if we get them back they'll probably be ruined."

"Who took them?"

Ingenuus stared at him. "Didn't you see, sir? The natives! Strolled into the field right under the groom's nose, shot a couple of slingshot stones at him, mounted up and jumped the hedge! Something's going to have to be done, sir. This can't go on."

"No," agreed Ruso, wondering if the daylight horse theft had been laid on as a distraction for the attack on the soldier. It seemed an elaborate and risky plan to punish the theft of one hen. But if "everyone" really did do it as the soldier had claimed, perhaps the natives had finally had enough of having their meager food supplies raided by foreigners bored with military rations.

36

"THIS IS WHERE it all started, sir," said Ingenuus, pausing beneath the sagging awning outside Susanna's snack bar. "The night before last. Felix was at this table here . . ." He led Ruso in and indicated a corner table. "We were over on the other side. If only the beer hadn't run out, we'd have been here to help."

The elderly woman now sitting at the table of the ill-fated Felix repaid Ruso's interest with a scowl.

He eyed the rest of the customers seated in the very plain surroundings of the snack bar. There was no sign of Tilla or Lydia. Nor were there any workmen snatching a quick bite to eat. Not a single loafer was idling away the morning with a jug of Susanna's unexpectedly good wine. Instead . . . he turned to Ingenuus. "Is there something I don't know?" he murmured, wondering if Ingenuus's insistence on a midmorning snack was about to violate some local custom.

"What sort of thing, sir?" asked Ingenuus, unhelpfully.

Ruso leaned close to the big man's ear and hissed, "They're all women."

The bandager, unembarrassed, surveyed the occupants of the tables across the top of his box. "Never mind sir, I expect they've left us some food." He headed for the counter. "Watch out, ladies!" He lifted the box to clear the head of the elderly woman, who clutched at the bundle on the table in front of her as if she feared he would steal it.

Ruso reluctantly followed his assistant along a path created by a hurried shifting of stools and skirts and shopping baskets and small children.

"This is Susanna," announced Ingenuus.

"Susanna who serves the best food in town," she corrected from behind the counter, as if this were part of her name. "Hello again, Doctor!" She nodded toward the tables. "You've got a good crowd to see you today."

"To see me?"

Before Ruso could digest this unwelcome news, Ingenuus put in, "Susanna can tell you all about it, sir. Felix was sitting there minding his own business and the native came in—"

"What can I get you, sirs?" interrupted Susanna.

"We've just come for a quick bite to eat," said Ruso, whose appetite seemed to have scuttled into a distant corner at the sight of all these female patients. "And I was hoping for a word with Tilla."

"So was I," said Susanna. "When you find her, tell her that her friend upstairs could do with some company." She gestured toward the trays of pastries and sausages laid out behind her, beyond the reach of prying fingers. "So. What can I get you? More of that Aminaean wine, doctor?"

"Just a splash," said Ruso, not wanting to be accused of practicing while drunk.

"I'm glad you enjoyed it, sir," said Susanna. "To tell you the truth, Doctor Thessalus wasn't very keen on us serving it."

"Really? Why's that?"

"I don't know. Gambax said not to put it out when he was here because he wouldn't approve."

Ruso hoped there was not some new and disappointing discovery about the dangers of Aminaean wine that had reached Coria before it reached the Twentieth Legion's medics. It seemed unlikely, but now he came to think of it, the wine had had an alarming effect on Claudia, who had never thrown anything heavier than a shoe at him before.

He ordered some nameless pastry thing by pointing at it. He felt he should do something about Lydia, but he did not know what. He wished he could find Tilla. Women were better at that sort of thing and besides, while he was housed in the infirmary, she would have little else to do.

Ingenuus was busy surveying the room. "Short staffed today?" he asked.

"Dari's gone to visit her mother," said Susanna. "She may be back, she may not."

"She'd better be back. She was the best girl you had."

"I'm sure you thought so," agreed Susanna. "But I hire girls to serve food, not flirt with the customers. This is a respectable family eating house."

"There's nothing wrong with a bit of innocent arm wrestling."

Ruso's efforts to picture an arm-wrestling waitress distracted him from the conversation, to which he returned as Ingenuus was indignantly assuring Susanna that, "I'm not telling everyone. I'm telling the doctor because he's interested. He asked to see Felix before he was cremated. Didn't you, sir?"

Ruso opened his mouth to explain about the postmortem, but Ingenuus had moved on.

"And you know what that ruckus was just now? A bunch of natives helping themselves to two of our horses! Broad daylight! I tell you, ever since that Stag Man started appearing, they think they own the place. Next they'll be—ow! Is there something the matter, sir?"

Ruso lifted his boot from Ingenuus's large toes. "We haven't got time to talk," he said, handing over the money for whatever it was Susanna had just placed in a wooden bowl and handed to him. "We need to eat and get across to the clinic."

"Well," put in Susanna, "if the Stag Man comes, we can count on you boys to defend us, can't we?"

"That's what we're here for," said Ruso, hoping he was right.

The mystery food item turned out to be some sort of cheesecake. In between licking his fingers, he explained quietly to Ingenuus that it was not a good idea to speculate in public about the murder and the Stag Man. "We don't want to make people worried."

"But I wouldn't be making them worried, sir," Ingenuus protested. "They're worried already."

37

THE EXERCISE HALL of the bathhouse was not an ideal place to hold a clinic. The women playing a surprisingly rough game of ball seemed to resent giving up one end of the room to benches full of ailing civilians. Even when the modesty of each had been protected by two sets of wooden screens—to the evident disappointment of those who thought the encounter of patient and healer should be a public spectacle—the high ceiling and concrete floor bounced back every noise, so that the whole hall was a constant boom of sound from which it would be difficult to pick out the words of a shy patient. Especially if that patient's Latin was not fluent.

"Ingenuus," said Ruso, praying Albanus would turn up at any moment with Tilla, "do you speak the local language?"

The man frowned. "A little, sir. 'How much is that'; 'Hey you get out of the way,' and so on."

"I don't think that's going to be of much use."

"I shouldn't worry, sir. Most of them can speak Latin if they want something."

The first people to sidle around the doctor's screen were the elderly woman, still clutching the bundle, and a small girl. Remembering Valens's first rule of dealing with women *(always get the name right)*, he greeted them politely. "Good afternoon. I'm Doctor Ruso. What are your names?"

The response from both was a blank stare. Ingenuus leaned across and murmured, "They're from the homeland, sir. Shall I translate?"

"Go ahead."

Ingenuus obliged. Instead of relaying the answer, he appeared to be arguing with it.

"What's she saying?" interrupted Ruso, frustrated.

Ingenuus coughed. "She's not been in this country long, sir. She's the widowed mother of one of the men. She's come with his niece. They've got nobody left at home so he's brought them over here."

"I didn't ask for a life history!"

"No, sir. I just happen to know. That's why she's not very well acquainted with the ways over here, sir."

"Surely she's acquainted with her own name?"

"Oh yes, sir. She just wants to know why she has to tell you."

It was not a good start.

One or two patients left when they discovered he was not Doctor Thessalus. One thought she had heard of Doctor Ruso: Her husband had even tried a bottle of his tonic. "But it didn't do any good, Doctor."

Another took the trouble to explain in halting Latin that she was very disappointed that he was not the other doctor, because the other doctor was a lovely kind young man and very handsome, and if he had murdered anybody it must have been their own fault.

When Ruso demanded, "Where did you hear this?" a flush spread up her neck and across her cheeks as she said, "At the market, sir. Everyone is saying it."

The news of Thessalus's confession could hardly have spread farther if Metellus had stood on the top of the ramparts and shouted it across the town.

One woman insisted that she knew what Doctor Thessalus would have said about her son's headaches, and that it was not what Ruso had just told her. There was a woman seeking infertility treatment and one who had very obviously been beaten up but insisted she had walked into a door, followed by an elderly man who explained in detail what the other doctor had told him to do last week, and then all the reasons why he had not done it.

There was a brief respite when one visitor had come to give rather than take: an attractive young woman with a scar beneath one eye who arrived with a baby on one arm and a basket of fresh herbs for the pharmacy on the other. Veldicca, a native apparently well known to the infirmary staff, seemed upset at the news about Doctor Thessalus. Ruso had to curtail Ingenuus's whispered explanation of the conspiracy theory currently circulating around the barracks. It would, he explained, get the bandager into trouble and besides, there were people waiting to be seen.

There were people with chronic pain, in need of a miracle and receiving only medicine and advice they had probably heard a hundred times before. There were hideous stinking ulcers to clean and dress and lectures to be given to their weary owners about hygiene and exercise and diet. There were people whose descriptions of their symptoms made no sense at all even though he understood all the words. Ingenuus was unable to explain what "He has feathers in his chest" meant, and "My knees are runny" was about as helpful as Thessalus's claim that his triangles were getting blunt.

None of the patients had called out Doctor Thessalus on the night of the thunderstorm.

A sickly three-year-old was followed by a perspiring man who shuffled behind the screens carrying a small pot with a lid in one hand and a stoppered jar in the other. He placed these offerings in the middle of the heavy table that Ruso had commandeered for his examinations, and said proudly, "There you are!" before standing back with his arms folded.

Ruso had thanked him, but explained that no payment was necessary.

"Oh, they're not gifts!" the man exclaimed. "You've got to look at them."

"I have?" said Ruso, eyeing the receptacles with a faint stirring of dread. "Perhaps if you could tell me what the problem is first?"

The man's only response was a nod toward the pots. "It's all in there," he said.

Ruso stretched out one arm and lifted the lid off the pot. It was, indeed, all in there, although how it had been got in there was a matter on which he did not care to speculate. He replaced the lid.

"Aren't you going to take a proper look?" demanded the man.

"That won't be necessary," said Ruso, twisting the stopper out of the jar and sniffing the liquid inside, which smelled just as he had expected.

"You're all the same, you people," grumbled the man. "I try to be helpful and nobody wants to bother. Well? What's the verdict?"

"If you just give me some idea of what the problem is before I . . ."

"Hah!" As if this proved some point he had been trying to make, the man snatched up his samples and marched out, declaring, "Call yourself a doctor!"

"He is very good doctor!" echoed a loyal voice from beyond the screen, apparently addressing the line. "Take no notice of that rude man!"

"Tilla!" Ruso stood on tiptoe and peered over the top of the screen. He could not remember a time when he had been more pleased to see her. "Tilla, come here, will you?"

By the time Ruso had finished washing his hands, Tilla had joined him. He sent Ingenuus around the screen to see how many more patients were waiting and apologized for the mix-up over the gate pass. "I sent Albanus out but he couldn't find you. Where have you been?"

"I see a friend, and just now I see Lydia whose man is dead."

"I came to tell you about him last night, but it was too late. How is she?"

"There is a storm inside her head," said Tilla. "But she is sleeping now." He reached for her sleeve. "Let me see that arm."

She straightened her elbow so he could slide the fabric up over the old scar. The bruising had spread. Most of the expanse between her shoulder and her elbow was purple now.

As he smoothed on the salve, he could not resist leaning forward and kissing her ear. "I missed you last night."

"I am staying with my uncle in the last house on the east road. Catavignus."

"Catavignus the brewer? Gray hair, mustache? Guild of caterers? He's your uncle?" So that explained why he thought he had seen the man before.

"Catavignus, the man who makes beer for the army," she said. "But he is still my father's brother."

"Will he let me visit?"

She shrugged. "Why not? You are an officer. He will probably ask if you want to marry my cousin. My lord, there is something I have to ask you. It is about a friend.'

Before she could explain, Ingenuus appeared and announced that only fifteen of the people still waiting were actually patients.

"Fifteen? Gods above! Tilla, I want you to stay here." Metellus would have to wait for his identity parade. He doubted Tilla could identify anyone anyway. "If we get any locals, you can translate."

"My lord, I have to ask you—"

"Yes, ask me. Later. Just stay here and help me for now. You'll put the women at their ease."

As the morning wore on, Ruso came to the conclusion that Thessalus must have been a remarkably public-spirited soul to run a free clinic. Treating the genuinely sick was fair enough, but at least half of the people here were time wasters who would not have come if it had cost them anything.

So his penultimate patient, a man with obvious injuries, came as something of a relief—until Ingenuus burst out, "What's he doing here?"

The thick tail of fair hair and the mustache said he was a local man. The bare feet and ragged tunic suggested he was poor. The splendid black eye, the split upper lip, the bruised cheekbone, and the hesitant gait—suggesting something about his person would only stay in the right place if he were careful not to dislodge it—said he had been in a fight. The man paused, looking from Tilla to Ruso as if he had been expecting somebody else.

Tilla seemed surprised to see him. She said something to him in her own language. He replied.

"I'm filling in for Doctor Thessalus," interrupted Ruso. "What can I do for you?"

"He is a man of my people," said Tilla quickly. "I will translate for you."

"Don't bother," put in Ingenuus. "He knows what I'm talking about. Don't you, sunshine?"

"I am here to see the medicus," insisted the man in a Latin accented like Tilla's. Ruso guessed the slight lisp was caused by the injury to his mouth. "I am a free man and there is no law against."

"You've had the only sort of treatment you're getting from us, pal."

"Thank you, Ingenuus," put in Ruso, overriding an objection from Tilla. "Go and tell the bath attendants we've nearly finished."

Ingenuus raised a hand in warning. "I'm not leaving you alone with him, sir. Not after what he did to Felix. I dunno what he's doing here, sir."

Ruso eyed the native, realizing he must be looking at the man Metellus had arrested only last night for murder. Surely Metellus could have found some excuse to hold him, even if the news of Thessalus's confession had leaked out? Under the circumstances, it was surprising that he had chosen to consult a military doctor.

The native, who was about his own height, appeared to be staring at him with a similar curiosity.

Steeling himself to treat the man as a patient like any other, Ruso ordered him to sit. He placed Tilla at a safe distance. There was no telling how a resentful local might react to a collaborator, no matter how friendly her offer to translate. Besides, he would rather the conversation were conducted in a tongue he could understand.

Ingenuus moved to stand beside the patient, one hand resting on the hilt of his unlatched dagger.

"When did all this happen?" Ruso asked, already knowing the answer.

"Some of it, two days ago. Much in the fort last night."

That lip should have been stitched at the time, but Ruso was not going to play about with it now. The man might well be coming to a nasty end anyway as soon as the murder inquiry was completed.

"Let's have a look," said Ruso. "Take off your shirt."

As the man did so there was a sharp intake of breath from Tilla. His well-muscled torso was purple and blue with bruising. His skin was spattered with blisters and burns, no doubt from some imaginative and painful method of questioning devised by Metellus. Ruso was crouched beside him trying to ascertain whether any ribs were broken when there was a sharp crack and the man's head jerked sideways. Tilla cried out in alarm.

"Sorry sir," said Ingenuus, who had just adopted the unusual approach of slapping a patient while the doctor was examining him. "Man was showing disrespect to your—" He paused, evidently not sure what the right word was. "To the translator, sir."

Ruso glanced at Tilla, whose face was impassive. "Go and wait out in the hall, Tilla."

"I am all right here."

He frowned. "You're distracting the patient. Go and wait outside."

She did not move. "The soldier should have respect, my lord. This is a man of my people."

"And not a good one." He stepped across to her and murmured, "He's a known troublemaker. You're better off not getting involved."

"He has done nothing wrong!"

"He speaks Latin, Tilla. We don't need you."

She glanced at the native and then walked out without looking at Ruso, her back very straight. Ruso turned to find Ingenuus resting the point of his dagger just beneath the man's ear and demanding, "Think you're funny, do you?"

"Put the knife away," snapped Ruso. Allowing a patient to have his face slapped during an examination might possibly be excused, but allowing him to have his throat cut was distinctly unprofessional.

"He winked at her, sir. I saw him do it."

Ruso took a long breath to steady himself. "Thank you, Ingenuus." He turned to the man. "You chose to come here for medical help," he said. "I will treat you, but only if you behave yourself. Agreed?"

"Are the bones broken?" demanded the man.

"There's no serious damage as far as I can tell."

"Then I go," he said, snatching up his shirt and turning his battered gaze on Ingenuus. "I will be standing up now, soldier. Don't be afraid."

"I won't," snarled Ingenuus. "But you'd better be."

When he stood, the man was a good handspan shorter than Ingenuus. Ruso followed him past the screens, keen to see him off the premises.

The native said something to Tilla as he left. She did not seem to notice. She was leaning against the wall with her arms folded, watching the middle of the hall. The women's bathing session had come to an end while Ruso had been behind the screens. The center of the hall was now occupied by two naked weightlifters with oiled muscles.

"Back to work, Tilla," he ordered her. "We haven't finished."

Two women were just vacating the empty benches where his patients had been waiting. The older of the two was clutching an overflowing basket. The other was looking at him through small unfriendly eyes.

"Sorry about that," he said. "I'll see you now."

The unfriendly one shook her head. "No need. I have waited so long, I have got better."

"You should talk to the doctor," urged her friend. "After all this waiting," but the woman seemed to have lost interest.

"Come back if it bothers you again," said Ruso, generous with his time now that none was being demanded of him.

"There you are, Tilla!" said a voice from the doorway. The silhouette of Albanus was standing on the threshold. "What are you doing here? This is the men's session!"

"My master is working," replied Tilla, not taking her gaze off the grunting weightlifters. "I am helping."

Albanus looked at Ruso for support. "But I've been looking for her for *hours*, sir!"

Tilla shrugged. "This is not my fault."

Ruso stepped between them and thanked Albanus for his fruitless efforts.

"I did hear something else about the murder, sir," murmured Albanus. "They arrested a man last night, but I think they've released him."

"Ah," said Ruso, not wanting to discourage his clerk by pointing out that he knew this already. "I see. Thank you. Incidentally, since you've now spoken to most of Coria, you haven't heard of any tonics being peddled locally, have you?"

"You mean cough medicines, that sort of thing, sir?"

"Not exactly," said Ruso. "I mean medicines with doctors' names attached. Specifically, my name."

Albanus's eyes widened. "You're selling a tonic, sir?"

"No. But somebody seems to think I am."

Albanus shook his head. "I haven't come across it, sir. Do you want me to buy you some?"

"Absolutely not. See if you can find out who's supplying it, then come and tell me."

He moved to stand between Tilla and the weightlifters, and was relieved when she did not step aside to retain her line of vision (what would he have done? Grabbed her? Sidestepped again so they moved across the hall in a kind of shuffling dance?). "Now, what was it you wanted to ask me?"

"It does not matter now."

He frowned. "You aren't sulking, are you, Tilla?"

"I told you. It does not matter now."

Three years with Claudia had taught Ruso that when a woman said something did not matter and refused to tell you what it was, it usually mattered a great deal—to her, if not to you. Frequently her way of punishing you for not knowing what it was in the first place was to refuse to tell you until you gave up asking. This was her cue to accuse you of not caring about her, otherwise you would have known what she wanted you to know without having to be told. Finally, if you were lucky, she would explain the latest way in which you had failed her expectations. If you were not lucky, she would explain *all* the ways. In detail.

It was disappointing to find Tilla heading down this path. The northern air was definitely making her more awkward.

"I need to talk to you about the man who came to the clinic," he said.

"Rianorix is a man of my people," she repeated.

He drew her into a corner away from eavesdroppers and explained about the murder. The noise in the hall was such that he had to place his lips very close to her ear to make sure she heard. This made it difficult to concentrate on what he was supposed to be saying, so the explanation was twice as long as it needed to be.

When it was over she said simply, "I know this, my lord. But he did not do it."

"We don't know that."

"You do not," she agreed. "So I am telling you."

"In that case, who did?" asked Ruso, wondering whether Tilla had picked up any local gossip that had eluded the army.

"It was the gods, my lord."

"I see." Of course it was. "You don't happen to know if the gods had any help from anyone?"

A crease appeared in the middle of her forehead. "I hear they send a medicus."

"I think that's very unlikely," he informed her.

"This is what I think," she agreed. "Medici do not listen to the gods."

Albanus was still waiting by the door. "You'll have to come with me to the fort," Ruso told her. "There's an officer who wants to talk to you."

She seemed anxious, as well she might after being questioned by Postumus. She asked, as he knew she would, what the officer wanted. He said he could not tell her. She asked why not. He said he was not allowed to, adding that it was nothing bad, and she would understand when she got there. "The officer needs your help," he said. "Just do your best."

The eyes looked into his own. "You do not trust me?"

He said, "That's not the point, Tilla. I was asked to say nothing. Would you rather I lied and said I didn't know?"

She did not speak to him all the way back to the fort and in through the gate. She still refused to speak to him when he delivered her to Metellus's office.

He drew the aide aside and murmured, "Half the town knows about Thessalus. It didn't come from me."

"I know," came the reply. "It's a damned nuisance. The governor's given strict orders not to give the locals any excuse to start trouble, so we've had to release the native suspect until we can get this wretched confession sorted out. We'll be keeping an eye on him, of course. But we don't want them claiming we're holding a man who can't possibly be guilty."

"Any sign of the—?"

"No."

Ruso said, "I need to talk to you later to try and pin down some facts about Thessalus. But if you have any problems with Tilla, come straight to me. She's my property and not to be touched. Agreed?"

"Don't worry, Ruso."

"And you should know that she's saying she knows the native and he's innocent."

Metellus smiled. "They always are," he said.

38

TWO WARDS WERE now pristine, sweet smelling, and empty. The orderlies were disappointed to discover that all their fine work was to be spoiled by the installation of patients before the governor had a chance to admire it. The pharmacy table was also a model of good order. Instead of a mess, it held a tray. On the tray was a bowl of some sort of broth, bread, a wine cup, and a small jug.

"Doctor Thessalus's lunch, sir," announced Gambax.

Ruso dipped a finger in the lukewarm broth. "Tastes all right," he observed, "but it's not very hot."

"It's been here some time, sir."

Ruso took a sip from the water jug and examined the bread before suggesting, "Next time, perhaps you could wait for me before you have it served up."

Gambax said "Yes, sir" with such studied neutrality that Ruso wanted to stomp on his toe. Instead he took a sip from the cup, and the sour taste of watered army wine took him back for a moment to the legion and his relatively innocent days at Deva. "That's fine," he said, replacing the cup. "Let's round up somebody to sit with him and head over there."

Thessalus was perched on the edge of the couch. Judging from the way he fixed his gaze on the tray, he was hungry. As he reached up to take it, Ruso noticed his hands were unsteady.

"My meals delivered by three men," Thessalus observed, looking up at them. "And a guard outside the door. I was never worth so much attention before."

"Gambax has come with your meal as you asked," explained Ruso. "I've tasted your food and I promise you there's absolutely nothing in it that shouldn't be. This man will keep you company for a while and I'll come and see you later."

"Why? Are you afraid I shall be lonely?"

"No," said Ruso, noting Thessalus's eagerness as he reached for the wine cup. 'I want to talk to you without the medicine clouding your brain."

Ruso leaned his elbows on the freshly scrubbed wood of the operating table, lifted a bronze clamp from his case, and slid the clip idly up and down, feeling the faint jolt as it bumped in and out of the grooves on the handles. Metellus was supposed to be delivering Tilla to the infirmary after he had finished with her. How long could an identity parade take?

He needed to talk to Metellus anyway. Now that the word was out about Thessalus's confession and the native had been arrested and questioned—if only briefly—he was not sure what version of the truth he was supposed to know. And what version of the truth everyone else was supposed to know, and whether they were different. He snapped the jaws of the clamp together and scowled.

If only he had kept his mouth shut, he would never have gotten involved in this.

Ruso placed the tip of his little finger in between the jaws of the clamp and winced as he slid the clip into the groove. The trouble was, despite his fortuitous discovery of the truth about the murdered bar girls in Deva—something for which he had received no credit at all—he really was not very good at this sort of thing. Moreover, he didn't like it. He certainly didn't like Metellus. What the hell was that man doing with Tilla? How long could it possibly take her to look at a few suspects, announce that she didn't recognize any of them—as she undoubtedly would—and then be escorted across to the infirmary? And why had he clipped this painful thing onto the end of his finger?

Someone was knocking on the door. He slid off the clamp, put it back in his case, and said, "Yes?" hoping to see Tilla. He would explain why he had not been allowed to warn her about the identity parade. He would make it up to her by buying her a meal at Susanna's. He would sit with her in public. What did it matter? They were only here for a few days.

The disappointment that was Gambax stepped in and consulted the writing tablet he was carrying as if it lent authority to what he had come to say. "Twenty-two-and-a-half denarii, sir."

"Ah," said Ruso, not sure what Gambax was talking about but hoping not to have to admit it.

"Doctor Thessalus usually lets me have the money right away, sir," said Gambax, still not explaining what the money was for.

"Twenty-two-and-a-half?" repeated Ruso, hoping to elicit more information.

"Yes, sir. That includes my costs for processing the herbs delivered by the woman Veldicca."

Evidently it was something to do with the clinic. "Perhaps you could give me a breakdown of the figures?"

Gambax looked as though he had just asked for something outrageously complicated. "Doctor Thessalus never asks for a breakdown, sir."

"I'm new here," said Ruso, conceding defeat. "And frankly, I haven't a clue why you're asking me for money."

"The cost of the clinic medicines, sir."

Ruso looked at Gambax's face and tried to detect some sign of humor or deceit, but failed. The man who gave up his time to run a free clinic and took his staff out on their birthdays had evidently reached heights of generosity that Ruso could barely imagine. "Does Doctor Thessalus pay for all the medicines himself?"

"Oh no, sir." The corners of Gambax's mouth began to twitch. "You did remember to charge everybody, didn't you?"

A glum realization began to dawn. No wonder he had been so popular. While he had been behind the screens, word had spread around the market that the new doctor was handing out army medical supplies for free.

"Twenty-two-and-a-half sounds about right," he agreed, unstringing his purse and spilling its contents onto the operating table. He had paid Lydia's rent. Now he had inadvertently made a donation to the ailing civilians of Coria.

It was another dilemma for those bright young minds.

A man gives money to a deserving cause by mistake. Is he in any way morally superior to a man who gives nothing?

"Thank you, sir," said Gambax, scooping the money off the desk with one sweep of his hand and sending it clattering into a wooden box. "I'll write you a receipt from the pharmacy."

After he had gone, it occurred to Ruso that a more suspicious man might accuse Gambax of deliberately leaving him in the dark and sending a bandager who did not know the routine.

He got up. He was going to find out what Metellus was still doing with Tilla.

39

TILLA STARED AT the row of faces in front of her: seven local men, some of whom she recognized. None of whom deserved to be stood squinting into the afternoon sun in the courtyard of an army headquarters building. One had blood dripping from his nose. Another had a swollen eye. There would be other injuries, deliberately inflicted where they would not show.

The medicus had delivered her to the same quietly spoken officer who had arrested Rianorix last night. At first she had not recognized him. The hair that had glinted blond in the torchlight was dull brown by day. As soon as she realized who it was she had wanted to beg the medicus to stay with her, but she was afraid the quiet one would tell him where he had found her last night. The medicus, who liked to think he was a reasonable man, would not be reasonable about that. So she had said nothing when he repeated, "Just do your best," and abandoned her.

The quiet one had led her into the courtyard and told her to say which of these men she had seen in the yard at the inn.

"I saw a god," she said. "These are men. I do not know any of them."

"Look again."

She looked again, noting a bent nose that was nothing to do with the army: It had been broken years ago in a fight with her oldest brother.

The men were staring straight ahead, showing no sign of remembering her although several must have been surprised to see her there. She said truthfully, "None of them was in the yard."

"Take a good look."

"I have taken a good look," she said, loud enough for them to hear. "I do not know them. You have arrested the wrong men and hurt them for no reason."

Instead of being angry, the officer smiled. "Come with me," he said.

She followed him out of the courtyard, past the guards, and straight down a wide paved street. Before they reached the gatehouse the officer turned off to the right and led her to what looked like some sort of deserted workshop or storehouse. The windows were secured with bars against thieves. He unlocked the main door and led her into a small room. The sole item of furniture was a solid wooden chair bracketed to the center of the floor. On the wall beside her hung four sets of chains, a knotted rope, and a long-handled iron tool that reminded her of blacksmith's pliers. Already she wanted to scream.

"Now then," he said pleasantly, closing the heavy door behind her and locking it. "You've put on your little show for your friends. They can't hear you in here. So tell me which one it is."

"I am already tell you," insisted Tilla, aware that she was losing her grip on Latin and angry with herself for betraying her fear, "I do not know those men!"

The officer shook his head sadly. "I do wish I could believe you, Tilla. I really do."

"I cannot tell what I do not know. Let me talk to the medicus. He will tell you."

"Oh, dear. I do so hate to get cross with attractive young ladies."

"I do not know those men. Please. Let me—"

"Not one of them? You've never seen any of them before in your life?"

Outside she could hear men shouting orders. The sharp screech of boot studs swiveling on paving stones. Someone laughing. She forced herself not to look at the dark stains on the floor around the chair. Rianorix had spent the night in this room. She had seen what this man had done to him. "I have seen some of them before," she whispered. "They live near here. None of them is the man in the yard."

The officer's smile looked almost relieved. "Thank you, Tilla," he said. "Or shall I call you Darlughdacha? That wasn't so very difficult, was it? Now tell me about your friend Rianorix."

40

'I WAS JUST coming to look for you,' Ruso said. 'Where have you been?"

Tilla was frighteningly pale.

"Are you all right?"

She did not answer.

Metellus smiled as he stood aside to let her enter the infirmary and assured Ruso that she had been very helpful. "Property returned in good condition as promised, doctor. I've told the watch captain you'll be escorting her out later."

He beckoned Ruso outside and murmured, "Any sign of Thessalus withdrawing his confession?"

"Not yet."

"I told the girl I'd give you a few moments alone together. I'd be interested to know what she says to you. Just watch what you tell her. I know she's very lovely, but she is a native."

"I'm not a fool, Metellus."

The aide smiled again. "I do hope not."

One of the orderlies was rattling a broom around the corners of the treatment room. Ruso took Tilla by the hand and led her into his temporary quarters. When she was clear of the door, he squeezed in himself and sat beside her on the narrow bed, observing, "You're pale."

No reply.

Perhaps she needed to be distracted. He tried, "I expect it's a lot more comfortable than this at your uncle's."

She said, "Yes," but hardly bothered to look around.

He put an arm around her shoulders. She gasped with pain.

"Sorry," he said, retracting the arm. "I forgot. Tell me what happened with Metellus."

"I would rather have the ugly centurion with his stick than that one," she said. "That one has things in his room that I do not want to think about."

"He promised me he wouldn't hurt you!"

"I am not hurt."

"So what happened?"

"Nothing. I am all right."

"It is not nothing," he insisted. "And you are not all right." He got to his feet and turned around in the small space between the bed and the door. "I should never have left you alone with him. Tell me what happened and I'll go and see him right now."

"He did not touch me."

"He frightened you."

She bowed her head. He saw the dark splashes of the tears in her lap. If Metellus had been within reach at the moment, Ruso would have punched his even features out of alignment.

More tears. He could not send her back to her uncle in this state. "I'll go and see him. I won't leave you alone with him again."

She gave a loud sniff, and whispered, "I am no good."

"They're desperate to catch the man you saw in the yard," he explained. "Lydia's man isn't the first one he's killed. But if you can't help, it isn't your fault."

She rubbed her fists into her eyes. "Last night a rude man will not let me in here. Now you take me in to look at some men of my people, and the officer with the smile of a snake wants me to get them into trouble."

"You can only do your best, Tilla. There's nothing to worry about. The accident wasn't your fault."

She slapped her hands down on her knees in exasperation. "Is not me I am worrying about! Is Rianorix!"

"Rianorix? The man at the clinic? He's not seriously hurt, you know."

"They are still asking questions about him," she said.

"Well, just tell them what you know."

"I know he does not kill that man. But they do not want to say the gods did it because that will show our gods are more powerful than theirs. And they will not blame the doctor because he is a Roman."

Ruso sighed. This was exactly the native reaction that Decianus had anticipated.

"The doctor has a lot of problems," he explained, "but really I don't think killing Felix is one of them."

"Well, it is not Rianorix. You must tell the officer he is wrong."

"Tilla, when your gods do things, do they send people to act for them?"

She thought about that for a moment. "It is likely," she said. "A stag is a messenger."

"So the stag would give someone a message from the gods to do something?"

She nodded. "We must find out who the gods send to kill Felix. You must talk to the men who are with him in the bar. Perhaps it is them. Perhaps it is somebody who wants to kill Felix and blame Rian for it. Perhaps it is anybody. I will talk to Susanna at the bar and we must find Dari and ask if she knows where he goes afterward."

"Dari?" Dari the arm-wrestling waitress? "What's she got to do with it?"

"Susanna says she is the last person talking to Felix before he goes. We must find out. Like you find out what happened to the girls in Deva."

"I can't just go trampling all over Metellus's investigation, Tilla."

"Why not? He is wrong."

"You're absolutely convinced Rianorix is innocent?"

"I know."

For a moment Ruso wondered if he should ask her what a native warrior would do with an enemy head. Where would he hide it? Who would he show it to? Tilla, whose kitchen duties were often accompanied by interminable songs about her ancestors, must know the stories. She could save the army hours of fruitless hunting and possibly a great deal of trouble with their own men. The killer's trophy, the head of a Batavian soldier, might even now be at the center of some ghastly magic ritual that Rome had failed to stamp out with the extermination of the Druids. According to Albanus, which force had led Rome's final assault on the Druid stronghold?

The Batavians.

Ruso did not know what Batavians believed about death but he was certain that none of them would believe Felix was resting peacefully while his head was still in the hands of the enemy. Worse, it would no doubt reappear in a show carefully orchestrated to cause the maximum alarm among the Roman forces. One question to Tilla might save them from all of that.

On the other hand, Metellus could have asked her that himself, and it seemed he had not. Maybe his investigation did need a little trampling upon.

"I'll talk to Metellus," he promised, reaching forward to slip a finger under a curl that was touching the corner of her eye.

"You must tell him Rian is innocent."

"Yes. Now, since we've got a few minutes' privacy . . ."

She grabbed his hand. "Not now. They will make me go before long and I have to explain to you why Rian is angry with this Felix."

He stretched out along the bed and drew her toward him. "Tell me lying down."

"You will not listen."

"I promise."

She rolled over to lie on top of him with her elbows dug into his ribs. "Even when we are small," she said, "my cousin Aemilia wants to marry an officer."

Ruso closed his eyes and slid his hands down to cup the curve of her bottom. He had a feeling this was going to be a long story.

41

YOU'RE SURE YOU haven't let him out of your sight?"
The orderly hesitated. "I just went next door to use the pot, sir. But I was only gone a moment."

"How long ago was that?"

"About an hour ago, sir."

Ruso shook Thessalus again. He lifted one eyelid with his thumb, but in the poor light it was difficult to make out where the black of the pupil ended and the deep brown of the iris began. Standing over his patient, he watched the rise and fall of the blanket with each labored breath.

"Did he leave the room?"

"He sat reading after lunch, sir. Didn't hardly move off the couch."

So wherever it was, it must have been within easy reach.

Searching the room would be difficult, not only because it was cluttered and badly lit but because what he was looking for was small and probably as dark as the eyes of the man it had temporarily doped.

"Did you bring anything extra in here with you?" he demanded, ripping the cloth down from the window and letting in such light as the thick and dirty glass could offer.

"No, sir."

Ruso shook the scrolls over the lunch tray he had inspected himself and crouched to run his fingers over the underside of the chair. "Did anybody deliver anything?"

"No, sir."

"Keep trying to wake him." Ruso bent to peer under the couch. He needed to confirm that Thessalus had taken poppy tears before beginning the messy business of forcing down whichever of the antidotes came first to hand: *wine, olive oil . . .*

The medicine must have got in here somehow. And if there were any left, it would still be in here.

Vinegar, mustard . . . (mustard?! Was that right?) rose oil . . . Would Gambax have rose oil somewhere? Olive oil would do. There must be plenty of olive oil in the kitchen. *Then induce vomiting.*

He examined the tray. He tasted the water again. It was still water. "Thessalus, wake up!"

The wine had been drunk, but the gritty dregs were no more bitter than when he had tasted it earlier. Army-issue wine might not have inspired his patient, but it would not have prostrated him either.

He eyed the body on the couch. It had the definite appearance of being drugged, and its hands and feet were cold.

He turned to the orderly, who was chewing his lower lip. "Why didn't you call me?"

"I thought he'd gone to sleep, sir," protested the man. "I thought a doze would do him good."

"He's certainly gone to sleep," agreed Ruso. "We'd better hope he wakes up again." He scowled at Thessalus. All that talking, and they were no further forward. It was as if the man wanted to destroy himself.

He crouched, put his lips close to the pale ear, and said loudly, "Thessalus?"

No response.

"Thessalus, someone needs the doctor!"

The muscles around the man's eyes twitched.

"Wake up. We need a doctor!"

Thessalus muttered something and tried to turn over, then halted halfway and winced. "Whaa?"

"Wake up!" called Ruso.

"Uh," said Thessalus, raising a hand to rub his eyes. "Am I asleep?"

Relieved, Ruso helped him to a sitting position. "Drink of water?"

Thessalus blinked and nodded.

Ruso had the cup in one hand and was about to fill it from the jug when he paused. He carried it across to the window, upended it, and peered into the hollow of the base. There, stuck into the recess, was a little wad of brown resin. Dried poppy tears.

42

I T WASN'T ME, sir. Absolutely not."

Ruso relaxed into his chair and reflected that this was the first time he had ever seen Gambax standing at attention. The man looked uncomfortable, as if he were not used to it.

"I was ordered not to give him anything, sir, and I didn't," continued Gambax.

When Ruso said nothing he added, "It was an *order*, sir. I never do anything I'm ordered not to do."

"Hm," said Ruso, suspecting that unless he were ordered to do it Gambax rarely did anything useful at all.

"I can show you where I wrote it down, sir," added Gambax.

Ruso noted with some satisfaction that he was now beginning to sound genuinely worried. "You're writing all my orders down?"

"Just the ones that contradict Doctor Thessalus's orders, sir. So I can remember who said what when. In case there's any query about it when he's recovered." Gambax risked a glance at him. "You said you wanted better record keeping."

"So," said Ruso, making a mental note to find more useful work for Gambax to do, "if it wasn't you, who was it?"

Gambax swallowed. "I don't know."

"You don't know."

"No, sir."

"You haven't by any chance decided to obey my order yourself while passing Doctor Thessalus's order on to somebody else?"

The surprise in Gambax's "No, sir" suggested that had he thought of that first, he might have tried it.

"Well, here's my next order," said Ruso. "Don't stop to write it down, just do it. I want you to find every man who was on duty just before lunch and send them all in here one by one until I tell you to stop."

The first candidate was Albanus, who denied all knowledge of tampering with Doctor Thessalus's lunch. "I know," explained Ruso, "but I have to treat everyone the same."

Albanus did, however, have other information. First, Doctor Thessalus had not returned to the fort until just before dawn on the morning after the murder, and second, the gate guards had just taken a message from a man who had not left his name but who wished to speak with Doctor Ruso. He would be waiting at the bathhouse to meet him as soon as Ruso was free.

"Then he'll have a long wait," observed Ruso.

Next in was the cook, who denied interfering with Doctor Thessalus's meals and demanded to know why whoever was complaining didn't have the nerve to come and say it to his face.

"Nobody's complaining," explained Ruso.

"Well, they hadn't better. I can only work with what I'm given, can't I?"

"I'm sure everyone appreciates that. I haven't heard any complaints about the food." Although he had heard several personal remarks about the competence and parentage of the cook, who was now looking as though he was not sure whether to believe him.

Moments later he heard the cook summoning the next man into the room with the words, "Your turn. Waste of time. If that stew's stuck on the bottom, it's not my fault."

The next man to waste his own time and Ruso's was the orderly who had now removed the straw from his hair. He was less irascible than the cook but equally clueless. In the brief interval that followed, Ruso wondered whether he should have lined them all up first and made a speech designed to inspire terror and confession. But despite having spent years watching centurions in action, he was not sure that he knew either how to inspire or how to terrorize. He would just end up looking ridiculous.

A rap on the door interrupted his musings. Ingenuus bent under the door frame, closed the door behind him as instructed, and responded to, "Good morning, Ingenuus. Stand easy," with, "It was me, sir."

Ruso blinked. "What was you?"

"Put the poppy tears under Doctor Thessalus's cup, sir."

"I see. Did you know I had issued an order that he wasn't to be given any?"

"You didn't order me not to, sir, you ordered Gambax. And Doctor Thessalus asked me to do it when I went to collect his breakfast tray."

Ruso rested his elbow on the arm of his chair, lowered his forehead into the palm of his hand, and closed his eyes. When he opened them the bandager was still standing there, supposedly at ease, but looking distinctly apprehensive.

"Ingenuus," he said with all the patience he could muster, "why do you think I gave that order?"

"Because you don't understand the situation, sir."

This was proving to be a most surprising conversation. "Enlighten me."

"I'm sorry, sir, I can't." At least the big man had the grace to blush.

"Are you telling me," said Ruso, "that there is a situation of which I'm not aware but everyone else—you, Gambax, Doctor Thessalus, for all I know everyone else in the Tenth Batavians—is?"

"I couldn't say, sir."

"And what if I were to order you to say?"

Ingenuus swallowed. "Then you'd have to charge me with insubordination, sir."

"I see." Ruso scratched the back of his ear with one finger. "This is all rather difficult, isn't it?"

Ingenuus's blush deepened. "Sorry, sir. But Doctor Thessalus asked me—"

"Of course he asked you! He'd ask anybody who walked through the door! That's his problem!"

"Yes, sir."

"From now on, you are not to give him anything he asks for without consulting me first. Understand?"

"But sir—"

"Do you understand?"

"Yes, sir," mumbled Ingenuus, his head bowed in misery.

Ruso leaned back in his chair, clasped his hands behind his head, and stared at the wall. He had never trusted Gambax. Now he could no longer trust Ingenuus. He was unlikely to get any sense out of Thessalus for a while and Metellus the aide was a self-confessed professional liar. Things had come to a fine pass when the only people he could rely upon were a clerk and a girl who was no friend of the army, and who believed she had meetings with gods in stable yards.

43

TILLA WAS BEGINNING to know what to expect. There were the shriekers, the starers, and the believers like Rianorix who whispered, "Have you come to haunt me, daughter of Lugh?" Ness was a starer. Then she launched herself across the doorstep and held Tilla close, crying, "You are home, you are home! I knew you were alive! Oh mistress, the goddess has brought you home at last!"

"Ness!" gasped Tilla, hugging the bony creature who had been their family cook for years and had only been saved from the raid by being at a relative's house nursing a broken ankle. "I thought I would never see you again!"

"I am not that old, mistress," pointed out Ness, recovering from her uncharacteristic outburst of affection. "Although your uncle and cousin are doing their best to work me to death."

"Are they here? I need to talk to my uncle. Rianorix was arrested."

"We know. Your uncle is out on business. Your cousin is in her room. I will tell her you are here."

Ordinary people grew thinner as the winter progressed, but the rich carried their weight through to the next harvest. So it was no surprise to see Aemilia plump and well fed. What was unusual was to see her pretty cousin confined to her bed with the sun still so far above the horizon, her wide blue eyes rimmed with red, and her fine clothes looking as though they had been slept in for several days.

"Cousin! Are you ill?"

"Daughter of Lugh!" Aemilia threw back the blanket, lurched to her feet, and flung her arms around Tilla. "Is it really you? Have the gods sent you to comfort me?"

Tilla's return of the embrace was wary. The cousin she remembered as fastidious smelled stale. Her hair was clumped and greasy. When her grip showed no sign of slackening, Tilla patted her on the shoulder and stepped back. "Veldicca tells me you have troubles."

"Everything has gone wrong!" Aemilia flung herself back onto the bed. "Where have you *been*? I have missed you terribly!"

Tilla opened her mouth to answer, but Aemilia carried on. "Everything has gone wrong, cousin, and I am all alone with nobody to help. Nobody understands!"

Tilla sat on the bed and eyed her cousin in the uneven light that entered the little room through the thick green window glass. "I am sorry to hear it."

"Such horrible things have been happening. You cannot imagine. Felix is—oh, I cannot say it—and Ness says Doctor Thessalus has gone mad and Rianorix is arrested and the builders have gone away and I am not with child after all and Daddy says I was a disgrace at the funeral but I couldn't help it, I really couldn't!"

"Rianorix has been released," said Tilla, grasping for an end in this tangled account.

"Oh, thank the gods!" Aemilia ran her fingers through her hair, leaving pale tracks running back across her scalp. "Oh cousin, it was not my fault! I never meant anything to happen to him, truly! But nobody will believe me!"

"You didn't mean anything to happen to Rianorix?"

"No, no—you don't understand!"

"You asked Rianorix to curse one of the soldiers, but you didn't expect anything to happen to either of them?" asked Tilla.

"No! When I thought I was with child I asked him to help me, but I didn't mean he should . . . oh, why is he so *stupid*? This is all his fault, and everything is ruined!"

Tilla had been right. Aemilia had not changed. She was not even interested in where her cousin had been for the last three years.

"I must look terrible," blurted Aemilia suddenly, groping beneath her pillow and producing a mirror. She peered into the polished bronze surface, gave it a vigorous rub against her sleeve, and peered again, tweaking her hair and muttering, "Oh, dear. Oh, dear . . ." She scrambled down to the end of the bed and began rummaging among a jumble of pots and vials and earrings and hairpins strewn across a small table. "If only your mam were here now! She would understand. She would know what to do."

Tilla closed her eyes and thought of the time Aemilia had refused to get off the swing, shouting, "Push me! Push me harder!" and then run crying to Mam, blaming everyone else, when she fell off. The time Aemilia had watched from a safe distance while the daughter of Lugh groveled about collecting eggs from the hens' cobwebby hiding places, then offered to help carry them and run to the house shouting, "Look at all the eggs I found!" The time when, finally exasperated, the eight-year-old daughter of Lugh had grabbed the cousin with the silly Roman name by the hair and shoved her into the nettle patch. The daughter of Lugh had been given a beating and the cousin with the silly Roman name had been given sympathy, a drink of warm honeyed milk, and crushed nettle stems to treat her stings. Whatever Aemilia did, Mam excused her on the grounds that she was a poor motherless child. Now Mam was not here to excuse her, yet still Tilla felt guilty for being angry with her. She said, "Rianorix is released, but they are still asking questions about him."

Aemilia turned, makeup brush in her right hand, mirror in her left, revealing one painted eye and one naked one. "Did he tell them anything about me? They won't come here, will they?"

"I don't know."

"It wasn't my fault!"

Tilla felt the muscles in her jaw tighten and took a deep breath. Getting angry with her cousin, she reminded herself, was like getting angry with a sheep for being stupid. It ruined your day and the sheep was too dim to care. "What Mam would say," she announced, "is that you should get up and wash and change your clothes and have something to eat and you will feel much better."

Aemilia sniffed. "Do you think so?"

"Yes."

"But how will that change anything?"

"Give me your clothes. I will hand them out to Ness. Does this window open? It stinks in here."

Aemilia sniffed again and looked as though she was about to cry. "Don't be angry with me, cousin. Please. I couldn't bear it if you were angry with me."

"You should be angry with yourself for what has happened to Rianorix. Do you know what the soldiers do to people when they question them?"

"You aren't angry? Are you sure?"

Tilla, unlatching the window, ignored her.

"You are so kind, cousin. Just like your mam. She was always kind to me when nobody else was. Oh, I do miss your mam!"

"So do I. Now give me your dirty clothes. And stop crying. The makeup will run and then you will have to clean it all off and start again."

Aemilia wriggled out of her tunic and began to release her heavy bosom from the creased and sweat-stained breastband. "Daddy and Ness are both angry with me," she said.

Tilla took the pile of crumpled clothing and opened the door. "I will fetch some water."

"Will it be warm?"

"I will see what I can do."

"Tell Ness not to give my silk tunic to the washerwoman. I don't want it lost!"

"Warm water, and the silk tunic is not to be sent to the washerwoman," repeated Tilla, wondering how she had become a servant again so quickly.

"Oh, cousin," cried Aemilia. "I am so happy to see you again!"

44

THESSALUS WAS LYING on the couch with his head propped on a cushion. His eyes opened as Ruso entered, but the rest of him did not move.

"Doctor." The voice was weak. Ruso noticed the dark hollows around his eyes.

"How are you feeling??"

Thessalus appeared to find this a difficult question. In the end he said, "Not good, I think. How are you?"

"Very well, thank you," said Ruso, and moved swiftly into, "I thought I'd drop in while I was passing," before any fresh confusion arose over which of them was the doctor and which the patient.

"I have news for you," he said. "Rianorix has been released. You have absolutely nothing to feel guilty about."

"I am a murderer!"

"You are troubled and confused. The medicine you have been taking to ease your mind has not helped."

Thessalus sighed. "My head is aching," he said. "Do you happen to have any—"

"Poppy tears?" suggested Ruso. "No." He peered at the man, who really did not look well. He reached for his case. "I've some juice of dried roses boiled in wine."

Moments later he handed Thessalus a cup.

"What is the thing that everybody knows except me, Thessalus?"

"I am too tired for philosophical questions."

"I need to know about the emergency call that came in on the night Felix was killed."

Thessalus did not seem to be listening.

"You came back from Susanna's," Ruso reminded him, "then you were supposed to be on duty at the infirmary but you were called to an emergency and went out again until dawn. Where did you go?"

Thessalus steadied the cup with the other hand and took a gulp of the medicine. "I'm sorry," he said. "I can't remember anything at all. It must be in one of the spaces."

Ruso said, "Spaces?"

Ruso looked at the boldly patterned plaid cloth that Thessalus had fetched from a box in the corner and was now holding out, draped across both arms. He scratched one ear. "I'm afraid I don't quite . . ."

"The spaces in my memory," said Thessalus, as if this would make perfect sense if Ruso could only make more effort to listen. "Look again." His forearms, which he had held pressed together, moved apart. The cloth that had hung in a loop between them stretched out to form a soft horizontal surface "Now. Watch." He drew his arms together again until they were touching from elbows to wrists, and adjusted their position so that the repeating pattern reformed perfectly across the two separate sections of cloth supported by his arms, leaving out the fold that hung between them. "You see? It looks the same, but what is missing?"

"The cloth in between?" suggested Ruso.

"Exactly!" said Thessalus. "And now?" He shifted one arm half an inch forward. The horizontal lines of the plaid shifted out of alignment. The join became obvious. What was not obvious—to Ruso, at least— was what this was supposed to illustrate about Thessalus's memory.

"This is how I find out," said Thessalus sadly, looking down at the fractured pattern. "The spaces are invisible. When the lines join up, how can you tell?" He glanced at Ruso. "When you sleep, how do you know how long you have slept?"

"By whether it's daylight?" suggested Ruso. "By the sound of the next watch?" He wanted to add, "By whether Tilla is up and lighting the fire," but Thessalus was already sufficiently confused.

"By whether the pattern lines up," said Thessalus. "Before, it is night . . ." he lifted his left arm, "and after, it is day." The right arm rose. "So," he said, moving his arms so the loop of cloth billowed between them, "you know there is something in between."

Ruso, who was beginning to grasp what he meant, said, "There are times when you can't remember what you've been doing? When you're awake?"

"What happens in between . . ." Thessalus stretched the cloth out again, "I have to guess."

"How long has this been happening?"

Thessalus shrugged. "When the patterns line up, who can tell?"

"Everyone has patches where they lose concentration," suggested Ruso. "Lots of people find if they're traveling and thinking about something else they sometimes forget whole miles. They know they've arrived but they can't really remember much about the journey." At least, he hoped there were lots of people. Maybe he was the only one.

"Not just minutes," said Thessalus. "Sometimes hours. A whole day once. Gone. Stolen. Is someone stealing my hours?"

"I think they're being drowned in poppy tears. And if you're only guessing at what fills the spaces, you may be guessing wrongly."

"I have dreams."

"Dreams seem very real at the time. But when you wake, you know they aren't."

"And the healing that comes in dreams?"

Ruso hesitated. He had never been sure about the trustworthiness of divine healing through messages in dreams, but he knew several people who claimed to owe their lives to it, and indeed he was hard-pressed to explain their cures in any other way. On the other hand, he could recall several cases where the gods had been given the credit but the doctor had done most of the work. "Healing is one thing," he said. "Nightmares are different." And this relative sanity was, he feared, a mere break in Thessalus's mental clouds that might soon close. "Tell me," he urged, seizing the moment, "what you remember about that night."

Thessalus looked sadly down at the cloth, then folded it neatly and set it beside him on the couch. "We came out of the bathhouse and went to Susanna's," he said. "It was Gambax's birthday. There was an argument.

Something about cows. A soldier was lying to a native. I remember thinking somebody should defend the native." Thessalus paused. "Then I woke up here, after a ghastly dream, with blood on my hands and my clothes." He looked apologetically at Ruso. "I looked at myself and I was not injured. I told myself I must have drunk more than I thought. That I had been to the infirmary on the way home and the blood was from a patient. Or that I had been to a temple that night and made a sacrifice."

"Tell me about the dream."

Thessalus bowed his head into his hands, raking back the hair with his fingers into a wild splay of dark curls. "I am holding a knife," he said slowly. "Felix is afraid. He is pleading. Begging me not to do what I am going to do with the knife. I tell him to be silent but he won't. He keeps saying he has no cows. I tell him he must pay, because I don't want to do it. And he won't be quiet. He tries to shout. I silence him with the knife."

"This is all a dream, Thessalus. Everything in it comes from somewhere else."

"The worst is yet to come," muttered Thessalus. "I said nothing. I washed my hands and clothes and ate breakfast and went to the infirmary hoping to find a patient whom I had treated the night before. When I got there I heard Felix was dead. I was already leaving the army for fear of what I might do in one of the gaps. Now I saw that it was too late. I should have gone before. I knew the native would be blamed and I knew I had to do something."

"This blood," said Ruso. "Did anyone else see it?"

"I saw it. I was awake."

"We both know what a strain it is to perform surgery," said Ruso. "I can see why you're convinced you've done something wicked but I think you're confused. A lot of terrible memories have combined in your mind and given you a frightening dream that just happens to have some coincidental links to reality."

A weak smile crept across Thessalus's face. "You would have me consult an interpreter of dreams," he said. "A clever theory. Spoken like a Greek."

"Thank you," said Ruso, privately thinking it was a lot more plausible than Plato's nonsense about triangles. "I'm going to do my best to find out where you really did go that night, Thessalus. Then we can straighten all this out."

Thessalus brightened. "That will be good. Then perhaps you can tell me what I did with the head."

45

R USO HAD INTENDED to consult Metellus before making any further inquiries into the murder, but finding himself alone with Gambax he decided to carry on his fictitious inquiries into night duties. After surprising his deputy by congratulating him on the cleanup, he said, "You said when you came back from Susanna's the other night, Thessalus was on duty but he was called out. I suppose in that situation you would cover for him?"

"Nobody asked me, sir."

"I'm not complaining. In fact, I heard you were called out yourself."

Gambax looked puzzled. "No."

"I must have been misinformed. I was told you went out again just before curfew."

"Oh, that. Like I told Officer Metellus, I went out to find Felix. I was worried about him."

This was a surprise. "I'm sorry. I didn't know he was a friend of yours."

"He wasn't. I was supposed to be meeting him over at his quarters, but he wasn't there. After that business at Susanna's, I thought I ought to go out and see if he wanted company on the way back."

"That was remarkably decent of you." Perhaps he had underestimated Gambax. Or perhaps on that night Gambax had reached that stage of drunkenness where all the world was his friend and he couldn't understand why people had to keep fighting when they should all be looking out for their mates. "You went on your own?"

"I didn't want to make a fuss, sir."

"And I assume you didn't find him?"

"I went over to Susanna's and across to the brothel and down to the inn. You can ask Metellus; he's confirmed it all. I wish I'd looked harder now, but his roommates said he often stayed out all night and not to worry."

"I see. Just out of interest, what were you supposed to be meeting him about?"

"Aminaean wine, sir. I heard that Felix had a supplier and I wanted to get ahold of some."

"For yourself?"

"For the infirmary, sir. I'm a beer man myself."

"Very good," said Ruso. "So did you ever find out where he was getting it from?"

Gambax had not. Felix had a vast range of business contacts. Yes, since the doctor mentioned it, most of the people in the bar probably had known him, but he had no idea why anyone other than the native would have wanted him dead.

"One last thing," said Ruso. 'I hear you told Susanna that Doctor Thessalus wouldn't approve of Aminaean wine?"

Gambax frowned. "Did I? I don't think so, sir. She must have misunderstood."

46

OFFICER METELLUS WAS in a meeting and could not be disturbed, neither to be asked if a visiting medic could interfere further with his murder inquiry nor to listen to complaints about the way he frightened his witnesses.

Meanwhile, Ruso and Albanus were slumped in a back alcove of Susanna's empty snack bar, separated by a table that held two large jugs and two cups. Ruso had offered to treat his clerk to a nonmilitary supper after evening ward rounds as compensation for his wasted morning hunting for Tilla.

Albanus clearly felt this was an important occasion. He had scrubbed most of the ink off his fingers and he smelled of hair oil. "Permission to ask a question, sir?"

"Albanus, this is supper. You're allowed to make conversation."

"Yes, sir. What I'd like to know is, now they've let the native go, who really did kill the trumpeter?"

Ruso scratched one ear. "I wish I knew."

"Was it Doctor Thessalus?"

"I hope not."

Albanus glanced around the empty bar. "Is it true it all started in here with an argument about cows, sir?"

"Ah," said Ruso. "I do know the answer to that one." He took a sip of wine before commencing. "Ever since she was a little girl, Tilla's cousin Aemilia has wanted to marry an officer."

Not surprisingly, Albanus looked bemused.

"Bear with me. This is one of those native stories that will end up as one of the interminable ancestor songs Tilla sings in the kitchen. Apparently her family friend Rianorix, who is a mere native basket maker, proposed to this Aemilia, and she turned him down. And—according to Tilla's sources—to sweeten the refusal, she told him she would always look on him as a kind brother. And because—again, according to Tilla—he is a softhearted fool, he swore he would always protect her as if she were his own sister. Are you seeing the connection now?"

"But Felix wasn't an officer, sir."

"Very good, Albanus. Aemilia set her sights on Felix, who by all accounts was very attractive to women and gave her the impression he was getting promoted any day now." Ruso paused, making sure he had the chain of events straight in his mind. "So, when Aemilia thought she was pregnant, she announced the joyful news to him, expecting him to push for his promotion and set the wedding date."

"Oh dear."

"Exactly. Felix disappeared like a rat down a sewer and Aemilia turned to her sworn brother to defend her honor."

"What about her father?"

"He didn't approve of Felix as a suitor. He'd forbidden her to go near him. Aemilia was frightened to admit she was pregnant."

"So Rianorix went and found Felix and murdered him?"

"Ah," said Ruso. "That's where Tilla's interpretation of events diverges from everyone else's. According to Tilla, he went privately to see Felix and explained that 'round here, a chap has to either do the decent thing or hand over five cows in compensation. After a couple of weeks with no cows and no wedding plans, Rianorix got tired of asking nicely. He began to call on the native gods to avenge Aemilia's disgrace. He came here to make a final appeal to Felix's honor in front of all his friends—which is what a native would do, apparently—and got thrown out. And then the gods brought judgment on Felix."

"Are you sure this Rianorix didn't simply bump him off to get the girl?"

"I'm not sure of anything," said Ruso. "Although as Tilla has pointed out, if he was going to do it, why would he have announced it first? And afterward, why did he wait around to be arrested?"

"He doesn't sound awfully bright, sir. Maybe he thought he was like the Stag Man. Invincible."

Ruso frowned. "The Stag Man isn't invincible, Albanus. You're starting to sound like Tilla. He's just a clever man with a fast horse and a bit of dead animal tied to his head."

"Yes, sir." Albanus reached for his drink. "Do you mind if I speak freely, sir?"

"Go ahead," said Ruso, wondering how many other men would ask permission before allowing wine to loosen their tongues.

"I don't blame that Aemilia girl for wanting to better herself. This isn't much of a place, is it?"

"I've been in worse," said Ruso, feeling it was his duty to try and cheer up his clerk, who had only volunteered to come with him out of personal loyalty.

"Yes, sir." Albanus picked up a crumb from the table and rolled it between finger and thumb before flicking it away.

"I can't actually remember when," confessed Ruso, reaching for his drink. "But you have to admit this is rather fine wine."

"The wine's all right," conceded Albanus, "and the scenery's quite pleasant. If you're partial to the sight of greenery. And if you don't know all the bushes could be hiding natives with grudges and antlers. But the town isn't up to much, is it? Have you seen that shop that says it sells everything?"

"Next to the butcher's."

"Yes. Well, don't build your hopes up." Albanus sighed. "Frankly, sir, I wish I'd brought a few more books with me."

"I can lend you some medical texts if you're desperate," said Ruso, wondering how desperate a man would have to be before he would read medical books to cheer himself up. Although he supposed some doctors' diatribes on why all their rivals were incompetent nincompoops might be mildly entertaining.

"Never mind, sir. I've only got another eighteen years, six months, and two days to serve."

"That must be very comforting," said Ruso, who was on a short-term contract with the army and could extricate himself whenever he wanted with little difficulty.

"How long have you got left, sir?"

Ruso coughed. "I haven't counted recently. Tell me something, Albanus. If you can translate Plato and read medical texts, what are you doing in the army anyway?"

"My father made me promise not to go into teaching, sir. He said the boys are badly behaved, the parents have no respect for you, and the pay isn't very good."

"So he suggested you sign up for twenty-five years in the legions?"

"Looking back, sir, I don't think my father knew very much about the modern army. I think he got all his ideas out of poetry books."

Ruso noted with surprise that he had nearly finished his wine. "Fathers don't always make wise decisions," he said.

"No, sir," agreed Albanus.

"Mine certainly didn't."

There was a clatter of crockery from behind the counter. Albanus looked up, then lost interest when Susanna-who-serves-the-best-food-in-town emerged with a cloth and began to wipe the tables.

It occurred to Ruso that too long in the provinces could turn a man into the sort of bore who hung around in bars telling his life story to soldiers who were too junior to escape. Thank goodness he was here with a mission. Not an official mission, since he had yet to talk to Metellus, but one he should be getting on with nevertheless.

He waited until Susanna was attacking the table next to theirs, and explained to her that he was trying to help Doctor Thessalus and would she mind answering a few questions? But before that, would she mind bringing over more of that wine?

Albanus was busy diving for the satchel that he had brought with him lest the Batavian clerks should raid it in his absence and steal his best pens.

Susanna said, "Officer Metellus already wrote everything down, sir. And that was the last of the wine."

Ruso gestured to Albanus to put the stylus away, and as he did so something occurred to him. "Can I see the amphora?"

"It's empty, sir, I promise you."

"I know. I'd just like to . . ." He tried to think of a suitable excuse. "I used to have a friend who exported it," he said. "If it was his I'll write and tell him where I drank it. He'll like that."

Susanna, fortunately, seemed to operate by the policy that the customer was always right no matter how blatantly he was lying. Behind the counter, Ruso heaved up the heavy clay container by its handles and scanned the surface for the vintner's mark. There, painted in long thin letters, was the expected AMIN . . . The writing faded into a clean patch where something else had been scrubbed off. He shook his head and expressed regret that this wine had not come from his fictitious friend. What he did not tell Susanna was that although he had no idea where it had come from, he had a very good idea of where it should have gone, and it was not into the mouths of paying customers at a snack bar. No, Susanna did not know where Felix had gotten it. She seemed surprised that anyone might have considered asking him.

"I know you've been through everything with Metellus," Ruso said, making his way back to where Albanus was waiting, "but it would help me to know exactly who was in the bar the night Felix died."

Susanna perched her ample bottom on the next table and sighed. "This is never going to end, is it?" she said. "Years of building up a respectable family business and now we'll always be the place where the trouble started." She spread her arms wide to indicate the bar. "Look at it. Where is everybody?"

"It's probably not you," suggested Albanus brightly. 'Everyone's frightened to be out in the evenings because of the Stag Man."

"If you could just tell me about that night—" put in Ruso.

"He's not real, you know," continued Albanus. "He's just a man with a dead thing on his head. And there are extra patrols out."

"Fat lot of good they're doing," retorted Susanna.

"That night?" prompted Ruso, realizing Albanus's sudden chattiness was inspired not only by the wine but by the appearance of the other waitress, the little mousy one he thought of—if he noticed her at all—as being "not Dari."

Susanna flapped one hand to send the girl away and described what had started out as a normal evening: the bar crowded, the staff harassed, and the customers no ruder than usual—until by some unlucky oversight the beer ran out. At this point several of the infirmary staff who had joined Gambax to celebrate his birthday expressed their disgust and went elsewhere.

"But Thessalus didn't go with them?"

"I should think he was glad to see the back of them," said Susanna. "He'd been paying for everything. So then it was just him and Gambax left there." She pointed to a table halfway across the room. "And some wagon drivers from Vindolanda next to them, and a merchant and a girl he was pretending was his wife in the corner, and Felix and his friends over by the door."

"If I needed to know, do you have names?"

"We get to know our customers, doctor. And we look after them. Not like some places I could mention, where they'd steal the fleas off your dog."

"Any reason why any of them might have had a grudge against Felix?"

She shrugged. "If they did, they kept it quiet."

"So then what happened?"

There was little new in what she told him. Thessalus had been trying to persuade an unusually cheerful Gambax that it was time to go home when there was a commotion over by the door, and Rianorix was yelling abuse as he was being shoved out into the street by Felix's cronies. Moments later he returned. Felix's friends seemed to find this very funny, and promptly threw him out again.

"What was he shouting?"

Susanna frowned. "Something about 'you will see what happens to men who don't honor their debts.' The rest of it was in British."

That would have been the curse, presumably. "And everyone in the bar heard this going on?"

"I was out the back sorting out a new beer barrel, and *I* heard it."

"The native didn't say what he would do to Felix?"

Susanna shook her head. "I'd have remembered."

"And then what?"

She shrugged. "And then nothing. Felix and his friends settled down, the merchant complained about the disturbance, the wagon drivers started shouting for beer, and Thessalus must have persuaded Gambax it was time to go. Thessalus is a good man, sir. I think it says a lot for a man when he's kind to his staff like that. Taking someone out on his birthday and seeing him home. Even when you could see he wasn't enjoying it much."

Ruso tried to imagine himself paying for a fun evening with Gambax, and failed.

"Was Thessalus acting strangely?" he asked. "Drinking too much?"

Susanna shook her head. "He was a bit quiet. That's all. I didn't see him again until he came in the next day. He was in a terrible state by then. His hands were shaky and his hair was all over the place. He came up to the counter and told me he'd killed somebody. He asked whether I thought he should confess to the prefect. I told him to go back to the barracks and lie down."

"Did you mention this to anyone else?"

"No!"

"Nobody at all?"

She fiddled with her shawl. "Well . . . when they arrested Rianorix later on, I thought they would know the doctor hadn't done it. I may have mentioned it to one or two people after that."

So that was how the story had escaped. Ruso decided not to tell Metellus that it was Susanna who had wrecked his plans for an easy conviction.

"But I told them not to tell anybody."

"Of course."

"He didn't say it was a secret," she added.

"If it was a secret," said Ruso, feeling sorry for her, "he wouldn't have told you, would he?"

She looked relieved.

He said, "I heard Felix was talking to Dari late that evening."

"Dari? She didn't have anything to do with what happened."

"Did you mention her to Metellus?"

"I didn't want to waste his time."

"Humor me for a moment," said Ruso. "Waste mine."

Susanna paused to pull the shawl forward over her hair and repin it. She said, "I think Dari owed him money. She gave him something, and I saw him get his note tablet out. Then I got rid of him. I didn't know Rianorix was lying in wait for him, did I?"

"Of course not."

"In the end I told him to go or he'd miss curfew." She cleared her throat. "To tell you the truth, doctor, I was annoyed. I've had to speak to Dari before about standing around chatting when she's supposed to be working."

"So Felix was a nuisance?"

Susanna folded her arms. "I didn't say that," she said. "I don't imagine he was much of a soldier, but he was good company. He had a way of talking to you as if you were the most important person he'd ever met." She wrinkled her nose. "'Course, I didn't fall for it at my age."

"Of course not," agreed Ruso, then wondered if he had said the wrong thing.

"Anyway," Susanna continued in a tone that suggested he was right, "we never had any bother with him. And frankly, I'd rather have him than some of the so-called heroes we get in here trying to bully my girls." She got to her feet. Now, gentlemen, can I get you something to eat? There's plenty left."

After Susanna had gone in search of food, Ruso swilled the last drop of Aminaean at the bottom of his cup and said, "Why do you think Susanna thought Gambax was telling her to hide this?"

Albanus looked blank. Ruso explained about Susanna's belief that Gambax had told her not to serve the wine in the presence of Doctor Thessalus.

With an uncharacteristic lack of charity Albanus said, "I expect Gambax was lying because he wanted it for himself."

Ruso grinned. "Travel has certainly changed you, Albanus."

"Well, sir, as Socrates would have said—"

"Ruso! There you are! I've been waiting in that miserable bathhouse for *hours!*"

Ruso never found out what Socrates would have said. Standing in Susanna's doorway was a man who should have been somewhere else entirely.

47

"VALENS!" SAID RUSO. "What the hell are you doing here?"
"I'm taking some leave. Move over." Ruso's former housemate
edged around the table and collapsed next to him on the bench.

"You're taking leave from the hospital? While I'm away?"

A weary grin spread across Valens's handsome and unshaven face.
"You're not completely indispensable, Ruso. They've brought a replace-
ment in on a temporary contract. And I have to say, he's no fun at all. So
I started to wonder how you were getting along up here in the wilds."

Ruso did not believe a word of this, but did not want to say so in front
of Albanus. "He turned to his clerk. "Perhaps you could go to the
kitchen and see if they can find Officer Valens some—"

"Anything," said Valens. "Anything at all. I'm starving."

The moment they were alone, Ruso said, "Right. Now tell me."

"It's not my fault," insisted Valens. "Really it isn't. None of this would
have happened if you and Tilla hadn't pushed off and left me on my
own in the house."

"None of what?"

"You remember the Second Spear?"

"Not with pleasure."

"Well, you know he had a daughter?"

"Gods above! Tell me you haven't?"

"Do listen, Ruso. It wasn't my fault. She found out you'd gone and I was at home alone and bored, and she started popping 'round to see me."

"With no encouragement from you, of course."

"Ruso, she's a rather attractive young lady—"

"Who stands to inherit all of the Second Spear's money."

Valens looked pained. "Money does not come into this. Anyway, you're quite right, it wasn't a good idea. So I told her it had to stop before her father found out. And that's when the trouble started. Are you going to finish that bread or can I have it?"

"What trouble?"

Valens sighed, and Ruso saw signs of the strain he must have been under for the last few days. "It's all a bit of a mess," he conceded. "I wasn't intending it to go quite like this."

"You were allowing a single girl to pop 'round and visit. Completely unchaperoned, I suppose. How did you think it would go?"

"I didn't sleep with her, Ruso. I swear."

"You might as well have."

"That's what she said."

"What else did she say?"

"I don't want to remember. You know what her father's like?"

The memory of one particular clash with the Second Spear made Ruso shudder.

"Well, she's inherited it. She's terrifying, Ruso. She's like . . ." Valens searched for a simile. "She's like a one-woman cavalry charge. I had to take to sleeping in the hospital to avoid her. That was when she went and told her father."

"Oh," said Ruso, needing no further explanation. "So what are you going to do?"

Valens shook his head. "I really don't know. I am genuinely on leave, by the way. It cost me a fortune to wangle it, which is why I can't afford a shave, and I'm going to have to ask you to pay for my supper, but I wouldn't have lived to spend the money anyway."

"And you really haven't touched her?"

"Of course I've *touched* her. I just haven't done anything irrevocable."

"You could try going back and telling him that."

The dark eyes widened. "Ruso, he's bigger than me. And so are all the men with swords who'll do whatever he tells them. I've been on the road for days. Sleeping in wagons in case he had people searching the inns."

"So now what are you going to do?"

"I was hoping I could stay up here with you for a while. Just until he calms down. I could help out with . . . well, with something or other. Anything, really." Valens brightened. "I could do your night duties!"

Ruso tried to remember any previous occasion upon which Valens had offered to do someone else's night duties. This simple offer was more alarming than all the fear and exhaustion betrayed by his friend's face.

He lowered his head into his hands. "Well," he said, "thanks for involving me in all this."

"I'm sorry. But you're my best friend. How much longer is your clerk going to be with that food?"

"I think he's taken a fancy to the waitress," said Ruso. "He's scrubbed the ink off his fingers and he's wearing hair oil. It's a dangerous time, spring."

Ruso circumvented the difficulty of explaining Valens's arrival at the fort by not bothering to try. He announced that an officer had arrived from the Twentieth and a gate pass was issued without question.

There was only a night porter on duty at the infirmary. "It's evening," explained Ruso to his bemused colleague, who was staring around the office in dismay.

"Gods above, Ruso, is this really how they do things up here?"

"No," said Ruso. "This is how it looks now that I've gotten them to sort it out." He was about to offer to take Valens around and introduce him to the patients when he heard the soft closing of the outside door. Metellus glided into the office and asked to have a word with him in private.

48

TILLA FELT HERSELF go rigid in the darkness. Something had woken her. Something bad. There it was again. That scrabbling sound. *Mice?*

No . . . mice did not sniff and sigh and mutter and bounce around enough to make the bed shake. Not mice. Aemilia was hanging over the side of the bed, groping for something under the mattress.

"What are you doing, cousin?"

Another sniff. "I can't tell you."

"Well, can it not wait until morning?"

There was a choking sound, then a sob. "It can wait forever!" wailed Aemilia. "It is no good now! What am I going to do?"

Tilla fought down an urge to shove her cousin out of bed. "Go to sleep," she suggested. "Or lie still so that I can. And be glad that Rianorix is no longer in chains because of you."

"You don't understand."

"You don't explain."

Another sniff, then a movement that led Tilla to suspect her cousin was wiping her nose on the sheet. "I suppose it doesn't matter now," said Aemilia. "Put your hand out."

After a moment of confusion in the dark Tilla felt something small and hard being pressed into her palm.

"Don't drop it," urged Aemilia. "It's very precious."

Tilla's fingers explored what seemed to be a metal ring with a complicated pattern that made the surface deeply uneven.

"Gold," Aemilia whispered. "With my name on it." Another sniff, another wipe.

"Who gave you this?"

"Felix."

Tilla yawned. "He gave you a gold ring?"

"It was our secret."

Tilla slid it onto her third finger. She had never worn a gold ring before. She did not expect to wear one again. It was a pity there was no light by which to admire it.

"Do you think I will see him in the next world, cousin? He said he didn't believe in that sort of thing, but you don't have to believe in something for it to be true, do you?"

"I suppose not," said Tilla, who privately thought that if the next world was reserved for people with honor, any soldiers who managed to make it there would be very lonely. "Is the ring the reason Rianorix was jealous of him?" Rianorix could make baskets all day and all night and still have no hope of affording a gold ring.

"No, no, cousin! The ring made everything all right. And then that horrible doctor went mad and . . . and . . ."

Tilla reached for Aemilia's hand and placed the ring on her finger. "I am sorry for you, cousin," she said. "Truly."

"I am going to wear it," announced Aemilia. "I know what everyone thinks. But he gave me a ring with my name on it. I will show them!"

"Tomorrow," agreed Tilla, snuggling back under the blanket. "Now we must go back to sleep."

"I will show them all." Aemilia flung herself back down on the mattress and sniffed.

"Good night, cousin. Sleep well with your beautiful ring."

"Good night, cousin."

"Cousin?"

"Yes, cousin?"

"One last thing. Do not wipe your nose on the sheet when I am in the bed."

49

R USO STOOD IN Metellus's very ordinary office in the headquarters building. Clearly this was not the room to which Tilla had
been taken for questioning. There was nothing frightening about three
folding stools, a table, a cupboard, and the rather fine bronze lampstand
that was enabling him to see them all.

"Wine?" offered Metellus, gesturing toward a flagon and a set of three
matching glasses. "It's rather good. I have an arrangement with the people down at the inn."

Ruso declined.

"Excuse me if I do," said Metellus, pouring himself a glass. "Aminaean," he said, holding the glass up to the light. "I wish I could say we
were celebrating the return of a missing object, but our searches continue." The flames of the lamps stretched and swayed in the glass as he
lifted it to his lips.

Tilla was right. Something about Metellus really did remind Ruso of
a snake. "When I spoke to you earlier—"

Metellus smiled. "You didn't mention that you'd chased off a gang of
natives single-handed this morning. Well done. It's a pity we can't make
more of a fuss over you, but we don't want to spread yet another tale to
frighten the good folk of Coria."

"That wasn't what I wanted to talk about," said Ruso, who had been so concerned about Tilla earlier that the natives in the back alley had completely slipped his mind. Evidently the victim had decided to report the incident himself.

"This Stag Man business has the locals very overexcited," explained Metellus. "They're starting to compete at army baiting, and of course every exploit adds to his reputation. This seems to have been a bunch of amateurs—which doesn't diminish your achievement, of course. You wouldn't have known that when you took them on."

"I want to talk about Tilla."

"And all over the theft of a hen, apparently. Any excuse."

Ruso felt he could not let that one pass. He said, "The natives thought they had a grievance."

Metellus shook his head. "There's a system for making complaints, Ruso. We have no thefts of hens reported. I checked."

"About Tilla—"

"How are you getting on with Thessalus?"

"I'm trying to find out what he actually did do that night, but that's proving a problem. Apparently he was out till dawn on a call, but my man can't track down where."

"Really? I wouldn't worry about it. Just confirm that he's insane."

"I'll keep looking," said Ruso. This was not the time to argue about who controlled the contents of military medical records. "About Tilla. I brought her to you as a witness for a simple identification, Metellus. We had an agreement that if you had any difficulty with her, you would get ahold of me. I want to know why that didn't happen."

"She refused to identify anyone."

"Then she was telling the truth. I was out in the yard that night as well. It was pitch dark and pelting with rain. I wouldn't have recognized my own brother."

Metellus gestured toward the flagon. "Are you quite sure you don't want a drink?"

"I don't want a drink; I want an apology. It's no wonder you have trouble with the natives if this is how they're treated when they're offering to help."

Metellus gave a sigh that sounded almost like regret, sat down and motioned Ruso to one of the other folding stools. He waited until they were both seated before saying, "What has she said to you about Rianorix?"

"I told you. She knows him. She says he's innocent."

"I see."

"You weren't able to crack him with your questioning, were you?"

"Not this time."

"Then maybe she's right. You should be looking for somebody else."

"Yes, Doctor," said Metellus, in a tone that reminded Ruso of a medic thanking a patient for some wildly inaccurate attempt at self-diagnosis. "I have thought of that. Which is why my men and I have already spoken to everyone who heard the argument in the bar that night, including the merchant couple and the men from Vindolanda, and confirmed their whereabouts later on."

"How about Gambax?"

"And Gambax, although it's hard to imagine why he should want to make a native sacrifice of one of his comrades anyway."

"I've been told Felix was seen with some sort of list of debtors at the bar."

Metellus frowned. "Really?"

"Audax didn't mention finding it on the body. If the killer got rid of it, then we should assume it was somebody who owed him money. So it wasn't Rianorix. Rianorix was asking him for payment."

Metellus brushed invisible dandruff off his shoulders. "I wasn't aware that the prefect had given you permission to investigate, Ruso."

"Perhaps it was nothing to do with the bar. Perhaps the argument happening on the same night was just a coincidence."

"I suppose Tilla suggested that?"

"No, I just thought of it."

Metellus savored a sip of wine before replying. "Tell me. How much do you know about this Tilla?"

Ruso frowned. "She's my housekeeper. She's been living with me since October."

"Inside the fort at Deva?"

"She couldn't do her job outside."

"And before that? What do you know about her background?"

Ruso explained about the cattle raid, Tilla's abduction from her burning home into slavery with the Votadini tribe in the north, and her arrival in Deva. The silence with which Metellus listened made him uneasy. Finally he stopped talking and said, "Are you waiting to tell me something?"

The aide exhaled very slowly, as if he was taking the time to think what to say. "The girl you know as Tilla," he said, "is going under an assumed name."

"I know that. The other one's too bloody difficult to pronounce."

"I didn't realize who she was until you brought her in this afternoon. She wouldn't remember me, but her family lived about an hour's walk northeast of here. Known troublemakers and notorious cattle thieves. The raid she told you about did happen, but it was a retaliation from the Votadini tribe after a great deal of provocation."

Evidently there were some details Tilla had chosen not to pass on.

Metellus said, "Has she mentioned Rianorix before?"

"Not till he turned up and caused a stir at my clinic," said Ruso. "He tried to flirt with her so I sent her out."

Metellus frowned. "Why not send him out instead?"

"He was a patient. It was a clinic, not a classroom."

"What did they talk about?"

Ruso shrugged. "I don't know. They were speaking their own language."

"Interesting."

"Not really," insisted Ruso. "If I could speak the language I wouldn't have her as a translator, would I? And if he's an old friend they would have things to talk about. Just because she happens to be Brigante—"

"Corionotatae, actually."

"Who?"

"Not exactly Brigante. There's a difference."

"Well, whatever she is, it doesn't make her a traitor," said Ruso, beginning to wonder what else Tilla had not fully explained to him.

Metellus nodded. "True enough. So you didn't know they'd spent the night together?"

"*What?*"

Metellus smiled. "No, I can see you didn't. Sorry."

"She was staying with her uncle!"

"When we went to arrest Rianorix last night, we found them curled up together like kittens."

Metellus's mouth was opening and closing and words were coming out, but Ruso's mind was too busy repeating, *So you didn't know they'd spent the night together?* to take them in. "She was with her uncle," he insisted. "It must have been somebody else," but even as he said it, he was aware that Tilla's use of Latin tenses was loose to the point where *I am staying with my uncle* could mean *I have stayed with my uncle, I will stay with my uncle,* or indeed, *I want you to think I am staying with my uncle but in fact I am doing exactly as I please.*

Metellus had stopped talking and was looking at him as if waiting for a response.

"Sorry, what did you say?"

"I said, she had regular access to military information—"

Ruso began to object, but Metellus continued, "She was on the loose in the yard when the sabotage took place, and she was heard talking to someone."

"We've been through this already," retorted Ruso. "Never mind what her family were. Tilla's a midwife, for heaven's sake. Midwives don't go around causing traffic accidents."

"Midwives are able to enter the houses of strangers, move about at all hours, and disappear at short notice with no questions asked."

"That's ridiculous. And whatever she saw in the yard, it took her by surprise."

"Perhaps."

"I was there," insisted Ruso, beginning to wonder if he had been as blind to reality in the yard as he had been to the real nature of the exchange in the clinic. "She told me she was praying to her gods." It sounded less convincing the more he said it. "Rianorix is an old friend of her family."

"Oh, he is," agreed Metellus. "And much more to her, from what I hear. Which makes her an unreliable witness and a dubious companion for a legionary officer."

"This is ridiculous!"

"Please don't shout, Doctor. My men are discreet but you never know who else is listening."

Ruso ran one hand through his hair and wished Tilla were here to tell him none of this was true. That Metellus had been misinformed. Instead, all he could hear her saying was, *You are mistaken about this. I am not a friend of the army.* "I still think she was telling the truth when she said she couldn't identify anyone," he said.

"Perhaps," agreed Metellus, "But frankly, I wasn't convinced we had many likely candidates in the lineup this time. That was why I didn't bother pressing her."

"Are you saying you knew it was a waste of time anyway?"

"Not at all," said Metellus. "You never know what witnesses will let slip while you've got them concentrating on something else. But your Tilla is a clever girl. If she knows about the head, she's keeping it very quiet."

"That's because she doesn't know."

"I would have thought Rianorix would have told her. They like to boast. But perhaps he's cleverer than he looks too."

"What's the matter with you people? If you think he did it, what the hell did you let him out for? Surely you're not really so frightened of the natives that you dare not arrest a murderer?"

"We have to tread softly at the moment, Doctor, since one of our own men is widely known to have confessed. But having Rianorix out there may work to our advantage. We may just catch a few bigger fish."

"Tilla's not a big fish! She's not a—" Halfway through the sentence he realized how ridiculous it sounded, but he finished it anyway. "She's not a fish at all."

"No, it's often surprising what you find when you pull the net in."

"It's ridiculous. Lock him up. His rebel cronies aren't going to go near him anyway while you're sniffing around."

"That depends on how obvious we are. My informers are very discreet."

"Well, so far they haven't been much use, have they?"

Metellus shook his head. "Frankly, Doctor, I didn't expect a man of your standing to be so attached to a native slave. Although she does have a certain rustic charm. I can see why you're so disappointed."

Ruso gritted his teeth.

"I'm afraid she's let us both down."

Ruso realized he was pacing up and down Metellus's office floor. Part of him wanted to rush off and confront Tilla. Part of him wanted to stay and prove Metellus wrong. About everything.

"Well, Rianorix hasn't led you to the Stag Man," he said, "And Tilla doesn't know who or what he is either. In the meantime, do you realize what effect seeing Rianorix free is having on the men—not to mention the rest of the natives?"

"It's not an ideal situation, I agree. As soon as you clear the path for us with Thessalus, I'll persuade the prefect to have him rearrested."

"You don't think he did it!" surmised Ruso suddenly. "You'd never have let him out if you thought he could tell you where that head was."

Metellus smiled. "Well done, Doctor. You're right: I'm not sure that he did it. He may well just be a loudmouth. But he's a rebel sympathizer. And he was making public threats against one of our men. In fact, you're quite right, we are considering the possibility that it was one of his cronies seizing a chance to cause trouble. For all we know there may have been several of them: We can't really control who's in the streets out there after dark. I'll try and get some names from him when we pick him up again. But someone will have to be put before the governor in three days' time. It won't be a local god and it certainly won't be Doctor Thessalus. Now. You need something to take your mind off all this. Are you sure you're not interested in hunting? Rumor has it the governor might—"

"No," said Ruso. "Definitely not."

"Pity," said Metellus.

50

RUSO BURST OUT of Metellus's office with an energy that
made the sentries guarding the headquarters shrine grab at their
weapons. He strode across the torchlit courtyard, then turned on his heel
and scrunched down the graveled street in the direction of the infirmary.
He was going to see Tilla. He just needed to collect a few things on the
way.

The sword swung against his thigh as Ruso shrugged on his body armor.
His fingers fumbled with the buckles and thongs that joined the iron
plates together. He lowered the heavy helmet onto his head and tied the
strips of leather beneath the cheek pieces. He was not going to put up
with any nonsense from anyone out there tonight.

Valens wandered out of one of the wards just as he was leaving his
room.

"Goodness, Ruso, where are you going looking like that?"

"Out," said Ruso, without breaking his stride.

The guard on the east gate saw the medical case in his hand and
opened up for him immediately.

The sound of his boot studs rang out in the quiet night, and he was
conscious of the brass belt fittings jingling with every step. As he passed

the shrine, a dog began to bark in one of the houses. It set off a yappy, irritating reply farther away. Ahead of him, a window squeaked open. It
closed again as he approached.

A rat scuttled across the shuttered entrance to We Sell Everything.
Ruso kept to the main thoroughfares and to the center of the street. Nobody, antlered or otherwise, was going to creep up on him and drag him
into one of those dark gaps between the buildings. Not without a fight.

He approached the last house along the east road. He knew he was in the
right place. The air was thick with the smell of the brewery next door.

By the third attempt, he was thumping on the door with the hilt of his
sword. A muffled voice from somewhere down the street shouted, "Hey!
Clear off!"

That was when he noticed that the shutter on the small window
nearby had swung open. A woman with an accent like Tilla's demanded
to know what he wanted. As soon as he stepped left to address her, the
shutter slapped back into the frame.

"Is this the house of Catavignus the brewer?" he asked the shutter,
hoping that she was still listening behind it.

"The brewery is closed," came the reply. "Come back in the morning."

"I'm looking for a girl called Tilla."

"Well, look somewhere else."

He tried, "I'm a doctor."

"Nobody is ill."

Were all the women of Tilla's tribe—whatever it was called—this difficult? Why couldn't she at least open the shutter to talk to him?

He was not going to bawl his name down the quiet street. He leaned
closer and said in a hoarse whisper, "I'm an officer with the Twentieth
Legion. Ruso. Catavignus invited me here. Tilla is my . . . Tilla knows
who I am. I have to talk to her."

There was a pause, then a reply of, "There is no girl called Tilla here."

"Darlughdacha," he corrected himself, trying to remember how Tilla
had taught him to pronounce it. "I'm a friend."

"I thought you said you were the doctor?"

"I am," he said, adding, "she has two names," lest the woman should
wonder why someone claiming to be a friend had got it wrong the first
time.

"No Darlughdacha either."

"She told me she would be here," he insisted. "She will be expecting
me." This was not strictly true, but he felt it would lend weight to his case.

Silence.

"This *is* the house of Catavignus the brewer?"

The voice confirmed that it was. Then it wished him good night. After that, he might as well have been speaking to a wall. As indeed he was.

Curled up together like kittens. Metellus's words seemed to echo around the empty streets as Ruso strode back past the deserted bathhouse, the shrine with a lamp flame wavering on it, We Sell Everything, and the alleyway where most of Felix had been found. The murder was something Ruso felt he should care rather more about than he did at the moment. And the fact that he did not care was *Tilla's fault.* He had behaved perfectly reasonably. More than reasonably: generously. He had traveled to the very edge of the civilized world out of consideration for her: something most men would not do for their wives or mothers, let alone for a slave. He had even tried to *help* that arrogant bastard Rianorix with the black eye and the gappy tooth and the silly horsetail hair. What a naïve fool he had been.

Unless Metellus was lying. But why would he do that?

He would give Tilla a chance to tell her side of the story. He was a reasonable man. He would ask her, calmly, to explain where she had been last night. Where she was *now.* That was the point. She had expressly said she was going to her uncle's house tonight. He had hinted that he might visit. So why wasn't she there?

Perhaps there was an innocent explanation. Perhaps Tilla had been called to . . . no. The woman behind the shutter had not said, "She has gone out." She had said they *did not have* a girl with either of Tilla's names.

He should have let Ingenuus cut Rianorix's throat at the clinic. It was too late for that now. Instead, he was going to leave him to Metellus.

Back at the infirmary, he found his bed already occupied by Valens. He woke him for a brief altercation, which revealed that Valens had assumed this to be the on-duty bed, while Ruso's proper quarters were somewhere else. "I did say I'd cover night duty for you," Valens reminded him. "Why *are* you dressed like that?"

"Never mind," said Ruso, shedding his armor and kicking it under the bed. "Just go back to sleep."

51

THESSALUS'S GUARD MIGHT have thought it was an odd time for a doctor to be visiting a patient, but it was not his place to say so. Within minutes Ruso was wrapped in a blanket on Thessalus's floor, staring up into the black space where the rafters would have been if he could see them. His mind refused to sleep. *All the words. Jumping around like frogs.* Ruso forced himself to listen for the breathing of his unsuspecting host over on the couch, and for a moment he understood the feeling Thessalus had been trying to describe.

Where was Tilla? Had she betrayed him? If she hadn't, why would Metellus lie to him?

What would he say to her when he found her? Worse, what if he didn't find her? She could have run off somewhere with Rianorix. She could have been planning it ever since they left Deva, and like a fool he hadn't seen it coming. She could be mocking him to Rianorix right now, just as she had mocked Trenus. *The body of a bear, the brain of a frog, and he makes love like a dying donkey with the hiccups.*

Surely she would find something better than that to say about him?

Curled up together like kittens. The thought made him shudder.

He rolled over. He must think about something else.

Despite his bold assurances to Albanus, he did not know who or what the strangely invincible Stag Man was, nor how long the army could keep on playing down the subversion he was raising.

Who had murdered the trumpeter? He didn't know that either. Tomorrow, if he couldn't get Thessalus to retract his confession, he would declare him insane. The way would be clear for Rianorix to be arrested and questioned again about the names of his fellow rebels. It was no worse than he deserved. If one believed in curses, then logically cursing a man was as bad as doing him physical harm.

Tilla's voice came back to him. *I know this, my lord. But he did not do it.*

Then he should have kept his mouth shut at the bar. And he should have kept his hands off Tilla. Metellus had investigated everyone else. Rianorix was the only logical suspect.

There was, however, the illogical one. Thessalus, the man who had been out all night and could not explain where—but did know how the murder had been committed.

Ruso had never met anyone quite like Thessalus before. He gave up his time to run a free clinic for people who largely didn't do what he told them. He was a good doctor but was so doped up with poppy that he was incapable of defending his patients against the laziness of his staff. He put up with a ghastly deputy and even took him out on his birthday, and then—according to him—committed a grisly and apparently motiveless murder in a back alley. It made no sense. Yet like a lot of his apparent nonsense about triangles and fish, there might be some sort of meaning if one could piece together the background.

Ruso rolled back, put his hands behind his head, and stared at the invisible rafters.

Thessalus had not chosen an easy calling. Only the sick would be truly eager to meet a man who spent his days with the ulcerated and unlovely, poking about in the dark and stinking recesses of humanity that most people would prefer to forget about. Ruso sometimes wondered why he had taken it up himself, since he frequently found his patients drove him more to exasperation than compassion.

Thessalus had evidently found it too much of a strain. Working with Gambax would not have helped. Unable to bring about the miracles demanded of him daily and possibly asked to collude in torture, a kindly and well-meaning man could easily find himself unable to sleep. So he would take a carefully controlled dose of something to lift himself above his worries. He would tell himself it would steady his nerves. Indeed, it would do so. He would take another dose the next night, believing he needed the rest and would wake refreshed and a better healer the next morning. He would tell himself he could stop at any time, and would always be on the verge of stopping. But knowing that "any time" was receding farther into the distance, he would come to distrust and despise himself. He would also begin to need more and more medicine to achieve the same effect. In fact he might need it merely to achieve the levels of calm he had enjoyed before he had started down this path.

All the time, beneath the false calm of the medicine, a worm would be burrowing. A little worm of doubt and shame, one that would whisper in his ear that he was not quite in control of what he was doing. Indeed, there might well be inexplicable gaps in time when he could not re-member what he had done. Sooner or later his confused and guilty mind, already filled with gory images from surgery, would latch onto some terrible deed and convince him that he had carried it out. That he had come home with Felix's blood on his hands. That the only way to avoid execution was to pretend his mind was completely gone and he was not responsible for his actions.

Thessalus had already ended his contract with the army because he knew he could not resist the poppy and he knew he was not fit to prac-tice under its influence. In a way, that was an honorable course of action. Many other men in the same position would have hung on as long as possible and pretended all was well.

But how did he know about the head? Only four people knew about that. Audax, the prefect, Metellus, and himself. Five people including the mur-derer.

Ruso sighed. In the darkness, everything was too tangled. He wished he could talk it over with—

No. He was not going to think about her.

"Is that Ruso?" said a voice from the direction of the couch. "Please. I need poppy."

He said, "Tell me where the head is."

"Haven't you found it?"

Ruso sat up. "Tell me where it is, and I'll believe you did it."

"I remember looking into his eyes." The voice was unsteady. "I re-member asking him where he wanted me to put it."

"You don't know."

"After that, nothing. Until I was back here with the blood—"

"Yes, we've been through that. You don't know, because you didn't do it. Who told you what happened?"

"No one. I only know what I can remember."

"I have been trying to think this through logically," said Ruso. "I realize poppy tears might confuse you. I suppose too much might give you bad dreams, or make you frightened or sick, and a big overdose would finish you off altogether. But I can't find any record of poppy making patients violent. You were sensible enough on that night to bring Gambax back from Susanna's. I imagine you were sensible enough to know that he wasn't fit to be left in charge of the infirmary. But despite that, you went out. You explained quite clearly to the gate guards that you'd had a call to a civilian emergency. Emergency calls are the sort of things people remember. They like to think they're helping. Yet I haven't been able to track that message down."

"I've told you—"

"I know what you've told me. Let me pass on what I've been told by somebody else. That Felix deserved to be punished and you were the instrument of the gods."

Thessalus let out a long sigh of relief. "That explains it!"

"Of course it doesn't explain it!" snapped Ruso. "I'm tired of being made a fool of, Thessalus." He threw back the blanket. "Apart from thinking you're Julius Caesar, you've demonstrated just about every symptom of madness in the book. Of course you have. You've read the books. What was it you said to Ingenuus that persuaded him to sneak medicine in here for you?"

"Please. Poppy is the only thing that works."

Ruso sprang to his feet. "Enough of this don't-touch-me rubbish about curing people by talking to them. You're going to get up, and I'm going to fetch a couple of lamps. Then you're going to get undressed and we're going to have a proper look at exactly what's wrong with you."

"There's no need," came the reply. "I can tell you. But you must swear not to tell anyone else."

By the light of the feeble lamp Ruso measured out a dose of poppy in wine and handed it to Thessalus. "That should ease it a little."

Thessalus nodded his thanks. When he had downed the drink, he rested back on the couch. "When I was an apprentice," he said, "I discovered I had quite a few fatal diseases."

"So did I."

"But then you learn to stop looking, don't you? So when this began—" he indicated his emaciated body—"I told myself I was just tired. Overworking. Out of balance."

Ruso nodded. There was no need to comment on the injustice of it. Thessalus was only twenty-four years old. He had already tried every treatment Ruso would have suggested. "If you'd told me the truth in the first place instead of babbling on about fish and triangles, I might have been more helpful."

"I kept it quiet because I was afraid they would discharge me, and I needed the money. Gambax just thinks I'm in love with the poppy tears. I had to tell Ingenuus because I was not brave enough to face the pain."

"He won't talk. He wouldn't even tell me."

"Have you ever thought," continued Thessalus, "how useful it would be if each of us was born knowing the time of our death? How many different choices we would make?"

"We might waste our lives trying to change our fate."

"I think we might spend them more wisely."

"You have done a great deal of good," Ruso assured him. "Men are alive now who would not be. The clinic patients speak highly of you."

"All of them?"

"Most. You know how it is."

Thessalus chuckled, then eased himself into a more comfortable position. "You have been good to me," he said. "Do me one last honor. Make them believe me."

"But I don't believe you. Nobody does. You didn't do it."

"My last wish is that I should be found guilty of this crime and that the life of an innocent native should be spared."

"But—"

"My liver is diseased—which I forbid you to tell them—but my mind is quite sound. If you testify otherwise, you will be lying."

"Everyone I meet here seems to want me to tell some sort of lie. And always for the best possible reasons."

"I'm sorry, Ruso. I know you mean well. But you're so determined to do the right thing."

"What's the matter with that?"

"You don't understand what the right thing is. Which makes you dangerous."

"And you're a man with nothing to lose. Which you seem to think gives you the right to make a fool out of me and everyone else."

"Nothing to lose?" repeated Thessalus. His hands rose to cover his face. His shoulders began to heave. For a moment Ruso thought he was crying, then he realized the movement was silent laughter. "Nothing to lose!" repeated Thessalus. "The gods have given me all I ever wanted, and now you're trying to help them snatch it out of my grasp!"

"Then don't just lie there, man!" snapped Ruso. "I'm the only one who's in a position to help you. Tell me the truth!"

52

WHAT WOULD YOU think," Thessalus asked Ruso, "if a man were taken sick and died, and you discovered the doctor who failed to cure that man had been secretly visiting his wife?"

Ruso winced. "I would think that doctor should have referred the case to a colleague."

"Even if that colleague were Gambax?"

"Even Gambax. He's not bad at his job, just lazy." The far end of Thessalus's blanket began to slide onto the floor. Ruso reached across to the couch and rearranged it. "How's the pain?"

"Easing," said Thessalus. "You're right, I should have sent for Gambax. Everything is so obvious now. But I thought people would wonder why I was sending for help to treat a simple fever."

"Even so."

Thessalus's smile was bitter. "Do you know, Ruso, even as he was slipping away, I really managed to convince myself there wouldn't be a problem? I had genuinely done my best. I wrote up all the notes afterward. I thought if nobody knew that I had been seeing his wife . . . it was Gambax who worked it out. I think he must have wondered why I insisted on sourcing the herbs myself instead of letting him do it."

"You've been seeing the herb woman? That's where you went that night?"

"I've been seeing the herb woman," agreed Thessalus. "Veldicca. Rianorix's sister."

Ruso stared at him. At last something made some sort of sense. He said, "You're dying anyway. You've confessed to save your girlfriend's brother."

They had met at the clinic, where Thessalus had guessed that his patient's "accidental" injuries had been inflicted, not by a fall as she claimed, but by a fist. It was not her first visit, and it would not be her last. His fury had risen with each successive "accident": each fresh crop of cuts and bruises meted out by a husband to whom he dared say nothing lest he make the bullying worse.

He claimed he could not remember how it had started. Perhaps a look. Perhaps a brushing of one hand against another as she laid out the herbs she was now delivering weekly for his clinic, and for which he was over-paying her out of his own salary. He did not ask what she did with the money. She did not tell him until much later that the man she called her husband was demanding the coins from her at the end of each market day.

The secret she kept from Thessalus, though, was as nothing compared to the secret she kept from her husband. And when the child was born with dark hair and its eyes turned the color of peat, she and Thessalus celebrated in secret. In secret, because although the husband was dead by this time, they were still in danger.

"Gambax is lazy, but he's not stupid. He saw Veldicca at the market one morning with our daughter and came straight back and told me he would do me a favor and keep quiet about my so-called murder of her husband."

"In exchange for what?"

"He never made that entirely clear. He just started taking time off whenever he wanted. Ignoring orders when it suited him. That's why I didn't ask to renew my contract here."

"You were planning to make a fresh start together?"

"We had to. I knew that even if I could prove I hadn't killed the husband, Gambax would say Veldicca had poisoned him with her herbs."

"Did she?"

Thessalus yawned. "Of course not."

"How do you know?"

"Ruso, don't you trust *anybody*?"

"Not women."

"Well, she didn't, I promise you." Thessalus tried to shift into a more comfortable position. "Of course, the irony is that we made all these plans expecting to live forever. Or at least for the foreseeable future. We would move south and marry in a town where nobody knew us. It wouldn't matter that Veldicca's family had disowned her for mixing with the army, because I would be setting up a practice that would support us both. But it matters now."

"She'll be left here with no family and no support."

"And possibly no infirmary to supply, either. You've seen what's going on around here. The governor will report back to Rome and Hadrian will have to do something. He might well pull out like he has in the east."

"Or he might send a lot more troops."

"Whatever happens, Veldicca and my daughter will need friends. I don't want her having to take in some other lout in a uniform just to survive. And actually her brother isn't a bad man."

"That's a matter of opinion."

"Seriously. They have a different way of looking at things, Ruso. They had a whole system of law before we came, and we've interfered with it. Rianorix's girl and her whole family was wiped out in a tribal raid a few years back, and instead of letting him demand a blood price or take revenge, we told him to leave it to us. And of course we did absolutely nothing. You can understand why he's angry."

Ruso did not respond.

"I imagine when his girlfriend's cousin Aemilia came to him for help, he saw the chance to redeem himself. And do to Felix the things he wanted to do to the raiders who took his girl. The same traditional punishment he threatened me with until Veldicca told him not to be so silly and stop listening to his daft friends. Are you still awake down there, Ruso?"

"Yes. So that's how you knew about the head."

"That was the difficult part." Thessalus yawned again. "When I heard they'd hidden the body I knew there was something badly wrong. I had to take a bit of a guess when I confessed to the prefect, but as soon as I dropped a hint about the head I could see I was on the right track. Have they really not found it yet?"

"No. Where would he have put it?"

Thessalus shook his dark curls. "I've no idea. I hope he hasn't passed it on to the Stag Man."

"So do we all. The four of us who know. It's being kept secret."

"I pretended to be confused so I didn't get tripped up by the details. Then you came along, and I had to be even wilder to keep you at bay in case you found out I was ill and the whole thing would start to unravel. It was a gamble, but it's worked, hasn't it? They've released him."

"For the moment. But they don't believe you did it."

"I felt terrible leaving Gambax in charge that night," continued Thessalus, oblivious to Ruso's caution, "but I had to go and warn Veldicca about what her brother was getting involved in. I thought perhaps she could go and talk to him. It might even help to reconcile them. She's quite amenable to a reconciliation, actually. But she's doing her best to dissociate herself from him until all this is over."

"Gambax went out as well," said Ruso. "But he came back before you did."

Thessalus gave a weak smile. "I was supposed to come right back, but I was too exhausted to get up on the horse. And then the storm broke. Veldicca made me stay the night."

"So you are at last admitting that you didn't do it?"

"I suppose I am, but if you ever report this conversation I shall deny every word." Thessalus reached down to retrieve the blanket, which had slid off his feet again. "Uh, that's nice. The pain's going." His eyes drifted shut. "I'm starting to float."

"And all this is to persuade Rianorix to look after his sister when you're gone? Couldn't you have found a simpler way?"

"Not if he was executed," mumbled Thessalus, his voice muffled by the pillow.

Ruso said, "His lost girlfriend wasn't killed, you know. She came back with me."

"Mm?"

"She told me Rianorix didn't do it."

"Mm."

"But she's been sleeping with him," added Ruso. "So she's probably lying anyway." He glanced across at the couch. Thessalus was asleep, floating on the poppy tears.

53

"ᴀᴇᴍɪʟɪᴀ!" ᴄᴀʟʟᴇᴅ ᴛʜᴇ voice. *"Ut vales, filia mea?"*
Tilla paused with one arm inside her overtunic, and frowned. Even in their own home, Catavignus was asking his daughter how she was feeling this morning *in Latin*. Perhaps her father's old taunt was right: Perhaps her uncle really did have a toga stashed away somewhere, ready for the governor's call to wrap himself in it and strut about as a citizen of Rome.

Tilla opened the door a crack and replied in her own tongue, "She is asleep, uncle."

"Child!" He slipped back immediately into the language of his ancestors. "Welcome home!"

Catavignus was grayer, and perhaps heavier, but otherwise unchanged. For a moment she wondered why he was not surprised to see her. Then she realized that Ness must have told him she was here. He had had time to prepare himself.

"I am sorry not to have welcomed you yesterday," he continued. "I was away on business. If I had been told you were coming—"

"No matter, uncle," she assured him. "Aemilia made me welcome."

"Aemilia, yes." He dropped his voice to a murmur. "How is she?"

Tilla glanced over her shoulder at a pile of jumbled blankets: all that was visible of her cousin. "Still asleep."

"Come to my office when you are dressed, child," suggested Catavignus. "We have much to talk about."

When she was dressed Tilla wandered along to the kitchen and moments later found herself enjoying not only soft bread and warm milk, but the luxury of knowing someone else had risen at dawn to fetch the water and sweep out the hearth and get the fire lit. She sat with her elbows resting on the scrubbed table, watching Ness's quick fingers checking supplies and seeing her lips move as she limped around the kitchen memorizing a shopping list.

She would have liked to speak freely with Ness, but what could she say? *I know now how it is to be a slave?* Of what help would that be to either of them? They had embraced last night, genuinely glad to see each other again, but today they had returned to their roles. The only useful thing she could do would be to get up off the stool and help, and that would embarrass both of them.

Ness finished counting and began to grope her way along the line of laundry, checking for dampness. "Were you expecting a visitor last night, mistress?"

"A visitor?" said Tilla, realizing she had forgotten to explain to anyone here about the medicus.

Ness slapped a dry pair of socks down on the table. "I knew he was lying!"

"Who was he?"

"Some drunken soldier. Did you not hear the banging on the door?"

"I must have been asleep," said Tilla. The family bedrooms were farther back in the house. Ness slept in the little storeroom facing the noise of the street, so that Catavignus did not have to feed a doorkeeper as well as a cook. "What did this soldier look like?"

"Like a man in a helmet in the dark. I got rid of him."

"Did he leave a message?"

"No."

"There is an officer I know," she confessed. "A medicus. It might have been him."

"It was very late." Ness was sounding defensive now.

"He is sometimes delayed by his patients."

"I am not here to let men in and out late at night. What sort of a house do you all think this is?"

Tilla grinned, drained her milk, and made her way out of the back door into the gray of a drizzly morning.

The yards of the house and the brewery were linked by a tall gate that was not locked. Pushing it open, she entered the brewery yard and paused to marvel at how much her uncle's business had expanded in just three years. Instead of a few sacks of homegrown barley and a collection of buckets and fat-bellied cauldrons beside the hearth, he now had a whole building devoted to the production of beer. Not only that, but at the far end of the yard, well away from the main building, the rain was dripping off the thatch of a little square house that had a narrow blackened tunnel disappearing under one wall. The soldiers must be drinking so much beer that her uncle had built a special hot floor to dry the sprouted barley.

A surly-faced boy emerged from the back door of the brewery with a bucket in each hand. He stared at Tilla for a moment, then dunked the buckets into the water trough. When he lifted them out, the trickle of water of which she had been vaguely aware became louder. She looked on in amazement as she realized that the sound came from a metal spout over the trough. Clear water was trickling out of the spout and refilling the trough. When the boy had carried the buckets back in, she went across to examine what she had seen and found another pipe leading away from the trough in the direction of the house latrine. She thought of the endless trips down to the stream on days when her mother told her to go and help Ness. The aching shoulders on the long climb back up to the house. The fingers numb with cold. The effort not to tip the buckets lest she should waste the water and have to traipse back down and fetch more. Now, her uncle's servants did not even have to leave the house. The hot floor was nothing compared to this. Catavignus had his own water pipe in the yard and a latrine that cleaned itself.

"Niece!" exclaimed a voice from the back door of the brewery. "Come in out of the wet."

She made her way across the damp paving stones and into the gloom. The surly boy was pouring the water into a hissing cauldron set over a charcoal fire. Her uncle did not introduce them.

The surroundings had changed, but the smell of the boiling mash was still the same. The smoke and steam made her cough as Catavignus led her down through the building past stacks of barrels and grain sacks. A gnarled old man who looked as though he had worked there for centuries paused from hooking down a bunch of dried flowers from the rafters when Catavignus yelled in his ear, "My niece, back from a long journey!"

The man nodded and grinned at Tilla, exposing both of his teeth.

"We just add the meadowsweet for the flavor these days," explained Catavignus, indicating the brittle bunches of flowers above her. "Demand is so high that everything is drunk before we need to think about preservation." He pushed open a side door. "We can talk in my office."

The only light slid in on a cold draft from a window that was open onto the wet street. *Office,* Tilla observed, was a grand name for a cramped storeroom with a desk that looked suspiciously like a military castoff under the window. She seated herself on the proffered stool and pointed to a glossy orange inkwell sporting a feather quill.

"Have you learned to read and write, Uncle?"

The crease between her uncle's brows deepened. "Of course. But I rarely find the time. I have a man who comes in to deal with that sort of thing."

"You are doing very well," she observed. "You have . . ." she counted on her fingers. "Ness, a boy, the old man, a man who does the writing you are too busy for, the woman and her husband up at the old house—"

"You have been to the old house?"

"Yesterday. Six servants, two houses, and a brewery with a hot floor and a water pipe!"

"The gods have been kind to me." The bow of acknowledgment was modest. "Coria is a good place to do business. I have formed a guild of caterers. Things are moving forward."

Forward. The word he had used in all those shouting matches with her father. *You must move forward. Seize the opportunity. Rome is the future.* As if the wisdom of the ancestors were of no value. Now, with Da gone, there was nobody to disagree with him.

She said, "I see you are trying to build a grand Roman house in a place that will never succeed."

For a moment he hesitated, then his face split into a warm smile that reminded her painfully of her father. "You have your da's directness," he said. "He would be proud."

Tilla wondered if that were true.

"If only we had known you were alive! But there was no ransom demand. We thought you were lost in the fire. Then last year we heard a rumor that you had been seen in the southern plains. I went down there to look for you. They told me a girl with your name had gone back to Deva to live with a soldier."

The words hung in the air, innocent enough, but clad in the armor of old arguments.

"I said nothing to your cousin," he added. "In case the rumors were not true."

She said, "They were true."

He nodded. "We all have to make changes, child. Your father was a fine man, but he was not always right about everything."

"The man I lived with is not a proper soldier," she insisted, conscious of evading the gaze that reminded her of Da. "Not really. He is a healer."

"I see."

"The family would have learned to like him." Perhaps. Or perhaps they would have refused to have anything to do with her, just as Rianorix's family had shunned Veldicca when she had rejected their chosen blacksmith and set up home with a soldier who had more patience with his bees than his woman.

Catavignus said, "Is this healer traveling with the Twentieth Legion?"

"Medicus Gaius Petreius Ruso."

Her uncle nodded approval. "I have met him. A good man. An officer. You have done well."

"Do you think so?"

"Your cousin will be jealous."

"I am not his wife," she pointed out. "I am his slave."

"His slave?" Catavignus frowned. "Well. We shall have to do something about that."

"We?"

"From now on, daughter of Lugh, we must look after each other. As family. You, me, Aemilia—and in time, if the gods are willing, your officer."

"Aemilia is not well," said Tilla, eager to change the subject.

Her uncle nodded. "She needs some womanly advice."

"Yesterday I advised her to get out of bed, wash herself, and eat properly. Today I shall advise her to go for a walk."

"Good. Did she tell you why she is behaving in this way?"

"Not exactly," said Tilla, not sure what Catavignus was supposed to know.

"She entangled herself with a very unsuitable young man. It has ended badly, as I knew it would. I told her at the time that she could do better, but what do I know? I am only her father. It is not easy for a man to raise a daughter on his own."

Tilla bit back the observation that he hadn't done it on his own: What about the succession of honorary aunties? The fat one with the wart.

The one with the slit up one side of her tunic that showed her thigh. The one who was always cleaning and who liked to grab passing children and wipe dirt off their faces with the cloth she had just spat on. None had stayed long, but there had been plenty of them. And now he had Ness to limp around after them both.

He was still talking. "We must make the most of you while we have you," he said. "They tell me your medicus will be moving on in a few days."

Tilla looked her uncle in the eye. "He will be moving on," she agreed. "I may go with him. Or I may not."

54

R USO THREW HIS blanket aside and concluded that floors these days were harder than they used to be. "I'll get some men to clean things up in here after breakfast," he said. "They've had plenty of practice now that I've had them scrub up the wards."

Thessalus reached stiff arms outside his bedding, stretched them toward the rafters, and sucked in a sharp breath. "Gambax kept promising me he'd get them to clean up, but he never—" He stopped. "Did I really hear you say last night that Rianorix didn't do it?"

"I said I've been told he didn't. It's not the same thing."

"But who else could it be?"

"That's the problem. Metellus is determined to have a culprit to present to the governor, and at the moment, guilty or not, Rianorix is his easiest option."

Thessalus dangled one arm over the edge of the couch and groped for his cup of water. "If he's really innocent, and we can prove it, I could get out of here. It's not much fun sitting here in the dark thinking up new lies to tell you. Especially when you take away my poppy tears."

Ruso leaned across to put the water in his hand, and gave him another dose of poppy. "Sorry about that."

"So who told you he was innocent?"

It was clear that Thessalus had not heard Ruso's final observation last night about his own strained relationship with Tilla and Rianorix. "It was an unreliable source."

"But we must follow it up!"

"I've tried."

Thessalus put the water down and tried to pull himself up to a sitting position. "Tell me everything. There must be something else we can try."

"We?"

"We can't see an innocent man executed!"

Curled up together like kittens. "Are we talking about you or Rianorix?"

"Either of us. Try harder. Please. I'm not brave, Ruso. I want to end my life in Veldicca's house, drifting away on the poppy tears. I don't want to be executed. I'm only doing this because I have to."

"I could save you from that right now by telling the truth about you."

"I'm a patient. You would be breaking a confidence."

"What confidence? You're in the army." Ruso sighed and folded up his blanket. Then he shifted the pile of scrolls out of the chair and told Thessalus everything he knew about the murder of Felix the trumpeter.

When he had finished, Thessalus said, "So. I'm asking you to help me save the man who's sleeping with your girl."

"A man who may well be guilty anyway."

"Please, Ruso."

Ruso put his blanket under one arm and pointlessly tucked in a stray corner. "The more I think about this," he said, "the less I like it. If you take another man's punishment, what about the others? What if he tells his friends and they all get the idea it's all right to butcher anyone who's offended them?"

"I don't think he'll go around boasting about it. Anyway, I'm not responsible for the peace of the province, Ruso, and neither are you. I'm responsible for my family. And I'd feel a lot easier in my mind if I knew you'd help me."

"I'm not promising to lie to the prefect."

Thessalus smiled. "I've already done it. It's not too difficult."

Ruso scratched one ear. "I'm sorry about the ease of your mind," he said, "But all I'm going to promise is that I'll keep trying to find out what happened. Then I'll decide what I'm going to do about it."

"What if the governor gets here before you find out?"

"I don't know," said Ruso, heading for the door and feeling like a coward. "I can't talk about it now. I've got to go to work."

55

R USO HAD BARELY got past "Days to Governor's Visit II" and established that Valens was still asleep in his bed when three men attempted to crowd into the treatment room at once.

First in was an overweight cavalryman with fuzzy splashes of blood seeping into the weave of his damp blue tunic who declared, "It's not me, it's him."

"Him" was a staggering comrade with a rag clutched against his arm. He too had been out in the rain and had blood on his clothing. It was also smeared on his face, on his fingers, and down one leg.

"Sit him down," ordered Ruso, turning to the third member of the trio, a flush-faced Ingenuus. "What have we got?"

"Sword cut, sir. Accident." Ingenuus glared at the friend. "I've already offered to help."

"He needs a doctor," insisted the bulky one. "Are you a doctor?"

Ingenuus squared his shoulders. "I'm a fully trained bandager!"

"Well, when the doctor's finished, you can bandage it, can't you?"

Ruso looked the man in the eye. "Thank you for bringing him in. Go and wait outside."

"But I'm his mate!"

"We'll call you when he's ready."

The man eyed him for a moment as if considering defiance, then appeared to think better of it and instead crouched beside his injured comrade. "You'll be all right," he assured him. "This one's a proper doctor. From the legions. He does this stuff all the time. That's nothing more than a scratch to him."

When the friend had gone, the injured man glanced at Ruso and murmured, "Thanks. He was giving me an earache."

Ruso pulled up a stool beside him. "Let's take a look."

The victim watched as the rag was peeled back to reveal a gaping but apparently clean cut. "Look at that!" he muttered as if offended rather than injured. "Clumsy bloody idiot. He's going to kill somebody before long. And it'll probably be me."

"How did it happen?" inquired Ruso, swabbing the skin with a cheap wine that added a duskier red to the scarlet.

"He's got the paws of a bear and the brain of a turnip, and some fool put him in a job where he could wave a sword about." The injured party sucked air past his teeth. "Ow! We're patroling about three miles out and some dozy Brits with an overloaded vehicle won't get out of the way. We ask to see their customs token and guess what? They've paid the tax, and they know they've got it somewhere, but they just can't lay their hands on it. So we tell them to pay up now or go back to the border and pick up another token. They start getting lippy, so we decide to teach them some manners, and they scuttle off in into the woods and start chucking stones at the horses. We go after them and turnip brain decides there's room for two abreast between the trees. If this is going to stop me riding, I swear I'll kill him. I'm trying to get into the governor's escort."

"It won't stop you for long," said Ruso, pressing the clean pad Ingenuus had just handed him over the wound and fearing he would soon be the one with the earache. "It's not deep, but you'll need a few stitches." He turned to Ingenuus. "Ready?"

"Me?"

"You can deal with this, can't you?"

Ingenuus shook his head and backed away. "Sorry, sir. I haven't done stitching yet. Doctor Thessalus was going to teach us."

"Time you learned."

The patient's eyes widened. "He's not learning on me!"

"No," Ruso assured him, "he's just going to get everything ready and then watch."

"Is this going to hurt?"

"I'll be as quick as I can. Do you want something for the pain?"

The man grimaced. "Just get it over with."

While Ingenuus was preparing the equipment, the man said, "If you don't mind me asking, sir, how is Doctor Thessalus?"

"About the same," said Ruso, choosing the vaguest of his selection of vague answers, which included *As well as can be expected,* and *Comfortable.* "Just get up on the table for me, will you?"

"Only some of the lads were wondering, sir," said the patient, lying down with his head resting on his uninjured arm. "We heard they were going to get him out, but instead that bloody basket maker's running around laughing at us. And now all his little friends are getting uppity as well. All they had to do was get out of the way. What's the matter with them?"

"You should have seen the basket maker yesterday at the clinic," put in Ingenuus. "Came strolling in . . ." he illustrated the movement with a sweep of the hand holding the needle "and looked like he wanted the doctor's translator to kiss his bruises to make them better."

"Holy Jupiter!" The patient was staring at the needle. "Haven't you got anything smaller than that?"

"The small needle, Ingenuus," suggested Ruso, catching his eye in time to stifle any objection that this *was* the small needle and making a mental note to remind him about not brandishing surgical equipment in front of the patient. He returned his attention to the man on the table. "Keep still now. Ingenuus, hold him steady, will you?"

"Perhaps you could have a word with headquarters, sir," suggested Ingenuus, passing the needle to Ruso and handing the patient a leather strap to bite on before continuing on a topic that was obviously of far more interest to him. "They'd listen to an officer. Perhaps they don't know what's going on out there."

"I'm sure they'll be keeping an eye on the situation and briefing the governor," said Ruso. He stabbed in the first stitch.

The patient grunted.

"Well done," said Ruso, drawing the thread through. "Won't be long now."

"Some of the lads might not want to wait for the governor, sir," put in Ingenuus, who had clearly not grasped that the purpose of this conversation was to distract the patient, not the doctor.

"Then they'll have to control themselves," snapped Ruso, knotting the thread and clipping it short. "This is going together nicely. You won't have much of a scar here." As the second stitch went in, the patient groaned and clutched at the edge of the table.

"We're not saying anybody's going to do anything," continued Ingenuus, unabashed. "We're just saying, if anybody did, nobody would care much. And whoever did it wouldn't be as stupid as he was and go 'round making threats in public beforehand, would they?"

Ruso glanced at him. "I shall be testing you later on stitching technique."

Ingenuus, as he had hoped, fell silent and let him concentrate.

56

D OCTOR!" EXCLAIMED CATAVIGNUS, hurrying to the
entrance of the brewery and elbowing aside the surly slave boy
who had opened the door. "Come in out of the rain! Would you like to
try our latest batch, or shall I send out for some wine?"

"Actually," explained Ruso, taking a deep breath before he stepped
into the fug and hoping Tilla had not been serious about Catavignus
asking him to marry her cousin, "I was hoping to have a word with your
niece. Darlughdacha."

Catavignus's smile could have signaled recognition, or amusement at
his pronunciation. Whichever it was, it vanished as he explained that his
niece—for whose safe return he could never thank Ruso enough—was
not there. She had gone to the baths with her cousin.

"It's not mixed bathing, is it?" said Ruso hopefully.

Catavignus looked shocked at the suggestion. He was not expecting
the girls back before the women's session ended at midday. "But allow
me to entertain you while you wait, Doctor."

Ruso excused himself on the grounds that he was on duty, politely
agreed to Catavignus's suggestion that they must talk some other time,
and then found himself floundering for an excuse not to attend the guild
of caterers' dinner tomorrow evening along with his delightful friend,

the officer Catavignus had had the pleasure of meeting at the bathhouse
yesterday. "And there's no need to worry, doctor," Catavignus assured
him. "My niece has told me all about your relationship."

"She has?"

"We live in complicated times."

"That's very true," agreed Ruso, who was intending to uncomplicate a
few things as soon as Tilla emerged from the sanctuary of the bathhouse.

"I don't blame you at all," Catavignus was continuing. "A man in the
prime of life should not restrain himself. And she is a very attractive
young woman."

"Ah—yes." Ruso edged toward the door. "I really do have to—"

Catavignus's "We'll talk about this when you have time" sounded
more like a threat than a promise. "But in the meantime," he added,
"please don't feel there should be any awkwardness over this ownership
business."

"Right."

"We will be honored to welcome you to our home whenever you
wish."

"Thank you," said Ruso, feeling less at ease with every reassurance.
"Just one last thing. Was your niece at home with you last night?"

Catavignus smiled. "Of course. We are all thrilled to have her back.
And the caterers will be delighted when I tell them you're coming to the
dinner."

There was someone else he needed to see while he was waiting for Tilla.
Ruso ducked in under the dripping awning and banged on the door of
the snack bar. A female voice called from within, "We're closed!"

"I'm not a customer!" called Ruso, wondering what sort of bar remained closed on a normal working day and whether he was interrupt-
ing some sort of crisis. Across the street, several men were lining up
against the wall of the bathhouse, sheltering beneath the overhang of the
roof. Susanna must be missing out on a good deal of business.

Just as he was about to give up, the door opened to reveal the waitress
who was not Dari.

"You're Albanus's officer."

"I've come to see Susanna," he said.

The girl disappeared into the gloom. "It's all right; it's not him! It's the
doctor!"

A distant voice shouted, "Which one?"

"The new one!"

A reply came from somewhere in the back of the building. "She says she didn't call for you," translated the girl, returning to the door.

"I didn't say she did," pointed out Ruso. "I need to have a word with her. But if it's not a good time—"

"It's the day of rest, sir."

"Right," said Ruso, baffled by Susanna's apparent lack of business acumen. "So can I talk to her, or not?"

The girl pondered that for a moment, then turned and called, "He won't go away!"

"Oh, all right!"

The girl retreated and Susanna appeared from a back room. "Excuse this," she said, pointing at the towel wrapped around her head.

Ruso noticed the pale splashes down the substantial expanse of her tunic and wondered if she bleached her hair herself.

"Still, you're a doctor," continued Susanna, reaching down behind the counter. "You'll have seen worse." She produced a flagon of ordinary wine, a water jug, and a cup. "What's so urgent?"

"Sorry to disturb you on the Sabbath," he said. "I didn't realize."

One unbleached eyebrow rose. "How do you know?"

"A guess," said Ruso, whose knowledge of her people's customs came from a grim visit to Cyrenaica, where the local Jews had practiced their tradition of rebellion with such fervor that the army had performed its equally time-honored response of massacring them. "Are there many of you here?"

She shook her head. "Just me. Singing the Lord's song in a foreign land, and largely unappreciated." She led him across to a table under a small window, and seated herself on the bench opposite him. "I can't say I'm doing very well at it, but I didn't ask to be widowed and stranded here among a bunch of quarreling pagans, did I? And so far I've been blessed with a good living. Now. What was it?"

Ruso poured himself a drink. "I'm hoping you can tell me some more about Dari."

Susanna sighed. "Why is it that men always need to talk about Dari?"

"I don't know," said Ruso. "I've never met her."

"Wait there," she said, and headed for the kitchen door.

Seconds later a remarkable bosom was followed out of the kitchen by a pert nose attached to a cheerful face.

Ruso suddenly understood the appeal of arm wrestling.

The girl placed both hands on the edge of the table and leaned forward in a manner that placed a fathomless cleavage exactly at Ruso's eye level. "Susanna says you want me."

"Please," said Ruso, gesturing to the bench and forcing himself to look the girl in the eye, "sit down."

In the privacy of the closed bar she seated herself with her back to him, then curled both knees up to her chest and swiveled around in a flurry of skirts. She used both hands to shift the bosom so it was resting on the table, and inquired, "What can I do for you?"

Ruso tried to concentrate. "I'm making some inquiries," he said, "about the murder of a soldier the other day."

"Poor Felix," she said, frowning. "I only found out last night. What a shock, eh?"

"So you haven't spoken to anyone else about this?"

"'Course I have. Everybody's talking about it. It's not a secret, is it?"

"Anyone official, I mean."

"Only you, sir." She leaned closer and dropped her voice to a husky whisper. "Ask me anything you want."

Ruso cleared his throat again and said, "You were working here that night?"

She nodded.

"Tell me what happened."

The account she gave added little to what he already knew. A busy night, a beer shortage, Rianorix shouting at Felix and twice being thrown out into the street.

"You know Rianorix?"

"Everybody knows him. He's the good-looking one who sells baskets at the market."

Ruso was already having enough difficulty focusing on the facts without being reminded of the charms of Rianorix. "And afterward?"

The girl wrapped a dark curl around her finger and pulled it toward her mouth. "Well, that was it, wasn't it? If Rianorix came back for a third go, I didn't see him."

"And when did Felix leave?"

"A bit later on."

"With his friends?"

"No," said Dari, suddenly monosyllabic. The curl sprang back into place.

"I heard he stayed to talk to you."

"What if he did?"

"What were you talking about?"

The bosom lifted off the table. The girl sat back and folded her arms beneath it. "What happened wasn't anything to do with me," she said. "We talked, and then he left. I didn't do anything. I didn't go anywhere. I was clearing up. Then we all went to bed. Ask Susanna."

"You were talking about money, weren't you?"

"Who's been—?" She stopped. "Her, I suppose? Nosy cow."

Ruso said nothing.

"Felix gave me a loan a few weeks ago to buy some new shoes. I said I would pay him that night and I did. That's all."

"And a few hours later he was dead."

"I told you, it's nothing to do with—"

"Did he say where he was going when he left?"

"It was a business arrangement, all right? He wasn't my boyfriend."

"What did you pay him?"

"Does it matter?"

Had the girl been more cooperative Ruso would not have bothered questioning her much further. As it was, she was giving the impression of having something to hide.

"Why did you leave town the next morning?"

"My mother was ill."

"And if I check with her neighbors they'll confirm that, will they?"

The girl sucked in her lower lip and chewed at it for a moment.

"It doesn't look good for you, does it?" prompted Ruso. "You're the last to see him, you hand over some money you probably don't want to part with—"

"How many times? It wasn't me! I was here all the time!"

"So why run away?"

Dari glanced around to make sure nobody was listening. "I had a reason," she said. "I can't tell you what it was."

"If they take you in for questioning," he said, "you'll have to tell them. And it will hurt. If you tell me, I may be able to keep it quiet."

"That's not much of a choice."

"It's the best offer you'll get."

The bosom sagged onto the table. "I didn't steal it," she muttered. "I found it. Finding's not stealing."

"You found some money?"

She frowned. "Of course not. I wouldn't have to tell you that, would I? Money all looks the same. I found a ring. Under a bench in the bathhouse. A gold ring. Felix wanted his money and I didn't have any. So I used it to pay him."

Susanna emerged from the kitchen and gave Ruso a look that said she was disappointed in him. He pretended not to see it. "Tell me about this ring," he said.

"It was one of those lattice patterns," she said. "So it looks fancy but it doesn't use much gold. There were letters in the pattern."

"Did you know what they said?"

She shrugged. "Not a clue. But it can't have been anybody's name or he'd have asked me how I got it, wouldn't he?"

Not, reflected Ruso, if Felix was simply going to use it to buy off Rianorix, who doubtless couldn't read either.

"It wasn't really stolen," she insisted, "but I knew there might be a fuss when he tried to sell it. So I thought I'd stay out of town for a while. Then I heard he'd been murdered the same night."

"So you guessed it was safe to come back."

She nodded.

"One last thing," said Ruso. "When you paid him, did he make a note of it?"

"He wiped me off his list. I watched him do it."

He got to his feet. "Thank you, Dari," he said. "You've been very helpful."

"It wasn't me."

"I know."

"And you won't tell anybody?"

"Not if I can help it," he said.

57

TILLA HAD BEEN surprised by the sudden cacophony of "Aemilia!" echoing around the hall of the bathhouse as a group of young women in the corner noticed their arrival. There had followed a flurry of greetings and compliments and surprise, as it seemed everyone needed to assure everyone else very loudly—in Latin—how lovely it was to see them and how Aemilia wasn't looking at all terrible and she was being wonderfully brave and—finally—who was her friend?

"This is my cousin," announced Aemilia, putting an arm around Tilla's shoulders. "Her name is Darlughdacha."

This seemed to cause some confusion. "Hasn't she got a Roman name?" demanded one of the girls.

"Does she speak Latin?"

Tilla eyed the eager faces framed with fancy hairstyles and decided that she did not wish to hear her beautiful name mangled by the lips of strangers. "Tilla," she said. "You can call me Tilla."

Aemilia pulled up a stool and introduced her to each girl in turn, declaring the names as if she were proud to have so many friends.

"I remember you," said Tilla, accepting the space on a bench beside a girl with a squint who was introduced as Julia but who had been called something very different when they had last met. She slipped back into the ease of her native tongue. "You lived in one of the houses near Standing Stone Hill. Your da used to work a lathe."

The girl tossed her head and replied in Latin, "Oh, that was a long time ago! Now I live here in a proper house."

"Julia has a son," confided Aemilia. "Her man is with the Tenth. Like—"

Tilla saw apprehension in the faces of the other girls.

"—my poor Felix," finished Aemilia. She gulped, and made a sudden grab for her purse. "We need some oil. Come and help me choose, cousin."

As Tilla followed her cousin across the hall, she was almost sure the jumble of echoed voices around her held a hiss of, "She really doesn't know, does she?"

Tilla adjusted her towel and leaned back against the wall of the warm room, closing her eyes to the sight of the painted dolphins leaping across the walls and, beneath them, the unpleasant things women were having done to themselves in the pursuit of elegance. She wished she could also close her nose to the stench of competing perfumes and her ears to the babble of voices laced with the occasional grunt from the massage couch and "Ow!" as the plucker of unwanted hairs delivered her own particular form of torture. The smell, the heat, and the noise were making her head ache. It was hard to imagine why anyone would want to come here at all, let alone turn up every day to be exposed and prodded by strangers.

She let out a long breath and let her head fall slightly to one side, mimicking sleep. Around her, the brittleness of the chatter became more obvious as she shut out the wide eyes and overeager smiles. It was as if, with few shared memories to link them, these women were so far apart that they needed to keep reassuring themselves by waving and shouting across the gap.

She thought of the long comfortable silences at home. The nights snuggled under warm blankets, listening to the low murmur of adult voices. The heavy crunch of another log being thrown onto the fire. The gentle trickle of beer being poured. Later, sometimes, the giggling and shuffling and gasping from her parents' bed that she and her brothers were not supposed to hear.

A sudden wail followed by, "Sorry, miss!" brought her mind back to the bathhouse. This, perhaps, was what people who abandoned their ancestors and surrendered their souls to the foreigners became. Brittle shapes, clinging to one another and shrieking to drown the shame.

Her mind was drifting above the conversation around her when she heard a change of tone and realized an argument was starting.

"Look!" her cousin was insisting.

Tilla opened her eyes to see Aemilia tugging off her precious gold ring.

"Look!" she repeated. "It is my name. In Greek. Aemilia."

The middle-aged woman standing over her gave a derisive laugh. "You can't read Greek!"

"Can you?"

"No," she retorted, "but I know what that says. It says, Long Life to Elpis. Ask anybody. That's my ring. And you're the little thief who pinched it from me last week."

58

R USO WAS LEAVING Susanna's when both of the girls he now needed to talk to emerged from the bathhouse and scurried along the wet street. Aemilia, the buxom daughter of Catavignus, was holding a towel over her head to protect her hair from the drizzle.

"Tilla!" he shouted. He was going to get this difficult encounter over before tackling Aemilia about the gold ring.

Both girls turned. Aemilia had clearly spent too long in the steam room and was still very pink in the face. Tilla said something to her and she hurried on.

"I want to talk to you," he said to Tilla, wondering who had given her that dress whose shade picked up the color of her eyes and why she was wearing perfume. "Where can we go?"

Tilla shrugged. "I have no house. I am not allowed in the fort because I am not a soldier. Soon I am not allowed in the baths because I am not a man, and Susanna's is closed."

"We'll sit outside," he said, heading toward the benches underneath the sodden awning.

"You will sit with me where everyone can see?" She sounded pleased.

Choosing the only table not under a drip, he realized she was not calling him "my lord" anymore. And he realized he did not know how to start this conversation. He had imagined speaking with her in private, but there was nowhere private to go.

Before he could decide how to begin, she said, "Do you know who it is yet who kills the soldier?"

He cleared his throat. "No."

"I have some new things to tell you. That Felix is a thief and a liar. He has given a ring to my cousin to keep her quiet. It was a stolen ring. She is shamed in front of all the women."

Ruso said, "Oh."

She chuckled. "And last night my uncle's housekeeper says she sends away a drunk, because I forget to tell her you are coming."

"Where were you the night before?"

The smile faltered. "With a friend."

"Rianorix."

She paused. "If you know, why do you ask?"

"Because I was hoping you would deny it," he said.

There should have been some sort of hesitation while she considered her shame. Instead she shot back, "I am visiting Rianorix, who is a friend of my brothers, who are in the next world, and that snaky one comes with his soldiers and—"

"What were you doing sharing a bed with him?"

"Why are you spying on me?"

"I'm not. I trusted you. I didn't want to believe it when they told me."

"Then choose not to believe it."

"You just told me yourself it was true!"

"There is one bed. One blanket. But I do not betray you with this man. That snaky one is telling you these things."

"I *trusted* you, Tilla. Holy gods, of all the men you could have chosen!"

She folded her arms. "The soldiers will not let me in the fort. I have to go somewhere."

"You had an uncle here. Or you could have stayed at Susanna's."

"Where I sleep at night is my own business."

He took a deep breath. "If you were my wife, I would divorce you for saying that."

"I am not your wife!" she retorted. "I am your housekeeper. This is what I hear you telling people. Housekeeper. You share a bed with your housekeeper!"

He got to his feet. "You made a choice, Tilla. I have never forced you. *Never.*"

"I am not your wife," she repeated, louder, standing on the opposite side of the table so their eyes were level. "And I am not your slave either. Do you know how Claudius Innocens gets me to sell?"

He did not. He had never wanted to turn over that particular stone.

"The wives of Trenus do not like Trenus coming to my bed any more than I do," she said. "So one day when he is not there, they sell me to a trader who is traveling past. I am never theirs to sell. So, I am never yours either."

"But I have a sale document," he said, feeling like a man falling over a cliff and grabbing at a leaf for support.

"False."

"Why didn't you say this before?"

"I try. You do not want to listen. You never want to hear things you do not like. Now listen to this. Rianorix is a man of honor and he does not kill that soldier, and I am not lying to you. And if you will not help him, I will."

He did not know what to say. He stepped back. The bench tipped over and crashed onto the ground. He kicked it out of the way and strode off into the drizzle.

He was some distance down the street and determined not to look around when he heard her shout, "And he does not have the thing the snaky one is looking for!"

When he marched back and grabbed her by the shoulders, she cried out in pain. He let go and looked around to see the barber and his wife watching with interest.

"Do you know what Metellus is looking for, Tilla?"

"No. They come to the house at night shouting, 'Where is it?' Rianorix does not know what they want or why."

"Do you know what I said to Metellus?" said Ruso, keeping his voice as even as he could manage. "I said that Tilla, who is a person I trust, told me that Rianorix didn't do it: You should be looking for another killer. And do you know what he said?"

"He tells you reasons why you should not trust me."

Ruso stared into her eyes for a moment and said, "Yes."

"And now you do not know who to believe."

"You spent the night with another man," he said, and walked away.

59

CATAVIGNUS TOOK A pinch from the contents of the bowl the ancient servant was holding out to him, bit into it, and nodded.

"Try some," he suggested to Ruso, who had just been shown into his office. The bowl contained some sort of grain.

"Barley," said Catavignus.

Ruso took a couple of the grains and wondered whether his host knew that the army considered barley rations to be a form of punishment. He bit warily, not inclined to sacrifice his molars for the sake of politeness. To his surprise the grains crunched between his teeth and the flavor was unexpectedly rich and nutty.

"Malt," explained Catavignus as the servant left. "Sprouted and dried at just the right time and temperature. That's the challenge of this business: getting the malt right. Do you know there are tribes across the sea who use good malt as currency?" He smiled. "If only we could all grow our own money. What can I do for you, Doctor?"

"I was hoping you'd allow me a quick word with your daughter now that she's finished at the baths."

"My *daughter?*"

"It's about Tilla," said Ruso, untruthfully.

"Ah, yes. In fact if you have a moment, I would like to speak to you myself."

Ruso, who did not have a moment, wished he had gone straight to the house and asked to see Aemilia instead of trying to observe social niceties.

"As you can probably see," said Catavignus, nodding toward the window, through which Ruso could see almost nothing, "this settlement has enormous potential."

Ruso, who had been expecting to discuss Tilla rather than town planning, grunted something that might have been assent.

"A fine location at a major river crossing and a road junction, fertile land, and plenty of local building stone for something more permanent. It's already a holiday destination for the men stationed up in the hill forts, and I've lost count of the number who say they'd like to move here when they retire. And we have the advantage of being right at the forefront of the empire."

"The forefront?" repeated Ruso, wondering if the man had chosen the wrong word to translate a native concept.

"On the prow of the ship. On the edge. A lamp shining civilization out onto barbarian ignorance. And a customs post always draws plenty of trade."

"I see," said Ruso.

"Of course it's all on a modest scale at the moment, but this is the time to invest. Get in at the beginning. That's why I've expanded the brewery and had a malt house built and a water supply put in. That's why the guild of caterers is very keen to do all it can to support the emperor's protectors. Because once the rebels are dealt with, Coria has the potential to become one of the finest towns in Britannia."

"Really?"

"Not only an ideal place for an ambitious officer to invest, but a good location to settle and raise a family."

"Ah," said Ruso. "So this is about Tilla."

Catavignus smiled as if he knew he had been caught out. "Pretty name. Did you give it to her?"

"I think she made it up."

As Catavignus said, "She is all we have left of my brother's family," the surly boy appeared and announced that the builder was here again.

"Tell him I've no more to say to him. Felix had the money. He needs to talk to Felix's centurion." Catavignus turned back to Ruso. "I take it you know what happened to my brother?"

"More or less," said Ruso.

"Ah. Yes. Well." Catavignus took an ominously deep breath. "He and his family farmed a plot of land just north of here. They were . . ." He hesitated. "My brother's family led a wild existence," he said. "There have always been cattle raids across the border, but my nephews made a habit of it. The northerners, of course, retaliated. One night I woke to hear the alarm horn being blown—we lived close by in those days—and rushed up there to find my brother's house burned and the haystack and the stores ablaze, and in the light of the fires . . ."

Catavignus lowered his head and appeared to be struggling to compose himself. "Excuse me," he said. "The memory is still painful. When daylight came we searched through the wreckage but the fire was so fierce we could not even account for all the bodies. I'm ashamed to say we all assumed my niece was among them. Of course if we'd known she was a prisoner, I would have taken steps to bring her back. So as the surviving head of the family, I can only say how very grateful we are to you for looking after her."

"She has worked for her keep."

"My niece has always been the flower among the brambles of my brother's family," continued Catavignus. "A delightful girl."

Ruso scratched one ear and tried to remember if he had ever thought of Tilla as "delightful." The word had possibly wandered into his mind, but if so, it had swiftly fled when confronted with the reality. "She's very attractive," he conceded. He might also have said erotic, eccentric, frustrating, obstinate, and very likely unfaithful, but not in front of her uncle.

"She tells me you treated her kindly. I suspect you were very patient."

"I've done my best," said Ruso, glad Catavignus had not witnessed the conversation outside Susanna's just now.

"Newcomers find our women headstrong at first, but I promise you they're well worth the effort of taming."

"Like your hunting dogs?"

Catavignus's smile reminded him of Tilla. "Like our horses," he said. "Visit her here whenever you like. My people have a tradition of hospitality. I'll see to it that you have complete privacy."

Ruso managed, "Thank you."

"We'll be honored to welcome you into the family."

Ruso's mind was echoing, *Into the family?* when the surly boy interrupted again to say the man from the infirmary was here to see the master.

Catavignus frowned and excused himself for a moment. To his surprise, Ruso heard the voice of Gambax outside.

Moments later Catavignus reappeared. "Always a pleasure to do business with the army." He sat down and smoothed his mustache with a forefinger. "A busy morning. Where was I? As I was saying, my people have many kinds of marriage to suit all situations."

"Marriage?"

"Spring is the right season. And it's quite common for the wife here to stay in the home of her kin. So if the husband has to be away on duty he can be sure she's safe and well looked after."

"Nobody's talked about marriage," pointed out Ruso.

"You mean you've not been bedding her?"

"Well, yes, but—"

"We'd be happy to reduce the bride price in recognition of the kindness you've shown her."

"There's a bride price?"

"Traditionally, yes, but a nominal sum will do. You've already been very generous."

Ruso swallowed hard. "Have you discussed this with her?"

"I'm talking to you first. Finding out your intentions."

Ruso shook his head. "I'm sorry to disappoint you," he said, "But my intentions in caring for your niece really weren't, ah—" He could hardly say that he had bought her from a rogue trader in a back alley. Nor, despite his own feelings about it, was it fair to tell her uncle she had slept with Rianorix. "I mean, I know she's very . . . I am . . . I have been very fond of her. But my first marriage wasn't a success. I'm not looking to settle down with a wife and family. Even if she did want me as a husband, which I doubt very much."

Catavignus frowned. "I'm sorry to hear that, Doctor. She does come with land as well, did I forget to mention that? Of course, as a military man you wouldn't be farming it, but I could put in a tenant and send you the rent wherever you're posted. Less a very small deduction for costs, of course."

"Land?" said Ruso, stupidly. "Rent?"

"Of course to an officer like yourself, a little rent here or there is nothing. I'm just trying to make the offer as fair as possible."

"I've never really thought of—"

"Don't worry, Doctor. I see what you're trying to say. I'll keep looking. Somebody will have her, I'm sure. Now, come with me, and I'll introduce you to my daughter."

Whatever either man might have hoped for in a meeting between Ruso and Aemilia, both were disappointed. Aemilia had retreated into her room and barricaded the door. Her father's insistence that a very important officer had come to see her only produced a howl of, "Go away!"

Catavignus explained to Ruso that his daughter was not well, and less politely to Aemilia that she was shaming the whole family.

"Go away!"

Ruso asked for a chance to try on his own. When her father had retreated he said quietly, "Aemilia, this is important. I know about the ring you were given by—"

"Go away!"

"Aemilia, I'm a medicus. Perhaps I could help—"

"Go away!"

"Please just let me—"

"Go away!"

"Aemilia, I know you saw Felix on the night—"

This time "Go away!" was preceded by a loud scream and followed by the dull boom of fists hitting the back of the door.

Catavignus appeared in the corridor, yelled at his daughter that she was a disgrace, that if she didn't open the door this minute she would be beaten.

Not surprisingly, this did not entice her out.

"Don't worry," said Ruso. "I'm used to this. Don't bother with the beating. I'll just come back later."

60

ALL THE WAY back to the infirmary Ruso was running over his alarming conversation with Catavignus.

My people have many kinds of marriage.

Of course there were many kinds of marriage. There were at least three. There was his brother's sort: the kind where the couple liked each other from the start. There was the sort contracted by the rich and powerful, where the couple didn't like each other—if they had even met—and probably never would, but the marriage cemented some form of political or financial alliance. Finally there was the sort where each found the other vaguely attractive—well, not unattractive—and where the families of both assured the candidates that they were eminently suited and it really was time that each of them married, so why not each other? After all, how long were they going to wait around being particular? Then they spent the next three years finding out that they didn't like each other at all, and wondering how much longer they would have to wait for the development of—well, if not affection, at least mutual comprehension. Then, after yet another misunderstanding, the wife sent a long letter home detailing all the husband's shortcomings. Instead of telling his daughter to pull herself together, the wife's father scribbled a terse note to the husband demanding that he shape up. After that, it was only a matter of time before the wife packed her many bags—or rather, had her slaves pack them for her—and booked a passage home at the husband's expense.

None of these seemed to be the sort of marriage Catavignus was suggesting. Certainly none of them covered the relationship he had enjoyed with Tilla before he had made the fatal error of bringing her home.

He exchanged a nod of greeting with the man from We Sell Everything, and made his way back through the gates to discover that Valens had commandeered his chair in the treatment room.

"Ruso! Where have you been? Come and sit down. Gambax, get him a cup, there's a good man."

When Gambax had gone Ruso frowned. "I'm trying to get the beer drinking under control here."

"Really? Gambax told me you and he had a drink together when you first got here. Then you asked specially to be put in the room with the barrel. I hope you're not falling into bad ways, Ruso. Beer's not good for you, you know. Bad for the membranes, makes you bulge, and produces flatulence. Dioscorides says so."

"Then why are you drinking it?"

"To be sociable, of course. Actually they seem to be a friendly lot here. I met some chap in the baths yesterday who invited me to dinner tomorrow. And another man dropped by just now to ask if you wanted to go out hunting."

"Metellus?"

"I thought about telling him I was your brother, but nobody would believe I was related to a miserable toad like you, so I told him the truth and swore him to silence. He seems like the sort of chap who can keep a secret."

"Oh, he is," agreed Ruso. "Secrets are his business. I hope you told him I was too busy?"

Valens's handsome face clouded over. "Actually, he seemed to think you'd enjoy it. So I said I'd cover for you here. You'd better hurry, they'll be going any minute."

"I've already told him at least twice that I won't go. And it's raining."

"Oh, don't be miserable, Ruso. A little rain won't hurt you. I'm doing you a favor—ah, Gambax. The doctor doesn't want a beer after all. He's assigned me to cover the infirmary for him while he goes off stag hunting."

61

Ruso's previous experience of hunting was limited, but even he knew that late morning was not the time to start and that this was a bizarrely equipped expedition. The mounted company he intercepted on its way to the east gate consisted of Metellus, a dozen fully armed cavalrymen, and six hounds in the charge of a mounted servant. A couple of riders had rolled hunting nets strapped to the backs of their horses as if this had been an afterthought.

"Are you expecting the stag to put up a fight?"

Metellus smiled down from beneath the brim of his helmet. Already the drizzle had started to coalesce on the metal surface and trickle down to drip on his cloak. "You can never tell with these British beasts," he said. "Hurry and get ready, Ruso. They're waiting for you over at the stables."

"I've told you several times—"

"You will want to join this hunt. Trust me."

Ruso reflected that if he had to count off on the fingers of one hand the names of people he trusted least in the world, Metellus would be among them. But his curiosity had been piqued. Valens could cover his duties at the infirmary. Thessalus was asleep. He did not know what to do with Tilla—even if he could find her—and Aemilia was probably still barricaded inside her room.

He went back to the infirmary to get changed.

The party rode out in silence along the north road for about a mile, then branched off onto a narrower road leading up into the eastern hills. The fort was out of sight now. They were following the course of what seemed to be a tributary valley. To their right, the pasture sloped away gently into a wooded glen. To their left was a patch of high flat land with a few animals grazing around the dark clumps of marsh grass. Just past the marsh they passed some foundation trenches that had been abandoned halfway through digging. A dog began to bark as they approached a ramshackle round house. The man in charge of the hounds ordered them to heel. A woman shouted at the house dog to shut up.

Farther along they paused outside a smaller round house that was in better repair. Two men in rough tunics and armed with hunting knives emerged and saluted Metellus. He dismounted and there was a brief exchange before Metellus beckoned to the dog handler, who took his animals into the house. Metellus turned back to talk to the two guards. They led him around to the back of the house. The dogs and the handler emerged and headed for the gate.

Curious, Ruso dismounted and slipped in through the doorway.

The place was as gloomy as all native houses, since most of the British had a strange aversion to the insertion of windows. It stank of burning. Ruso stepped to one side so he was not blocking the light. Something crunched beneath his boot. The ground was strewn with the black skeletons of charred wicker, and above him the thatch was scorched. He moved forward, picking his way through a scatter of smashed baskets and an upside-down crib whose neatly woven base had collapsed into its walls as though someone had jumped on it. He coughed as he inhaled the ash that was still floating in the air from someone tipping over the fire irons into the hearth. He was beginning to realize whose house this was. On the far side, a wicker chest had been upended and a collection of clothes tipped out onto piles of dead bracken and blankets that must have once served as a bed.

Behind him, Metellus said, "This is where we found the pair of them."

Ruso said, "Why would I want to see this?"

"Come outside."

Obediently, he followed the aide out of the door and around past a meager woodpile to where a brown blanket lay over something on the rough grass. As soon as he saw the shape, Ruso knew what was underneath.

Metellus glanced around, then beckoned him across. They both crouched down. Each took a corner of the blanket. The first object to appear was an empty sack, besmirched with soot. Ruso steeled himself and lifted the blanket higher.

"You can finish your postmortem now," said Metellus.

62

AEMILIA WAS STILL in her room. Her insistence that she was not to be disturbed left Tilla—who was sharing her room—with nowhere to go. Finally, still agitated by the argument with the medicus and uneasy at being idle while someone else did all the work, she wandered into the kitchen and asked Ness if there were anything she could do to help.

"To help me?" demanded Ness, surprised.

She was given some dry laundry to fold, but it was obvious that despite having complained of overwork Ness was discomfited by her interference.

"So," said Tilla, holding up an undertunic to gauge where the center was, "How is it, working for my uncle's family?"

"They took me in when I was without a home," said Ness, folding a garment herself at twice the speed. "There is plenty of money for housekeeping." After a pause she said, "And Miss Aemilia needs someone to look after her."

"And my uncle?"

Ness shrugged her thin shoulders. "He is not changed."

"No," said Tilla. "That is what I thought." She put one of a pair of large gray uncle-style socks inside the other and said, "I shall go and take my cousin something to eat."

"She already has something," was the surprise reply. "She took a jar of honey in there with her."

Clearly Aemilia was not planning to starve.

"How are you now, cousin?"

Aemilia eyed the forefinger she had just been licking. "Everyone is laughing at me."

"No, they are not."

"I am shamed."

"You were deceived. Everybody knows you did not steal that ring. If you had, you would never have worn it in public."

Aemilia sniffed. "I have been thinking about the ring," she said. "I am sure Felix did not know it was stolen."

Instead of saying, *Yes, he did, that is why he asked you to keep it a secret,* Tilla sat down on the bed and dipped a finger in the honey.

"Nobody will want me now."

"Of course they will," urged Tilla. "You are pretty and kind and friendly." It was a pity she could not truthfully add "clever," or "hard-working." "Your da has a good business," she said. "And he is building you a new house."

"Yes!"

Surprisingly, it was the mention of the ridiculous house that seemed to cheer Aemilia. Tilla felt her cousin's sticky fingers wrap around her arm.

"Once the rebels are dealt with—and Daddy says they will be, very soon—lots of people will want to live here. It will be safe to move out to the edge of town. But without Felix . . ." Her grip loosened.

"Last week," she said, "we had a man turn up with a gang to make the heating tiles for the baths. We haven't even got the foundations in yet. Felix said Daddy shouldn't have sent them away because we were lucky to get them. But we weren't ready for them. Daddy was worried about how much everything's going to cost. And it's even worse now because without Felix we don't know who they are to get them back when we want them."

"Did Felix make enemies, Aemilia?"

"All the girls were jealous of me."

"They would be your enemies, not his. What about his business associates?"

She shook her head. "He had difficult customers, but he never bothered me with things like that. He said I took his mind away from his business problems."

"Can you think of anything at all that could help Rianorix?"

Aemilia chewed a fingernail. "I didn't mean this to happen," she said. "But if he didn't do it, they cannot hurt him, can they?"

This was hopeless. If anyone were going to help Rianorix—and it was very unlikely the medicus would do so now—Tilla would have to do it alone.

If only she had chosen to walk back to town that night.

"Once the rebels are got rid of and the house is all finished," said Aemilia, "everything will be better."

"Perhaps," said Tilla, wondering what possible difference a house could make.

"We have most of the furniture, and I ordered the fabrics from the weaver last week. When it is finished, we shall invite your officer to dine every night."

"He is not my officer."

"He is truly fond of you, cousin. I saw how he looked at you."

"He does not trust me."

"It is a pity he is a doctor, so you will never know where he has been putting his hands, but he *is* an officer, and in a legion too! Do you *know* how much those officers are paid?"

"Not as much as they spend."

"And he is rather good-looking, in a cross sort of way."

Tilla shrugged. "Who cares?"

"You do," said Aemilia, dipping her forefinger in the honey, raising it high in the air, and placing her open mouth beneath to intercept the thin stream of gold.

63

THE HUNT FOR Rianorix had begun in the early morning when the men assigned to surveillance of his house realized he had been out of sight down at the stream with the water buckets for a very long time. They had then wasted time in a desperate search for him, before looking in the sack dumped in the grass behind the house and realizing they were in even bigger trouble than they thought.

Ruso's participation in the search had begun with his joining the huntsmen and dogs at the east gate for a considerable amount of milling around to no apparent purpose, followed by a ride out to the last sighting, the grim and secret discovery of the head of Felix the trumpeter, more milling around, and finally much excitement and galloping about. They had leaped over walls and ditches, plunged down steep slopes, picked their way through forests, and bowed flat to duck under the branches that scraped along helmets and plucked at clothes. They had thundered across open fields and followed hidden trails only to find that their quarry had doubled back, waded off through the stream, or gone around in circles.

Rianorix was never sighted. The dogs became tired and distracted as the trail grew fainter. Finally huntsmen, horses, and hounds beat a weary and mud-splattered retreat in search of a hot meal, but not until they had returned to the start of the chase and reexamined Rianorix's home. A small cart in an outbuilding was deemed worth stealing, as was his ancient pony. Some of his clothes found their way into the cavalrymen's saddlebags before his home was burned, his gates torn down and trampled in the mud, and his fences knocked flat. The men who knew what had been found on the grass behind the house had been sworn to silence on pain of death. They were the ones who led the destruction and neither Metellus nor Ruso made any effort to restrain them.

The rain had stopped but the light was fading by the time they reached the fort. Ruso glanced back at the horizon and saw a thick smudge of black smoke rising into the evening sky. He thought of Rianorix and Tilla curled up together like kittens on the bracken bed, and of the severed head of a man who had betrayed his lover. And he felt sorry for Thessalus, willing to sacrifice himself for a man who could commit such a hideous murder. He felt sorry for him, but he was not going to back up his lies. Ruso would tell the truth, Rianorix would be rightly executed according to the law, Thessalus would die peacefully in Veldicca's house, and Veldicca . . . Veldicca would survive somehow. Women did.

He groped behind him, checking that the blanket containing the gruesome evidence was still firmly strapped on. He knew now that Felix had died from a massive fracture to the back of the skull: one that could have been inflicted with the stone he had found in the alley. The neatness of this discovery brought no satisfaction.

Ruso shifted in the saddle and shivered. There was scant warmth in leather riding breeches on a wet day, and the rain had soaked through patches in his cloak and chilled his shoulders. He would be glad to get back to the fort, and to hand over his grim burden for secret cremation.

Metellus was riding beside him with a smile playing on his lips. Despite failing to catch Rianorix, the man seemed to think they had done a fine day's work.

64

R USO COLLECTED A bowl of leftovers from the infirmary kitchen for himself and found Valens stretched out on an empty bed discussing horse breeding with the wounded men Ruso had met on his arrival.

"So," said Valens, swinging his legs down from the bed and following Ruso to the treatment room. "Will it be venison tomorrow?"

"We didn't kill anything," said Ruso, settling into his chair before Valens got there. "Anyway, you and I will be at the guild of caterers dinner celebrating the imperceptible start of the British summer."

"Ah yes. I forgot. Hosted by the fine Susanna who I'm told serves the best food in town. Although the menu will be a bit restricted because Susanna has some odd ideas about diet."

Despite not wanting to take up his own invitation, Ruso felt an irrational pang of jealousy that Valens should have been similarly honored without being a putative family member.

"Apparently Catavignus has designs on Susanna," said Valens, hitching himself up to perch on the treatment table. "Or maybe on her snack bar."

Ruso poked unenthusiastically at the leftovers with his spoon. "How is it you've hardly gotten here and you've found all this out?"

"Albanus and I have been chatting," said Valens. "His favorite waitress doesn't want to work for Catavignus. Oh, by the way, I went across with Thessalus's dinner and gave him the poppy tears he asked for. Nice chap. Why can't we tell anybody that he's ill?"

"It's a long story."

"And speaking of dinner, what have you done with the lovely Tilla?"

Ruso explained that she was staying with her uncle.

"You don't seem very cheerful, Ruso. Have you two fallen out?"

"I'm busy. And it's military personnel only inside the gates."

"Oh dear. That must be frustrating for you."

Ruso sighed. "There's a native," he explained. "A close friend of hers. Everyone except Tilla thinks he's a loudmouth murdering bastard."

"You *have* fallen out."

"Meanwhile, Catavignus wants to know whether I'm going to marry her." He scowled. "It's not funny."

"Sorry. Tell you what. Why don't you leave it all behind for a while? I'll relieve you here, and you go on up the road to join the rest of our men."

"I can't, I've got to report back to the prefect. Why don't you go yourself?"

Valens frowned. "Because they'll all know who I am, Ruso, and somebody will tell the Second Spear. Have some sense."

Ruso busied himself scooping up the leftovers, which seemed to consist of cabbage doused in brown juice, and mused upon the shattered skull of the unlucky Felix the trumpeter. He would have liked to think of it as conclusive evidence, but there was something wrong about its opportune appearance inside a sack on the grass behind Rianorix's house. The native must have known he was under surveillance, or he would not have run away. And knowing that, why would he leave behind the one thing that could prove his guilt?

Ruso had grown increasingly uneasy about it on the ride back to the fort. When he had raised the matter Metellus had simply suggested that Rianorix had not wanted to be caught carrying the grisly burden and as a final act of defiance, he had left it for them to find. Perhaps he had hoped it would distract his pursuers and buy him some time to make his escape. Whatever the reason, its recovery was good news. The Stag Man would not get his hands on it. There would be no native spell casting around it at secret gatherings, and the good folk of Coria would never know.

When Ruso had asked, "Why didn't you find it up there before?" Metellus had replied, "Obviously, we didn't look hard enough last time.

He certainly hasn't brought it home since. Even those dimwits on surveillance duty would have noticed that."

"It all seems very convenient."

"We need to be seen to be keeping order. Ruso. The native won't be
much of a loss."

"But what if—"

Metellus raised a hand to silence him. "Don't worry. If we find out
later that it was put there by somebody else, we can arrange their quiet
disappearance."

"And that's justice?"

"Rianorix got himself into this mess. He was issuing threats against a
Roman soldier in a public place. There are people who would say that's
disrespect for the emperor. This isn't just an isolated quarrel in a bar, you
know. You need to take a wider view."

Ruso had frowned. "I've always thought," he said, "That the wider view
is an excuse not to look too closely at the details you don't want to see."

"Has it ever occurred to you, Doctor, that you think too much?"

"Frequently," said Ruso, wondering how he was going to break the
news of the day's events to Thessalus. "And I think you're on very uncertain ground with this."

"Fortunately for the security of the border, Ruso," Metellus had
replied, "what you think doesn't matter."

Valens was still talking. ". . . And if I told her I wasn't thinking anything," he said, "which I wasn't, usually, she just kept on asking until I
made something up."

*All Thessalus's plans had been thwarted. He had brought disgrace upon him-
self for nothing.* Valens appeared to be waiting for some sort of an answer.

"Sorry, what did you say?"

"I said," repeated Valens, "did you have trouble with Claudia asking
what you were thinking all the time?"

"What? Oh. Not for long."

"How did you stop her?"

Ruso frowned. "I seem to remember sitting on a garden bench," he
said, "and she started chattering about the sunset, or something. She
seemed quite happy so I let her get on with it. Then she got hold of my
hand and asked me what I was thinking about. So I said, 'The treatment
of anal fistulae.'"

Valens grinned. "That was particularly imaginative."

"No it wasn't. I was answering the question. After that she never asked me again. Now that I think about it, she didn't speak to me for the rest of the evening. Valens, where was Gambax last night?"

"Gambax? I've no idea. In the barracks, I suppose. He wasn't here. It was just me and a bandager. Why, should he have been on duty?"

"I need to talk to Albanus."

"I told him to clear off after the evening meal. I expect he's gone to try his luck with Susanna's girl. He'll be back soon; it must be nearly curfew."

"Albanus didn't say anything about the work he was doing for me?"

Valens frowned. "Oh, he was worried about something as usual. Something to do with the administration. He didn't seem to want to talk to me about it."

Ruso got to his feet. He needed to talk to Aemilia about that business with the ring, but it was too late to go visiting her at this hour. He would go across to see how Thessalus was and find a way to tell him what had happened.

He had barely sat down in Thessalus's chair when there was a hammering on the door and the guard informed him that he was wanted back at the infirmary for an emergency. When he got there, an orderly was hurrying down the corridor with extra lamps. To his surprise the squat figure of Audax emerged from the treatment room.

"It's your lad," he said.

"My—?"

"Your clerk. Found him down the same alley."

Albanus lay pale and unconscious on the table, his face and clothes covered in blood. Valens was crouched beside him, holding the lamp dangerously close and gently probing the matted hair on the back of his skull.

"What is it?" demanded Ruso, picking up the scent of Albanus's hair oil and dreading what he was about to see.

"Depressed fracture, I think. Hurry up with those lights, will you?"

Ruso said, "Was he conscious when you found him?"

"He was muttering something," said Audax. "Dunno what." He drew Ruso aside and murmured in his ear, "At least he's all in one piece. I'm off down there now. Got to clean another bloody stag picture off the wall. This is getting out of hand."

65

"HOW MANY OF you buggers have we got here now?" demanded Audax. "There's the skinny one locked up with his brains on the boil, there's you, and now your mate's turned up. And still you can't fix him."

Albanus had opened his eyes and muttered a few words late last night before lapsing back into unconsciousness. This morning he was lying in a bed with his head swathed in linen bandages barely whiter than his face. The smell of the strong vinegar Ruso had used to check any bleeding of the membrane around the brain still lingered in the air.

Ruso, who had been up half the night tending him, yawned and leaned against the wall. He felt this was his fault. He had brought Albanus to this wretched place. He should have thought to warn him about that alleyway. He should have ignored the Batavians' cover-up schemes and told him the truth about the danger that lurked in the streets of Coria. Worst of all, he should never have asked him to interfere in Gambax's affairs.

He could say none of this in the presence of Audax. Instead he said, "It's just wait and see now."

"Never mind waiting and seeing," retorted Audax. "You want to give him a dose of Doctor Scribonius." He thrust forward a fist containing a square bottle of greenish glass with an inch of dark liquid swilling around inside. "I'll bring some more over later."

When the centurion had gone, Ruso sat on the edge of the bed and watched the faint rise of his clerk's chest with each breath. He laid one hand over the cold fingers. "You're not going to die, Albanus," he assured him. "We're not going to lose another man from the Twentieth. We won't let you go."

For a moment he thought there was some flicker of movement behind the eyelids. "Albanus?" He waited, but there was no further sign. He tucked the clerk's hand in under the harsh gray blanket and summoned Ingenuus to sit with him. "Any problems, send for Valens," he told him. "Don't let Gambax anywhere near him. And don't give him that tonic till we find out what's in it."

Gambax was busy smudging out one stroke of the "II" after "Days to Governor's Visit."

"Where were you last night, Gambax?"

"Polishing my kit, getting ready for the governor. You said Doctor Valens was on duty."

"So I did," agreed Ruso, leaning against the wall and folding his arms. "Doctor Valens is on duty again now. He's the only one allowed to touch Albanus. I shall be out."

He waited until Gambax had finished and gone back inside. He was alone with the images of the gods. Since arriving at Coria he had neglected one of them completely and never bothered to find out the name of the other. He asked forgiveness of both. Then he stretched out his arms to the image of Aesculapius, and prayed for the life of the clerk he himself had failed to protect.

He only became aware of someone standing behind him in the street when he had finished speaking.

Metellus thought he might like to know that a certain object had been discreetly and respectfully disposed of, and as soon as Rianorix was apprehended—which, thanks to information just received from an informer, he soon would be—the matter would be settled. "Perhaps for the sake of pacifying the locals, we should get you to confirm that Thessalus's confession was never credible because of the state of his mind."

"I can't say that," said Ruso.

Metellus sighed. "I do hope you're not going to be difficult, Ruso. Although it doesn't matter much now anyway: We have the evidence, and it's obvious that he must be unhinged or he wouldn't have confessed. As soon as we catch Rianorix—"

"You need to look at Gambax."

"Gambax? Oh dear, Ruso. Has that girl been working on you again?"

"I'm pretty sure he and Felix were working some sort of scam with the infirmary ordering system. That's where your fancy wine came from. I checked the amphora and the official mark's been scrubbed off it. Gambax must have been buying it in for medicinal purposes and selling it to Felix, who distributed it. Only Felix was distributing it a bit too widely and Gambax realized he was going to get caught. Gambax must have seen the chance to finish him off and take over the distribution himself. Now I think he's found out my clerk is onto him, and he's tried to finish him too and blame the whole thing on the Stag Man. When Albanus wakes up I'm sure he'll confirm it."

Metellus shook his head sadly. "Go and lie down, Ruso. Nobody's going to go around murdering people over a few amphorae of wine."

"But if he thought he would be caught and punished—"

"You surely haven't forgotten the evidence you carried home yesterday?"

"He could have hidden that somewhere and then taken it up there at night when he found out that Rianorix had been released and we were still looking for somebody else. Rianorix got up in the morning, saw it, panicked, and ran."

"This is all sounding rather desperate."

"You know Gambax was outside the fort somewhere when Felix was killed."

"I told you. We checked everyone's whereabouts. All the people he said he'd been to see actually saw him, and none of them noticed he was covered in blood and carrying a severed head. Perhaps they just forgot to mention it."

"He could have seen them before he met Felix." Ruso was aware that he was sounding desperate. "You should at least check his movements last night. Find out if he really was in the barracks polishing his kit when Albanus was attacked."

"Ruso, the governor is arriving in the morning. I have better things to do than pursue your—"

"Who was it, then? You think Rianorix came back into town last night and tried to murder my clerk? Or did the Stag Man decide to pay a visit?"

Metellus gave him a long look. "I will of course be investigating the attack on your clerk. Let me know when he wakes up, and I'll come and talk to him. In the meantime, I have to go and welcome another of your girlfriend's former bedmates."

"What?"

"Trenus of the Votadini. He's been disarmed at the border and escorted into Coria for tomorrow's meeting with the governor."

"Trenus is a thief and a murderer," said Ruso. "Tilla didn't stay with him willingly."

"Really? She was there for at least two years."

"She couldn't get away. If you want a clear-cut example of justice for the natives, why don't you arrest him? She'll testify."

Metellus shook his head sadly. "This is exactly why I warned the prefect about involving an amateur. Your loyalty is commendable, but not appropriate."

"I suppose you're going to tell me it's not that simple?"

"The Votadini are a self-governing friendly tribe, and the governor will be hoping to enlist their help in flushing out the Stag Man. If we invite one of their people to a meeting and then arrest him, there will be enormous political implications. I suppose you do understand that?"

"What I understand," said Ruso, "is that we're more interested in doing the easy thing than the right thing."

Metellus shook his head. "No, no. We are interested in doing the thing that will get the right result. And the right result is that we keep order and make sure the taxes are collected."

66

THESSALUS WAS AS upset as Ruso had anticipated at the news of the gruesome discovery behind Rianorix's house. "But I think Tilla's telling the truth about him," said Ruso, moving the scrolls to sit in the chair. "He didn't do it. I think Gambax did." He explained about the wine deal.

To his surprise, Thessalus laughed.

"I didn't know about the wine," he said, "but I had a fair idea about other things. Bedding, clothing, kitchen equipment, tools . . . Anything you can legitimately buy for the infirmary or any of the medical facilities along the border, all of whose supplies come through us, you can overorder. I'm pretty certain he was passing the surplus on to Felix and I suppose they were splitting the profits."

"But when Felix took a stupid risk and supplied medicinal wine to the bar where you drank—"

"Ah. I'm afraid that's where your theory falls down," said Thessalus.

Ruso stopped. "Why?"

"I couldn't be seen to be drinking it, it's true, but Gambax knew I dared not upset him because of what he knew about me and Veldicca. He probably told Susanna to keep the wine out of my way, but even if I did see it, what would I do?"

"Oh, hell. I don't know. Maybe they fell out about something else. He was definitely on the loose out there when Felix was killed."

Thessalus shook his head. "We're running out of time, Ruso. And Metellus has his evidence. You have to decide what you're going to do."

Ruso scratched one ear. "I'll try and get some sense out of Aemilia. Felix gave her a ring he didn't receive until closing time that night. She must have been the last one to see him alive."

"I mean about me. You can't prove anything about Gambax, and you said Metellus has checked out everyone else who was in the bar. The only realistic chance of saving Rianorix is if I'm convicted in his place."

Ruso reached idly for a scroll, perused the name, and put it aside.

He tried to frame his dilemma in one of those educational questions for bright young minds to ponder. *A man is asked to lie so that an innocent colleague who does not have long to live can take the punishment of a man who has coincidentally stolen the first man's . . .* gods above. By the time the tutor got to, *What should he do?* the students would be just as confused as Ruso himself.

He said, "If they convict you, what happens afterward won't be pretty."

Thessalus took a long breath. Finally he said, "I'm just hoping they'll make it quick because I'm an officer."

"You don't have to—"

"And I've got more to go on now, remember. I can remember hitting him on the back of the head with a rock. I can remember hiding the head up near Rianorix's house. I suppose he found it and didn't know what to do with it."

"Nobody's going to believe that. They'll know I told you."

"They won't *know* anything unless you tell them. They'll be guessing. And they'll do whatever's politically convenient. Just get me in front of the governor, Ruso. Let me try and convince him. You aren't going to let me down, are you?"

67

MISS AEMILIA WAS not receiving visitors at the moment. No, she was not unwell and in need of a doctor. If he really had to know, she was getting ready for the caterers' dinner this evening.

Ruso explained that his visit was extremely important. Ness informed him that nothing was more important than the caterers' dinner and besides, he was not to go upsetting Miss Aemilia just when she was feeling better.

"How about Tilla? Is she here?"

"No."

"I need to talk to her urgently too. About something else. Where is she?"

"Out."

Ruso gritted his teeth. "I want to warn her," he said, "that the man who caused all the trouble with her family is in town."

"She knows," said Ness.

There was a movement behind her and Aemilia appeared. Her face was unnaturally white and one stray curling rag had escaped from the bright green cloth wrapped around her head. Ruso recognized the early stages of female preparation for an evening out. At this point the effect was alarming rather than attractive, and in the days when she was still interested in what he thought of her, Claudia had shooed him out of her bedroom until the job was complete—a task that could take anywhere from several minutes to several hours.

"My cousin is not at home," Aemilia said as calmly if she had not screamed, *Go away!* at him last time he was there. "We don't know where she went. There was somebody she did not want to see."

He said, "Did she go by herself?"

Aemilia had said *Let me just finish getting ready and I'll come with you, Cousin,* but Tilla had said she was in a hurry, picked up a cloak, and run out the door.

"Was Trenus the person she didn't want to see?"

"He came to visit my father," said Aemilia. "She heard them arguing and ran away."

"Did she say where she was going?"

"Somewhere safe," said Aemilia, unhelpfully.

Ruso took a deep breath. "While I'm here, there's something very important . . ." The final words were spoken at rising volume, because Aemilia was retreating from the door. "I need to ask you some questions!" he shouted. "Aemilia, please! It's about Felix!"

"You can ask the mistress questions at dinner," said Ness, pushing the door closed in his face. "She has to get ready."

68

THERE WERE, RUSO reasoned, only a limited number of places
a visiting chieftain with a rough reputation could be lurking in a
place like this. If Trenus were in the fort, Metellus would know. If he
were not, he would be in a bar, a brothel, or the bathhouse. Ruso hoped
he wasn't going to have to search them all. He was supposed to be working at the infirmary. He needed to get some sense out of Aemilia. He
needed some proper evidence against Gambax. He needed to check on
Albanus. He was supposed to be doing any number of important and urgent things, none of which included hunting for a visiting tribesman in
defense of a woman who had betrayed him, but suddenly that seemed
more important than any of them.

Trenus was not at Susanna's, and no one would have been interested
if he had been. The little waitress was blotchy faced, and Susanna's
head covering kept sliding off and having to be yanked forward again.

"Two of them!" she muttered across the counter, furiously and ineffectively rubbing at an old stain with a cloth. "Two customers attacked
in one week!"

Ruso agreed that it was very bad luck.

"Why me?" she demanded, her hand pausing in midrub. "I ask you,
what sin have I committed that this should happen to me? I close on the

Sabbath. I don't envy anybody anything. I don't eat the food offered to Apollo-Maponus. I admit it's served in my house, but what can I do? There's only me here. I don't eat it myself, and it's too late to cancel the caterers now. You'll be there, and Doctor Valens . . ."

"Don't worry on our account," said Ruso generously. "You can say you're canceling out of respect for Albanus."

"But all the caterers will be making things to bring, and the pastries are in the oven, and the duck's been stuffed!" She sighed. "If we cancel now, people will say we're giving in to the rebels. But I swear if that young man survives, I'll never host another one of these things. Never mind what the caterers think. That's the end of it."

Ruso crossed the street. Someone in a place this size was bound to have noticed a visiting chieftain.

The barber was busy with another customer but greeted him like a long-lost friend. "Doctor! I won't be a minute!"

"Don't rush, Festinus," Ruso urged him. "I just want a word."

Moments later the customer was clutching a wad of bloodstained linen against his jaw, and Ruso had been directed to a bar on the far side of the west gate.

"Step right in, sir! What'll you have to drink? Will it be wine, beer, mead?"

"No thanks," said Ruso, who had drunk enough overpriced vinegar in seedy bars to know better. From the look of the customers eyeing him from the table in the waiting area, they were wishing they hadn't bothered, themselves.

"Of course for our selected clients we do have"—here the woman propelled him in by the arm and gave him a frightening leer as she stage-whispered—"*Doctor Ruso's special love potion.*"

"*What?*"

The secretive wink was even more frightening than the leer. "Very effective, sir. You'll be impressed."

"What did you call it?"

"Special love potion, sir. As used in all the best establishments in Gaul."

Ruso peered at the face again, wondering if underneath the paint—which had sunk into the wrinkles around her eyes, making her look even older—there was a patient from his clinic, who was trying to apply one of the first rules of salesmanship: Address the customer by name. But try as he might, he could not recall the violently red hair. Nor the black teeth. "What," he said, turning to make sure he was leaning against a solid wall and not one of the curtained-off alcoves in which the real business was conducted in this sort of place, "did you say the name of the potion was?"

The stink of breath-freshening pills surrounded him as she stood on tiptoe to whisper again, "Doctor Ruso's, sir."

"And he sold you his potion, did he?"

"Oh, no, sir. We get it from a supplier. He imports it from a famous specialist."

"I see," said Ruso, postponing further inquiries because at that moment, deeper into the gloom of the interior, a curtain was pushed back and a hefty black-haired man emerged, fumbling as he attempted to knot his belt.

Ignoring the owner's assurance that Cynthia would be free to entertain him in a minute, Ruso eyed the man's braided hair and drooping mustache and said, "Trenus?"

Behind him, he heard a bench scrape back across the floor. The two customers who had been lounging over the table were on their feet, and much taller than he had expected.

One of them asked something in the local language. Not for the first time, Ruso cursed his laziness in not bothering to learn it.

"He says," explained Trenus, "who wants to know?"

"I do," said Ruso, relieved to find that the man spoke good Latin and moving aside lest the two bodyguards should think he was trying to trap Trenus in the building. The owner, he noticed, had retreated behind the planking that served as a bar.

Ruso said, "I hear you paid a visit to the local brewer this morning."

"What's that got to do with you?"

"In case Catavignus didn't explain something to you, I'll do it. Stay away from his niece."

Under the mustache, Trenus's mouth spread into a smile. "The blond?"

"You know who I mean," said Ruso, hoping to avoid pronouncing her native name.

"What I did for that girl," said Trenus, "was a kindness. She was supposed to go up in smoke with the rest. Not that I ever got any thanks for it. You're her latest victim, then?"

"If you ever lay a hand on her again," said Ruso, "if you so much as look at her—you'll answer to me. Have you got that?"

Trenus held up a hand as if requesting a pause. "I'll just translate that for the boys," he said.

There followed a rapid exchange that Ruso could not understand, then all three looked at him and laughed. "What will you do then, eh?" inquired Trenus, pretending a genuine interest.

Ruso paused in the doorway. It was all very well trying to defend Tilla, but he had no idea what he could do that would either frighten or impress a man like Trenus, who was now standing between his henchmen with his thumbs hooked into his belt and his head cocked to one side, waiting for an answer.

What was it Tilla had said about this man? *The body of a bear, the brain of a frog, and he makes love like a dying donkey with the hiccups.* None of that seemed especially helpful at the moment.

"I'm only one man," Ruso conceded. "And you've got two bodyguards. So at the moment, all I could do is run away."

"Hah!"

"Not only that, but I hear you've got important friends. I hear the governor's invited you to dine with him in the fort."

"What's that got to do with you?" repeated Trenus.

"Nothing," said Ruso. "I'm just a humble medic." He pointed at the woman hiding behind the bar, whom he suspected of clutching some kind of hidden weapon. "She'll tell you all about Doctor Ruso. Specialist in potions and poisons, temporarily in charge of the fort medical service."

Trenus glanced at the woman as if he were wondering whether to believe any of this.

"Did you know there are some poisons so deadly that a man can be killed just by having a vessel painted with it touch his lips?"

"You're lying."

"Am I?" Ruso smiled. "Enjoy your dinner, Trenus."

69

B ACK AT THE house next to the brewery, Ruso informed Ness that as a legionary officer he was ordering her mistress to talk to him.

"My mistress is not in the army."

"Tell her it's about stolen jewelry and withholding evidence from a murder inquiry."

Moments later, Aemilia appeared. She had taken out the curling rags. Her eyes were wide with alarm and fresh paint beneath the unnaturally springy hair. "I didn't know it was stolen!" she began. "I haven't done anything wrong!"

"Can I come inside? You won't want to discuss this on the doorstep."

Aemilia glanced over her shoulder at Ness, and then stepped back to allow him in. Ness ushered them both into a small room painted dark red and crammed with furniture. Ruso sat on an overstuffed couch that had been polished into slipperiness, and Aemilia seated herself in a wicker chair on the far side of a flotilla of small tables. Ruso wondered whether Rianorix had woven that chair.

She said, "About yesterday. You called at a bad time. I was upset."

He said, "I know. I'm not worried about who the ring belonged to, but

I have to ask you some questions. It's very important for Rianorix's sake that we find out exactly what happened on the night Felix died. You saw Felix that night, didn't you?"

Her fingers strayed toward her mouth. "Yes."

"Did he come here, or did you meet somewhere else?"

Her voice was very small. "He came here."

"Do you know if anyone else saw him? Anyone hanging around, or visiting the house? Gambax from the infirmary does business with your father, doesn't he?"

"Not that night. There were no visitors." She ran a hand through the artificial curls. A long pin dropped out and landed in her lap. She picked it up and twirled it between thumb and finger. "He said we would get married," she said.

Ruso tried to think of something comforting to say. Instead all he could come up with was, "Who do you think killed him, Aemilia?"

There was an audible click as she bit through a fingernail. "I never meant all this to happen."

"I don't think Rianorix did either. He was only asking him for money."

She frowned. "For money?"

"For five cows."

"Then it was all lies," she said flatly. "Everything he said was a lie."

Ruso waited, not sure which of the men she was talking about.

"I have tried to tell myself Felix meant what he said," she continued, "even though it was not his ring. But that is the honor price. He must have told Rianorix he would never marry me."

"I'm sorry," said Ruso, ashamed of having upset the girl and still no further forward in the hunt for the murderer.

She said, "Rianorix was asking the proper compensation to the family for a broken promise of marriage."

Ruso leaned back. The back of the couch creaked under his weight. He wondered if Felix had grasped the importance of what was being asked of him. "What if that compensation was refused?"

"I don't know. My uncle used to say that in the old days the Druids brought justice. I suppose they would ask the man's people to pay." She looked at Ruso helplessly. "But the Druids are gone, and Felix's tribe is across the sea. The army wouldn't pay us, would they?"

"No."

Her chin rose. "Then he got the punishment he deserved," she said. "I must tell Rianorix I am sorry."

"Who killed Felix, Aemilia?"

She picked up the hairpin and a comb. "The Stag Man," she said. "Now, would you like to know where to find my cousin?"

70

TILLA KNEW NEITHER of the muscular young men who blocked her path, but she recognized some of the faces of the people gathering around them. There was one of the women she had seen at the clinic. There was the husband, whose nose her brother had knocked to one side. Another was a neighbor from across the hill who had been one of the children piling onto the swing in the oak tree outside her house when the rope broke and they all fell in a heap in the mud. The others were strangers. Finally Rianorix, busy chaining up the barking dog, noticed the cluster of people around the gate and headed down to see what was going on.

"I am Darlughdacha," she told them. "Come home to join the Gathering."

"We know that," said the man with the bent nose. "And we know you traveled here with the legionaries."

"We all have to survive as best we can in these times."

"We heard that you were living behind their walls down in Deva."

"That is true."

"So why are you here?"

Tilla looked him in the eye. "This is my uncle's land," she said. "And

that paddock and the house beyond it are on the land that was farmed by
my family. Why are *you* here?"

"You must have seen many things inside the fort," said one of the
strangers, tucking his thumbs in his belt. "You will know how the soldiers store and prepare their weapons. How they send messages and
arrange their supplies. How they order their guards."

"I was a housekeeper," she said. "I can only tell you how they prepare
their dinner."

"You walked through the fort with your eyes shut?" demanded the
man with the bent nose.

"I find it is the best way," said Tilla. "Then I cannot identify people
and get them into trouble. And if my brother were here he would knock
you down again for insulting me."

The woman said, "Let her stay and help me until the Messenger gets
here. Then we can ask him."

"She could be a spy," pointed out her husband.

"What is the matter with you all?" demanded Rianorix. "We know
her."

"You could be a spy too," grumbled the man. "Why was it they let you
go, eh? Did you do a deal with them?"

"Of course he did not!" retorted Tilla. "Even the Romans understand
that the gods made someone else execute that soldier after Rianorix
fasted against him. First you insult me, then you insult a man whom the
gods have favored. You should be more careful."

The grumbler scowled. The wife offered Tilla a small shrug of apology. One by one, they stepped back out of her path.

Tilla entered the gate and followed the path toward the house that had
been commandeered from her unsuspecting uncle and his servants. She
had passed the servants on the road, hurrying into town. They had been
given an urgent message summoning them to help with the guild of
caterers dinner. She had not believed a word of it, but they had, and they
would not be back until morning.

71

RUSO MUST HAVE looked anxious because the owner of We Sell Everything called after him, "All right, sir?" as he sprinted past on his way back to the fort.

When he found her, he would tell her how he had tackled Trenus for her, while Rianorix had fled to save himself and left her behind. He would not mention that he had been there when Rianorix's house was burned. If she did not know that, she would not ask what he had done to prevent it, and he would not have to admit that he had done nothing at all.

He was exchanging a hasty salute with the guards on the east gate when he heard a familiar and disrespectful yell of, "Hey, Doc!"

"There you go," announced Audax, thrusting a full bottle of dark liquid into Ruso's hand. "Got the last one. Some other bugger had his paws on it. But I told the trader it was for you. Worked like a charm. Must be nice to be in the legions. Straight to the front of the line every time."

"Really?" said Ruso, who was wondering how easy it would be to commandeer a horse without an official order, especially since they would all be being washed and polished for the governor's inspection in the morning.

"He says he knows you."

"Really?" He would need something fast. He needed to catch up with her before she found Rianorix's house destroyed and was either waylaid by Metellus's lookout men or wandered off somewhere else.

"He says you did some business at Deva," said Audax.

"Really?" He would tell the grooms he was on a mission from Metellus. It was almost true.

"Fat belly, Gallic accent, hair combed across the top of his head. Asked to be remembered to you. Name of—"

"I know what his name is," said Ruso, finally paying attention and recalling a man he had hoped never to have the misfortune to meet again. He knew, now, who was selling Doctor Ruso's Love Potion.

"He did open his eyes for a moment," said Valens, leaning back in Ruso's chair, which he had now moved into the isolation ward, and folding his arms. "Tried to say something, but I couldn't catch it."

Ruso slid his fingers under Albanus's thin wrist and felt for a pulse. "Gambax hasn't been in here, has he?"

"No, and if he had I'd have shooed him out like the madman you seem to think he is. Audax was in again just now, though. He's decided we're all incompetent and we can't manage without him. He said he was bringing somebody else."

Albanus's breathing was shallow and his pulse disconcertingly weak. "Who?"

"Another doctor, I think."

"Not Scribonius?"

"He's dead, Ruso."

"I know," said Ruso. "Years ago. But his reputation isn't." He held out the bottle of tonic. I had a quick taste. I think it's just dates in hydromel with garlic."

Valens pulled out the stopper and sniffed the liquid. "Smells disgusting. Are you thinking of inflicting it on Albanus?"

"Only if we run out of better ideas."

"Fair enough." Valens put the bottle on the table by the bed and stood up. "Since you're back, I'll nip off and hunt down some lunch."

Ruso withdrew his hand from the pulse. "You carry on enjoying my chair. I'll tell the cook to bring you something."

Valens looked pained. "I'm not a *patient*, Ruso. I don't want anything that's good for me. I want something *nice*. Washed down with something drinkable."

Ruso headed for the door. "I promise I'll bring something back for you."

"Back from where? You're not going out again and leaving me here, are you?" Valens frowned. "Holy Hercules, I sound like somebody's wife."

"Where else are you going to go, anyway?" demanded Ruso. "Over to hang around at Susanna's, or back to sit around the bathhouse and chat with Catavignus?"

Valens shuddered. "Not there. It'll be bad enough at this dreadful dinner tonight. I swear the minute he met me, that man was sizing me up as a suitable prospect for his daughter. I've already been offered the taster's tour of the brewery with the purpose-built malt house and had to listen to his eulogy to the kindness of the army plumbers who popped in his free extension pipe from the bathhouse. They do seem to be awfully fond of their beer around here. All of which makes the brewery a wondrous prospect for a business partnership, apparently."

"You don't know anything about business," said Ruso, recalling that his own approach from Catavignus had included some tale about having invested in the plumbing himself. "And I've got to go out. I'll see you later."

"I don't know anything about beer either," agreed Valens. "But that doesn't seem to worry him. I seem to be fated to be pursued by fathers."

"Why don't you tell him all about the Second Spear?" suggested Ruso. "That should put him off."

Valens frowned. "I thought I might expect a little sympathy from my closest friend," he complained. "A little brotherly understanding. A little—"

"A little piece of advice," said Ruso. "Stay away from women." He glanced around the lime-washed walls of the isolation room. "You should be safe in here while I go and track down Tilla."

72

RUSO URGED THE horse on up the road they had taken on the day of the hunt, speeding past a cluster of native houses where a couple of men were stacking piles of wood in preparation for tonight. While he and Valens made polite conversation with Tilla's family and the guild of caterers, the less civilized locals would be up here celebrating the arrival of summer in their traditional manner: gathering together to burn things.

Apart from the obvious disadvantage of having to mingle in the dark with people who might want to chop his head off, Ruso could not help feeling that if one were compelled to attend a social event, a bonfire—even one with British food and interminable British ancestor tales—would be a lot more fun than being trapped around a dining table with a bunch of foreign cooks and businessmen offering investment plans. One would hardly even need to dress up. The serious business of the native event, as Tilla had explained to him during a particularly boring stage of the journey north, was over very quickly. Something to do with purifying one's cattle by driving them between two fires. Presumably there must be some arrangement for keeping celebrants and livestock separate. Or some ancient saying promising that He Who Sits in a Cowpat Is Twice Blessed, or something.

By the time he swung off the main road, the sun was low in the sky. There was still no sign of Tilla. He was beginning to realize that this lone sortie had not been one of his better ideas. He wished he had at least worn his sword, but he had entertained some vague and ridiculous hope of being mistaken for a civilian. He spurred the sweating horse on, overtaking a couple of native families who he trusted would not attack him in front of their small children. He hoped he was not too late to catch up with Tilla, and not for her sake only. He did not want to be riding across these remote hillsides on his own after sunset. The tale that he was conducting a search for a local girl in order to take her to safety was scant protection at best, but at least in daylight he could hope to see any assailants before they struck, and try to dissuade them from murdering him. After dark, he would not see them coming.

It was a surprise to find yet more natives ahead of him, but there was nothing he could do now except hurry past them. To his relief they edged a white-haired grandfather out of the middle of the path when they heard the hoofbeats approaching, and in return he tried not to let the horse splatter them with mud as he cantered past.

The path wound around a wooded bank and opened out above the valley he remembered from the hunt. On his left was the high marshy ground. Ahead were the abandoned foundation trenches and the ramshackle round house, but instead of containing a woman and a dog, the place was crowded with natives. Dozens of them. Many had turned to watch his approach. They were reaching for weapons.

Ruso reined the horse in and glanced around. The families he had passed on the road had been reinforced by men carrying staves and clubs.

Ahead of him, the gate was open. At the top of the yard a barking hound seemed to be trying to strangle itself by leaping forward and being jerked back by the limits of its chain. Beyond its range, natives without weapons were clutching jugs and bowls and armfuls of wood and piles of dried bracken. The smell of roasting meat drifted past the gate.

There was no way to run from this. He would have to hope that Tilla was here and would help him talk his way out of it. And that none of these people had seen him in yesterday's hunting party.

He swung down from the horse and led it in through the entrance. Two men carrying heavy sticks approached him. "I've come to fetch Darlughdacha," he shouted over the sound of the dog, hoping he'd got the name right and they understood Latin.

"What do you want with her?"

Other men appeared, surrounding him. A couple were eyeing his horse. A man with a bent nose nudged his companion and nodded toward the frantic dog, raising his hand to his throat and making a slashing motion. His companion nodded. The man with the bent nose strode away.

Ruso said, "Her family have sent a message."

"What is this message?"

"Hurry up and come with me or she'll be late for dinner."

Some of the men chuckled. Behind them, he could see a woman asking a companion what he had said. Farther up the yard the dog yelped and fell silent.

A figure emerged from beneath the dilapidated porch of the house. As it approached Ruso could see that the black eye was fading to yellow. The lip was healing.

"She has nothing to say to you," said Rianorix. As he added, "You are not welcome here," Tilla came out of the house and walked down to stand beside him, still wearing the dress that matched her eyes.

Ruso made an effort to keep his voice calm. "I don't believe you killed the soldier," he said to Rianorix. "If it's any consolation, Aemilia says she didn't mean any of it to happen. Now if you value either of the girls as much as you say you do, you'll let Tilla come back with me and go to her uncle's dinner."

"I have always said that I did not kill the soldier. And I know what Aemilia meant. But now your men have put that soldier's head in a sack outside my house because they want to execute a native man and not their own officer."

"I think someone else did that," said Ruso. He wanted to say "Gambax did that," but found he could not. On reflection, it did seem very unlikely that anybody would murder someone over a few amphorae of wine. "In the meantime," he continued on safer ground, "Thessalus is doing his best to save your miserable ungrateful skin in the hope that you'll manage to do something sensible for once and look after your sister. Frankly I think the poppy's addled his brain. But if that's what he wants, I'll help him. I don't like you, and I don't think you deserve help, but I seem to be on your side."

Rianorix put his arm around Tilla and gave a lopsided smile. "Look around you, soldier. It is too late. The gods have woken. The people are gathering. We don't need your help."

Ruso glanced around at the armed men, the women bustling about with jugs and bowls, the youths discussing the horses tethered under the trees, and the throng of children chasing one another around the pasture.

He looked at Tilla, standing with the native in the place where they had been brought up together. Playmates. Friends. Lovers. A shared history into which he, who had only known her a matter of months, was struggling to intrude. He said, "I'm surprised to see you letting a man speak for you, Tilla."

She laid a hand on Rianorix's shoulder and then stepped away from him. "I will escort you down the path," she said. "You should not have come here."

She said something to the other men in her own language. They dropped back, but he heard their footfalls behind him as she led him back toward the gate.

"You shouldn't be here," he urged her.

"These are my people. This is my uncle's land. The house that was on my land is burned again. By you, this time."

"Stay away from him, Tilla."

"This is my home."

"This is an illegal gathering. There are far too many people and there's nobody here to supervise it. Metellus is bound to have informers here. Don't get involved."

"Is a feast and a bonfire," she said. "This is what we do. We do not need the army's help to welcome summer."

"Come back with me now, before it's too late. You can put on one of Aemilia's fancy outfits and we'll go to the caterer's dinner together. If you really want, I could think about getting married."

He could hardly believe he had said it. Perhaps he hadn't. Tilla did not seem to have noticed. All she said was, "I will not dine with that man."

"Trenus won't be there. I've found him and I've spoken to him. He won't come near you."

"I am talking about my uncle."

"Oh, for goodness' sake! Does it matter what you think of your uncle? Come back with me now before you get yourself onto one of Metellus's security lists."

"I was listening outside the window when Trenus was visiting the brewery. My uncle is shouting, 'You were supposed to deal with her.'"

"With who?"

"Me. Trenus is supposed to get rid of me in the raid. With my family all dead, there is nobody to argue with my uncle. Nobody to cause trouble."

"Tilla, that's . . ." Ruso stopped. It was not preposterous. It made perfect sense of something Trenus had said.

"And then my uncle opened the door and saw me, and he knew I had heard."

"Trenus told me you were supposed to have gone up in smoke with the rest of them," he said. "Are you saying your uncle deliberately set the raid up?"

"Now you see why I will not come back."

"He did that to his own brother?"

"Yes. That is why he came too late to help. Why he never sent for me."

Ruso scratched one ear. He had seen Catavignus as ambitious rather than ruthless, but if he were really prepared to sacrifice his own family . . .

He rubbed a hand across his eyes. He had been a fool. It was obvious. There was Felix's unsuitable courtship of Aemilia. The missing list of debtors. Catavignus's desire to get rid of rebel sympathizers. "I have to get back," he said. "I have to talk to—"

His mind formed the word *Susanna,* but before it reached his lips, something crashed against the back of his skull and the ground rose up to meet him.

73

THERE WAS A squeak and a grinding, and the pig carcass over the fire began to turn.

"And then when she had taken a drink from the cup she handed it to her bridegroom, and—" The old man who was telling the story stopped and scowled at the boy clutching the handle of the spit. The carcass rolled back into its former position, rocking violently with its truncated legs splayed in the air. Dripping fat crackled and hissed into the embers, which flared in the fading light.

"And the bridegroom drank from the cup too. And she laughed when she saw that he had drunk all of the poison, and she said, 'This is my vengeance for the wrong you did me!' Then she died and went to rejoin her true husband, and the bridegroom died there too, in front of all the guests, and instead of holding a wedding feast they held . . ."

"A funeral!" shouted several voices.

"A funeral," agreed the old man solemnly.

This dismal tale of justice and revenge was a familiar favorite, and there were murmurs of appreciation and a few cheers from the old man's supporters among the crowd gathered around the fires. Someone else stepped up to sing a song.

Tilla glanced over her shoulder toward the house. The moon was clear

now but her eyes were still dazzled by the bright flames and it was difficult to make sense of the silver and black world beyond them. She
thought she could make out the shapes of the guards standing by the sagging porch. She wondered how the medicus was feeling. Alone in the
dark house, listening to the crowd outside filling up with beer and
bravado, he would be afraid.

She did not expect them to do anything serious to him—she had already told them he was a good man and probably not a spy—but then,
she had not expected them to take him prisoner either.

"There was no need for that!' she had pointed out as the men were
dragging him toward the house. "He was leaving anyway."

They said he had seen too much.

"Now the soldiers will come looking for him."

They had looked at one another, then back at her. "Do they know
where he is?"

She said, "I cannot tell you what the soldiers know."

"Why did he come here?"

"Perhaps you should have asked him before you hit him on the head."

They told her that she had not changed while she had been away. It
was not meant as a compliment.

"My da would never have attacked a harmless soldier like that."

"Your da was an old man," they had said, flinging the struggling
medicus face-first onto the ground and twisting a rope around his wrists.
"We're running things now."

74

TILLA MADE HER way down to the trees where the horses were tethered. There were about a dozen animals in the line now. All were still saddled. Girths had been loosened and reins tied for safety, but it was clear that most of the riders were expecting to leave tonight. That was good. The black horse with one white sock that the medicus had brought was in the middle of the line, stretching its neck down to tuck into the long grass. Sizing up the other animals, she settled on a neat-looking dark bay that seemed to have no distinguishing features. That would do nicely for herself. It looked like an intelligent horse. It looked like a fast, fit, well-kept horse. It looked like . . .

She moved toward the animal. "Cloud?" she murmured. The mare reached down to nuzzle her hand, looking for a titbit she could not offer. Tilla moved along the horse's flank, sliding one hand down the inside of the front leg and feeling the smooth weight of the hoof in her hand as the animal obediently lifted the leg. With her other hand she brushed at the dried mud coating the long coarse hairs. There, just visible in the stark light, was the little patch of white.

She was turning to leave when a voice said, "Hey!" A skinny figure was lugging two buckets of water from behind the lines. "No touching the horses, all right?"

"She is a fine animal," said Tilla. "Is she yours?"

"My master's," said the youth, placing a bucket in front of the mare.

"You keep her well."

The youth lowered his head and mumbled something, clearly flattered.

"Who is your master?"

"I'm not allowed to say."

"I am looking for a good horse like this. Do you know where he bought her?"

"My master don't buy horses," said the youth proudly. "People give them to him."

"And who gave him this one?"

The certainty faded. "I'm not allowed to say nothing. Not unless he says I can."

Tilla smiled. "You are very loyal," she assured him. "That was the right answer. But if your master gives you permission, tell him the person who wants to know is the daughter of Lugh, whose family used to live on this land."

"I have come to check on the prisoner," announced Tilla, handing the heavy jug of mead to one of the guards outside the house.

As he said, "Nobody's allowed in," his companion emerged from the black shadow of the porch, lifted his club, and slapped it slowly against the palm of his hand as if he were testing its weight.

"I need to check his injuries," she explained. "We don't want him to die."

"He's not badly hurt," said the guard. "He was putting up a good fight when we gagged him."

"He is a good man," urged Tilla, raising her voice in the hope that the medicus might take some reassurance from it even if he did not understand the words. "He gives people medicines. Let me see him for a moment."

"We don't need foreign medicines. We have our own."

She slid up her right sleeve. Her skin gleamed white in the moonlight. The scar was a faint dark streak. "I was near death and he saved me. My arm was broken and he mended it."

"And from what we hear, you've paid him back," said the guard.

"Is it honorable to treat a healer in this way?"

The guard shrugged. "Don't ask us what's honorable. We've got our orders." He took a sip of the mead, then crouched and balanced the jug on the ground next to the wall. "Not bad. Thanks. We'll enjoy that later. Bring us some food when you start serving it, will you?"

75

A SECOND STORYTELLER, a much younger man, emerged from between the fires. He lifted the hood of his cloak to survey an audience whose lips and fingers glistened with pig fat and who rested against one another with the relaxation of a people well fed and alcoholically watered.

The young storyteller leaned forward. *"Long ago . . ."* His voice was just quiet enough to ensure that everyone kept silent, *"There was a time before memory. There was a time when the gods walked on the earth. And the people . . ."* he paused for dramatic effect. *"The people lived in peace and prosperity."*

"Ah!" came the response from one or two voices at the back of the crowd, as if he had reminded them of something delightful whose existence they had forgotten about. As the man recounted the lost wonders of the past, Tilla craned forward to get a closer look. She felt Rianorix's breath against her ear as he whispered, "We could move closer."

She shook her head. The moonlight was as stark as lightning. She did not need to be closer to know that she had seen this man before. "What's his name?"

"They just call him the Messenger."

"Do you know him?"

"Sh!" came a voice from behind, the meaning emphasized by a poke in the back.

"And all was very well," continued the man, *"until into this land there came . . . ,"* He crouched and glared at a child in the front row, *"the Gray Wolf!"*

"The Gray Wolf!" repeated the crowd. There was hissing. The child began to cry.

When the noise died down the man continued, *"The Wolf was greedy. The people knew he had stolen the crops from the south, killed the animals, and burned down the houses, and many warriors had died trying to resist him.*

"So when they heard the Wolf was coming they made offerings to the gods and sharpened their weapons and mounted their best horses and stood on the north bank of the sacred river, fierce and proud. Then the Wolf opened his mouth and showed his sharp teeth and his slavering tongue, and the children trembled and the men drew their swords and the women raised their spears . . . but the Wolf did not attack. The Wolf summoned his servants.

"On that soft grass south of the river, the servants laid out a banquet. There were fine wines and flowing honey, roasted meats and warm spices from the East, all laid out in golden bowls with silver spoons. The people saw the feast and wondered at it, but the men kept hold of their swords, and the women kept hold of their spears.

"When the meal was served the Wolf licked his lips with his slavering tongue, and he smiled and showed his sharp teeth, and he said, 'Come across and dine!' "

"Don't do it!" yelled a voice from the back of the crowd.

The storyteller bent to address someone at the front. "Would you dine with a wolf?"

The reply was inaudible.

He moved along. "Would you?"

"No!" came a child's voice.

"Not even for fine wines and warm spices and flowing honey?"

"Yuck!" responded the child. There was laughter.

"Good boy." The storyteller nodded and resumed. *"But the people of old were not as wise as this child. They smelled the wine and the spices, they saw the golden bowls and the silver spoons, and they lowered their swords and their spears and asked one another, "What does this mean?"*

The man went on to describe the arguments between people who wanted to trust the wolf and people who did not. Tilla breathed into Rianorix's ear, "Have you heard this story before?"

"No."

"Neither have I. He said it was an old story of our people."

"So? He's a storyteller. They tell lies for a living."

"Shh!" came a voice from behind.

"The wolf, seeing the people were divided, said, 'Why not put me to the test? Why not come across and try a little of the wine, have a taste of the roasted meat, a sniff of the spices? See for yourselves that I come in friendship. Look, I and my servants will stand back while you eat.'

"Some of the people began to move forward. Others seized hold of them and tried to stop them, saying the Wolf was not to be trusted. But the trusting ones said, 'The Wolf offers hospitality. It is rude to refuse.' So they made their way across the stepping-stones and ate and drank. And the Wolf stood back and did nothing. And when the trusting ones had eaten and drank, they turned to the others and said. 'See? There is nothing to fear. Come across and dine with the Wolf.' "

"Would you dine with a wolf?"

"No!" said a child's voice.

The man nodded. "Good girl. *But the people of old were not as wise as this child. The ones who had held back looked across at their companions eating and drinking and said, 'The feast is safe. The Wolf is a friend.' And they began to sheathe their swords and put down their spears and walk over the stepping-stones toward the banquet. Only one boy looked across at the Wolf and saw the sharp teeth and the slavering tongue and said, 'We have everything we need on this side of the river. We should stay away from the Wolf's fine food and his soft words.' But no one heeded the boy except an ugly old woman, who was too lame to cross the stepping-stones.*

"So all the rest of the people crossed over the river and sat down to dine. And when they had sat down, the Wolf secretly called up all the wild dogs, and the wild dogs leaped on the men and tore them to pieces!"

There were cries of "Traitor!" and "Shame!"

"Then the Wolf's servants rounded up all the women and children and made them into slaves!" More hisses and protests rose into the night air.

Tilla had to concede that he did it well. If she had not recognized him, she would have been impressed. As it was, she was wondering what he was up to, and what she should do about it. This was not a traditional story. This was a very dangerous story. He had not even bothered to conceal the meaning in a riddle. Everyone had seen the soldiers who carried the image of the emperor wearing a wolf pelt instead of a crest on their helmets. It was a foolish story to be telling when nobody really knew—even among an invited gathering like this—who could keep a secret and who was a spy. And what if the children talked?

"Then the Wolf and his wild dogs came across the river and plundered all the fruits of the land, stealing all the treasure and burning the houses, while the boy and the old woman fled to a cave high in the hills. And in that cave the old woman grew older and uglier, while the boy grew into a man."

Predictably, the young man wanted a wife. Equally predictably, the old woman pointed out that there was no one to be had except herself, and the young man was not impressed. While Tilla was wondering what the old women in the audience would make of that, the young man went in search of the Wolf and shouted across the river,

" 'How much will it take to buy back one of my people?' "

"The Wolf thought for a moment, and said, 'Bring me all the silver in the land. Then I will give you a woman your own age for a wife.'

"Then the young man went away very sad, because he knew there was no silver in the land. The Wolf had already stolen it.

"When the old woman saw that the young man was sad, she asked him why. He told her, 'Because there is no silver in the land to buy a wife.'

"The old woman shook her head, and said, 'Never bargain with a wolf. Take me as a wife.'

"The young man wrinkled his nose. 'You are old and ugly,' he said. 'I want a wife of my own age.'

" 'And do you trust the Wolf?' asked the old woman.

" 'I do,' the young man said. 'But I have no silver.'

"The old woman replied, 'You are a fool. But if you give me one kiss, I will tell you where to find the silver.'

"The young man looked at the woman's old, gnarled face and thought he could not bear for his lips to touch such skin. But then he thought it was not such a bad price to pay for a wife, so he took a deep breath, closed his eyes, and kissed the old woman on the cheek.

"And she said, 'You must go out in a boat at midnight at the next full moon and harvest all the silver from the waters. Take that to the Wolf. See if he will give you a wife.'

"So the young man went out and harvested all the silver of the moon and the nighttime grew black all across the land. Then he went to the river where he saw a beautiful young girl tied to a tree across the water, and he sent the silver across on a raft to the Wolf.

" 'Now release me that girl for a wife,' said the young man. The Wolf counted the silver. He shook his head. It was not enough.

" 'But that is all the silver in the land!' cried the young man. The Wolf smiled, *showing his sharp teeth and his slavering tongue. 'Bring me the gold, then,' he said."*

Tilla pressed closer to Rianorix and whispered, "The gold will be the sun. I need to go to the bushes. Too much beer."

The guards were still standing outside the house. The mead jug was still propped up in the same position by the wall.

"How is the prisoner?"

"Sh. We want to hear the story."

"The story is not true," she retorted. "He is just making it up."

"So? It's good."

"Let me see the soldier. I can find out if there are others coming."

"It's no good asking us." The guard pointed his club in the direction of the storyteller. "You'll have to talk to him."

76

*T*HEN WHAT MORE *can I give you? There is nothing else! You
promised!'*

*"The Wolf's laughter rang across the water. 'If you want her, you must come
across and get her yourself.'*

*"The young man knew the Wolf could not be trusted, but he must have a wife.
A wife of his own age. He could hear the girl calling to him. Just as he was about
to step forward onto the first stone he heard a movement behind him and smelled
the smell of wild dog and he knew in a flash that this was a trick: The Wolf had
him surrounded. So he leaped aside and drew his sword, and thrusting it this way
and that into hot bodies that grunted and snarled at him in the blackness, he
made his way back up the bank and fled to safety."*

"You were right," murmured Rianorix in her ear. "It was the sun. And
he had to kiss the old woman on the lips."

*"The old woman sat beside the fire, waiting. 'Well?' she said. 'The land is
dark by night and dark by day. The crops have died and birds are silent. You have
no wife your own age, and the rest of our people are still held prisoner. A fine deal
you have done with the Wolf.'*

"Do not nag me, woman,' replied the young man. 'You are not my wife.'

*"Then the old woman took him by the arm and led him to her bed, saying, 'I
am not your wife. But I am all you have.'*

"*Then the young man cursed the old woman. And when he had finished cursing the old woman he lay on the bed and wept, and when he had finished weeping he lay on the bed and thought, and when he had finished thinking he took the old woman in his arms and took her for his wife.*

"*When he awoke it was still black as night, for the land was dark by night and dark by day. But standing above the bed, shimmering in the firelight, was the tallest, the most beautiful, the most terrifying woman he had ever seen. On her head was a golden helmet. Her hair flowed down to her waist, and her cloak was fastened by silver brooches with precious stones set in them. In her hand was a flaming spear. And the woman hurled the spear into his pillow and cried, 'Awake at last, son of Brigantia!'*

"*The young man did not dare ask who she was. He looked around for the old woman. There was no sign of her.*

"'*Long have I waited,' said the shining woman, 'and with much patience.'*

"*The young man trembled, and did not know what to say.*

"'*Long have I waited, and with much patience, listening to the cries of my people in slavery, watching the Wolf steal the goodness from the land, watching while you plunge the earth into darkness with your foolish bargains!'*

"*The young man knelt at her feet, but the woman said, 'Do not grovel. Sons of Brigantia should not grovel.'*

"*So the young man stood, and followed the woman out of the cave as he was ordered. And outside were two magnificent horses, a white one for her and a black one for him. Before they mounted, the woman turned to him and said, 'Son of Brigantia, will you save your people?'*

"*The young man said, 'I will.'*

"'*Will you fight for them and for their freedom against the Gray Wolf and all his armies?'*

"*The young man looked into the woman's eyes and he knew that by her side, he would never be afraid. He said, 'I will.'*"

The storyteller suddenly bent and glared at a young child in the audience. "Son of Brigantia, will you save your people?"

The child said something.

"Louder," urged the storyteller.

"Yes!" came the reply.

The storyteller turned to the child's companion. "Will you?"

"Yes!"

There was a cheer.

The storyteller rose to his full height. "Sons and daughters of Brigantia, will you save your people?"

The crowd cheered louder, shouting, "Yes!" and "We will!" From some-where a chant began to spread, "Death to the Wolf! Death to the Wolf! Death to the Wolf!" until Tilla felt herself swaying in time to the words and the air around them was alive with the roar, "Death to the Wolf! Death to the Wolf!"

Suddenly the chant died away as if the storyteller had given a signal. A lone voice cried, "Death to—" and faded amid the derision of his companions.

"Children of Brigantia!" The storyteller's voice dropped to a whisper. "It is no easy thing to kill a wolf. For a wolf is cunning."

There were murmurs of agreement.

"And a wolf is strong."

More murmurs of agreement.

"And a wolf is brave."

"But we're braver!" shouted a voice from the back. There were yells of support.

"Yes." For the first time that evening, the storyteller smiled. "*So it was with the young man. Once he had turned to the wise old woman, he found the courage of his ancestors, and he rode down to the river and fought with the strength of fifty men. The people who were held captive rose up with him and there was a terrible battle. The Wolf, seeing what was happening, disguised him-self as a dog and fled. At last every one of the Wolf's followers lay on the ground with his head hacked from his body. Then the young man and the people marched back over the river carrying the gold of the sun and the silver of the moon, and the crops grew again and the birds sang and the people prospered in the land.* But remember this, my children . . ."

The storyteller paused, surveyed his audience, and continued softly, "The Wolf is still out there, waiting. Waiting with his soft words and fine promises." He paused again, then raised his voice. "Would you be de-ceived by a wolf?"

"No!" was the unanimous shout.

"Would you bargain with a wolf?"

"No!"

"What would you do with a wolf?"

"Take his head!" roared a voice from the back of the crowd.

"Take his head!" yelled the crowd, stamping and clapping and swaying in time to the words. "Take his head! Take his head!"

As the chant rose to a crescendo, Tilla gasped. Figures were leaping out from between the fires. Wild, naked men with painted bodies and spiked hair pranced in front of the crowd, brandishing shields and flaming torches. A man on horseback was moving among them: the storyteller, now with antlers sprouting from his head. Then another figure emerged into the light. Not dancing. Stumbling. Dragged forward, his hands roped together, his face pale and wide-eyed with terror.

"Take his head, take his head!"

It was the medicus.

"No!" shrieked Tilla, springing to her feet and scrambling toward the fires, tripping over legs and cloaks and children. "No, he is a good man!"

Behind her she could hear Rianorix shouting, "Leave him alone!"

"Take his head!" howled the crowd.

As she reached the front, she was seized and dragged aside. As soon as she hit the ground, a body landed on top of her. She struggled to get up, but her captor was sitting on her, crushing her so she could hardly breathe. She tried to kick at him, but he seemed not to notice. Seconds later someone else landed beside her. Over the chant she was conscious of a flurry of grunts and punches and gasps, and then beyond all of them a new rhythm. A harsh, relentless rapping of swords on shields. Getting closer. The chant of death giving way to shouts of "Soldiers!" and suddenly she could breathe again.

All around her was running and confusion, feet trampling over her, the blare of army trumpets, screaming as people fell into the fires, and the roar as the soldiers charged into the stampeding crowd.

77

IT'S ALL RIGHT, Ruso! It's me."

The words finally penetrated the terror. Ruso stopped struggling and lay still while Postumus ripped off the gag. He spat the vile taste out of his mouth and forced himself not to tremble while the centurion's knife tackled the ropes around his swollen wrists. He shook his hands free and placed a clumsy fist on Postumus's arm, muttering, "Thank you!" as he struggled to his feet. "I can't tell you how glad I am to see you." He tried an experimental step and found to his relief that he was still able to walk. "They were going to tear me apart."

"I told you I wanted to get my hands on that bastard," said Postumus.

"Did we get him?"

"Dunno."

A familiar figure emerged from the shadows and stood with his back to the fires, surveying the chaos.

"What's Metellus doing here?"

"It's his operation," said Postumus, sheathing his knife. "I just brought a few of our lads over as backup. And you should be bloody glad I did, because if we hadn't gone in just now he would've left you there for the chop while his men crawled about getting into position."

Ruso looked up from massaging his wrists. "You overruled Metellus?"

"Let's just say I must have misunderstood his signal in the dark."

Later, his painful joints shifting with the motion of the borrowed horse that was carrying him back toward the town, Ruso was joined by a second rider. The man's face was shadowed by the rim of his helmet, but the words, "What the hell were you doing out here on your own?" identified Metellus.

"Looking for Tilla," said Ruso, glad to have a chance to explain. "Have you seen her?"

Metellus jerked a thumb back over his shoulder. "With the other prisoners."

"I was trying to help her. I thought I'd be safe."

"You should know by now. You can't trust them."

"I know," said Ruso, glancing at the ghostly shapes of the moonlit cavalry escort ahead and checking that the soldiers and shuffling prisoners were too far back to overhear. "Listen. I've had some more thoughts about Felix."

"Don't start that again, Ruso. You've caused enough trouble for one night. If we hadn't had to charge in and rescue you before we were ready, we'd have caught the whole lot of them. Including the Stag Man."

"We didn't get him?" Ruso was incredulous.

"We saved you instead."

"Oh. That was very decent of you."

"Doing so was quite frankly neither the easy thing nor the right thing."

"No," Ruso agreed, wanting to add, *Which is why you didn't give the order to do it, you lying bastard.* Instead he said, "I understand there was some confusion about the orders."

"You're supposed to say, 'You should have left me and captured the Stag Man,' " said Metellus.

Ruso wondered whether anyone would stop him if he leaned across and grabbed Metellus by the throat.

"There's been a development," said Metellus. "Your clerk has woken up and told us the last thing he can remember is taking a shortcut through an alley with Gambax."

"I knew it!" Poor Albanus, the victim of an attack that might have been avoided if only his officer had not asked for his help in snaring a man who had been stealing from the infirmary. "So, I was right after all."

"Apparently you were," agreed Metellus, and yawned.

Ruso yawned too, and glanced at the sky. There was no sign of dawn yet. Tonight, he would not notice the inadequacies of the bed, nor the presence of the barrel. Tonight, that little storeroom would be Nero's golden palace.

"You'll be happy to know," said Metellus, "that Gambax will be tried for the attempted murder of the clerk as soon as the governor can fit it into his schedule."

Ruso forced himself to sit up straight, ignore his aching muscles and aching head, and concentrate. "I wanted to talk to you about Gambax. I've changed my mind. He wouldn't have killed Felix over a squabble about where they were selling the wine."

"So you accept it was the native?"

"Not the native that you mean. It was Catavignus."

For a moment all he heard was the steady plod of hooves and boots and the sobbing of a child in the crowd behind them. Then a deep sigh came from Metellus's direction. It was followed by, "How hard did they hit you on the head, Ruso?"

"It all fits."

"That's what you said about Gambax."

"Listen," urged Ruso. "I've spent the evening lying on the floor in a stinking hut thinking about this, because it was the only way to take my mind off wondering what the natives were going to do to me. Catavignus fell out with Felix about a business deal, and he didn't want him to marry his daughter. He owed Felix money, probably to do with this house he's supposed to be building. He overheard the argument in the bar while he was delivering the beer, which he did in person because he's got designs on Susanna—"

"And you can prove this, can you?"

"We'll need to check that part with Susanna," said Ruso. "Felix went to visit Aemilia and give her a ring to shut her up, and Catavignus followed him from the house. They probably walked down the alley together, because Felix wouldn't have realized—"

"I'm sorry, Ruso. I don't have time for this. Catavignus is our strongest local supporter *and* our main beer supplier. You're the man who's just ruined a major security sweep and you work with a bunch of madmen, layabouts, and runaways. In addition to which . . ." Metellus steered his mount closer until Ruso felt the soft warmth of the horse's flank pressed against his knee, "How did the head get to where we found it? Our friendly local brewer would have to have been wandering around the countryside in the middle of the night carrying a severed head in a sack."

"Why not?" said Ruso. "He used to live up here. He'd know the way in the dark. He'd know how to get to that house without your guards seeing him. You can't prosecute Rianorix while there's a chance it could be him."

"We can prosecute whomever we want," said Metellus as they turned the horses left and up onto the main road. "And even if we didn't, we could always execute Rianorix for his part in tonight's escapade."

"He tried to save me tonight!" insisted Ruso, "He and Tilla were—"

"Did he? I saw him jump up out of the crowd and follow her. I'd say he was trying to stop her from intervening."

"But—"

"You were confused, Ruso. It was night. Your life was under threat. There was a crowd baying for your blood. You don't know what you saw."

Ruso rubbed the back of his aching head. "What will happen to the prisoners?"

"They'll all be questioned. Somebody must know where we can find the Stag Man. Then it'll be up to the governor. I expect he'll execute one in ten, or something. Nothing too drastic. After all, they didn't actually kill you."

"Tilla and Rianorix tried to help me tonight," insisted Ruso. "The man you want is Catavignus. You can't trust him. He's obsessed with furthering his business. He did a deal with Trenus to fix that cattle raid, and now he's killed one of your men. If you don't prosecute him now you'll regret it later."

"I'll regret it immediately if I accuse him with nothing to back it up."

"There must be evidence," insisted Ruso. "It's just a case of taking the trouble to find it."

"You seem very confident."

"I am," said Ruso, wishing he were telling the truth.

"Hurry up and find it by morning, then," replied Metellus. "But you'd better come up with something better than coincidence and supposition. Because if you upset our tame local without good cause just as the governor arrives, you'll be wishing I'd left you with the natives."

78

"GODS ABOVE, RUSO, look at you! Where have you been?"
Ruso surveyed the lamplit wreckage of spills and leftovers that was all that remained of the guild of caterers' dinner. A lank-haired woman in a dingy tunic bent down, peered at the floor, and retrieved a lone shoe from under a table. She turned it over, looked around for something to do with it, then placed it in the middle of the table and carried on piling dirty crockery onto her tray. "I went to look for Tilla," said Ruso. "I got delayed."

"Well, you might have sent a message!" Valens lowered his voice. "I've had a very difficult evening on my own."

"So have I."

"And you didn't even send Tilla."

"I know," said Ruso, who had last seen her being marched toward the fort with the other prisoners.

"My host offered me vast quantities of drink, far too much food, and a chance to form an alliance with the brewing trade. I was hoping for an emergency call, but everyone back at the infirmary is disappointingly healthy. Even Albanus let me down."

"Sounds better than the evening my hosts offered me," said Ruso. "I'd better go and apologize to Catavignus for not turning up."

Valens wrinkled his nose. "Not looking like that, I wouldn't. Where have you been, a farmyard? There's mud on your clothes, straw in your— is that blood?"

"Probably."

"And you smell of cows."

"I'll tell him I fell off my horse. Back me up, will you?"

Valens shrugged. "Why not? I can't think how else you'd end up like that."

Catavignus was splayed across a chair in the far corner of Susanna's kitchen. He seemed unaware of Ruso's arrival. "*And* another thing!" he announced, flinging one arm wide to illustrate the vastness of the additional thing he was about to reveal.

Susanna, clearing a space on the table for more dirty crockery, greeted Ruso and Valens with obvious relief.

"I have never, ever looked at another woman since I saw . . ." Catavignus's expression slowly rearranged itself into one of surprise. "Doctor! The food's all gone. We'll find you a drink." Raising one finger to indicate a pause, he leaned forward and narrowed his eyes. "You don't look well."

Catavignus was effusive in his sympathy when he heard about the fictitious riding accident. Ruso doubted he would remember it—or very much else—in the morning. Finally Ruso suggested that the two medics would walk Catavignus back to his house.

"I'm very busy," said Catavignus, indicating the kitchen with another expansive sweep of the arm. "Lots to be done. Clearing up."

"Oh, clearing up is for women and servants," said Ruso. "Come on, we'll walk back with you. You can show us around the brewery."

Catavignus nodded. "Good idea," he said. "Very good—oops. Can't get up. Very low chair."

As Ruso and Valens took an arm each and hauled him up and out of the kitchen, Susanna gave them the sort of smile Catavignus was probably hoping for and was never going to get.

Ruso had no particular plan when he extricated Catavignus from Susanna's kitchen and waved aside the servants who had offered to help. He merely hoped that, since the man was probably guilty and definitely drunk, some sort of admission might slip out. Had he been less tired himself, and in less of a state of nerves after his ordeal with the natives, he might have been able to devise an ingenious sequence of questions that would lead to a confession. As it was, he could only interrupt Catavignus's sentimental ramblings with a heavy-handed, "Just as well there's three of us. You know what happened to Felix."

"Felix!" exclaimed Catavignus, tripping over an invisible obstacle and sending the three of them lurching sideways into the empty street. "Dead."

"What exactly was it the natives did to him?" demanded Valens, steering back in the right direction and oblivious to Ruso glaring at him across the back of Catavignus's neck. "Nobody seems to know."

"Nobody knows," said Catavignus, shaking his head. "Nobody knows about Felix. Terrible."

"What do you think happened to him?" asked Ruso.

"From what I hear," chipped in Valens before the suspect had time to answer, "It was quite unpleasant—steady now. Right turn. Nearly there. Shall I knock?'

"When was the last time you saw him?" asked Ruso.

"Can't see anybody now," said Catavignus. "Very tired. Always tired after the guild of caterers' parties. It's all the organizing, you know."

The servant was unbolting the door. Running out of time, Ruso tried one last desperate move. "Catavignus," he said, twisting to look into the man's face and enunciating his words very clearly, "Did you kill Felix?"

Catavignus looked past him and smiled. "Aemilia!" he exclaimed. *"Ut vales, filia mea?"*

"Of course she heard, you idiot!" hissed Valens, pulling up the blankets over the now snoring Catavignus. "Why do you think she rushed off to her room? What on earth got into you to say something like that?"

"Because it's true," muttered Ruso miserably. It seemed a poor justification. Aemilia had already endured the loss of both her lover and her dignity. Now he had given her fresh cause for grief.

"Perhaps," suggested Valens softly, "you might do me the honor of joining me in our host's reception room to consume some of his wine and explain what on earth is going on."

"I'll tell you on the way back," said Ruso.

"Back to where?"

"The infirmary. They'll need some help treating the injured."

79

THERE WERE THIRTY-FOUR of them. Tilla knew that because she had heard the guards counting them as they were herded into the corner of the big courtyard where she had seen the men lined up to be identified.

The army did not seem impressed with their prisoners. They had captured mostly old people and mothers with young children: the ones who had not been able to run fast enough. The storyteller and the naked warriors had vanished into the night.

When the soldiers charged, Rianorix had grabbed her and tried to shield her. By the time they scrambled to their feet they found two Batavians with drawn swords standing guard over them. The soldiers had laughed—not kindly—when they recognized Rianorix.

She lifted her head. The moon was being assisted by smoky torches, and all around her the yellow light flickered over shapes huddled on the cold gravel, sharing whatever cloaks and blankets they had managed to keep hold of in an effort to keep warm.

The old man next to her heaved and coughed, the jerking of his head made visible in the darkness by the white stripe of bandage. When the doctors had been allowed in to treat the injured, she had feigned a sprained wrist, but the medicus was not there and Valens only had a chance to murmur, "Are you all right?" before assigning her to a bandager and turning his attention to the next person in the line.

She had wanted to talk to the medicus. To explain to him that these people did not deserve to be punished. They were ordinary families: farmers and weavers and carpenters gathered for a traditional celebration spiced with the excitement of secrecy—and, yes, with the camaraderie that came from sharing their complaints about the Romans. But the celebration had become something she could not have foreseen. Under the leadership of the Stag Man, or the Messenger, or whatever he called himself, these ordinary folk had taken the medicus prisoner, worked themselves up into a frenzy, and threatened to murder him. As the big soldier she remembered from the clinic looped a bandage around her thumb and back around her wrist, she tried to think what she could say in her people's defense. There was not a lot.

Within what seemed minutes of arriving, the medical staff had been ordered to leave. "We just want them alive enough to talk," one of the officers had explained to Valens.

"You know who they will want us to talk about," she whispered to Rianorix.

"They won't find out anything," Rianorix assured her. "Nobody knows where he comes from. He's very careful."

"But they all suffer for him."

"If we want freedom, sister, some of us will have to be prepared to suffer."

It sounded like a speech he had heard at a meeting. "But not him," said Tilla. "He is very careful."

They paused as a guard walked past. When he had gone Rianorix hissed, "He is our best hope. What is the matter with you?"

"There is nothing the matter with me!" she retorted in his ear, frustrated at the constrictions placed on the argument by the need not to be overheard. "You are the one who needs to open your eyes. I can see that he is bringing nothing but trouble."

"And what do your friends the Romans bring?"

She grabbed his wrist. "The Romans are not my—"

"No talking!" called out one of the guards. As one of the people translated the order for the benefit of those without Latin, he yelled again, "I said, no talking!"

Over in the corner, a baby began to cry. A small voice wailed, "I'm cold!"

There were several hisses of, "Sh!"

The old man began to cough again.

Thirty-four people. Children and mothers and grandparents.

He is our best hope.

Thirty-four people.

We just want them alive enough to talk.

"The Romans are not my friends," she breathed. "But I am not fool enough to follow everyone who opposes them."

"You are much changed, daughter of Lugh."

"And you are just as stupid as ever," she retorted.

"You there! Stand up!"

Tilla put a hand on Rianorix's shoulder to urge him to stay down. She gathered up her skirt and got to her feet.

"Come over here!"

She was aware of heads lifting, frightened eyes following her, bodies shuffling to let her pass as she picked her way across to where the guard stood. Before she was near enough to be hit, she stopped. "I would like to see the commanding officer," she announced in Latin, her voice clear in the silent courtyard. "I have some information to offer him."

80

I T WAS STILL dark when Ruso realized that he was awake. This realization was followed by the niggling sensation that there were things
he did not want to think about. But no matter how much he tried not to
disturb them, the worries had woken with him and were already yawning, stretching, and preparing to accompany him for the rest of the day.

Tilla: his girl, who had run away to Rianorix when she was in trouble and
was now held prisoner with other natives over at headquarters. The girl to
whom he had rashly offered marriage and who hadn't even noticed.

Thessalus: incurably sick and begging him to save the man who was
stealing Tilla away from him.

Aemilia: betrayed by her lover and now, if he succeeded today, about to
learn that she had been betrayed by her father as well.

Albanus: the clerk who was lying in bed with a fractured skull because
of the inquiries he had made at Ruso's request.

Catavignus: the murderer against whom there was no evidence.

Metellus: the schemer whose carefully planned security raid he had
ruined.

Then there was the carpenter he had failed to save. Even when Ruso
had been minding his own business, he hadn't succeeded in doing anything useful.

He curled down under the covers and put his hands over his ears, but the whisper accusing him of being a bungling fool still filled his head. He came up for air, turned over, and sighed. He opened his eyes and stared at the looming shape of the barrel, just visible in the gray that was creeping around the edges of the shutters. He could only have been in bed an hour or two at the most, having been delayed at the infirmary dealing with injuries that were more the result of men charging around by moonlight with drawn weapons than of any resistance from the fleeing natives.

How could anyone feel this tired and yet not sleep?

He rolled onto his back and tried to breathe slowly and deeply.

Did you kill Felix?

Of course she heard, you idiot.

He sat up, punched his pillow until it was fat and soft, then threw himself back down on it and tried to convince himself that things were not so bad. He must pull himself together. Make the effort to find something to look forward to.

Batavian hospital porridge for breakfast was not much of a reason for rejoicing. *It is officially summer* was no better. *You are getting out of this place soon* was no consolation when he added, *probably without Tilla.* The dearth of any other reasons for cheer left him feeling more depressed than ever.

He had no idea how much time had passed when he heard movement in the next room. It seemed that Valens, who had spent what was left of the night on a mattress shifted into the treatment room, was no longer sleeping. Ruso glanced at the barrel. He could make out the iron hoop around the base now. He pushed back the covers.

It was dawn, Valens was already awake, and anyway, this was important.

Valens wandered back from the latrine and grunted when he saw Ruso. "Do they need both of us?"

"It's not a call," explained Ruso, sitting on the end of Valens's mattress and wrapping his own blanket around his shoulders. It might be summer, but it was not warm.

"Good," replied Valens, climbing back under the covers and hauling ineffectively at the other end of the blanket Ruso was sitting on. "Uh, gedoff."

"It's morning."

"Go away."

"You're awake."

"No'm not."

"I need to talk to you."

"Me?"

"I know," said Ruso. "But there isn't anybody else."

"It is all a bit of a mess," agreed Valens. "You will keep getting involved in things, Ruso. Anybody'd think you didn't have enough to do."

"I was asked to take this on," pointed out Ruso. "Well, some of it, anyway."

"Still, look on the bright side. There's a nine in ten chance that Tilla won't be executed. Catavignus will probably forget what you said—"

"Aemilia won't."

"Well, if it's true, she'd have to find out sometime, wouldn't she? Best of all, the governor'll be here today with the new man to run the infirmary, so you can clear off and leave it all behind."

"But it's not sorted out."

"Never mind. You've done your best."

"What am I going to say to Thessalus when he finds out they're going to execute his brother-in-law?"

"You'll think of something." Valens yawned.

"Let's go over it step by step."

"Let's go to sleep."

"There'll be time for sleeping later. Listen. I'm not meant to tell anybody this, but I suppose it won't matter. Since you aren't really anybody anyway."

"Thanks."

"Officially, I mean. Officially you're not here. So listen. When Audax found Felix's body, somebody had cut his head off with his own knife."

"Oh dear. That's messy."

"Exactly. He was probably dead already by then, but even so, it would have been pretty messy. Rianorix could have just run off in the dark and gone home to clean himself up. But Catavignus—"

"Would have to change his clothes before going home in case he was seen," said Valens. "Obviously. Are you telling me you haven't thought of that before?"

"I only found out last night what a nasty piece of work he really is," pointed out Ruso. "And the next minute somebody threw a sack over my head and tied me up."

"I suppose that did make it difficult to get to dinner."

"So, what happened to Catavignus's bloodstained clothes?"

"Perhaps they went to the laundry."

"There's no laundry here."

"Really? What do they do, then?"

"I don't know. I just leave everything outside the door and it comes back clean a couple of days later."

Valens sighed. "No laundry, no forum, no amphitheater, no decent shops . . . you know, I'm beginning to think women have a point."

There was a clatter from the kitchen, followed by the screech of yesterday's ashes being raked off the hearth. Ruso tried not to remember the comfort that morning sound had once given him. He said, "Tilla would say ask the staff. I need to find a way of questioning Catavignus's housekeeper."

"Only if you think any of this is actually worth the bother," said Valens.

"How else can I prove that he's guilty?"

"Never mind that. For some bizarre reason, you want to prove Catavignus guilty to save Rianorix. Yes?"

"I want to prove him guilty because he did it. But yes, there are reasons why Rianorix has to be helped off the hook."

"But you already know they're planning to nail Rianorix up on another charge. Really, Ruso. You might have bothered to think all this through before you woke me up."

"I think we should both be trying to save a decent colleague from the disgrace of a false murder confession," pointed out Ruso. "And for whatever reason, Rianorix was trying to help me last night. Metellus can say what he likes. There were plenty of other witnesses." He got to his feet. "The trouble is, he's the one they'll believe. I need to talk to the prefect before Metellus gets to him."

"Not at this hour."

"He'll be awake," insisted Ruso. "He's having a visit from the governor today."

81

No ONE IN her family who had any honor had ever been inside the fort, and yet here she was again, this time standing in front of the desk of the commanding officer. She lifted her chin. She was not going to look submissive. Or nervous.

"I will tell you what I know," she announced, "if you promise to let the prisoners go."

The man reclined in his chair, looking faintly amused. "And what is it you know?"

"Not until you swear to let them go."

He said, "I will decide what your information is worth when I hear it."

She looked into the deepset blue eyes. This was a man whose people had been crushed by Rome and who now oppressed others on the emperor's behalf. How could he be trusted? On the other hand, what choice did she have? She said, "You must give me your word as the emperor's servant that if what I say is good, my people will go home."

"You have my word," he agreed, as if he still had some honor to lose.

"My name is Darlughdacha," she said. "Three winters past, in the time of year when the wheat was beginning to ripen, my home was raided by thieves under the command of Trenus of the Votadini. My family was killed, and I was taken as a slave. All our animals are stolen. One of the animals is a good bay mare, five winters old, dark all over with a few white hairs above the nearside front hoof."

She was interrupted by a quiet voice from behind. "Can I have a word, sir?"

She turned to see the snaky one standing behind the door. The prefect beckoned him forward. The snaky one hissed in his ear for a moment. The prefect nodded. The snaky one slithered back to his place.

"It seems you are better at recognizing horses than people," said the prefect. "I hear you failed to help us identify the man who caused the wagon accident. I also hear that your father and brothers were known troublemakers."

"Is that why you do not give justice when Trenus raids our land, burns our house, murders my family?"

"That took place under my predecessor," explained the prefect smoothly. "I'm sure he would have dealt appropriately with any complaint. Now, what is it you would like to tell us?"

Tilla clenched her fists. She must stay calm. She was here to save the living as well as avenge the dead. "I have seen that horse again last night," she said. "And then when I see the younger storyteller—the second one—I remember where I have seen him before too. Three times now. Once in the yard at the Golden Fleece inn. And once riding along the hillside when the accident happens. And before that at Trenus's house where he comes to share supper and accept the gift of the bay mare stolen from my family."

The prefect's eyes flicked across to the other man. "Metellus?"

"She's got a motive for discrediting Trenus, sir. And last time she was questioned she said nothing about seeing this man before."

"I do not lie," insisted Tilla, concentrating her gaze on the prefect and wishing the snaky one would stop interfering. "If you trust Trenus, you will be a very sorry officer. He is pretending to be your friend while he is supporting this man who stirs up my people against you."

Again the two men looked at each other.

"Do you know where we can find this storyteller with the horse?"

"No, sir. He is very careful. But Trenus must know someone who can tell you."

The prefect beckoned the snaky one to him again. There was another whispered conversation.

When they had finished she said, "Now can the people go?"

The snaky one stepped aside. The prefect sat looking at her, tapping a thumb on the edge of his desk. "Rome has no quarrel with the Vota-dini," he said. "Why would Trenus want to cause trouble here?"

"I only tell you what I know, my lord. I do not know what is in his mind."

The thumb tapped the desk again. Finally he said, "You were a slave to him for how long?"

"Two years, my lord."

"You know his people."

"Some of them."

"You could be very useful to us."

"But my lord—"

"Give us something definite on Trenus's connection with the Stag Man and we'll release your people. You have my word."

82

R USO AND THE nymph were watching the rising sun gilding the top tiles of the prefect's roof when two people emerged from his office.

"Tilla!"

She turned to look at Ruso as the guard hustled her along under the portico.

"Are you all right?"

"Eyes front!" snapped the guard, giving her a shove that made her stumble, and they were gone.

Moments later another familiar figure emerged. Metellus strode past the nymph and accosted him. "Your girlfriend," he said, "is nothing but trouble."

"What's she done now?"

"Amazing how taking hostages jogs their memories, isn't it? She's suddenly remembered where she saw Stag Man before."

"She's what? Let me talk to her!"

Metellus snorted. "If I were you, I'd stay well away. You don't want to be dragged down with her. Try thinking with your head for a change, Ruso."

Before Ruso's head could come up with a reply, the house steward approached.

"Prefect Decianus will see you now, sir," said the steward, his tone suggesting that if it were up to him, he would have told Ruso to come back sometime next year.

In the light of what Metellus had just said, Ruso wished he had.

"You were supposed to report back in time for Metellus to organize a prosecution case," said Decianus, lifting his arms while a crouching slave adjusted the folds of his tunic, "Instead of gallivanting over the hills getting yourself taken prisoner by barbarians."

"Sorry, sir."

"Are you injured?"

"Not really, sir."

"I hear your deputy's been arrested for trying to murder your clerk. You haven't exactly restored order in the infirmary, have you?"

"The clerk was investigating a fraud in the infirmary accounts, sir."

"What else have you got for me?"

What Ruso had had, until moments ago, was a plea for mercy on behalf of the undeserving Rianorix and an insistence that both he and the innocent Tilla had been trying to restrain the crowd last night.

Now it seemed that Tilla was not so innocent after all. And if she had been lying to him all along about knowing the Stag Man, perhaps she had lied about Rianorix. Perhaps he really had murdered Felix. On the other hand, Catavignus had a motive, and he had an opportunity, and . . . And Ruso was suffering from lack of sleep and a headache and he did not know what to say about any of this. He could not come up with any words until he had had a chance to unscramble Metellus's latest revelation.

"I'm told," prompted Decianus, "that you now think Catavignus the brewer carried out the murder. I take it we have evidence?"

"I was hoping to get something this morning, sir."

"You mean no?"

"Not yet, sir."

The slave finished tweaking and lifted the prefect's breastplate from the stand. Decianus motioned him to wait. "I've got the governor arriving in a matter of hours," he said. "I've still got one man who's confessed to a murder and another one who probably did it. You've had days to sort this out, and we're no farther ahead."

"You've got Rianorix in custody again, sir."

"We could have done that whenever we wanted. We'd have the Stag Man as well by now if it weren't for you."

"Yes, sir."

"So have you got anything useful to tell me?"

"The infirmary's been cleaned out and tidied up and is ready for the governor's inspection, sir."

"I heard you had to bring in reinforcements."

"A professional colleague volunteered, sir."

"So you didn't even manage that by yourself."

"No, sir." There was no point in arguing. "Sir, I need to ask you something."

Decianus sighed. "Go on."

"I was hoping you could release the girl Tilla—the one you just saw—to help me gather evidence this morning."

Decianus lowered his head and pinched the bridge of his nose between his thumb and forefinger. Looking up, he said, "Is this some sort of practical joke?"

"Sir?"

"Did she put you up to this?"

"No, sir."

"I suppose you'd like me to release the basket maker as well?"

"No, sir. We can do that if we find some evidence against Catavignus."

"Catavignus is on our side, Ruso, and it's time you learned to stand on your own feet instead of calling on colleagues and women to help you out. You've already told Metellus that your deputy did it. Next you'll be telling me it was you. I'm not surprised the legion thought they could spare you. You're as mad as the Greek and twice as useless. Now clear off, I've got more important things to do."

83

VALENS, WHO HAD evidently abandoned all hope of sleep, looked up from examining an ulcerated leg. "Successful visit?"

"Not exactly," said Ruso.

"Thessalus is asking for you."

"Tell him I'm trying to sort something out."

"He said to remind you the governor's due at midday."

"Not now he isn't," put in the owner of the leg.

"Really?" said Ruso, his hopes lifting.

"My mate just saw a dispatch rider who said he passed them about an hour ago out on the south road."

"Are you sure?"

"It's true, sir," put in the orderly. "Only it's less than an hour now because I heard it three patients ago."

"Miss Aemilia is at the baths, sir."

"No matter," said Ruso. "It's you I want to talk to. It's about laundry."

He followed Catavignus's housekeeper into the kitchen. He was rewarded with the sight of limp garments festooned across the back of the room. "We've got no space for any more," said Ness, surveying the drooping lines of twine. "There's a woman you could talk to down on the bridge road. We sometimes send out there when we've got too much."

"It's not for me," said Ruso, trying to ignore the feminine underwear draped across the nearest line and examining the tunics beyond for the vestiges of bloodstains. "I'm trying to find out something about the laundry here. Whether you've been asked to wash anything—unusual."

"Unusual?"

"Ah—unusually soiled. Or perhaps you've found something that somebody's had a go at washing by themselves. In the last few days."

The woman frowned.

"I wouldn't be troubling you with this if it weren't very important."

"I'll have to ask the master, sir."

"I'm asking you."

She folded her arms. "I couldn't answer questions about the household without the master's permission, sir. Or Miss Aemilia."

"I know," said Ruso. "Which normally would be admirable, but it's vital that you tell me right now."

"Shall I wake the master, sir?"

"No!"

The woman looked relieved.

"I've been given the prefect's authority," insisted Ruso, not adding that it had now been rescinded.

"I don't answer to the prefect about my laundry. If the master or Miss—"

"I'll find Aemilia."

As she followed him to the door the woman said, "Sorry not to help you, sir," and actually sounded as though she meant it.

The elderly bath attendant raised a hand to halt him in the doorway. "Sorry, sir. This is the women's session."

"I know," said Ruso, "It's a woman I'm after. Aemilia, daughter of Catavignus the brewer. Can somebody fetch her for me?"

The man looked around nervously. "Are you family, sir?"

"Yes," lied Ruso. "And it's urgent."

The man shook his head. "I don't think you are, sir. I—oh!"

Ruso had grabbed him by the arms and lifted him off the floor. "Sorry," he said, putting the man down again to one side, "but I really haven't got time to argue."

The female scream was a ghastly sound at the best of times, but when several of them did it together in a room with a bad echo, the effect was hideous. Ruso clapped his hands over his ears and shouted, "Has anyone seen Aemilia?" over the cacophony, but nobody seemed to be listening.

A glance around the hall revealed that he would have to go deeper into the female sanctuary that was the Coria bathhouse before the sounding of the midday bell.

The cold room was empty. It was in the warm room that the real trouble started.

"A man!"

"Get out!"

"Aemilia?" ventured Ruso with his head around the door, his gaze darting about wildly in an attempt not to settle on any undressed females except the one he needed to talk to.

"Go away!" shrieked a woman whose vast and dimpled thighs seemed to be keeping her anchored on the bench as she lunged at him with a towel.

"Could somebody please—"

"Help!"

"Help, a man!"

The crashing open of the cold room door behind him warned Ruso that the attendant had fetched reinforcements. He ignored the shrieks as he strode across to enter the hot room.

The heat and the additional screaming—they had obviously heard what was going on next door and got themselves ready—both hit him at the same time. They were followed by a splatter of hot water in the face, a hail of bathing equipment, and a flurry of buffeting towels.

"Out!" screamed his tormentors. "Out, out, out!"

"Where's Aemilia?" yelled Ruso, ducking to one side and trying to shield his head with his arms.

"Out!"

He finally retreated when they started to beat him over the head with their wooden bath shoes.

Back in the warm room he was seized by three bath attendants and a couple of scantily clad women. The bath attendants were apologetic and applied no more force than necessary. The woman weren't and didn't.

"I was told she was here," he insisted as they bundled him back through to the hall. "I didn't mean to—"

"Stop!" called a female voice. "Please, stop! Doctor, it's me!"

Ruso and his handlers paused. One of the women gave him a final kick to remind him not to do it again.

"I was having my hair washed," explained Aemilia, wrapping the towel tighter around her ample frame.

"I need your permission to talk to your housekeeper."

Aemilia pushed a strand of wet hair behind one ear. "I knew you would come sooner or later," she said sadly. "I'll get dressed. You can talk to me."

They were standing in the meadow behind the bathhouse, far enough away from the buildings for only the grazing horses to hear what they were saying. Aemilia's hair was lank and dark with damp, and her eyes looked hollow. He realized she was older than he had thought.

"I need to know what happened, Aemilia."

She lifted her skirts above the grass and began to walk slowly along the top of the meadow. "I have tried to believe that the doctor did it," she said, "Or the Stag Man. But I can't."

Ruso, in step beside her, said nothing.

When she said, "What will they do to him?" he knew she was talking about her father.

"Tell me what happened."

"I met Felix through Daddy. Felix was interested in investing some money in the brewery. Then he lent Daddy the money to start the new house and introduced him to the builder. But the builders had hardly got going when they raised the price. Daddy was cross and said if he'd been told the truth about how much it was all going to cost in the first place he would never have started."

This sounded horribly like the tale of Ruso's family shrine to Diana.

"Felix said Daddy should have asked the builder for proper figures right from the start."

It was exactly what Ruso and Lucius had said to each other when they found out the extent of the debt.

"Daddy told me to stay away from him, but by then I thought I was having a baby. I didn't dare tell Daddy. But Daddy was still being nice to him because Felix had a lot of business connections and he didn't want him to cause trouble in the guild. That's why I couldn't believe Daddy would do anything to hurt him."

"Did your father know that Felix had come to see you after he left the bar that night?"

"I have thought about this," she said. "I thought he was asleep in bed but he must have heard us."

"Did you hear your father leave the house after that?"

"No. But I woke up later to hear him banging on the door. Ness had locked up and gone to sleep, and he couldn't get in. I got up but she was already there. So I went back to bed."

"Did you see him come in?"

"No. It was dark. Ness was just carrying a small lamp. I heard her say something, and he told her not to make a fuss." Aemilia's fingers crept toward her mouth. "He said it was only a nosebleed and he was all right now."

"I see."

She hung her head. "When I first heard about Felix I was frightened that he might have done something terrible. Then I told myself I was being silly. He is my father! And then the doctor confessed and I thought I must be wrong." She turned away from him, gazing down across the meadow to where the horses were swishing their tails against the flies.

"Does your father often get nosebleeds?"

"No."

"Did he say where he went that night?"

"He told Ness he had been to check something at the brewery."

Ruso said, "Do the brewery staff sleep on the premises?"

"The foreman sleeps in the loft, but he's very deaf. Daddy has a key. He could go in there without anyone knowing."

So the story might have been true. He said, "Where's your father now?"

"When I left, he was ill in bed," she said. "He is usually ill after the caterers' dinners."

"Do you know what he was wearing that night?"

"There was no blood on his cloak," she said dully. "I looked. Under that, the tunic with the blue stripe that is lost in the wash." She paused. "Could he have taken his cloak off before he . . . ?"

"Yes," said Ruso. "Yes, he could." After he had stunned Felix, the brewer had been clear thinking enough to realize that the mutilation that would help to incriminate Rianorix was going to incriminate him too if he wasn't careful.

"We shall have to apologize to the washerwoman," she said. "The tunic never went there, did it?"

"What do you think he might have done with it?"

She shrugged. "Anything."

"Was it the sort of thing lots of people wear? Or could it be identified as his?"

"It was an old one," she said. "But it was expensive. He bought it from a trader from Londinium. It was a very fine weave."

"He won't have dumped it where someone might find it, then," said Ruso, glancing down toward the river and hoping it was not wrapped around a lump of stone lying on the bottom.

"Ness has already searched the house for it," said Aemilia. "She couldn't remember sending it to the washerwoman, but I think she didn't know who else to blame."

"Tell her to search again," said Ruso. "And this time we'll help her."

84

RUSO KNELT BESIDE the blackened slabs of the firing hole by Catavignus's malting floor. They had already caused a disruption inside the brewery and scrabbled fruitlessly through the damp malt that had been loaded onto the floor ready for drying. This was the last possible hiding place he and Aemilia could think of.

"Do you clean this out every time you light it?" he asked, peering past the kindling into the murk of the low tunnel that led under the raised floor of the building to the flue.

"It won't need doing today, sir," the slave boy assured him, bending toward the kindling with the glowing brand he had just fetched from inside the brewery.

Ruso grabbed his wrist. "Don't."

"Miss Aemilia?" The youth looked at her in the hope of being saved from this interfering officer and allowed to get on with his work.

"When was the last time it was raked out?" asked Ruso.

"About a week ago. The barley ran out so the master had to wait for them to send some down from the granary."

"Do it now, will you?"

"Rake it out?" The slave looked understandably appalled. "I've just got it ready to fire! The malt needs to be dried now or it'll go over. The master's very particular."

"Please," said Aemilia, taking Ruso by the arm. "Do as he says."

"But miss, your father—"

"I'll tell him it was my fault."

"Have you noticed any odd smells in the burning lately?" inquired Ruso as the slave knelt by the hole and began to gather up the kindling.

"There's always odd smells," grunted the youth, reaching for the rake and crouching to insert it at an awkward angle. "If it burns, it goes in here."

Ash began to pile up outside the mouth of the tunnel. The youth's hands and arms and knees were smeared in soot. He had a black mustache where he had wiped his nose on his arm. "I can't get any more out, sir. You'll have to get a little kid to go right inside if you want it done properly."

"We haven't time," said Ruso, imagining what a ghastly job it would be.

"I'll just get something to put this ash in, miss."

When he was gone Ruso took the rake and poked at the crumbling flakes of wood ash.

"Nothing," said Aemilia.

He took a deep breath, got down on his knees, and reached an arm into the stinking black depths of the flue. He could feel the soft powder rising in the air, entering his nose and eyes and coating his skin. This, he realized with disgust, was where Catvignus had hidden the sack containing the head until he had decided to deposit it as evidence outside Rianorix's house. He groped about in the grit of the ash that remained on the floor, ramming his shoulder farther in, praying for one of Tilla's miracles. He realized he was no longer interested in proving anyone's innocence or guilt. He was desperately hoping to prove—to himself, if nobody else—that he was not a total fool.

His fingers closed around brittle half-burned sticks. Scraps of broken pot. Then something thin and woven and pliable. He drew it out, blew off the dust, and lay it on top of the brushwood waiting to be burned. He and Aemilia stared at it.

It was a scorched fragment of old green rag.

Ruso swore.

Aemilia said, "That's an old tunic Ness was using for cleaning."

"I suppose Ness can testify to what she saw that night," said Ruso, disappointed. "It's not very conclusive, though."

A nosebleed would surely make stains very different from those of an attack on another human being. The tunic would have been just the evidence he needed, but he was not going to find that evidence now. In the distance, a trumpet sounded. Ruso scrambled to his feet and looked over the wall of the yard and down toward the river. A carriage with a large escort was making its way across the bridge. A red-cloaked formation of Batavian cavalry, glittering and immaculate in the sun, was trotting down the road to welcome it.

"I've got to go," he said, wiping the soot from his hands onto his tunic. "What shall I do?"

"Talk to Ness. Find out exactly what she saw and tell her she must talk to officer Metellus." It might make a difference, although Ruso suspected not. "I'll be back as soon as I can."

Behind him, he heard the slave begin to restack the kindling in the stoke hole.

85

IT WAS A good morning for burglars. Inns were abandoned, houses deserted, the forge and the carpenter's workshop fallen silent. Even the painted whores had emerged into daylight, jostling with shoppers and slaves and traders and veterans for a position by the side of the road. Small children wanting a better view were trying to clamber onto the backs of older brothers and sisters. A mother was urging a toddler to wave at the cavalry, perhaps in the hope of a surreptitious wink from beneath the brow of a polished helmet as its owner rode out to meet the man who was bringing the authority of the emperor.

It was a good time to be a burglar. It was also a good time to sidle up to a man and murmur over his shoulder that he might like to follow you to somewhere more private.

Trenus's bodyguards closed around her immediately, but he motioned them to stand back. "What do you want?"

Tilla murmured, "Have you forgotten me so soon, my lord?"

He turned and looked her up and down, taking in the pinkened cheeks. The low neck of the blue tunic.

She forced herself to slide a hand around his thick waist. She hoped he would not notice that the borrowed sandals were too big.

"You ran off," he said.

"You should ask your wives who took me," she said. "And ask them what they did with the profit."

His eyes narrowed. "My wives? What profit?"

Her hand slid lower. "I have missed you, my lord."

A smile twitched beneath the mustache.

"Quick, while my uncle is not here." She moved away from the crowd and stepped toward a gap between two houses.

Incredibly, he seemed about to follow. Then he seemed to regain some grip on common sense and glanced at the bodyguards. One pushed her aside and strode into the narrow alleyway. The other gestured to her to follow him.

The alley smelled of urine and the walls on either side were green with old dampness. She thought, *Only a fool would come down here in the company of an enemy.*

There were footsteps behind her. Trenus was following while the other bodyguard watched the entrance.

Moments later there was a cry ahead of, "Clear, boss!" and she emerged into the daylight to find the bodyguard leaning against the back wall of the house, gazing across an empty yard with his arms folded. Just as she remembered Trenus's other men doing years before. As if what was about to happen to her was nothing to do with them.

She thought, *If I had a knife I might take him now.* But of course she had not been allowed a knife. Besides, back at the fort, thirty-three people, who should have known better but who did not deserve to die, were depending upon her.

So when Trenus emerged from the gap between the houses, she seized his hand, led him under the cover of an almost-empty wood store, and said crisply, "I have to speak with you, my lord."

Her arm was rammed up behind her back. The smell of his breath made her want to vomit. "Let me go!"

"I didn't come here to talk."

"Let me go, or I will tell you nothing."

He slackened his grip, frowning. "What can you tell me?"

"It is private," she said. "Tell your man to stand farther away."

He eyed her for a moment, then gave the order.

"Farther still," she demanded. When the man was out of earshot she said, 'I know you are helping us to get rid of the Romans. If my people knew that, they would feel as I do. But they might wonder why. They might think you were trying to get rid of the army so you can take what we have for yourself. They might ask whether you can be trusted."

"That's my business."

"They will not follow a man who will not give his reasons."

"And they've sent a girl to tell me that?"

"No. What I want to tell you is that the soldiers have the Stag Man's horse keeper among the prisoners in the fort. Sooner or later someone will give him up. And the Romans will find a way to make him talk."

There were cheers from the street. They must have caught sight of the governor. Trenus said, "Who told you?"

"I saw him. I was taken too. But the Romans trust me. I'm with an officer, and Catavignus is my uncle. They think I'm on their side. They don't know that I remember the Stag Man and I remember him coming to your house to collect the horse. If that prisoner talks you are in danger."

The noise from the street grew louder. The bodyguard was distracted, trying to peer down the alley.

"And you're telling me this," said Trenus, "because you like me?"

"I never liked you," she said, pulling her arm free. "And I don't like you now. If you touch me again I shall scream *rape*." Nobody in the noisy crowd would hear, but she hoped he would not think of that. If only she had a knife. "When my uncle heats the mash, he leaves the windows open to clear the steam," she said. "I was outside in the street. I heard you arguing with him. I know now why he thought I was dead. And I know that I owe you a debt."

"Catavignus wanted us to finish the lot of you," said Trenus. "In return for the livestock. But I thought that was a waste."

"You showed me mercy," she said, forcing herself not to be distracted by what she could see going on behind him. "This is why I am warning you now. Get out before the army arrests you." She hesitated. "And think about giving my people reason to trust you."

He grinned. "Tell your people the Votadini don't like being told what to do by Rome any more than you do. When the time comes, we'll be there."

"Good." Tilla smiled, and stepped back out of the way. "You have told me everything I wanted."

Too late, he sensed movement behind him.

As the soldiers dragged Trenus and his hapless bodyguards off toward the fort, Metellus appeared. "Nicely done," he said. "And I understood

nearly every word without the interpreter. If anyone asks, we've just rescued you from an attempted rape."

"Do not speak to me," she said, rubbing the pink off her cheeks and
kicking off the sandals she had borrowed from the maid of the prefect's
wife. "I owed him a debt, and I have paid it."

"So I gather," said Metellus. "You should be working for me. Have we
really got the horse keeper?"

"No. And I would never work for you."

"But you just have," pointed out Metellus. He turned to a soldier who
had appeared from the alley. "All going smoothly out there?"

"Fine, sir. All cheering like they mean it."

"Excellent." He seized Tilla by the wrist. "I don't imagine you want to
pay us another visit, so stay out of trouble."

She lifted her chin. "The others should go free."

"Of course. You have the prefect's word. When we have time, we'll let
them all out."

"You will not hurt them?"

Metellus frowned. "I don't remember that being part of the agreement."

86

THE PRISONERS WHO had been cluttering the headquarters courtyard had been shifted somewhere out of the way, the waste buckets removed, and the gravel hastily raked into military lines. Ruso's preparations had been less precise. They had consisted of rushing into the infirmary, ducking his head around Albanus's door, and saying, "Glad to see you awake!" before wiping off the worst of the soot, flinging on his best tunic, seizing the sword he had failed to sharpen, diving into armor that looked remarkably clean considering he had forgotten to ask anyone to polish it, and strapping everything up on the run across to headquarters.

As he slipped onto the end of the row of officers beside Metellus, he realized the aide was also out of breath. Mercifully the governor was still taking his time. Staring straight ahead, Ruso murmured, "Catavignus came home late on the night of the murder in bloodstained clothing."

"Not now, Ruso."

"Where's Tilla?"

"You stink of soot."

Audax, stationed at the end of the row opposite, glared at them.

"The servant saw him," Ruso insisted, struggling to talk without moving his lips. "His daughter heard him say he'd had a nosebleed."

"I shall be glad when this is over," muttered Metellus. "Even Gambax is trying to pretend he knows who did it now."

Ruso risked a glance at him. "What's he saying?"

"Who cares? If he knew, why didn't he come forward when it happened? He's trying to do a deal to save himself."

Ruso was not able to argue, because at that moment the governor strode into the courtyard.

Everything that could gleam had been polished, including the top of his head. Everything that could jingle or glitter had been attached. Leaving his flunkies lined up by the entrance, the governor made his way around the silent and rigid rows of Batavians, with Decianus one pace behind, inspecting and commenting and pausing to chat with several of the men. Each side was clearly determined to impress the other, and Ruso curled his toes in frustration. He wanted to know what Metellus was going to do about Catavignus. He wanted to know what had happened to Tilla since she had been marched out of the prefect's house. Instead, he was compelled to stand like a statue while the governor—admittedly the nearest thing to a god that was likely to visit Coria this summer—wandered about at his leisure.

The great man was progressing down Ruso's row. He could hear the crunch of footsteps on the gravel. Somewhere ahead of him, a man tried to stifle a sneeze. There was movement in front of Ruso now. The footsteps paused. Ruso hoped the great man would not inhale too deeply and choke on the stink of soot.

"Has this officer come straight from duty?"

"From the infirmary, sir," agreed Decianus.

The great man moved to stand directly in front of Ruso. "I take it things are busy at the infirmary?"

The required answer was, *Yes, sir*. The appropriate tone was one of enthusiasm, gratitude for being singled out, and a sincerity that would imply that Ruso's scruffy turnout was the result of heroic and self-sacrificial devotion to the emperor's service. *Yes, sir.*

"No, sir," said Ruso. "I've been trying to catch a murderer so that you don't end up condemning an innocent man to death later today."

There was a brief and terrible silence, during which the whole courtyard seemed to hold its breath. "Very good," said the governor benignly, and moved on down the row, leaving Ruso wondering if he had heard anything at all.

87

WHEN HE WOKE up cold and dripping with three angry women standing over his bed, Catavignus must have thought his hangover had turned into a nightmare.

Aemilia put down her empty bucket. Tilla nodded at Veldicca, who lifted the second bucket and poured the stream directly onto his nose so the others had to dodge back to avoid the splashing. He tried to reach out to defend himself. From her hiding place in the corner, Ness laughed, because she was the one who had tied his hands together. He opened his mouth to protest, and Tilla rammed in the dirty sock. Only when he tried to sit up did she put the kitchen knife to his throat and say, "You said the Romans would bring us peace and justice, uncle. We have come to help them. Get out of bed."

He blinked the water out of his eyes and looked around at them. She wondered if he knew why they were there. No matter. All being well, there would be plenty of time to explain.

Catavignus, of course, had a great deal to say for himself, but since she had tied the sock in place with his belt and Ness had pulled a sack down over his shoulders, all that came out as they prodded and dragged him across to the malt house was an agitated moaning noise. After much stumbling—helpfully corrected by Ness jabbing him in the ribs with the other kitchen knife—they lined him up in front of the open door of the malt house, gave him a good shove, and enjoyed the sight of him falling face-first into the warm grain. Tilla slammed the door before he could get to his feet.

"And do not expect the men to come!" shouted Aemilia as she slid the lock across. "I have given them the day off!"

There was no response from inside the malt house.

"Perhaps we have killed him," suggested Veldicca, tucking the key inside her breastband.

"We will think of that later," said Tilla, slipping the knife into her belt and glancing around at her coconspirators. Ness, grimfaced as usual, seemed to be waiting for orders. Aemilia was wild haired and as flushed as if she had just come from the steam room. Veldicca leaned against the wall and folded her arms. "What now?"

Tilla, suddenly aware that she had not given a great deal of thought to what would happen next, pushed the hair out of her eyes. "He has a right to know why he is a prisoner," she said. "We will all tell him our grievances. Who's first?"

"Me!" insisted Aemilia, pushing her way past Ness to sit on the stone step and bang on the door with her fist. "I know what you did, Daddy. Do you hear me? You tried to turn Felix against me, and then you followed him and killed him! You have ruined my life and I hate you!"

There was a series of grunts and moans from behind the door, then a hefty thump from inside that made the lock rattle.

"Lean against it," ordered Tilla, wishing they had tied him up more thoroughly. He was a big man. The door was thick, designed to hold the heat in, but the lock was only there to keep out the curious and it did not look strong. If he shoulder charged it, they could be in trouble. "Veldicca and Ness, fetch something to wedge the door." She leaned closer to Aemilia. "I'll hold the door. Go and stoke the fire."

"Me?"

"Of course you! As hot as you can. I don't know how long we can keep him in there. It won't kill him, but it will give him a good fright." She braced herself against the door and shouted, "Better sound the alarm, uncle! You are being attacked!"

There was more moaning and grunting from within, but no further attempt to break out.

"Surely your family will come to help?" she cried. "But no, perhaps they will not! Perhaps they are the ones who arranged it! Perhaps they want you out of the way so they can get on with making lots of money from the army!"

She moved aside as Ness and Veldicca maneuvered a heavy table out of the back entrance of the brewery and rammed it against the door.

Aemilia ordered Ness to bring more wood. The servant eyed her as if wondering whether to argue, then limped toward the neat stack of split logs under the eaves of the brewery.

"How's the malt doing in there, uncle?" called Tilla, glancing up at the smoke that had made its way under the floor and was billowing from the top vent of the flue.

"Sh!" Veldicca had her finger on her lips. "Shout at him quietly, daughter of Lugh. They will hear us in the street."

She was right. They had got rid of the brewery staff, but if they were overheard, then some passerby might be misguided enough to fetch help.

Veldicca reached over the table and rapped on the door with a stick. "You had my brother falsely arrested and tortured, Catavignus!"

Ness took the stick from her. Tilla put a hand on her arm. "You do not have to do this," she assured her. "There may be trouble afterward." They both knew that a slave who attacked a master would be shown no mercy.

Ness pushed her aside. "I have waited a long time for this," she said, and rapped the stick against the heavy wood. "Is the malt drying well, master?" she called. "Is there anything else I can get you? You are lucky to have me, you know. I could have been killed along with my old master and mistress."

A muffled bellow of "Get me out! You're all mad!" came from behind the door.

"Oh, good!" announced Tilla, secretly worried that his voice would carry into the street. They had no way of quieting him now: He had probably wrenched his hands free and the doorway was too narrow for more than one person at a time to tackle him. "You can talk to us! Perhaps you can tell us why we should not set light to the thatch and leave you to burn like you left my family!"

88

RUSO HAD NOTHING to lose now. Feeling slightly guilty about Valens's complaints that he hadn't meant he would cover *all* of Ruso's duties, he walked out of the east gate and back to do battle with Catavignus. It was probably hopeless—why would a man confess when there was nothing to prove him guilty?—but he could not think of anything else to try.

There was no answer from the house next to the brewery. It seemed even the servant was out. He was about to try the brewery itself when he heard something odd going on behind it. Some sort of native chanting, interspersed with a rhythmic thump. The sound evoked the hideous memory of last night. He shuddered. He was about to turn back and fetch help when a voice he knew very well indeed called some sort of command. There was a pause, and then the chant began again. He hurried to the back of the brewery, flattened himself against the wall, then peered around into the yard.

A fierce fire was crackling in the stoke hole where he had groped in vain for the missing evidence this morning. Tilla and her friends were circling the malt house, chanting something over and over again, each of them clutching a burning brand in one hand. At the end of the chant they beat the brands against the thatch. Embers broke off. The larger pieces rolled down the thatch and fell into the mud beneath. The sparks and smaller chunks sank down into the straw. The chant began again, the circle moved on, and the thatch began to smolder.

Tilla, Aemilia, Ness the housekeeper, and Veldicca, the secret lover of Thessalus were circling around the malt house in some peculiar native ritual perhaps designed to call down the gods to save Rianorix. He supposed it had as much chance of success as anything he had tried himself.

It was only when he heard a muffled male shout that he realized they had somebody trapped in there.

"Stop!" he yelled, scrambling over the wall and dropping down into the brewery yard. The chant died. The women halted, looked first at him and then at Tilla, the smoking brands still raised in their hands.

"Help me!" cried the voice, in Latin this time. "Get me out!"

Aemilia looked flushed and excited. Tilla had a kitchen knife tucked in her belt, tangled hair, and an expression that suggested if he came too close, he would end up locked in the malt house himself.

"Help!" came Catavignus's voice again. "Is there anybody out there?"

"It's the doctor!" shouted Ruso.

"Apollo-Maponus be praised! They're trying to roast me to death!" The door rattled. "Get the key!"

Ruso looked Tilla in the eye. "What are you doing?"

"This is justice."

He took a step closer.

She reached for the knife.

Ruso moved to one side and saw the table wedged against the door. "This is murder."

"He betrayed my family," she said simply. "He cannot deny it."

"I deny every word of it!" roared Catavignus. "Get me—" The sentence ended with a scream. "The roof's on fire!"

Ruso seized one leg of the table and hauled it clear. As he moved toward the door two firebrands were thrust in front of his face and he felt the jab of Tilla's knife over his right kidney. "This is our business," hissed Tilla in his ear. "He is one of our people."

"Bring him to the governor for trial," insisted Ruso, straining away from the heat of the brands scorching his face. He could hear Catavignus coughing and beating on the door of the malt house. "The law—"

"This is our law," insisted Tilla. "You think we will get justice from you? He is a friend of the army. You will find an excuse—"

"Have him tried by the governor, Tilla. Otherwise you'll all be in terrible trouble for this."

"Why? What is one more dead native to the army?"

"Don't be naïve. He's their friend. Their beer supplier."

"Hah!" she said. "This is what I tell you, they will not kill him!"

Flames were rising from the thatch in several places. Catavignus seemed to be flinging himself against the door in a last desperate attempt to escape, and Ruso realized he had just argued himself into a circle.

He twisted around, trying to look her in the eye. "Tilla, I'm ordering you to hand over that key!"

She leaned over his shoulder. Her smile was almost pitying. He could not order her to do anything at all, and they both knew it. What he did not know was whether she was prepared to use that knife.

"Confess, man!" he yelled, tensing himself ready to flail and kick his way free. Even if she stabbed him, he might still be able to get over the wall and shout for help before they caught up with him. "Confess and—"

"Stand aside!" roared a voice he was not expecting. A squad of soldiers vaulted over the walls of the yard and surrounded the women with the points of their spears. Audax stepped forward, jammed a crowbar under the door lock, and prized it open. A filthy figure stumbled out in a billow of smoke, choking and gasping for air.

Audax was giving orders for the fire to be put out and Ruso was extricating himself from among the women when Metellus appeared at the back entrance of the brewery. He saw Tilla and shook his head sadly. "What did I say to you earlier?"

"He is a murderer," said Tilla. "He betrayed my family. You heard Trenus say it!"

Metellus frowned. "Did I?"

"Stop playing games with her, Metellus," put in Ruso. "He killed Felix as well."

Metellus sighed. "I might have known I'd find you here in the middle of it."

Ruso seized the spluttering Catavignus by the shoulder. "Susanna says you were there delivering the beer when Rianorix came and threatened Felix," he said. "But when I first met you, you told the barber you didn't know anything about it."

"I can't remember."

Ruso hauled him to his feet and dragged him across to the water trough. When the latest soldier had filled his firefighting bucket, he plunged

Catavignus headfirst into the cold water. The man's arms flailed wildly while his long hair floated on the surface like waterweed. Ruso pulled him out again. "That should help clear the smoke from your eyes," he said. "Felix had his debts list with him when he saw Dari. It wasn't on his body. You destroyed it so you wouldn't have to pay the builder."

"The builder was useless!"

Whatever else Catavignus had to say about the builder rose as bubbles. When he emerged, gasping, Ruso pushed his nose toward the malt grains bobbing on the surface. "Tell the truth!"

"Help me!" shouted Catavignus. "Metellus! Tell him to stop!"

Metellus folded his arms and leaned back against the wall of the brewery.

Strands of wet gray hair were plastered down Catavignus's face as Ruso yanked him upward. "Gambax saw you with Felix that night." said Ruso.

"Nonsense! I was never—"

Ruso put him under the water again, trying to think what he could say that would compel Catavignus to confess. Pulling him out, he said, "Gambax has been arrested for attacking my clerk. He's singing like the wind in the trees, trying to do a deal. So it doesn't matter. We don't need your confession, we've got a witness."

"I need protection!" Catavignus spluttered, squirming in Ruso's grip. "I demand protection! Metellus, tell him who I am!"

Ruso glanced across. "He's a native brewer," said Metellus. "He's a man who did a deal with a neighboring chieftain to get rid of his own brother's family."

"But I helped you!" shrieked Catavignus. "You said there would be protection!"

"He's lying," said Metellus.

"This is the army, Catavignus," said Ruso, pushing the wet head downward again. "There is no protection for natives. Sorry."

While he was under, Ruso turned to Metellus. "It *is* Catavignus that Gambax is accusing, isn't it?"

"Yes."

"Phew," said Ruso.

Metellus frowned. "But I still don't see why Gambax didn't come forward and say what he'd seen right away."

"Because he was blackmailing you, wasn't he?" demanded Ruso of the struggling Catavignus as he hauled him out of the water. "That's what Gambax does."

89

THIS IS JUST like old times!" exclaimed Valens, leaning back against the wall of the isolation room and handing Ruso the smaller of the wine cakes he had just liberated from the prefect's kitchen.

"Not really."

"No, of course not," said Valens. "Sorry, I forgot. I must say it's a bit rich, her taking up with a native after all we've done for her. Still, it hasn't been an entirely wasted trip, has it? You've rescued the reputation of a colleague and you've pinned down a very nasty murderer."

"That doesn't give me much pleasure," said Ruso, remembering the faces of the women Catavignus had wronged as they circled the malt house.

"That's because you like to be miserable," said Valens. "Did I tell you our friendly brewer of fine beer is claiming he did everything at the request of the army? He says Metellus asked him to help clear up undesirables."

"How do you know?"

Valens grinned. "You should have joined the governor's hunting party today, Ruso. Fresh air, good exercise, and a chance to meet influential people and help them kill things. And it gave most of the Tenth an afternoon out, making sure we weren't ambushed by ungrateful natives."

"So are your influential friends going to reward Catavignus for clearing up the undesirables?"

Of course not. Nobody wants it to look as if we can't keep order without the help of the guild of caterers."

"They make a shambles and call it peace," said Ruso, misquoting a famous historian.

"Desolation, sir," came a voice from the bed. "They make desolation. It's from Tacitus."

"Pleased to see you're feeling better, Albanus," said Ruso.

"No thanks to you lot," observed Audax from the doorway. "If I hadn't gone and got that tonic, he'd be dead by now."

"Must be good stuff," said Ruso, wondering if Valens had administered it or poured it down the latrine.

"Hmph," said Audax. "Tell that to the young whippersnapper who was in here this afternoon. How many bloody doctors have we got hanging around here now? Four? World's gone mad."

"We're not officially supposed to be here," explained Ruso. "The whippersnapper's taken over. He's brought in his own clerk, and he's going to tell the prefect that the survival of the infirmary without Thessalus must be thanks to Gambax, who may have been a violent criminal and a thief, but was obviously a marvelous deputy medic."

"We're surplus to requirements," agreed Valens. "That's why we're hiding in here with our favorite patient."

"Well, one of you do something useful and fetch me a beer."

Valens shook his head. "Sorry. The whippersnapper doesn't approve of beer."

"He doesn't approve of a lot of things," agreed Ruso, recalling the new man's outrage at his treatment of Thessalus.

"Why's he in this miserable hole?" the new man had demanded, assuring Thessalus, "Don't worry, you won't be stuck here much longer. We'll get you out somewhere with a bit of light and fresh air and better company." He had turned to Ruso. "He needs a properly controlled diet, pleasant surroundings, and full-time nursing. Why isn't he in the infirmary?"

"I'm sorry, Thessalus," said Ruso, not intending to explain to the new man about the abandoned murder charge. "I suppose I should have thought about putting you out in a convalescent billet in the town."

"Of course you should," said the whippersnapper, glaring at him.

This, decided Ruso, was the ideal posting for such a man. He could spend the long empty evenings composing diatribes against the stupidity of his colleagues. "There's a local woman who supplies medicines for the clinic," he said thoughtfully. "Veldicca. She might take him in."

"I'd like that," agreed Thessalus.

"But she's not cheap," added Ruso.

"That's hardly the point, is it?" said the new man. "We should be doing the correct thing, not the cheapest thing. Especially for a colleague."

"You're right," agreed Ruso.

"Thank you, Doctor," said Thessalus. "I can't tell you how grateful I am to you. I've been getting a bit downhearted, shut up in here."

"It's nothing," the new medic had said with a smirk, as if the sick man's thanks were intended for him. Behind his back, Thessalus caught Ruso's eye and smiled.

Valens's eyes widened as the sound of the trumpet penetrated the peace of the isolation room. "Heavens, is that the time? I must get going. Did I tell you I'm dining at the prefect's house tonight?"

"With the governor?"

"You really should have come hunting this afternoon, Ruso. You never know when good contacts might come in useful. Tell you what, some of the great man's underlings will be down at the public baths about now. I'll introduce you."

"No thanks," said Ruso. "But I'll walk across with you. I've just remembered some unfinished business."

The two surplus medics made their way out through the gates where, a couple of hours earlier, Ruso had stood and watched the weary native prisoners shuffling past. Decianus had kept his word to Tilla, but not before names had been recorded, evidence taken, and backs flogged. All had taken place well out of earshot of the governor—who could not be expected to have to put up with the noise that men and women insisted on making when in pain—but within sight of their children, who needed to be shown that threatening to butcher a Roman officer was a very bad idea.

"Still here?" Metellus had inquired, having appeared from nowhere as usual.

"I'm leaving in the morning," said Ruso. "I thought you were going hunting?"

"I would have," explained Metellus. "But unfortunately I was delayed by having to prepare a murder case and deal with this lot. Look pretty harmless now, don't they? But they would have torn you to pieces last night."

"I know," said Ruso, watching Rianorix wince as he forced himself to march out of the fort with his head held high.

"Incidentally, how did you know about Gambax being a blackmailer?"

Ruso shrugged. "Just a lucky guess. Tell me something. Was it you who gave the order for Tilla's family to be got rid of?"

"Me? Of course not."

"And the water being supplied to the brewery had nothing to do with paying for services rendered?"

"Absolutely not."

"Good."

Metellus shook his head. "As I told you before, you have a vivid imagination."

"No you didn't," said Ruso. "You told me I think too much."

There was no sign of the released natives now. They must have scattered into the countryside to nurse their wounds and their indignation.

"Does he really sell everything?" inquired Valens as they passed the shop.

"I doubt it," said Ruso. "I've never been in there."

"Really?" said Valens. "He's grinning at you as if you're his best customer."

"We've developed a silent acquaintance," explained Ruso. "I keep seeing him, but I can't think of anything to say to him."

"I'd keep it that way," suggested Valens. "You'll only be a disappointment to him when he finds out how boring—what's the matter?" He peered down the street, following Ruso's gaze. "Oh, holy gods! Is that who I think it is?"

Ruso eyed the mounted figure being escorted by four legionary cavalrymen past the shrine to the god whose name he never had gotten around to finding out. "I believe so," he said, noting the handsome face, the square jaw, and the broad shoulders that recalled the Second Spear. "She's very like her father, isn't she?"

90

RUSO ENTERED THE bathhouse alone. At the sight of him, Claudius Innocens stood up so fast that he almost knocked over his table and smashed his bottles of potions on the hall floor. "Doctor, sir!" he exclaimed, hastily steadying the table and shifting a couple of pots to the back of the display before rearranging the strands of his hair across his bald patch. "What a pleasure to see you again!"

"If only it were mutual," said Ruso, observing that Innocens seemed greasier than ever. "What are you selling?"

The man's smile was probably supposed to be encouraging. "Tonics for every condition, sir. All guaranteed recipes from the great healers and using only the purest ingredients. Special prices for you, sir, of course. What would you like to try?"

"Have you got any Doctor Ruso's Special Love Potion?"

Innocens's smile froze. His gaze dropped to the pots and bottles. "I'm not sure we've got anything like that, sir. But if you give me the recipe I'd be pleased to get it made up and we'll come to an arrangement about the profits."

Ruso reached for one of the pots Innocens had moved to the back. Clumsily chalked on the side was a phallus. "Is this it?"

"That's, ah, that's—"

Ruso turned the pot around to find his own name chalked on the opposite side.

"Somebody gave them to me, sir," Innocens protested. "But they haven't gone very well. I won't be selling any more of them. Once I've got rid of these last few—"

"No more."

"No more, sir. Of course." Innocens picked up a similar pot, spat on it, and began to rub at the chalk inscription. "Perhaps a new name would be the thing."

"If you must do it, at least pick the name of somebody long dead," suggested Ruso. "Like you did with Scribonius."

"Ah, yes, sir! Now that is a good seller. As used by centurions—I'll be able to say, 'As used by legionary doctors,' as well now, sir, won't I?"

"Not if you want to live," said Ruso. "And that reminds me. You remember the slave girl you sold me?"

"The blond girl? You got a bargain there, sir. I hope you're still happy with her?"

Ruso was not going to answer that. "There's a native in town who used to think he owned her," he said. "A very violent man from the north who got home one day and found out his wives had been persuaded to sell his favorite serving girl to a dodgy trader. That native's probably talking to the governor's men right now."

Innocens's eyes widened. "Really, sir?"

"Really," said Ruso.

Innocens bent down past his belly and pulled out a wooden box full of straw from beneath the table. "As ever, sir," he said, swiftly stacking his bottles in the straw, "it's been a pleasure to do business with you."

91

RUSO LEANED OUT over the rough logs of the palisade. A last trace of morning mist still hung over the river. He could hear the faint clatter of hooves as a messenger cantered south across the bridge. To the east, a road patrol was riding out toward the hill country. He did not turn to look north. Tilla had made her choice.

He had arrived early at the house next to the brewery, only to find it locked and deserted. The brewery foreman had told him the women had gone away somewhere. Probably for a long time.

He had tried to tell himself that Tilla's farewell message had been lost, but since the men here all knew him by now, that was unlikely. The truth was, she had not sent one. The last time they had spoken, she had pulled a knife on him.

Ruso surveyed the shabby little town that had sprung up to service the fort.

He's claiming he did everything at the request of the army. He says Metellus asked him to help clear up undesirables.

Metellus would continue to deny all knowledge of Catavignus's treachery to his own people, of course. Quite possibly Decianus, by taking the wider view, had managed to avoid knowing the details anyway. It was apparent from their conversation this morning that Decianus was only told what Metellus wanted him to hear.

"Ruso!" he had said, drawing him to one side after morning briefing. "Leaving us, I hear?"

"It's been an interesting week, sir."

"You weren't much help in the end," Decianus observed. "The governor never went near the infirmary. Metellus had to excuse your performance at the parade by telling him you were a mad medic called Thessalus who'd gotten loose by mistake. And then he tracked down the murder evidence by himself."

"Yes, sir," said Ruso, with what he hoped was the correct amount of enthusiasm, gratitude, and sincerity. Sometimes, it was just easier to say what people wanted to hear.

Getting rid of Felix, of course, had not been part of anybody's wider view. Catavignus had just seized the opportunity to solve his own debt problems and get rid of an unsuitable suitor for his daughter. Implicating Rianorix had been a smart move, though. Rianorix was a known rebel sympathizer who had asked awkward questions about the loss of Tilla's family. Once he had made a threat against a soldier he was definitely ripe for clearing up.

He supposed they would execute Catavignus. It was a messy solution to a messy problem. And an ironic one, because the man had been struggling to establish, in his own twisted way, a civilized town full of loyal Romans on the very edge of the barbarian world.

The proprietor of We Sell Everything was standing outside his shop with his arms folded. Behind him, a small figure was sweeping the step. The trouble was, prosperity here depended on the presence of the soldiers, and the presence of the soldiers depended on the whim of the emperor, and that was beyond mortal prediction. By the time Thessalus's daughter had children of her own, this fort could be sunk back into the ground, the bathhouse in ruins, the houses rotted away, and sheep wandering over the great green swell of rampart on which he was now standing. Or, whoever was emperor could have decided to launch another building project like Deva: a grand reminder of Rome's power set in stone. That had been Catavignus's vision. It was a fine vision for a ruler with legions at his command, but played out on a smaller stage by a provincial brewer with a borrowed knife, it was simply—

Ruso's deep musings skidded to a halt. He clattered down the steps, dodging past a surprised sentry who was halfway up, and sprinted toward the gates.

"Tilla!" he shouted, sliding on the gravel and barely bothering to return the salute of the gate guards who stepped aside to let him pass. "Tilla!"

She paused, using one knee to lift the big brass cooking pot around which her arms were encircled. She was back in her own clothes now: the old blue tunic, the shawl, and the battered boots.

"I didn't want to leave without saying good-bye," he said. "I didn't know where to find you."

"Aemilia will stay away until it is all over," said Tilla, not needing to explain what she was referring to. "Rianorix is no friend of the Romans but he will make sure the brewery men do their work for her."

He could not resist saying, "What does a basket maker know about brewing?"

"The men know what to do. And they know that if they fail, he has the power of the curse. Look what he made Catavignus do to Felix."

"I suppose so," he said, realizing sadly that he would never now have the time to argue her into a more rational position.

She seemed not to know what to say either. "I have come into town to buy this," she told him, lifting the pot. "Rianorix has nothing left, and we do not trust him to go shopping."

"I see." What was he supposed to say now? That he hoped they all cooked many fine meals in it and lived to a happy old age?

"Dari liked you so much she has run away to Ulucium to find herself a legionary," said Tilla. "Lydia is working for Susanna now."

"Ah," said Ruso. "Good." No doubt Lydia and her child would find a home here among the rest of the strays washed up on the shores of the empire.

Tilla was looking past him and down the street. "Is that—?"

He followed her gaze. "Yes," he said, seeing Valens and his very new wife. "They spent most of the night trying to make the Second Spear a grandfather. I know because I was in the next bedroom."

"She is allowed into the fort?"

"Valens seems to have weaseled his way into the governor's favor," explained Ruso. "Or perhaps the gate guards didn't dare to argue with her."

"Or perhaps because she is a Roman."

Ruso shrugged. "Perhaps."

"Where will you go now?"

"I haven't decided," he said. Going west would reunite him with Postumus and the men from the Twentieth. Going south would take him back to Deva, where he could slot into the role Valens had vacated. He doubted the army would care which of them was at which post. He had a feeling that sooner or later they would all be going north anyway, unless Rome found a new and painless way of rooting out the Stag Man and any other similarly minded rabble-rousers from the relative safety of the tribes beyond the border.

"And I suppose," he added casually, "since you're inexplicably fond of him, you'll marry Rianorix and have lots of blond babies."

"Blond babies, yes. That would be nice."

"Yes." He scratched his jaw. "Good." He was not going to beg. He had decided as he lay awake last night that the most dignified way to deal with the loss of Tilla was to pretend this had been his intention all along. As if he were releasing a pet creature back out into the wild before it became too dangerous to live with. "In that case," he said, "I suppose I should thank you for, um . . . well. You know. Lots of things."

She glanced down at her scarred right arm, curled around the cooking pot. "And I must thank you too. I will pray for you."

He hesitated. "I do realize you meant well with the stolen money."

"And you with the room at the inn."

"Yes," he said. "Tell me. Would you have used that knife on me?"

She paused. "I would have been sorry afterward."

It was not the answer he had been hoping for.

She shifted her grip on the cooking pot again.

He said, "I expect you'll want to be getting back."

"I have to take this," she said, glancing down into the pot.

"Yes," he said. "Well, um—this is rather difficult, isn't it?"

"I will make it easy for you," she said, turning her back on him and walking away.

92

THE GOLDEN FLEECE was open for business, but Ruso was not going to make the same mistake twice. There was plenty of time to get to the next town before dark, and he had stocked up on food at Susanna's. He had also salved a small part of his ailing conscience by leaving the last of the stolen money with Susanna, who had promised to pass it on to Aemilia as an investment in the brewery. Finally Susanna had revealed that she was the one who had summoned help to get Catavignus out of the burning malt house.

"I'm in your debt," Ruso said.

"I never liked the man," she said, "But he was a fellow member of the guild. And if we don't help each other in a place like this, what hope is there for any of us?"

He slowed the horse, reached into the saddlebag, and drew out a sausage in pastry. The secret of happiness, he reminded himself, was to enjoy simple pleasures, and not to spoil that enjoyment by thinking about the past. Or the future. About how empty the house would seem when he got back to Deva. Or about how different things would have been if he had never volunteered for this wretched posting in the north. Valens was wrong. He didn't like to be miserable. Being miserable was no fun at all.

He had just sunk his teeth into the pastry when he heard fast hoof-beats approaching from behind. He nudged the horse aside to give the messenger plenty of room.

Instead of passing, the rider reined in his horse and drew up alongside. Ruso sighed and prepared to abandon his lunch for another medical emergency.

"Where is your chair and your boxes?" demanded an unexpectedly familiar voice.

"I'm having them sent down later," he said, staring at her. "You haven't ridden all this way to remind me about lost luggage, have you?"

She said, "I have been walking home with the cooking pot and thinking about you."

"I see."

"And about Aemilia. And about Rianorix."

"I see."

"You are right; I am very fond of Rianorix."

"That's obvious."

"He is brave and honorable and handsome, even with his front tooth knocked out."

"I wouldn't know."

"He is like a brother to me," she said. "We were children together. I understand his mind."

"I see."

"But he is not very clever," she said. "Aemilia tells him to do things and he does them. He is selling the beer to Susanna who is selling it to the army. He does not like the army. But he is happy because he can give all his friends free beer."

"I see."

"He would have died for Aemilia," she said. "He would not die for me."

Ruso did not know what to say.

"So I tell him I am not going to marry him. He can ask her if he wants."

"I see."

"You are saying *I see* a lot. Never mind what you see. What are you thinking?"

He surveyed her for a moment, wondered if she had stolen the horse, and decided he didn't care. "I am thinking," he said, "that the sun has brought the freckles out on your nose. And I am thinking that it will be very lonely back in Deva without you."

"I will tell you what I am thinking now," she said. "I am thinking that perhaps you are still wondering whether I want to marry you."

"Ah." So she had heard after all. He shifted in the saddle and wondered what to say. The last person he knew who had withdrawn a proposal to a British girl had ended up dead in a back alley.

"But I do not want to marry you because you are foreign and you do not trust me."

"You did threaten to stick a knife in my back," he pointed out, feeling relieved and faintly ashamed.

She said, "You were working for Metellus."

"So were you."

She did not reply. He broke off half of the pastry and handed it to her. Ahead of them a native couple were bumping toddler twins along the road in a handcart.

"Tell me something, Tilla," he said. "In this place the man is expected to bring money to the marriage and the girl's family doesn't have to pay a dowry?"

"That is right. A bride price."

"Hm."

She said, "Now what are you thinking?"

"I am thinking," he said, "that if you promise to keep away from the knives, perhaps I should introduce you to my stepmother."

AUTHOR'S NOTE

There was "serious trouble" in Britannia at the start of Hadrian's reign, but fortunately for novelists hardly any of the details have yet come to light. What we do know is that shortly after this story is set, the need to separate the Romans from the Barbarians became so pressing that the border was solidified into Hadrian's Wall.

The Tenth Batavians rode into existence during the planning of the novel. At present nobody knows who manned the wooden fort that stood at Corbridge in 118. Present-day visitors to the site will find fascinating remains, but Ruso would have been a great-grandfather by the time most of the stones now visible were laid, and the civilian settlement that once spread across the surrounding fields can only be seen in archaeological records and crop marks. The river, of course, remains.

Lest anyone should wonder, there is plenty of evidence for the widespread consumption of beer and wine among Batavian and other units stationed farther along the border at Vindolanda. Sometimes authors don't need to make things up.

The Votadini, however, deserve an apology. For all I know they may have been a fun-loving and friendly bunch not at all given to rape and pillage. Apart from their names, we know precious little about most of the British tribes in the area at the time, and all the contemporary histories were written by Romans. I hope any ancestors watching from the next world—and their descendants—will forgive the guesswork, invention, and slander with which I have padded out the available sources.

Anyone who wants a more dependable account of the times will enjoy:

Women in Roman Britain, 2nd ed., Lindsay Allason-Jones
Garrison Life at Vindolanda: a Band of Brothers, Anthony Birley
Roman Medicine, Audrey Cruse
A Brief History of the Druids, Peter Beresford Ellis
The Gods of the Celts, Miranda Green

ACKNOWLEDGMENTS

This book would have been considerably worse without the generous assistance of several people.

Georgina Plowright, Dr. Martin Weaver, Barbara Evans Rees, and Terry Frain all provided help with the archaeology. Lindsay Allason-Jones advised on Roman rings, Alison Samuels advised on Latin, and Veldicca would have had fewer problems with her bees if she had consulted David Chantler. (Incidentally, "king" bees can be found in the works of Pliny the Elder.)

Suggestions and sources on medicine ancient and modern were kindly provided by Professor John Scarborough and Dr. Vicki Finnegan.

Mari Evans, Gillian Blake, Peta Nightingale, and Araminta Whitley gave a huge amount of editorial advice, and Kathy Barbour, Guy Russell, Sian Parrett, and Kate Weaver read through the manuscript and made helpful suggestions.

None of the above holds any responsibility for any errors which may have resulted from my inexpert mangling of the help they provided.

Finally, thanks to family and friends who put up with my grumbling, to Lynda Preston, who now knows far more about the Romans than she ever wanted to, and to Andy Downie, a husband of (almost) infinite patience.

A NOTE ON THE AUTHOR

Ruth Downie is the bestselling author of *Medicus*. She is married with two sons and lives in Milton Keynes, England.